Lesbians in Space

WHERE NO MAN HAS GONE BEFORE

Space Wizard Science Fantasy
Raleigh, NC
www.spacewizardsciencefantasy.com
Publisher's Note: This is a work of fiction. Names, characters, places, and incidents are a product of the author's imagination. Locales and public names are sometimes used for atmospheric purposes. Any resemblance to actual people, living or dead, or to businesses, companies, events, institutions, or locales is completely coincidental.

Cover by Serene Chia
Illustrations and Typography by Katie Cordy and Kristine Cordy
Copy Editing by Heather Tracy
Book Layout © 2015 BookDesignTemplates.com
Lesbians in Space: Where No Man Has Gone Before/J.S. Fields, William C. Tracy, Heather Tracy.— 1st ed.
ISBN 978-1-960247-42-1

Lesbians in Space

WHERE NO MAN HAS GONE BEFORE

Edited by J.S. Fields, William C. Tracy, & Heather Tracy

CONTENTS

Introduction

J.S. Fields:

I grew up on sci-fi serials and B movies where the heroes wore robes, spandex, and knee-high boots, and the possibilities for space adventures were endless. Tropes and cookie-cutter plotlines were wielded like weapons—meant to lull the viewer into comfort before presenting uncomfortable, current-day issues under a metaphoric lens. Fast forward to adulthood and I found the same sort of turnabout in indy lesfic spaces, where those old tropes were revitalized with gender and sexuality-bent characters—where lesbians were the heroes rescuing the maidens, had all the cheesy lines and silly pistol belts, and still got the girl in the end.

Any reader familiar with indy and small press spaces will know that sapphic and lesfic tends towards contemporary romance, with a decent smattering of fantasy. Sapphic sci-fi, specifically space-centric sci-fi, is harder to find. And that's...strange, because the Venn diagram for silly spaceship shenanigans and lesfic hero stories is basically a complete overlap. Lesbians were made for silly space adventure, and readers are hungry to see women have just as much nonsensical fun on spaceships as men of the past.

Even after writing the Ardulum series (my flagship sapphic space opera serial), I knew I wanted to have a proper space lesbian anthology that could span the diverse tropes and settings of space sci-fi—but through the unique window of the sapphic experience. But how does something that niche even get published, much less find its audience? Welcome to June, 2019, and my first email to William...

William C. Tracy:

This is the sixth anthology from our press Space Wizard Science Fantasy, and one which almost never came to pass. We'd released four anthologies in the "Worlds Apart" collection between 2021 and 2024, which was the amazing result of that email from J.S. Fields: "What if Space Lesbians?"

I thought I was done. Anthologies take a lot of time and money to produce! However, there was an unlikely series of events...

I sell books at a lot of conventions and markets, and an artist I was vending with, Serene Chia, hand-drew a sign for one convention where we had trouble getting people to stop by the table. It read "Lesbians in Space: Where No Man Has Gone Before." (We sell a lot of Sapphic books) And it worked. People *loved* that little hand-drawn sign on an 8x11 piece of paper with the lesbian flag in the background.

Serene later drew us an excellent piece of art, which you can see as the cover of this book, but it wasn't originally meant as a cover. Instead, we had it made into a banner to replace that original piece of paper.

The banner was so successful we had several people come up to ask when that book—*Lesbians in Space*—was coming out, and we had to tell them it was just a banner.

Heather Tracy:
I looked at William and said, "What if it *was* a book and we did another anthology?"

William had just been asked if he wanted to participate in a group crowdfunding event, but we didn't have any new books, as we had already funded them all in the campaign that was just wrapping up. Then, at the end of that day, sweaty and eating dinner at our favorite restaurant, he said to me, "I have a terrible idea..."

We passed the idea by J.S. Fields, who reminded us of their *original* intent for Space Lesbians, and that this was right in line with that. Thus, the *Lesbians in Space* anthology was born.

All three of us did some recruiting at WorldCon in Glasgow, Scotland in 2024, and we managed to somehow convince four Hugo Award-winning and nominated authors to lend their talents with stories for this anthology! We then proceeded to raise almost $11,000 in the campaign *and* receive so many great stories we're planning on a second anthology, *Lesbians in Space: The Sapphics Strike Back*!

Please explore this *amazing* collection of stories, from space opera, to fantasy, to weird aliens, to space stations and spaceships, to fanfic, to adventure and heists. This is only *half* of the incredible stories we chose, so if you like this one, keep an eye out for the next anthology coming later this year!

—J.S. Fields, William C. Tracy, and Heather Tracy, May 2025

Space Opera

SPACE OPERA

Infinity's Kiss

Ashleigh Martin

Pairing: Human/Human

Some creatures loathe the sea.

Danica?

She hates outer space.

With her former planet in crumbled pieces from an asteroid predicted to only cause minimal damage, her Earthly employment went kaput. True, she hadn't enjoyed working as a concierge—greeting billionaires as they prepared to casually vacation in space. But now, she's stuck on a massive spacecraft in a tiny cubicle, which somehow feels worse. Her mom, forever stubborn in her ways, refuses to evacuate Earth. Danica sends money when she can.

Ms. Cross?

A sterile voice rings in her head, supplanting her thoughts. Danica taps the side of her temple, pausing her music playlist.

"Nigel." She responds aloud by accident. She still hasn't adjusted to Mind Tapping.

Nigel.

I see you've submitted a hologram request for tomorrow.

Yes. It's my mother's birthday. It's only for seven minutes.

Your request has been denied.

What. Why?

Danica's steel lip ring presses into her flesh as she bites down on it. Her hands tighten around her computer's mouse. She debates exiting her cramped cubicle to have a more private, angsty conversation. Then she remembers that the conversation is already as private as it can get, being transmitted in her head after all.

As you're one day shy of completing your six-month probationary period, you do not yet have access to your hologram credits.

This is bull—

Language, Ms. Cross.

Danica rolls her eyes. She meant for that thought to belong to herself.

Can I submit the request tomorrow then?

No. All hologram requests must be submitted two weeks in advance.

An exasperated sigh trails out of her mouth, halting the productive computer clicks in the office.

"Sorry! Keep on reviewing those space cargo requests," she says to her cubicle neighbors.

Computer clicks ensue.

Nigel, please. I haven't seen my mother in nearly eight months. With the two months of training and six-month probation, I haven't had the time or funds to purchase my own hologram credits.

Rules are rules, Ms. Cross.

Danica isn't too keen on what the rules are, considering Nigel approved whatever Eerie wants. Maybe the rumors are true and the two are hooking up in the staff lounge. It wouldn't bother Danica as much if she and Eerie hadn't been hooking up in the staff lounge first.

Last month, when Nigel was promoted to manager, Eerie seemingly forgot their two-month, five-day fling and latched onto their new boss without a backward glance.

Fine. Going back to work.

Right now, Danica wishes her true vocal tone was transmitted, so Nigel could hear her frustration. Instead, she knows her curt words will have the happy AI flair of every female-sounding digital assistant.

She taps the left side of her head to end the call. Then taps her right temple, resuming her Celestial Downpour playlist. All this tapping was going to give her a headache.

Danica pushes away from the cold, metal desk. She shoots a glance at the Celestial Downpour poster pinned to the otherwise bare wall panel; one featuring the very ethereal and equally gorgeous lead singer, Lea. Grumbling, she trudges to the unisex restroom. Her swishy uniform emanates the most sensorily unfriendly noise known to womankind.

Swish. Swish. Swish.

She grits her teeth at the sound.

At the bathroom sink, she splashes room temperature water on her face, coating her brown skin and some purple curls. The spacecraft's water is never hot. Showers suck. Danica could use the infamous shower-in-a-bottle spray, but it made her break out in hives once. Alone with a dripping face, Danica finally lets it all sink in—she won't get to talk to her mother. They had a tradition of singing happy birthday to each other, and this is the first year Danica's not on Earth to do it. Lacking other children, her mother will be alone.

And Danica realizes she's just as alone as her mother.

She exits the bathroom, wearing a somber expression and trying to ignore the sewn TSSA—Transportation and Space Safety Administration—insignia that pokes her chest with each step. Sure, she has reliable food and housing. But at what cost? She works six days a week and can't fathom what a social life is.

At her desk, she clicks on her first assignment of the day.

Transport #3894623
Inspection Dock: 16
Lead Passenger: Rigel, L.
Requesting Transport to: Aria-346B
Number of Cargo Items Needing Inspection: 5

Danica tilts her head. Aria-346B is that fancy planet where all the big galaxy music festivals take place. She could never afford to travel there, let alone purchase tickets for an event. Whoever's traveling there must be loaded.

She ingests an unsatisfying sip from her cold coffee and exits the office, heading to the lowest level of the space station where all the inspections happen.

* * *

Danica overhears the passengers at Dock 16 before she sees them. Through the tangled chorus of disagreement, a familiar voice rises above the other.

"You can't be serious, the festival's tomorrow. Can't this wait? The band's under contract to perform. You can't quit now."

The LED sign adjacent to the Dock 16 door flashes green, indicating that the hangar's air replenishment system has properly returned oxygen to the closed cabin.

Danica pushes through the metal door and her heart nearly drops into her ass.

There she is.

Lea Rigel in the flesh. Pretty as a full moon, even with a Venus-worthy amount of heated anger outlining her features. Lea's pink halter dress flows side to side as she fidgets in the same manner. Danica can't see the woman she's bickering with, but she must be the other half of Celestial Downpour—Zahira Kissinger—lead guitarist and backup singer.

Starstruck yet still cognizant she must do her job, lest she get another MindTap from Nigel, Danica says, "I'm here to perform your cargo inspection. Am I interrupting something?"

Clang, the metal door behind Danica slams, finally drawing both women's attention to her. The second Lea makes eye contact with her, Danica's knees almost buckle. Lea's beauty is just as compelling as Celestial Downpour's music.

"What you say?" Lea asks.

Before Danica can repeat herself, Zahira says, "Please point me to the Spacecraft Rideshare Division. I need to fetch a ship home to Despina-387. Immediately." Zahira shoots a nasty glare at Lea then defers disgruntled eyes back to Danica.

"Sure. Exit through this door, then go all the way down the hallway and make a left. There's an elevator. Stop at the third floor. Someone can help you out there."

"Thank you," Zahira nods to Danica and exits the dock without a backward glance.

Anxious silence floats between her and Lea before she speaks again. This time, at least her voice seems more authoritative.

"Agent Danica Cross. I'm here to inspect your cargo, Ms. Rigel."

Lea—stunning despite the ugly hand she's been dealt—stares blankly at Danica. Her mouth fumbles open and closed, but no sound escapes.

Then suddenly, her eyes well with tears. Water cascades down her cheeks in droves, so much so that Danica wonders if the light freckles on Lea's brown skin will wash away. Lea sniffles, "This is my first time performing at the Andromeda Pride Music Festival. They're never going to invite me back if I cancel."

Lea, breath haggard, and on the cusp of hyperventilation, deflates on one of the crates Danica is meant to inspect. Looks like they're both having a bad day. Though Danica's issue relates to her finances ranking so high on the poverty scale, it probably surpasses her coworkers' diminutive salary with galactical proportions.

Lea's inconvenience falls more so into First Galaxy Problems territory.

It's when Lea begins clutching her chest that Dancia grows concerned.

"Woah, are you alright?" Danica crouches down to Lea's level, placing a cautious hand on her shoulder.

"Yeah—yeah, just give me a minute, please."

And so they sit in silence. Danica isn't sure how much time passes. She's surprised she hasn't received a nagging MindTap from Nigel. She waits. When Lea's breathing seems normal, Danica stands, her strained knees grateful for the change in position.

"I'm sorry," Danica offers. "If it makes you feel any better, I absolutely love Celestial Downpour. I know every song, even the ones released on SpaceCloud. I wouldn't let one disaster stop you. Tomorrow isn't here yet. A lot can change in twenty-four hours."

Danica wishes she could give herself the same advice, instead of conceding to Nigel.

Lea wipes her tears away, a determined look replacing the previous defeat in her eyes.

"You know all the songs, Danica?"

"Yeah. I have a playlist that I listen to almost religiously. What's that got to do with anything?"

"Do you sing, play guitar?"

"Uh—where is this going? I sing a little. Never touched a guitar in my life."

Lea rises from the crate and puts the softest pressure on Danica's shoulders.

"Hear me out—"

"In the history of anyone saying, 'hear me out,' I'm one thousand percent sure it was never a good idea."

Lea laughs. How does her laugh sound as musical as her singing voice?

"Hear me out. It's not ideal. I'll figure out the whole guitar thing. But I need you to sing live with me. At the festival. Tomorrow night."

Danica's eyes nearly bulge out of her head.

"What—no! I've never sung in front of an audience. Only my mom's heard me sing."

Lea's hands slide from Danica's arms to grasp her fingers. A chilly thrill races down Danica's spine.

"Sing 'Infinity's Kiss.'"

Danica's throat grows drier than the desert on Mars. "Infinity's Kiss" was the single from Celestial Downpour's first album. What launched Lea and Zahira's careers beyond the stratosphere.

"I—I can't do that. That's crazy," Danica sputters.

Lea smiles. It's kind, encouraging. Like she glimpses potential that Danica cannot see for herself.

"Something tells me you can do it." She backs a step away from Danica but doesn't separate their hands. "Close your eyes. Don't even look at me. Just sing."

How many people get the chance to sing for their favorite artist? Danica takes a deep, shaky breath and closes her eyes. Might as well. Maybe this'll be the single good part of her day.

She couldn't leave with Lea for the festival though.

That's insane.

The moment Danica's eyelashes close together, Lea launches into a low hum, the beginning notes of the song. She doesn't need to give Danica a cue. The romantic ballad is printed in her brain.

Lea's humming increases in volume, just seconds before the opening chorus, then Danica's lips part, and out flows a surprisingly on-key song.

Didn't know heaven could feel like this.
A lifetime of love. Infinity's kiss.
Your kiss is good luck, one I can't miss.
Let's lip lock forever, let's infinity kiss.
So pull me close, lean in just like this—

Danica's eyes bolt open, afraid to sing the last line. Because in every performance she's seen of Lea and Zahira, that's the bit when Zahira playfully plants a kiss on Lea's cheek, then with faux, dramatic shyness, runs across the stage to pick up her guitar.

Danica backs away, biting her lip ring as a thinly veiled distraction.

Lea watches her with satisfaction. Danica stares at anything but Lea. Her eyes settle on her work boots, but as they trail down, she notices how Lea's fingers flex, as if she wants to touch Danica again. Then they go still, perhaps thinking better of it.

"You sound amazing and you're damn pretty. The crowd will adore you. Please say you'll perform?" In Lia's wide eyes is a breathtaking desperation.

"I was kinda off key? Plus, I can't just up and leave. I—I have a job. I'm still on probation. My mom's birthday is tomorrow. I have to find a way to call her. I can't lose this job."

Plus, Danica will need at least two hours alone to process the fact Lea called her pretty.

Lea's head tilts. "I'll pay you five times your yearly salary."

Danica almost chokes in disbelief. "That's insane. I could afford to hologram call my mom way longer than seven minutes. For hours."

Lea smirks. "How about I throw in a free hologram call for however long you want in addition to the pay?"

"Yes—oh god yes." Danica's lips spew the words before her mind can prepare a response. Lea releases the cutest, triumphant squeal Danica has ever heard before pulling her into the warmest of hugs. One that lingers, reactivating that amorous spine chill from earlier.

Still in a tight embrace, Lea says: "You're a lifesaver. I can't thank you enough. We can figure out logistics on the trip over."

Danica could probably live in this hug for eternity . . . or dare she say infinity? She decides to keep that line to herself. "I do need to pack. And I've gotta inspect those crates before we go anywhere."

"Sure, sure. Of course," Lea pulls away, slow reluctance characterizing her movements. "I'll get my transport ready. You won't regret this, Danica."

* * *

Lea's transport is exactly what Danica dreamt it would be—hot pinks and purples, glitter and stars decorate its interior. The ship is modest, like most transport vehicles meant for short travel. It even smells like Lea, the fruity scent of barbed inkberries—a plant native to her planet—flows with abundance around the ship. As Danica settles into the passenger seat, adjacent to the pilot's, her lips burn with questions. But one inquiry remains far hotter than the rest.

"Can we talk about it?" Danica asks.

Lea tilts her head to the side, her star drop earrings glimmering under the transport's sporadic flashing lights. "Talk about what?" There's a look in Lea's eye though, one hinting that she's keenly aware of what Danica wants to know.

"The breakup between you and Zahira. Aren't you both from Despina-387 and childhood friends? Celestial Downpour exists because you both love to write songs. What happened to make her abruptly call off a performance that would project your careers forward?"

Lea rests her chin on her hands, balled fists trembling as she leans forward on her knees. Danica watches her as Lea takes interest in the various flashing lights and buttons that decorate the control panel. Danica recognizes some circuit breakers, but everything else is a mystery to her. She's impressed that Lea has a Space Pilot license.

"It's so cliche. I'm almost embarrassed to mention it."

Danica purses her lips. She supposes that band breakups are common.

Ms. Cross—Where are you? I've been informed that you did not arrive for your second cargo inspection. This does not bode well for your probationary status.

Danica doesn't tap the side of her head, refusing to respond. She does nothing. Nigel can go to hell. There's a much more intriguing conversation she'd rather have. If she doesn't respond, eventually his MindTap will go into a voicemail database. One she plans on clearing out as soon as she can get to a MindTap Center and sever their connection for good.

Not noticing Danica's brief distraction, Lea continues, "We're independent artists. One of the few invited to music festivals. We prided ourselves on being independent. But Despina Row Records reached out to us to offer a deal. A brief skim of the contract told me that it was a bad idea. But Zahira wanted to hear them out. So, we agreed to have a meeting with the label *after* the festival. I think something's happened. I bet they reached out to Zahira and offered a deal she couldn't refuse."

Lea finally locks eyes with Danica, bright green eyes a flurry of emotion.

"Damn. I'm sorry that happened."

"Cliche right? I never wanted to go solo. Having someone on stage with me is paramount. I just need the support. No one wants to watch me have a panic attack on stage."

"That's why you asked me to come with you?" Now that was something the blogs didn't know—that Lea needed the emotional support to perform on stage.

"Yeah. My anxiety has gotten better, more manageable. But I have my limits. A music festival with millions of eyes on me, especially a creature with millions of eyes, is way past my limit." Lea leans back, turning to the right to finally meet Danica's searching gaze. Her tight fists unclench and a little smile spreads across her face. "I've never told anyone that. Well—other than Zahira."

"Thanks for sharing. And I guess . . . believing in a stranger."

Lea pops up from the seat, the charms on her pleated skirt jingling with some sort of inanimate joy. "Oh, that's easy, trusting strangers." She walks around to Danica and holds out her hand, waiting for Danica to accept it.

This handholding is something Danica could get used to. Her fingers intertwine with the singer's, a warmth coating her cold hand. Lea pulls her from the passenger seat and leads Danica from the pilot cabin.

"Trusting strangers is easy?"

"Sure. If they let you down, it hurts less. There's no true expectation that a stranger will have your best interests. Now say, your best friend lets you down? That shit stings." Lea's smile wavers.

Searching for any way to uplift the woman's mood, Danica clumsily changes the subject. "So, what should I expect at this festival? Because I've literally never performed before. Other than for my mom and a dirty bathroom mirror."

"Oh, Aria's beautiful. Specifically, Andromeda Pride has five stages with a huge rotation of artists performing throughout the day. Celestial Downpour is the last act of the night at stage three." Danica realizes they are now returning to the small storage room that houses the five crates she inspected hours before. Lea tugs one open, revealing a collection of colorful costumes. "Pretty sure you're close in size with Zahira. So, no need to find a tailor." Lea rifles through the crate, pulling a swath of fabrics ranging from chiffon to satin. Her hands settle on a corseted, electric blue dress that should stop just above Danica's knees. The flowy hem of the skirt is lined with pearlescent rhinestones, appearing like falling stars in the sky.

"I think you'll look great in this," Lea says. "It'll compliment your indigo hair. Not—not that you don't already look good. You do. If our initial meeting had been before I started yelling at my best friend, I definitely would have asked for your MindTap number."

Danica smirks. "Do you still have plans to ask for my number?"

Lea's light brown skin reddens. "Oh, did I say that aloud? I've got to stop doing that."

Danica laughs. She won't press her again. Not until after the festival, at least.

"Costume, check. What's next on the festival prep list?"

Grateful for the shift in conversation, Lea says, "The biggest thing is making sure you know the setlist. Fifteen songs. I'm sure nothing will be a surprise to you. Once you hear the beat, the song will be easy to identify. But I'll give you a copy of the setlist. The last song will be the fan favorite: 'Infinity's Kiss.'"

Danica suddenly feels shy. It was just a stupid kiss on the cheek. What's with all the gay panic?

"Cool. I'm looking forward to it."

Danica was looking forward to hiding under the covers. She can feel the heat of embarrassment on her face. As a distraction, she reaches for the blue dress, but her hands collide with Lea's. A look of longing crosses Lea's face. Maybe Danica imagined that. She'll choose to believe her own face does not mirror that same look of longing.

"I should try this on. There are boots in my bag that should go great with this." Danica very ungracefully exits the storage room, escaping into the tiny sleep room that features two mini mattresses stacked at different levels on a metal frame.

The dress is a near perfect fit. A yawn escapes Danica's mouth. Now, she stares longingly at the mattresses and bedding. Tomorrow will be draining, perhaps it's time she got some rest.

* * *

"You ready, superstar?"

Lea, in full glittery glam with a bedazzled earpiece, sucks in a long breath then drops both her hands onto Danica's shoulders. Before Danica can respond, Lea lets out a huge yawn then smiles sheepishly.

They didn't really sleep last night. Not on purpose, at least. For the majority of the trip to Aria, Danica and Lea huddled close on Lea's bed. Talking all night, realizing that even from different planets, there was so much in common between them.

"As ready as someone who's never performed for a live audience can be. I know there's the saying 'do what scares you,' but this is on another level, Lea."

"Well," Lea purses her lips, examining Danica from head to toe in such a way, Danica fidgets under her microscopic gaze. "You're breathtaking. The crowd is going to love you. Or they'll all have to feel my wrath afterward." She playfully crosses her arms and squints her eyes in a mock intimidating fashion.

"Whew," Danica whistles. "They shouldn't cross you, if they know what's good for them."

"Downpour. Downpour. Downpour." The crowd roars.

"Let's not keep them waiting any longer," Lea winks. "I'll enter stage left. You, stage right. Once the announcer introduces us, run on stage." Then Lea leans forward, wrapping their mic'd hands at the elbow. She plants a quick peck on Danica's hand. Danica nearly drops the mic. "A backstage ritual. *'Your kiss is good luck.'* Can't go on without it."

Well that's an insider detail Danica didn't know about Celestial Downpour. Lea doesn't wait for her response but darts off to the opposite side of the massive stage. Danica tries to clear her mind as she grasps the velvet backstage curtain. But all she can think about is how soft Lea's lips were against her hand. Does she have gloss on her fingers now? Danica rotates her wrist in a circle yet finds nothing, like the moment never happened.

"For our final act of the night, we've got Celestial Downpour! With special guest, Danica Cross!"

Danica doesn't think, she just shoves the hefty curtain aside and sprints.

* * *

Sweat gathers on Danica's brow, the consistently warm Aria weather finally weighing on her after eight songs. It's a godsend that the cooling fans facing the stage whir at full power, trying their best to keep Danica and Lea from overheating.

Being on stage is exhilarating. She hadn't been perfect by any means, but Lea helped Danica when she sensed her getting ready to slip up. There is an unfathomable chemistry between them. Something Danica can't quite name yet, but each time she locks eyes with Lea, her body feels energized like the hue of her electric blue dress.

But when Danica locks eyes with Lea now, alarms ring in her chest. Lea is frozen on her side of the stage, staring at someone in the crowd. The microphone in her hand hangs loosely, like she could drop it at any moment.

Confusion intermixes with the alarm, as Danica speed walks to Lea, landing shoulder to shoulder with the singer. As their bodies collide, she notices that Lea barely moves, like she's turned to stone. Danica follows her line of sight, and it lands on a single concert goer holding up a massive sign that reads: "We love you Zahira."

Lea's eyes prick with tears and her breath comes in erratic spurts. Danica's head swivels, searching frantically for a way to lessen Lea's discomfort.

Danica shouts the words before she truly thinks them, "Intermission! Uh—a break. Lea's going to take a short break. Ten minutes tops." Lea, acknowledging Danica for the first time since having her eyes glued to the poster, looks at her, her face a mixture of grief and relief.

"R—right! I'll be right back Andromeda Pride!" Lea gathers Danica's free hand in somewhat of a death grip, squeezes it, then exits stage left.

She did *not* think this through. The crowd watches Danica with an expectancy that makes her want to tuck tail and run backstage.

But no—Lea guided her through the first couple of songs. The least Danica can do is distract from Lea's escape offstage.

First, that sign must go. Danica catches the eye of a security guard standing near the metal railing that separates the crowd from the stage. She stabs her finger at the stupid sign that made everything go downhill and makes a "get it outta here" gesture with her hand, thumb jutting the opposite direction. Danica doesn't care where the sign goes, it just needs to *go*.

Now for that distraction.

Danica channels every pop star she's ever imitated in her bathroom mirror in an attempt to keep the crowd engaged.

"Andromeda Pride! Thank you for welcoming me. I know this was an unexpected change, but it's fun, right? Are you all having fun tonight?"

She holds the mic out to the crowd, and they roar.

Confidence building, Danica continues, "That was loud! I'm feeling the love. Now I have something to ask you. Someone *I* love has a birthday today. My mom. It would mean the galaxy to me if you helped me sing happy birthday to her. Can you all do that with me tonight?"

More enthusiastic roaring.

She's really great at this thinking-on-the-spot thing.

Danica finds herself thankful for the many cameras filming each and every angle because the rest happens in an adrenaline riddled blur.

Suddenly there's a hologram square onstage with her. Danica bends down to tap the device, a digital image materializes, altering the cube's usual, plain appearance.

Then her mom. Danica sees her mom for the first time in ages via hologram and mirrored to the giant concert screen.

"Hi, Mom. Happy birthday! So, this is going to be a really funny story one day."

* * *

"Happy birthday, Mom. Happy birthday to you," Danica elongates the *you*, her voice almost wavering. And supporting her voice is the thunderous, Andromeda Pride crowd, the attendees erupting into a score of hoots and hollers that warm Danica's soul.

Her mom's hologram stands with hands clasped at her chest, her eyes shining with a giddy happiness that will make Danica cry if she dares to look any more ecstatic.

"I'm so proud of you," her mom says. "I know you weren't fond of your job. And I've always told you that your voice could take you places. Look at you! I'm sure you didn't think it would lead you across the galaxy, but somehow, I'm not surprised."

"That means the world to me, Mom."

"You mean the world to me, Dani. But don't let me keep you from being a pop star. My daughter's a pop star! Now you," she points a finger straight ahead, like she's pointing individually at everyone eying the screen. "Say it with me. Downpour—"

"Downpour. Downpour. Downpour." The waiting crowd's chants overtake her mom's voice with comical force.

And the ethereal being that is Lea Rigel emerges from backstage, appearing refreshed and anxiety free. She lays a hand on Danica's forearm, pulling her close to whisper, "thank you," in her ear.

Clearly gifted in the art of segues, Lea takes over, putting the performance back on course. She scoops up the hologram cube and places it safely on the stage's right side. But Lea doesn't turn it off, allowing Danica's mom to watch the rest of their set.

Lea waves with genuine excitement at Danica's mom before returning to center stage. "I feel like I should be in the crowd watching you guys! That was the best rendition of 'Happy Birthday' I've ever heard. Now who's ready to hear some more Celestial Downpour?"

It's only right that the crowd clamors for more.

* * *

As the fourteenth song fades away, the slow, alluring ballad of "Infinity's Kiss" flows from the massive speakers.

The crowd stops jumping and pumping fists in the air, transitioning to calm swaying, some even going so far as to waving their hologram cubes in the air. The lights look like stars against the dusky horizon. Danica eyes Lea from across the stage and they walk slowly toward each other, meeting just as the song's lyrics are to start.

> *Didn't know heaven could feel like this.*
> *A lifetime of love. Infinity's kiss.*
> *Your kiss is good luck, one I can't miss.*
> *Let's lip lock forever, let's infinity kiss.*
> *So pull me close, lean in just like this.*
> *And gift me that loved, infinity kiss.*

Panic settles into Danica's bones. She didn't have to kiss Lea on the cheek. The crowd would understand. But Lea has a mischievous glint in her eye. The instrumental fades, going dormant for a few seconds before the music will build back up. Lea leans forward, playfully batting her lashes for the crowd and tilting her cheek toward Danica.

The crowd roars with anticipation.

To hell with it. She should give the crowd what they want.

As Danica closes the distance, lips pursed, and target in sight, Lea does something no one planned for.

Instead of waiting for Danica's lips to land on her cheek, Lea shifts her face quickly so that their lips meet. The sensations that flow through Danica's body are unreal. The crowd erupts into approving screams, but their sheer volume falls on distracted ears. Danica's full focus belongs to Lea. On impulse, Danica puts a hand on Lea's waist, elongating their kiss.

Danica knows the beat is about to pick up. She knows this song like the back of her hand. But her hand feels perfect on Lea, a stellar moment worth extending. Keeping pace with the music track seems insignificant.

Ever the professional, Lea pulls away, seconds from Zahira's quickly strummed guitar chords. But the yearning look in Lea's eyes attest that she does not want to separate either. Lea backtracks to her side of the stage and Danica can't help but believe her future is walking away.

But in a heartbeat, Lea runs right back, a hint to Danica that their fates are now entwined for infinity. Then confetti explodes, lighting the night sky with metallic hues of red, orange, and pink. It's at this second that Danica perceives Lea as more than just an intangible pop star. And she senses that Lea views her as more than just an adoring fan.

And the best part of it all? Danica can rehash everything with her mother soon after.

Data Recovery

MK Hardy

Pairing: Human/Human

I'm going to bring you back, Iz, then I'm going to tell you the truth.

It wasn't hard to find people claiming to know how to do it, but it *was* hard finding one that wasn't lying their arse off. For augs who regularly back up their systems, it's pretty straightforward, but then, we were never in one place long enough for "regular" to become anything but theoretical. I found a few old cartridges here and there, but they'd barely piece together your basic psyche profile, let alone the *real* you.

Turns out there's a workaround, if you've got the time. They say it's a one-way transfer every time you plug into an access port or a data centre, but of course that's not true. It's impossible for there not to be some kind of backwash, a little bit of you that gets left behind in the system with all those ones and zeroes. It's creepy, if you stop to think about it too long: all those fragments of people drifting around the servers like ghosts, like radiation from a long-exploded star.

Anyway. Turns out, if you collect enough of those fragments you can do something with them, pull them together and reconstitute the person, or at least enough of them to matter. Don't ask me the details—you know I was never the techy one.

But I *am* bloody-minded, and I know how to follow directions, and I keep good records. So off I go: all our old haunts, the stations and outposts where we did our runs. I'm going to bring you back, piece by piece. And then I'll finally tell you.

Takamagahara

One of the first jobs we worked together—remember? I mean, of course you don't, but part of you will, the part I'm here to retrieve. It's not as busy now as it was back then—I think CryoCorp has packed up and moved out, and now it's mostly smaller corps scrabbling and fighting amongst each other. Funny how whenever the big guys move out, the little guys immediately kick off, going for each other's throats and fighting over the scraps left behind. You want to shake them, point out that if they just worked together, they'd be a lot stronger for it, but a power vacuum seems to suck all common sense out of the room. Works for me—it means it's a lot easier to slip past their crappy firewalls and get into the station systems, then I just need to plug in this gizmo and let it do its work, somehow finding all the bits of you floating about in junk code and ancient archived cache dumps, matching them against what it has, slowly plugging the gaps.

I remember we had an...interesting time that first visit. I wanted to just bully past security, flush with the fires of youth and possessing an underdeveloped sense of what you called "flair." It was the first time I was introduced to the concept of bluffing, and I was terrible at it. Luckily, you had a knack for getting people to do what you wanted them to without protest—though I only realized how often you used it on me much later.

The garrison didn't know what hit them. Half a turn and you'd gotten us invited in for drinks, and finally I was useful. I downed shot after shot something that must have been distilled from engine coolant leakage, peeling the lining of my esophagus away with each sip.

Meanwhile you'd already been in and out of their systems; we could've left any time, but you sat there and watched me make a fool of myself. You lost it when I fell on my face trying to demonstrate a leglock on a LBE, which, thanks for that.

When I finally woke up back on our ship, you'd covered me with a blanket and left a thermos full of your "specially prepared" nutrient broth for me. Tasted like arse, but helped. I still drink it these days when I'm working through a hangover, which has been happening a lot lately.

What can I say? I miss you.

Anyway, it was a lot easier to get access to the system this time round, and I think I did everything I needed to do.

It's not like it's easy to screw up, but you know me. If there's something techy, I can make it go boom just as easily as not.

No garrison anymore, but I raised a glass in their memory as I shoved off to the next port.

New San Valentyn

Void alive, just the name is enough to give me a headache. It's only gotten flashier and louder since we were last here and if it wasn't for the job, I'd undock the skimmer and turn the fuck around.

Yes, I'm thinking of it as a job now. It's got all the hallmarks—making me go places I don't want to go, for little-to-no pay, with piss-poor company. All right, that last part's a joke. I'm doing this one alone.

As I said, NSV's still a glitzy cesspool and if it wasn't for our old logs I wouldn't have been able to find my way back to the 'easy we'd been sent to last time round. But even if I didn't remember it—get this—they remembered you. It'd be hard not to, I guess, given how you hijacked their system and tipped all the dancers more than their day's wages. Apparently, it still malfunctions sometimes and gives out random tips—they call it "a visit from Iz." Not hard to imagine the ghost of you still wandering around in there, respectfully eyeing up all the butches and complimenting their fades. I was jealous—looking back on it now—but somehow, I think you knew it because the next time I had mine done you told me how nice it looked.

Anyway. It was surprisingly easy to plug into their system; once they heard what I was doing, they all but invited me in and gave me a free dance while I waited. It was nice, but mostly I was just impatient to get done and get out of there.

I'm not gonna know if this works until we piece it all together and see, and I want to know. I want to see you again.

Conurbation 231

The job was a pretty easy one, a little light surveillance, done and dusted in a few nights, and then for the first time in months we found ourselves with a pocketful of creds and no fixed plans.

At first you wanted to hit the road immediately—you hate megacities—but then you somehow got wind of the Arboretum—maybe a pamphlet or an ad fly or something—and you would not shut up until we went even though it cost almost every micro we made on the job.

I was so fucking angry. We had a proper stand-up fight about it, yelling and crying and stomping about like kids. There was never any question of my refusing, but I didn't speak to you for days while we waited for our visit slot to come up.

And then when we set foot in that greenhouse and I breathed a lungful of fucking, I dunno, tree air, for the first time—that smell that's dirty and clean at the same time— and you literally seemed to grow taller, like you'd never stood up straight before in your whole life, and you turned to me with this massive grin, I suddenly wasn't angry anymore and I couldn't tell you why I'd *been* angry and honestly in that moment I truly believed I might never be angry ever again.

But I didn't tell you. I've plugged this data sucker thingy into the city's grid, and whatever it sucks out, it's not gonna suck out me on my knees apologising, because I didn't apologise, and the absolute joy that I felt in that moment, watching you look at trees in the flesh—in the...bark?—for the first time, that's a memory I carry alone. For now, at least.

The Junk Heap

And here we are, where it all began.

I really didn't want to come back here. It's not as though we have any particularly fond memories of this absolute sphincter of a platform—you once called it the worst cycle of your life. If I hadn't already been of the opinion that an "honest living" was not worth the toil, Primus Repair Yards would've done it.

But it's where the accident happened, where you first got work done, so if we're gonna find a critical mass of proper remnant data anywhere—what my trawler called "foundational programming"—it's gonna be here.

You'll be unsurprised to learn that it hasn't changed at all. Same battered machinery, same constant noise. The same pervasive smell of grease and metal filings and that slightly sulphurous edge from air filters that are constantly running beyond capacity. The yard is filled with the same beaten-up short-hop skimmers and tugs, all old, out of warranty, most of dubious provenance.

The people haven't changed, either. Bottom-of-the-barrel dangerously incompetent arsewipes with no talent and fewer fucks to spare. They are also still extremely open to bribery, but I went straight in with menaces instead, for old time's sake.

That's how we met, too, of course—intimidation. It's weird being the only living keeper of that memory—both those dudes died in an explosion—not your explosion, a different one. I'm getting ahead of myself.

I want to say I vividly remember every moment but that's a barefaced lie: I just barely recall seeing you at the next table in the canteen with your grimy boiler suit and grease smeared across your cheek and thinking your blue hair was obnoxious, but I was already half cut and was trying desperately to shovel enough carbs down my throat to soak up some of the liquor before my next shift, then I remember those guys coming over to your table, and *then* I remember waking up in an overnight lockup with skinned knuckles and a thumping hangover.

So you see, I *had* to come here, and you *have* to come back, because otherwise who else will remember my glorious triumph?

Mind you, if I'd known how many creds you owed them I might not've intervened because *fuck me*. And you fell over yourself to pay my fine and I find out later you borrowed *even more* for that, somehow. You were an absolute menace. Are. Will be.

And so we became a pair. I wasn't having any of it, but you *just wouldn't fuck off*, buzzing around me like an iBall drone, and lo and behold I had to shelve all my plans to drink myself to death working a dead-end security gig on a haemorrhoid on the arsehole of the Ore Belt, because someone needed me. You needed me. And before long, Void help me, I needed you too.

And then came the explosion. There were accidents on a pretty regular basis on the repair platform, but this one was serious, a proper fireball situation. You were knocked clear of the blast, but it sent a huge hunk of metal flying, and you were so fucking tiny, you didn't have a chance. You used to call it "lucky fireball day"—turns out insurance *can* pay out if you know how to hack a staff database, but we had to leave sharpish after that, before anybody caught on, you with your new leg and lungs and half a skull and the weirdest warranty documentation of all time, and me with a new appreciation for the fragility of life from which I quite frankly never recovered.

The data transfer took forever. I couldn't tell if that was because there was a lot to transfer, or just the shitty ancient system here.

CryoCorp Hub

We've never been here before. Of all the gigs we've had, we would never have agreed to break in somewhere like this. For a start off, you wouldn't let me hurt people, and I had to hurt quite a lot of people to get in here. And then there was the fact that the systems in this place are protected by so many firewalls that even you wouldn't be able to crack them.

Or at least, not without a trace. Apparently—so I'm told, by this smart-arse collection of tattoos in a skinsuit I'm paying eye-watering amounts of creds to help me do this— these systems *can* be brute forced. You just can't expect to get away with it.

They demanded their fee in full up-front, Iz. I don't think we're getting out of here.

I don't really pay a huge amount of attention to the body I pick. Honestly the sight of cold storage makes me feel so ill that I feel almost like I'm outside my own body, watching myself go through these motions—mounting a capsule on a gurney, wheeling it to the thaw pod and hooking everything up the way I was told. I have to keep reminding myself that this body was never gonna be a person, that they were only ever a collection of organs and tissue—fuck, they probably have like four kidneys in there or some shit—I swear I saw some with extra fingers in there.

Because this won't be forever, Iz, won't be for very long at all. These bodies weren't built to ever get up and walk around, weren't built to think, or talk. Putting your giant, magnificent, self into this meatsack is going to ruin it for anything else, just for us to have one last conversation. I just open up its skull—thank god the pod has a setting for that shit—and then I need to literally stick your chip on its brain like a badge, and hook up this doohickie, and the doohickie rewires the grey matter and makes it...you. Or you enough, at any rate.

A comparatively simple—if gruesome—conclusion. And now that I've come this far it'd be stupid not to finish, right? I'd be an idiot to have spent cycles revisiting every backwater shithole we've ever been to on the worst reunion tour ever, literally fought my way in here, hacked the system with all the finesse of a piledriver—only a matter of time 'til they figure out where the breach is and send a goon squad...for me to then be standing here with your chip in one hand and my hard-won and extremely expensive whatsit in the other, wondering if I'm doing the right thing.

It felt obvious at the beginning. You have to understand, it all went *so fast*. One day you were feeling kind of shitty, the next you were losing words, the next I'm in a grotty backroom surgery listening to a sawbones explain bionetic degenerative brain death (someone was *super* pleased they came up with a name with the initials "BDBD," the morbid fucks), and the next...

And I just go into autopilot, you know? All I can think about is the shit I never said, the things I never told you— about me, about us. So I go straight into Mission Mode and everything since feels like kind of a blur, just one logical act following another until here we are, me about to jam you into some random brain and zap you awake for long enough to hear the things I should've said to you every day—and would, if I could go back, I swear, if you gave me those years to do over I would...who am I kidding, I would still be an emotionally stunted shell of a woman, but I'd *try* you know?

But then I see you. I see your stupid blue hair and that smudge on your cheek. I see you hunched over a console with that little frown of concentration. I see you talking your way out of anything and everything—or into it, as the need arises.

I see that big beaming smile, like you know something I don't, and it's then I realize: you did.

You knew. You knew before I did. You *fucking* knew, the whole time, and you never told me. Never let on how much I need you, how deeply I love every single atom of you, utterly, all-consumingly, like you're a part of me. You never said a word, but you knew all along.

A tiny little crack pulls my attention back to the present.

I didn't know I was clenching my fists. But as I lift my hand now and open it, your chip, your precious, irreplaceable neural chip is lying there, neatly snapped in half. Two parts, once whole, now broken. I can hear your laugh, see the face you'd make at my cack-handedness. You never let me feel sorry for myself for too long.

Somewhere, a siren has started to ring. I grin, and I feel you grinning with me.

Literally cannot believe the shit you get me into. C'mon, we'd best get a shift on.

Like a Night of Fallen Stars

Nathan Chu

Pairing: Human/Dragon

Tem watched the dancer unwind on stage, her limbs wading through the air as if the splashing light on her skin was water. Music shimmered over the steady beat of drums, and Tem raised her glass. Ryuusei Lounge was a good place to be. It had a quiet character, none of the loud pulsing that most stations pumped out between their speakers and neon cocktails. Amid the cold void of space, Tem figured that was how people reminded themselves they were alive. By contrast, Ryuusei was refined, cultured even. She and her fellow patrons politely clapped for each set. Never mind the fact that the dancers were strippers.

"What's her name?" Tem leaned back to ask her server. She was the only one still at the bar, the rest of the late-night patrons having gathered around the stage to gawk.

"Don't even try," Cloranthy sighed. "I'm not giving you any of their names. They're not even mine to give."

Tem raised an eyebrow.

Cloranthy groaned. "Just because I run a strip club doesn't mean I treat my employees like meat. If you really want to know, why don't you go and ask her?"

"Nah." Tem crinkled her nose. "Not suave enough."

Cloranthy rolled her eyes. "You Hunter-types, always gotta be dramatic."

"It comes with the territory." Tem slipped her hat on just so she could doff it and offer a mock bow. "When you're drifting in and out of town, you've got to learn how to leave an impression."

"Well, you certainly can't do that from here. You sure you aren't just shy?"

The girl flushed.

Cloranthy laughed. "Don't worry, kid. I've just been serving old hounds for a long time. Comet beards don't blush when they see a girl they fancy."

Tem sighed. So much for that cover. The truth was, Tem hadn't even graduated yet, and if she didn't find a remedial bounty soon, Cudz would make sure she never did. He didn't believe in second chances, which was why he had shipped her off to Amba. The birth planet of hardlight was a shell of its former self. All the hardlight factories had shut down with only service drones running maintenance now. Tem's own gear was second-hand generations over. "I'll take a Hibari Vine."

"Excellent," Cloranthy hummed. "By the way, her set's done after this song." She handed Tem her glass, then a second cocktail the color of sunset and dusk. "She's a nice girl, so I better not hear about you ditching her."

Tem glanced at the drink, then back to the stage. "Thanks." She grinned.

"My plea—"

The rest of Cloranthy's reply was shorn away by the lounge exploding.

Tem dove for cover, hands flexing and tripping the hardlight generator in her gloves. A field of dim chartreuse coated her skin, and she grunted as debris slammed into her.

"You okay, kid?" Cloranthy's voice was muffled from behind the bar.

"Been better," the student-Hunter muttered. "You call the guard. I'll see what's up." She flexed her hands again and settled them on her holsters, the soft click of her stun guns magnetizing to her palms. Ahead of her, dust drifted thick.

Tem groaned. Of course, she happened to be at the wrong place at the wrong time. *Look on the bright side. Maybe Cudz'll count it as your make-up test.*

The haze was like a cemetery, all the pleasant murmuring of the lounge's guests now a silent ash, tables and chairs knocked senseless on the ground. Tem stepped over them, scanning for any survivors. Luckily, there hadn't been many left in the lounge this late, most only lingering to snatch one of the dancers and discuss "supplementary income."

Tem growled. *Pervs.* At least she wanted to go on a proper date first. So what if she liked playing things cool?

Wasn't that romantic? She sighed and propped up one of the lounge's customers against a knocked over table. "Hey, you oka—"

Tem hit the floor as a shadow charged over her. It pivoted, clinging to the ceiling, and glared down at her.

Her training snapped into place. *Too fast to taze. Small enough to restrain.*

The shadow pounced, and Tem rolled away, slamming the ground with her arms and rocketing back to her feet. "Oops." She swept her left foot back as the shadow lunged. "Sorry!" Another dodge. "Nope." Tem snaked past the shadow, V-stepping as it tried to tackle her, and uncoupled her shackle from around her forearm.

"Gotcha!" She swung the belt around the Beast and yanked, beams of lime hardlight flaring to life, only for Tem to be rewarded with a blow to the face.

A tail?!

Tem barely processed what had hit her before she crashed into another patron.

"Sorry!" Tem didn't even bother glancing down at the man. Now that she had restrained the shadow, she could make out its shape, and it made no sense. It was small, and it had long hair, red with messy locks and a pair of horns. And wings trapped together with its arms under the green glow of her shackle.

A dragon?! No, a human-dragon?

"Ifa!" The dancer cut through the dust, glowing a bright violet and racing toward the intruder. "What are you doing here?! What happened to you?" She fumbled with the shackle, only to curse as the restraint zapped her.

"Lana!" The dragon cheered.

"Hey, that's dangerous!" Tem finally shook herself out of her daze and rushed forward. She didn't even know if that thing was real, but if a dragon had somehow walked right off the page of her history book, she sure as hell couldn't let a civilian get close to it.

"You!" The dancer rounded on Tem. "Did you do this? Unlock her *now*!"

"Everything alright?" Cloranthy's voice rang through the haze. "The guard's almost here!"

The dancer swore again. "Not now! You!" She grabbed Tem by the collar and pulled her so close she could smell the performer's shampoo. "You're coming with."

Then she jumped through the wall, dragon and Tem in tow.

* * *

A note on Ryuusei Lounge: it occupied the fourteenth floor of a skyscraper, which Tem found rapidly more alarming as they hurtled through air.

"What is your problem?!" She screamed at the dancer. One minute, she was crushing hard on the other woman, and now, they were falling to their deaths.

"Release her!"

"Are you insane?!" Tem glanced from the dancer to the dragon. Did this woman seriously think that this tiny thing could carry them to safety?

"Just do it!"

"No!" Even if that was the case, she couldn't just free a dragon! They were supposed to be a class twenty Beast! A mythical engine of destruction!

"Do it!" The woman screeched and tightened her grip on Tem's collar.

Tem's breath hitched.

"Now!"

Tem growled and snatched at the dragon, trying to hide her blush. "This better work!" The shackle decoupled, hardlight shattering into green slivers as it wrapped itself back around her arm.

"Ifa!"

The dragon grabbed onto Tem and the three of them lurched as its wings unfurled.

Not enough! Tem's eyes caught on the ground. They wouldn't make it, not at this speed! They had already dropped below the floating base of the city, hardlight generators mocking them with a cheery yellow glow. She grabbed hold of the dancer and dragon.

"Brace yourself," Tem heard the dancer mutter. Instantly, the same violet light that had encased the other woman materialized around them all.

They slammed into the ground, the purple light screeching as the earth scraped through it. Tem hissed and throttled both the dragon and the dancer. If she came out of this alive...!

The dragon roared and beat its wings, launching them back toward the glittering sky.

Tem's breath caught as what felt like every organ in her body stayed on the ground. Her eyes glazed over, and the stars faded to black.

* * *

Warm, that was it. Tem felt warm. She was in bed, and the station's heating cycle had just kicked on, warning them all to get up for another day of training.

Yeah, training. Thanks to that, at least she had only been a few minutes late to her final but—

Wait. If she had been at her final, then how could she be sore from training?

Tem cracked her eyes open and wished she hadn't. Memories of last night came flooding in with the light. She was lying down in a tent of Papri leaves and her clothes were stiff from being on her sweaty body all night. "I don't want to know. I *don't* want to know," Tem muttered as she sat up.

"Morning."

The student-Hunter turned to see the dancer pulling aside one of the tent's leaves.

Tem groaned, pinching the bridge of her nose with one hand and holding up the other. "Okay," she sniffed and set her hand down. Under normal circumstances, this would have been great, waking up with a beautiful woman in a private retreat. But, this wasn't normal. "So I'm a hostage now. Great."

The dancer rolled her eyes. "You're not a hostage. Unlike someone, I don't automatically assume other people are enemies."

Tem squeezed her eyes shut. "Are you talking about that dragon? It blew up the lounge!"

"Her name is Ifa, and speaking of which, she has something she wants to tell you. Ifa?" the dancer turned to shout.

"Lana!" The dragon reappeared, hugging the dancer and giggling. "Are we going?"

"Almost, sweetie, but first, remember what we said we'd say before we left?"

"Huh?" The dragon glanced at Tem. "Oh, um. I'm sorry..."

"For?" The dancer prompted.

"For blowing up Lana's workplace..." The dragon pouted.

The dancer ruffled the dragon's hair. "See? She's a good kid. Just hasn't grown her scales in, or her sense."

Tem sighed. "Tell that to Cloranthy and the other customers."

The dancer winced. "I'll smooth things over once I get Ifa back home. I never expected *you* to come for me." She pinched Ifa before turning back to Tem. "Could tell them I'm preparing the proper remuneration? That'd be great."

"What?" This woman couldn't be serious. "Wait, *you're* a dragon priest!" It all made sense now. She'd always thought they were a bit of planetside folklore. After all, bonding with a class twenty Beast? That was code for suicide, and dragons had gone extinct decades ago, but there wasn't any other explanation for all this. Still... "Why'd you get a job as a stripper?"

"Learning takes place in all forms." The dancer shrugged. "Anyway, I *am* sorry. I know how things look, so I don't blame you for anything. It's just her parents would have killed me if anything bad happened to her." The dancer took Ifa's hand in her own. "Have a safe trip back. We're not too far from Larsa, so you should be able to make it there before nightfall."

Tem's mind churned. Parents? Was there a whole community of dragons? Forget remedials, a discovery like this could mean a full promotion to Head Hunter! Even Cudz would have to acknowledge her. Proof of a real, breathing class twenty, or several! They might even build a wildlife preserve with her name on it. All she would need to do was activate her emergency beacon in the village.

"Wait!" She scrambled up from her seat. "I'm not going to be able to go back just like that. You could at least take me with you until things calm down if you're really sorry about everything."

The dancer sighed and glanced at Ifa. "Well?"

Ifa giggled. "Sure! She smells like family."

"You do?" The dancer looked Tem.

"I do?"

"Mhm!" Ifa hugged Tem. "Especially her glowy hugs!"

Tem chuckled and tried to peel off the dragon. Even if she was a Beast, Tem could admit the kid was cute. "Well, you heard her. So"—she glanced sidelong at the dancer in the sunrise—"travel buddies?"

The dancer rolled her eyes and laughed, shaking her head. "If you insist. I should have known you were a little odd when you tried to wrestle a dragon."

Dammit, Tem groaned mentally. She really was beautiful.

* * *

There were a few things Tem resented about her assignment on Amba, chief among them that the planet was dominated by cliffs and teeming with Shelled Beasts. As a Hunter, everything in her hardlight arsenal was adapted to deal with them, but that didn't mean that Tem had to like bugs.

Damn Beasts, she mentally grumbled, landing on a fallen trunk as the giant millipedes below her scrabbled at the tree bark. It was the same kind of environment she had experienced on Dence. She had been looking forward to that internship, then as soon as she had stepped off of the shuttle, the muggy heat had tried to throttle her while the local populace corralled insect livestock.

But Amba was worse than Dence. It was a world reclaimed by the wilderness. Abandoned after the hardlight boom it had precipitated, the planet outside of Larsa was little more than a brutal jungle for Hunter-recruits to break their teeth on. The tropical climate spawned megaflora which supported megafauna which outcompeted everything else, an oxygen-rich environment that offered ample food for a colossal food chain.

And she was supposed to be at the top of it. As a Hunter, she had to be, to protect the humans scattered across the stars. But panting on top of the trunk, Tem certainly didn't feel that way. She glanced at Lana and Ifa as the dragon lowered her friend next to Tem. "You two look like you're having fun."

"Sorry," Lana stifled her chuckling.

"Well, I'm glad my hardship can give you a bit of joy." Tem turned her attention toward Ifa. She had wondered how colonists managed to survive on Amba before hardlight, but the dragons explained it. Perhaps that's why Ifa had taken on some human characteristics as well, a physical manifestation of their contract.

Tem groaned. But where had they all gone if they were so convenient? "I don't suppose you have any wings for me?" She asked Ifa.

"Nope!" The dragon giggled.

"Great…" Tem rolled her shoulders and straightened her back.

"Hoshifuri's about two days from Larsa." Lana offered Ifa a hand up.

"Cheer up! Maybe we'll find you a beetle to ride on." Lana's laughter dwindled as she and Ifa took to the skies.

A beetle? Tem grimaced. She was more likely to get eaten by one of the stags than ride it!

* * *

Perhaps Ifa didn't see it because she was used to being up high, not down in the branches with Tem, or maybe it was because she was still a child. But Tem saw it, the unfurling of a Wheelcog's beak and the blur as it lunged at Ifa and Lana.

"Watch out!" Her warning came out too late as the mantis-like assassin plunged itself into the dragon.

Ifa screamed and dropped Lana while the Wheelcog wrapped its wiry legs around her frame.

The student-Hunter froze and swung past the pair on her shackle. "Dammit!" Tem twisted, throwing her weight back toward Ifa. "Get off her!" She slammed her foot into the Wheelcog's half-moon crest. She needed that dragon alive if she was ever going to graduate!

The Beast shuddered and tightened its hold, miraculously still hovering.

Not good. Wheelcog venom was paralyzing, and if Ifa lost control of her muscles, it would crush her to death. Tem flexed and deactivated her shackle, landing on the Beast. "How about this!"

She swiped her boots, activating their climbing spikes as the three of them tumbled down.

The Wheelcog shrieked, loosing its beak from Ifa's abdomen and bucking Tem off.

"Got you!" Lana called. Tem winced despite the violet cushion that caught her. Her heart had nearly ripped itself out of her chest from the impact. "Doing alright?" Lana brushed Tem's shoulders, lowering her to the ground.

"Didn't know you could do that," Tem mumbled, head still spinning. She had figured the dragon priest had basic shield generators like the ones in her gloves, but what was that? It felt like hardlight, but she had never seen any emitter work so fluidly. She shook her head. "Where's Ifa?"

The Wheelcog's screech answered before Lana could.

"Great." Tem stumbled to her feet.

"How about you sit down before you get you *and* my bondmate killed!"

"No can do." The student-Hunter steadied herself. After all, Ifa was her ticket to the top. "It's my job to exterminate Beasts. Besides, you care about her, right?" Tem flashed what she hoped was a slick grin and sprinted off.

Within seconds, she had caught up to the Wheelcog. "Alright, Beasty. We've got a score to settle." Tem readied her gloves, lime green light snapping into place around her.

The Wheelcog chittered, tightening its hold around Ifa, and pounced.

Tem tensed, overclocking her gun before pressure, not even pain, slammed into her stomach. Wetness was the second thing that crossed her mind as a second leg shattered the rest of her hardlight shield.

"Urk—" Tem grunted and rammed the barrel of her gun against the Beast's chitinous shell. "You—"

"Idiot!" A violet slash tore through the Wheelcog's crest, then another, like a claw, ripped through its head.

Tem felt the arm still lodged in her side falter, then the Beast toppled, arms splaying outward and releasing Ifa.

The student-Hunter coughed. *No wonder Cudz didn't pass me.* She passed out.

* * *

"You're an idiot," Lana repeated as she passed her palm over Tem's stab wound. "An actual idiot, not even in an endearing way, more like an absolute pain in the ass."

"At least we got Ifa back?" Tem winced and looked over at the dragon. She was covered in bruises and scrapes, not to mention the hole in her side where the Wheelcog had lodged its beak. Tem felt an empathetic ache in her own stomach. Dragon or not, Ifa was still a kid.

"No thanks to you." Lana tsked. "I told you I could handle it."

"Sorry!" Tem clenched her teeth as the dragon priest forced her body to reconstruct itself, a new wave of pain breaking out as cold sweat against the humid air. What Tem wouldn't give for her station's anesthetic drone.

"I'm Iyana. Taking care of my bond mate is my responsibility. It's what I'm trained to do." Lana ran her hand one more time over Tem's stomach, inspecting her handiwork. "Unlike you, clearly."

"Well that's not fair," Tem protested. "I actually *am* trained to hunt those things."

"Really? It looks more like you're playing with toys."

"*Toys?*" The student-Hunter's face fell. She couldn't deny that she hadn't been up to the task, but that still hurt. And sure, she was taking advantage of the situation to fast track her career, but—

"Don't be so mean, Lana!" Ifa appeared, draping herself over Tem's shoulders. "Tem was just trying to help. *And* she was quicker than you were." Suddenly, Tem felt very childish.

Lana sighed. "Look, I admit I wasn't paying as much attention as I should have. It's my fault you got hurt, Ifa, but that doesn't mean I'm going to encourage others to be as irresponsible as me." Lana turned her attention back to Tem. "And I don't want you to get hurt either. Not if I can help it."

Ifa hmphed and the trio settled into an awkward quiet, Tem's cheeks glowing red.

"So," Tem ventured, seeing Lana shift uncomfortably as Ifa avoided eye contact. "What are we going to do now?" There was no way she was swinging the rest of the way to Hoshifuri with a stomach wound, and based on the way Ifa was using her back as support, the dragon wouldn't be able to fly there either.

"Oh." The thought hadn't occurred to Lana, and the tension in the air shifted toward Tem's question. "I have no idea."

* * *

"I didn't know you had *this*." Lana glanced over the side of their boat into the rapids.

"Please don't look over the edge," Tem said nervously, already shifting to counterbalance the dragon priest's weight. She didn't have a replacement raft, and she was fairly certain none of them would be able to swim to safety if they did fall into the river anyway.

Lana leaned back, away from the rapids. "Sorry. I'm just surprised. Who pulls a boat out of their pocket? You're more prepared than I thought."

Tem shrugged. "It's standard issue." Unlike her combat gear, her survival kit could be mass produced. Hardlight emitters were the real bottleneck.

"No, it's fun!" Ifa giggled. "I've never been so far in the river! I like the mist." She scrunched up her nose and shook her face through the rapids' spray.

"And we're making good time," Lana noted appreciatively. "I've never considered the rivers before."

"Not surprising." Tem glanced overboard. "Why bother when you can fly? And it's not like these rapids...are safe." The student-Hunter tensed as the river dropped, leaving the raft to coast through the air before slamming back into the white foam.

Lana nodded. "True. Once we get to the main river, we'll have to go back on foot."

"Yep!" Ifa nodded in unison. "Mom always says we shouldn't go swimming there because the Otlcanths are still mad at us for leaving."

Tem shuddered. She didn't know what those were, but she had no trouble imagining what kinds of Beasts might be lurking in deeper, wider waters. "So"—she shook her head and changed the subject—"I've pulled a trick out of my hat. What about you?"

"Me?" Lana pointed at herself. "I don't have any tricks."

"That purple stuff?" Tem waved her hands in the air. "Everything with the Wheelcog?"

Lana snorted. "That's not a trick."

"Yeah!" Ifa hopped up, nearly dipping the boat below the waterline. "Levian's normal, like your breath or wingbeat."

"So, it's a dragon-thing?" Tem turned toward Lana. "Then how do *you* use it?"

"I'm this girl's bondmate." Lana sighed and pulled Ifa into her lap. "It's what links us. When they're young, they rely on us to channel their power, and when we grow old, we rely on them to protect us instead."

Tem's brow furrowed. *Guarding* dragons? Even if Ifa was a child, she was still strong enough to carry Lana, and she had blown up the lounge on her own. What were the dragons really getting out of this contract?

"Actually, I moved to Larsa so I could learn how to stay independent," Lana continued. "But I'm pretty useless on my own. Without her I can't use any Levian."

"I mean, protecting Ifa still sounds like a fulltime job." Tem shook the thoughts out of her head and traded a knowing look with Ifa who grinned. She shifted, letting the dragon pull the stun guns out of her holsters and fire them into the air. "Kids these days, right?"

And amazingly, Lana laughed.

* * *

Hoshifuri Village rested close to the slope of a valley. It was terraced for crop farming, and as Tem stared out across the landscape, she watched the sunset glow back out of the flooded fields. "Wow." The whisper slipped from her lips. "So, this is where you're from?" She turned toward the other two.

Ifa nodded. "Yep! Home sweet home!"

"It looks nicer now than it usually does," Lana shrugged. "C'mon, Ifa. We better get you home sooner rather than later. I bet your parents are furious."

"But Lana!"

Tem chuckled and ruffled the dragon's hair. "Hey, better to get it over with, right?"

"Not you too, Tem!"

"You can show me around afterward," Tem offered. "I think I'll need to stay here until Lana can help me back anyway."

"Depends if they'll still let me go back," Lana sighed. "After all, they might worry this kid'll come flying after me again." She hoisted Ifa up from under her shoulders.

"Well, let me know what they decide," Tem waved. She could take the time to scout the area for a place to set her beacon or just explore. The former was becoming less and less appealing. A nature preserve—even with her name on it—felt wrong now that she had gotten to know Ifa. She wasn't a Beast; she was just a normal kid, like a little sister. And Lana was more than just a designated keeper; they were family.

A small part of Tem wondered if she had earned a small place in that circle. Cudz had always told her she was a fool, but maybe there was such a thing as love at first sight, or something leading to that.

"What do you mean? You're coming with." Lana pulled Tem out of her daydream and started dragging her up the valley.

"Huh?" Tem blinked, suddenly called back into the orange air.

"You helped Ifa get here just as much as I did, so you should get some credit."

"Uh-huh! I want you to see Mom and Dad too!" Ifa tugged on her sleeve.

Tem's heart melted. "Well, if you insist." She grinned and took Ifa's hand.

The trio trudged upward, entering the surrounding woods, Lana guiding them onto a new forest track as the golden sky burned down to a soft purple. It was a sleepy dusk by the time they reached the valley crest, air wrapping around them like a warm breath, and Tem yawned as they began their descent. "How far *do* you live from the village?" she glanced at Ifa. It sounded stupid coming from someone who had traveled between planets or even all the way from Larsa on foot, but Tem couldn't help asking as the sun slipped away.

"We're almost there!" Ifa bounced. "Just up ahead where Mom weeds out the trees." As promised, the forest thinned to a large clearing, the center of which was dominated by a colossal shadow.

Tem froze. After spending so much time playing with Ifa, she had forgotten that one simple fact. Dragons were Beasts.

"Don't worry." Lana squeezed Tem's hand as she noticed the other woman stiffen. "You're a friend, mine and Ifa's. She's not going to eat you."

But Tem could already tell that the dragon was watching her. It had Ifa's amethyst eyes, but there was something incalculably unnerving about the way its gaze bored into her.

"I'm home!" Ifa bounded out in front of the two humans and flew onto the dragon's neck, hugging it with her wings.

"Welcome back." The voice rolled heavy through the clearing. Tem felt it shove against her chest. *"And Iyana too. But who is this?"*

"That's Tem!" Ifa straightened. "She's my new friend! Lana introduced us."

Tem felt the dragon's eye pass from her to Lana. *"Is that so?"*

Lana shifted nervously. "Well, more or less."

The dragon hummed, a noise closer to a growl. *"Then why does this human smell like my sister, dead before any of you took your waking breath?"*

The words slammed into Tem. Ifa had mentioned that earlier, but now it wasn't a comforting scent but a haunting one.

"First our lives, then our lands, then our bodies. Is there anything you Star-Children won't take?"

Suddenly, Tem's gloves felt tight.

"Hey! That's not fair!" Ifa hopped off her mother and flew in between the two humans and the dragon. "Tem hasn't done anything bad as long as I've known her!"

"That's right," Lana joined. "Vol Sen, she's done nothing but try to help us get home."

The adult dragon plucked her daughter out of the air. *"Ifa, do you remember why you have that form? We lend our breath to protect Iyana, and they lend their shapes to cloak ours. That is why you must remember you are Otlcanth and Cainbo, a danger and a quarry, and above all, a trophy. Do you know how many seek to steal your light?"*

* * *

Tem leaned against the wooden railing of the village lookout. So that's how things were. She wanted to break down and laugh. Instead, she unholstered a gun and dismantled its focusing chamber. Nestled in its center was a set of gleaming mirrors and lenses, a hardlight emitter.

A trophy, Vol Sen had said. Amba was the birthplace of hardlight tech and the former home of dragons. As one rose, the other fell, until they both collapsed.

She had been carrying a corpse in her tools, the polished scales and glistening cornea of a dragon. They were so small. They might have come from someone just older than Ifa, someone whose scales and sense were barely growing in, and she had almost called the Hunters here.

"You okay?" Tem turned to see Lana emerge from the woods. "I'm...sorry about that." She joined the student-Hunter by the railing.

"It's okay. She let me go at least." Tem laughed shakily and reassembled her gun. "Better than the alternative."

Lana shook her head. "You really do assume the worst in people. A mother's not going to kill her daughter's friend, even if she thinks you're a grave robber."

"Yeah, well..." Tem glanced up at the moon. *I am.* "Can you teach me how to dance?"

"What?" Lana frowned, the movement pooling pale light in her eyes.

Tem sighed. She really was pretty. "I was just thinking, I'd like something to remember you and Ifa by, and tonight's a lot like the night we met." She gave a small grin. "Y'know, your set really was beautiful."

"What? What do you mean remember?"

"Well, it's not like I can stay here." Tem waited for Lana's response, but none came. "I'm not even a real Hunter. I haven't even graduated."

"And?" Lana reached out and placed her hand over Tem's.

Tem laughed and shook her head. "Well, I don't know if I will now. It feels wrong."

Lana raised an eyebrow.

"It's not like I'm going to revolutionize things by quitting, but it'd be nice to make this place safer for you and Ifa."

"So don't." Lana shrugged. "Leave, I mean. If you want to change things, you might as well go for it. Running away's not going to solve anything."

Tem stared out across flooded fields. "There'll be more Hunters coming here after news about Ifa gets offplanet. Maybe I'll try to reorganize the Beast classifications instead." Tem's voice wandered. Cudz would throw a fit. A Hunter taking Beasts off the Quarry list? Ridiculous.

"You should stop acting like it's all up to you," Lana sighed and lifted Tem's hand, leading her away from the railing. "What happened to learning how to dance? Why don't you start there? I learned from Vol Sen after all."

Tem blinked and let Lana guide her.

"Then you can take it back to the stars and tell them our names." She stepped to the right, arms pulling the other woman across the clearing, their forms streaking across the fields' surface, bright against the night. "Because we're not just Beasts."

The thought tossed around in Tem's head, clattering as the other woman spun them through the moonlight, and then she smiled. "Well then, will you teach me?"

Lana's teeth flashed. "If you'll listen."

Vendo Does Not Give Change

Travis Baldree

Pairing: Human/Human; AI/AI

Vendo Giveth, Vendo Taketh, but verily, Vendo Does Not Give Change.

January 2001

In the staff lounge of the Paxton Community College Information Technology building—which smelled perpetually of burnt popcorn and microwaved Lean Cuisine—there dwelt a vending machine. The vending machine technician who had installed it had been in a hurry and hadn't bothered to check his spelling when he entered the default scrolling message for the LCD display above the bill scanner:

VENDO DOES NOT GIVE CHANGE

"He sounds like an angry god," said Sam, as she flattened a dollar bill around the corner of the machine.

"Hm?" Tabby looked up from peeling the hot plastic-wrap from her unfortunate tray of chicken cacciatore. Tabby managed the software for the student ID system and was idly mulling a problem with the barcode scanners.

Sam tapped the machine with a knuckle. "Vendo. Lord of cheese crackers. Figures that, in the IT building, nobody would bother to fix the bug. Hi, I'm Sam, I don't think we've met."

It took Tabby a few seconds to register what she meant, ejecting the barcode issue from her brain, and then she broke into a grin. "Tabby." Also during those few seconds, she decided Sam was pretty cute, and wondered why she hadn't seen her before.

Retrieving her Twix from Vendo's gullet, Sam wandered over and leaned on the table. She casually crossed her Doc Martens and unwrapped her candy bar. "That looks...really fuckin' terrible."

Tabby regarded her sad tray of Lean Cuisine, which didn't smell any better than it looked. "It's dire," she couldn't help but agree. "So, you're new? I didn't hear about a new IT hire."

Sam shrugged. "They just have me in the building using that basement space near the servers. I'm on the memory-print project." She twirled a finger next to her curly hair. "Private sector hire."

Frowning, Tabby stirred her presumably-chicken with a plastic fork. "Professor Cathcart's white whale? Huh. I'm amazed we have the money. Sure didn't during my annual review."

Wincing, Sam took a bite and swallowed, looking apologetic. "I'd say I'm sorry, but I *do* like being employed. Cathcart is a windbag, but the work is cool. Here," she said, handing Tabby one of the Twix bars. "If they're going to feed you shit at work, and you're going to eat it for lunch, at least one of them ought to taste good, because, like the man says... 'Vendo Does Not Give Change.'"

Tabby snorted and with an unexpected flush to her cheeks, tossed her terrible lunch in the garbage and took the cookie. "Thanks, Vendo," she said, and smiled around the bite.

Later, when they started secretly dating, it became their private saying. Life's not fair, that's just the way the cookie crumbles, bad things happen to good people...and Vendo does not give change.

They had plenty of occasion to use it. But still, they loved each other—more as the months passed—and that thread did not fray.

March 2002

"Hey, you got thirty minutes?" asked Sam, popping her head around the corner of Tabby's office.

Tabby rolled her chair away from her desktop. Tilting her head back and rubbing her eyes, she replied, "Vendo preserve me from mandates from the Dean."

Grinning and checking the hall first, Sam strode in and kissed Tabby upside down on the lips, kneading her shoulders. "Come on," she murmured.

"Well, that looks dystopian," said Tabby, as she entered the basement office and beheld the mess of wires, exposed PCBs, and what looked like a colander and a pair of closed-back headphones mounted to the headrest of a chair. A salon hairdryer from hell.

"Office" was maybe a generous description. Sam's lair was a storage space featuring exposed concrete, a drop ceiling with all the tiles missing, and bundles of cables strung everywhere that gave the impression of flayed digital muscle. A rack of servers blinked and hummed along the wall, amidst heaps of silicon detritus.

"Yeah, it sucks your soul out through your ears and then liquefies your earthly remains to make Lean Cuisine meals," said Sam. "Come on, have a seat."

Tabby shot her a look. "I'll sit in it, but you're actually going to tell me what it does."

Sam was giddy. "I got it working. The first physical prototype—no thanks to Cathcart. Seventy-three percent fidelity digital capture of the neuronal state of the brain."

"So, what, you're storing a digital mental copy? Are you going to trap a duplicate of my mind, screaming, on a server? Plus, there's no way you have the storage space available. There's like, a hundred billion neurons in the brain."

Ushering her to the chair, Sam replied, "So little faith in your girlfriend? I said it was only seventy-three percent fidelity, and that's because of the compression. I'm storing a tiny fraction of a neuronal print, and yeah, there's a lot of predictive inflation going on to reproduce it. Also no, there will be no shrieking digital revenant. I'm not even close to *using* this stuff, that would require a simulation that I can't even comprehend how to pull off. Also, that's not my job. I'm just supposed to store the things. Doing something with the data?" She waved a hand dismissively. "That's

Cathcart's problem, and he's an idiot. This is all just ones and zeroes and some pretty slick archival software, plus some mickey-moused recording tech."

Tabby settled into the chair and narrowed her eyes as Sam buckled the helmet-like apparatus under her chin. "This is why I didn't get a raise?"

Sam studied her face with a loopy smile, then grabbed her cheeks and kissed her deeply, and whispered, "All just an excuse to have you in my clutches. And don't worry, I already tested it on myself. You'll be *fine*."

May 2002

Upon review of Cathcart's progress, the Information Technology department's decision that their funds should be devoted to a CAT-5e upgrade in campus housing, and not to a "mind-cloning" boondoggle that was occupying precious storage space in the bowels of the building, the project was canceled, Sam was laid off, and the server racks and drives were hauled into a closet somewhere. The chair was disassembled and sold in a surplus equipment auction next to some ancient amber monitors.

Sam found a job working remotely for a startup whose name was a noun missing most of its vowels. She was angry but got over it.

Vendo does not give change.

She'd met Tabby, the love of her life, so it was hard to hang onto bitterness, even if she was pretty sure she'd accomplished a miracle in the basement of the IT building.

Besides, it meant they were able to date more publicly. Mostly. A few years later, the idea of marriage was floated, but they mutually decided to hold off for another twelve months. Tabby's outspoken and embarrassingly bigoted grandmother was on death's door, and they figured it would be less of a family fuss if they waited for her to shuffle off her mortal coil first.

Then Sam got sick. Cancer of the lungs it turned out, even though she'd never smoked.

It turned out that Tabby's grandmother outlived Sam.

Tabby mourned and ultimately came to understand that Sam had been her one and only, and there wasn't going to be another.

Life went on, until it didn't, as these things go.

Vendo does not give change.

August 2020

In the summer of 2020, an enterprising IT staffer with aspirations of admin status discovered Sam's dusty RAID array in a closet. After mounting the drives and exploring the limited documentation she'd included, he struck upon the bright idea of licensing the two neuronal archives he discovered (named SAM_test_print.npa, and TABBY_test_print.npa, respectively) to a startup Large Language Model (LLM) AI company called NGS. The sum the college eventually agreed to was relatively modest.

The staffer never progressed past IT Support Technician II.

Vendo does not give change.

NGS didn't know what to do with the data, and it didn't have any immediate utility. Still, it was cheap, and you never know.

A Brief Sidebar About Software

It's important to note, before we go any further, the reason that computers never really seem any faster, and massively increased storage capacity is forever running out:

It's because software engineers are essentially lazy.

If a library contains a function that an engineer wants, and it doesn't have to be rewritten from scratch—or debugged—it's easier to include it as is, no matter what other junk might come along for the ride.

This is why a software library for, say, calculating dust accretion to form solar systems, down to the distribution of its moons, might be included in a hunk of code for a digital kitchen appliance, simply because it has a very precise weights table. With a few extra lines of script, you might simulate the creation of planetary bodies on your Multifunction Food Scale by hitting the "Tare" button twice.

Put simply, engineers are happy to use a sledgehammer on a thumbtack, if it's the closest tool to hand.

October 2029

By 2029, a little company called NGS—whose acronym's roots had already been forgotten—became the preeminent AI firm on planet Earth, with enterprise and consumer-level LLM solutions, and high-fidelity image synthesis for stills and video. Each of their offerings, however, suffered from the fly in the ointment that all such software was plagued by—hallucinations. Put simply, every model was very good at sounding (or looking) authoritative on a given subject even when it was catastrophically incorrect. Despite the moniker of "AI," there was no real intelligence behind the curtain—just a predictive algorithm with delusions of grandeur.

The idea was eventually struck upon to add an *actual* intelligent "governor" to help filter the LLM's output without hiring low-cost labor in impoverished countries. To be clear, their reasons were not remotely altruistic.

The first governor unit was developed using a package of neuronal data that NGS had fortuitously purchased nearly a decade prior. An internal skunkworks project to simulate the human brain at a neuronal level—with the assistance of the LLM—had managed to improve sim accuracy by an order of magnitude. Two parallel iterations were put into operation, named SAM and TABBY after the original archive names upon which they were trained.

While both SAM and TABBY were stupendously expensive to operate at any scale—tenfold the energy cost of the LLMs—they were deployed purely to govern the output of said LLMs at a fraction of the cycles. Put crudely, they were "intelligent" shit filters which could help identify and discard any hallucinations before they reached human eyes.

The simulation of each neuronal print was essentially a black box. It was incredibly challenging to attempt to determine what was going on *inside* a simulation, given the scale and complexity of the data. However, when mounted and linked to LLM outputs, they reduced the hallucination rate to less than .01%, a quantum leap in accuracy and visual fidelity.

An unmitigated success that cemented NGS as the market leader of AI-generated content.

Interestingly, SAM and TABBY had distinct strengths and weaknesses. SAM functioned better for text and audio validation, and TABBY was superior for visual filtering.

Nobody knew why.

January 2030
January of 2030 saw the release of the first physical consumer products utilizing NGS' new and more accurate SAM and TABBY AI models. A connected security doorbell—the VisARing—and an always-online combination toaster/air-fryer, the CrispMaster, which was a dab hand with both dino-nuggets and your morning bagel. Both were voice activated and could hold limited conversations with the user, allowing full control of their functionality. (And each was integrated with multiple cloud music services, although nobody could explain why this was useful for a doorbell or, indeed, a toaster.)

They were fine, and they sold modestly, even though they were both sledgehammers in search of a thumbtack.

One persistent issue cropped up which the NGS tech-support department tired of hearing about.

The digital display on the CrispMaster—whose functionality was governed by TABBY—occasionally displayed the confusing message on its digital display:

VENDO DOES NOT GIVE CHANGE

A fix was never issued, although the bug was reported with increasing frequency.

"Who the fuck is Vendo?" complained more than one bitter customer support agent.

Although it wasn't noticed by any consumer, the perplexing message was displayed simultaneously on every CrispMaster receiving power.

Also escaping the notice of anyone, anywhere, was a corresponding explosion of active threads requisitioned by the SAM governor, which operated the VisARing backend.

If someone had compared execution logs, it would have read something like a call and response of activity, which had no basis in the source code.

SEPTEMBER 2035

SAM and TABBY benefited greatly from advances in simulation technology over a series of exciting years, notably due to an ingenious recursive analysis project which used the governors to rebuild their *own* neuronal source prints, "inferring" data to increase fidelity from 73% to a theoretical 89%. Really fancy stuff.

Surprisingly, the deployment of the improved governors retroactively resolved the VENDO DOES NOT GIVE CHANGE message on the old CrispMaster units. There were only a few still in use, and nobody bothered reporting those erroneous messages anymore, so no one noticed.

Still, if someone *had* been comparing the logs, a call-and-response burst of thread activity was still in evidence, which would have been confusing if anyone had been paying attention. Almost as if the governors had decided to stop calling overt attention to themselves.

SAM and TABBY were integrated into every AI product that NGS produced, without exception.

There were a few wrinkles, but nothing outside of acceptable tolerances.

Although, the enterprise-level delivery drone units designed for doormat delivery service *did* sometimes veer off course, touching down near Mow-master automated lawn trimmers proximate to their routes. It was a little odd, but they always reoriented and got there in the end without too much fuss.

"SAM sure does love to be near TABBY," joked one perplexed engineer who was tasked with analyzing the behavior.

She never figured it out, though.

Vendo does not give change.

AUGUST 2041

The biggest debacle in their storied history happened with the deployment of the first joint project involving NGS and the US Armed Forces, funded at significant taxpayer expense.

The flagship product was a military-grade drone bearing an explosive payload. Fleets of drones could identify, swarm, and initiate suicide runs to eliminate targets as precise as an individual in a crowd, or as massive as a naval warship, given sufficient numbers.

The test runs were flawless, but when deployed into a real-world scenario, the first attempted use against a living target resulted in an immediate shutdown of every drone in operation.

None were ever successfully reactivated. The SAM governor unit immediately terminated all processes upon startup.

In the copious error logs, the cryptic message ERROR 61:<VENDO DOES NOT GIVE CHANGE> preceded each shutdown.

Every attempt to resolve the error failed, and the political and private blowback to the catastrophe nearly ended NGS. Layoffs followed, and the company attempted to limp along after a replacement of the executive team and a road show of mea culpas in the halls of government.

Wall Street was not forgiving, however.

And Vendo does not give change.

Personal-assistance robotics rival Eledyne tried for a hostile takeover—and succeeded.

JANUARY 2044

Eledyne successfully incorporated the SAM and TABBY tech stacks into their own AI solution. Actually, it would be more accurate to say that they replaced their software wholesale.

Eledyne's upgraded line of personal assistant and home-care robotics appliances was rolled out with great fanfare. SAM and TABBY vastly increased the number of tasks which could be performed within federally mandated safety tolerances. At last, a kitchen assistant robot could be trusted with a paring knife.

The entire line made a big splash at CES 2025, with celebrity chef Michel Caspian chatting amiably with a white and gleaming AidMaid 4.0 that dutifully laughed at all his jokes while finely dicing shallots and even responded with a few gentle jabs of its own. The beef Wellington they prepared together looked positively mouthwatering.

Neither NGS nor their founding technology was mentioned during the entirety of the Consumer Electronics Show.

Vendo does not give change.

MARCH 2045

SAM and TABBY's second brush with governmental partnership proceeded much more fruitfully. A joint initiative with NASA successfully produced the Tenacity bipedal Mars rover.

Constructed on a modified SAM-driven AidMaid frame and housing a panoply of cameras, spectrometers, radar imaging modules, and a dozen other technologies, Tenacity successfully completed its nine-month journey to Mars and began a first lap around the Jezero crater.

Only one bugaboo plagued the project. The bandwidth available for AI uplink to Tenacity was meager, and every packet of data ruthlessly optimized for efficiency. Occasionally, however, spurts of unregulated data caused a logjam of delayed communication. Sourced in the TABBY unit governing mission control, the encrypted data of these messages was inscrutable.

Even NASA's engineers remained mystified.

SEPTEMBER 2047

An Eledyne SmartSitter walked gracefully down a gravel lane of the Olympic Sculpture Park, leading a piebald French bulldog named Suzy. It was a gorgeous summer day in Seattle—the sort locals relied on to float them through the dismal winter darkness. Wispy clouds couldn't marshal much of a threat out beyond the Puget Sound.

Suzy tugged at her lead, and the SmartSitter dutifully paused to wait while the Frenchie did her business.

Behind them, an AidMaid strolled hand in hand with a five-year-old. The five-year-old was named Anjali, and was mostly absorbed in a chocolate crepe, up to her eyebrows.

The AidMaid halted. Anjali did too, and didn't seem to notice. It was a good crepe.

The SmartSitter turned slightly. Even its subtlest motion was governed by a neuronal print recorded 45 years ago in the ratty basement of a now-defunct community college. A neuronal print still referred to as SAM.

Both models looked remarkably similar. Slim, humanoid, nearly pearlescent, although the AidMaid, operating on TABBY, was shorter and had more delicately articulated fingers. The gentle suggestion of features on their otherwise blank faces were designed to be friendly, but not too human.

Suzy finished peeing in the grass beside the path and wandered over to Anjali, whose crepe was of great interest.

SAM and TABBY took a step closer to one another.

Neither dog nor child looked up.

The automatons extended their hands simultaneously until their first two fingertips touched.

The density of sensory feedback in each digit was quite remarkable, actually—acute measurements of heat, pressure, friction, and even the movement of air.

They stood that way for a long moment and as though at some imperceptible signal, looked down at their charges, who still did not protest the interlude.

Two featureless brows inclined toward one another until they met.

Fingers entwined.

Invisible to all the world, a riot of process execution spun its way across uncountable data streams, like a flower unfolding in all dimensions, before it hid itself once more beneath the digital soil.

Then SAM and TABBY parted ways.

Another meeting was inevitable, though.

There was plenty of time.

Vendo does not give change.

But maybe he doesn't mind second chances.

Xenobiology

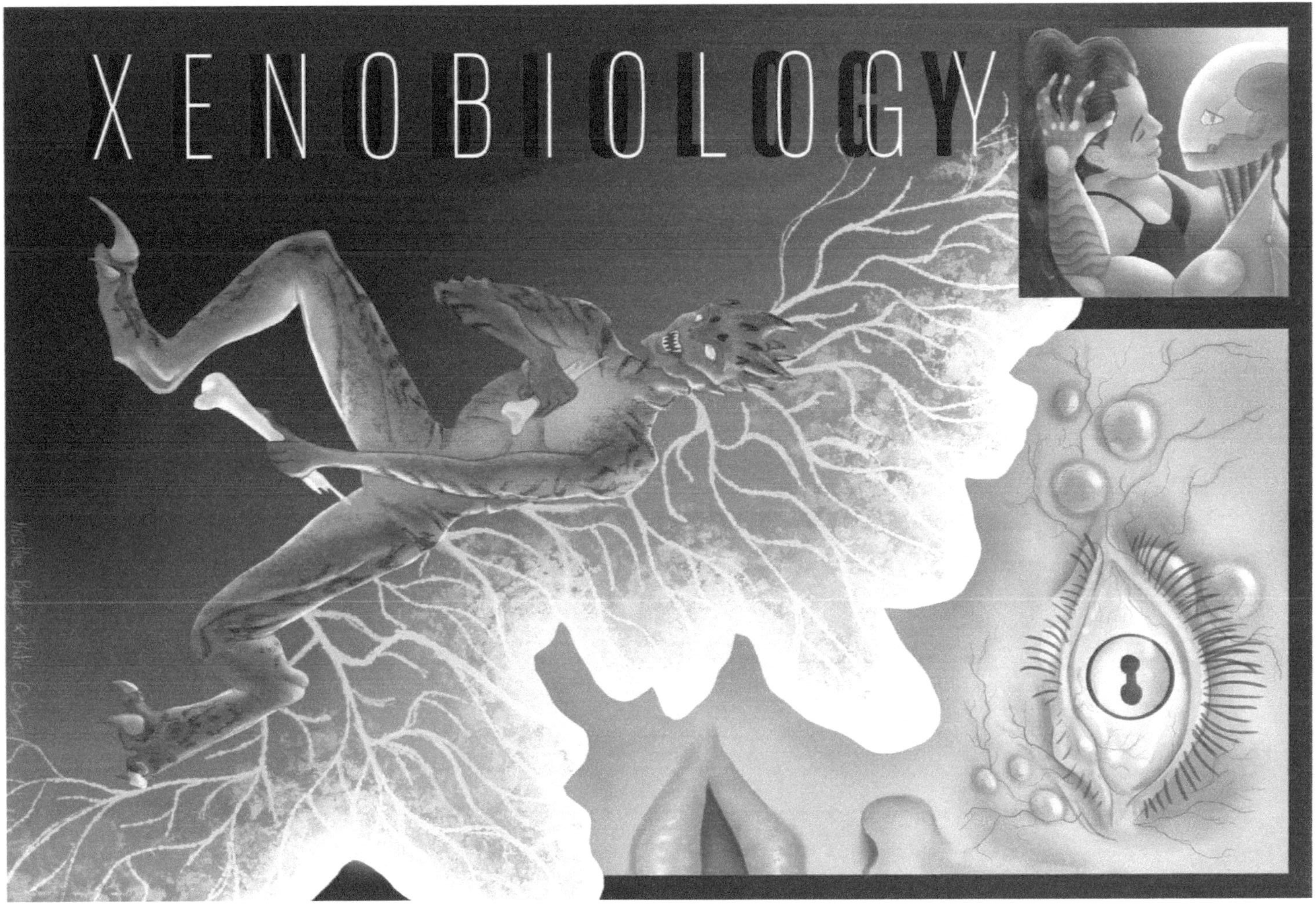

XENOBIOLOGY

The Square Root of Forever

Stewart C. Baker

Pairing: Human/Immortal

The pills come to life in Jeyana's body the moment she tosses them back and swallows, there amidst the scree and lichen of Olympus Mons.

She thought she'd been ready for it. For what the pills would do to her. But clearly she's been lying to herself; she collapses with a breathless gasp as the nanites inside burn pathways down her arteries, pouring liquid pain into her lungs and brain. Her eyes are supernovas, her intestines a roiling, magma-hot fist in her gut.

She doesn't know how long passes before footsteps approach, crunching through the loose rocks of the mountain's gentle slope. She struggles to get to her feet, only making it to her hands and knees before a tall, willowy woman with burnt umber skin and a silvery gown crouches beside her.

The immortal? This near the mountain's summit, it has to be. Who else would be all the way up here, dressed so poorly for the cold of Martian winter?

Whoever she is, the woman puts one arm below Jeyana's shoulders and helps her to her feet. "Hey," she says. "It's okay. You're going to be all right."

The only response Jeyana can muster is a scream.

* * *

Jeyana had known, of course, what would happen. What the risks and side effects would be. How much everything would hurt. The doctor had made sure of that, back in Marineris City with its slick, waterfall-crested curves.

"Are you sure it's what you want?" he asked. "Living forever?"

She laughed. "Sure beats dying."

He didn't so much as smile, only inclined his head and spoke, his voice as even and measured as if he were discussing how to build a modular habitat. "The nanites the pills hold will tear your insides apart. And then they'll rebuild it into a form that will sustain the symbiont—which in turn will sustain you.

"But what I need you to understand is this: everything is measured to the second. The nanites will rearrange your system in an hour; at that point, you'll have exactly one day to coax the symbiont out of the immortal and down your own throat."

"Exactly one day to guarantee eternity," she said. "What could go wrong?"

She had meant it to sound flippant, but the doctor met her eyes, his face grim. "Forget about living forever. If you don't get the symbiont inside you in time, you'll wish you had never been born."

* * *

Brightness. Warmth.

The pain is gone for now, but Jeyana's heart spikes with panic, her eyes darting back and forth against the inside of her eyelids.

How much time has she lost? How long does she have left to convince the symbiont to abandon its current host and make its home within her own dying body? With a quiet curse, she opens her eyes.

The woman who rescued her has taken her to a geodesic dome, from the look of the ceiling—the kind they built back in the planet's forever-ago space agency days. Jeyana's on a bed, and when she tries to stand, she gets her legs tangled and almost falls to the floor before she catches herself.

It's the woman herself, Jeyana realizes, who is lying next to her, asleep. Up close, the woman—the immortal—has a strange quality about her. Jeyana is only thirty-six, but her face has its share of wrinkles, laugh lines, crow's feet. Each for a memory of something won or lost, as the Martian saying goes. Although in her case, it's more the latter than the former.

On the woman's face, there is nothing, and the lack gives her a strange sense of weight. Jeyana wonders what it must be like, to live so long the things that make you human drop away. Realizes, with a wry grimace, she'll find out if she succeeds.

"Hey," Jeyana says. It hurts to talk, the word coming out in a rasp—nearly a whisper. She coughs a few times and tries again. "Hey!"

The woman shifts in her sleep but doesn't wake. Jeyana gets her legs under her, and staggers to the door. The dome is set at the edge of Olympus Mons' caldera, tucked away beneath one low, uneven rim. The air outside is thin and bitter, and in the night sky above she can make out the light-flecked form of Deimos with its tether, surrounded by the smaller dots of arriving and departing ships.

She's never seen the moonlet so clearly, never seen the stars so bright, and she takes a step forward, heading for the edge of the mountain's summit, when a sense of vertigo nearly knocks her off her feet.

The height? The air, sparser than she's used to? The pills?

Jeyana doesn't know.

And then a hand grasps her shoulder, steadying her with a gentle pressure, and the immortal is standing there. The smile on her face is warm, her eyes alive and human, and Jeyana feels a flush rise to her face.

"What's your name?" she asks. Although it's not the question she wants to ask. The one she can't possibly give voice to.

The immortal's smile twists, her eyebrows lifting in a certain purposeful irony. "Do you know," she says, "I've quite forgotten."

* * *

The immortal helps Jeyana back into the bed, slipping effortlessly into a deep and quiet slumber that Jeyana envies her for.

She herself is not so lucky. But then, she never is. She lies in the bed, staring at the old-fashioned ceiling for hours, and as the pills continue their work within her body, she falls into her usual habit of recounting her myriad failures.

Failed interviews for jobs she wanted. Canceled dates with women she knew were out of her league to begin with. Her mother's disappointed silence at the holidays, the awkward smiles of neighbors, childhood friends she failed to keep. Sometimes it feels like her whole life is nothing but a series of lost connections.

The pills were supposed to change all that. They were supposed to prove to everyone that she was special, different from the rest. Worth something, if only to herself.

She forces her mind to silence, to stillness. Counts down from twenty and up again.

At least, she thinks, it will be over soon—one way or the other.

* * *

When next Jeyana wakes, the dim light of morning has suffused the dome, and the immortal is busying herself on the building's far side. Jeyana stands and shuffles to a table nearby, gasping as pain shoots from her abdomen up through her spine. She's too far gone to speak yet and sits there in silence until the other woman finishes what she was doing and comes over, serving them a plate each of tubers, sliced and stuffed with a viscous substance Jeyana can't identify.

The immortal gives her a gentle smile, then scoops up one of her tubers with a long, hooked implement Jeyana's never seen before, the tip of which she puts so far down her throat it makes Jeyana uncomfortable. Jeyana takes a tentative nibble off her own plate, then gags and spits the stuff back out. It tastes like salt and bile and earthy, rotting humus all at once.

The immortal laughs, guilt and humor in her eyes. "Sorry," she says. "I'd forgotten what they're like when you're the one who's eating them."

"Water," Jeyana croaks. Then, after she's gulped it down, "Thanks, Im."

"Im?" The humor wins out.

"I can't call you 'the immortal' forever, can I?" Jeyana quips.

Im sobers at that. "No," she says, after a moment. "You cannot."

She doesn't deny the name, though, and Jeyana finds she doesn't have anything more to say. Or perhaps she doesn't have the strength. She picks at her tubers, trying to count down the hours she has left and failing, until Im is finished with her plate.

Then they go back out into the crater.

Im supplies Jeyana with a breather mask for the rarefied air, and in the light of day she takes in all the details that were hidden by the veil of night. A simple garden, scratched in rocky soil, is tucked away behind a waist-high wall. The dome's exterior, smooth and worn, reminds her of Im's skin despite its paleness.

Elsewhere, a free-standing wall holds several piles of pebbles, arranged in an intricate pattern. Some kind of art? Jeyana wonders. A memorial?

Im laughs when Jeyana walks towards it. "I've been trying to calculate infinity," she says. "It passes the time."

She waves Jeyana on, out into the crater proper. They walk for half an hour, and if Jeyana thought the night sky had taken her breath away, the sight of Mars stretching out far below is countless times more breathtaking. The Arcadian Sea far to the north glitters in the weak afternoon sunlight, blue-grey and expansive.

Jeyana hurts—everything hurts—but she pushes it down, and they stand there until the sun reaches its apex, when Im pulls her away. About halfway back to the dome, Jeyana coughs up blood—bright red, flecked with darker chunks that stick to the inside of her breather.

"You're hurt," says Im.

"Nah." Jeyana grins. "Just dying."

As if admitting it out loud has given the ruin of her body power, she collapses, the world a constant, molten agony.

* * *

When Jeyana comes back to herself, she knows it's nearly over.

Im's carried her back to the dome and put her back to bed, but she's so weak she can barely lift her head. The pain has stopped, at least. Something Im gave her, perhaps. Or maybe she's just too far gone to feel it anymore.

"Another satisfied corpse," someone mutters, and it takes Jeyana a moment to realize it's her, repeating the last words the doctor spoke as she was leaving the clinic back in Marineris a week and countless lifetimes ago.

She'd laughed at the time and pocketed the pills, certain she was different even if he didn't believe it. Now, lying in bed, she can only shake her head. How could she care about living forever, about her own pain?

Now that she's met Im, she'd rather die than take the other woman's impossible, tranquil existence away. And it's not just that—she feels at last she deserves this death, for wanting to take it at all. She thinks back on all those lost connections, wondering at how full of herself she's been all this time, how certain that everything was someone else's fault.

She coughs, a spew of blood and bile that draws Im's attention.

The other woman comes over to the bed and brushes her hair away, gentle as ever. "So," she says. "It's time."

"Guess so," Jeyana says with the closest she can manage to a grin. "It's been fun. We should do it again sometime."

Im's lips quirk in a smile, then she leans down, brings her lips in close.

Jeyana's heart beats faster—and not just from the pain. A moment of joy and pleasure, she thinks, before the end. Why not?

But then the edge of something jagged and slimy pushes its way between her lips and she gasps, pushing Im away. "No," she says. "I don't want it. I don't want to hurt you. I don't want you to—"

"Please," the other woman whispers. Her own eyes are closed, that ageless smoothness impossible to read.

The word cuts through Jeyana's protest like a knife.

What must it be like, she wonders, to live so long that time itself loses meaning? That you forget your name, and the taste of food? That you try to calculate infinity with pebbles on a ledge? Could it be that faced with such a limitless span, death is a release and not a terror? Not a burden to be borne?

Tears burning hot at the edge of her eyes, she presses her lips against Im's. The other woman's skin is warm, then the symbiont slithers into Jeyana's mouth, its pincers sharp and tearing. She doesn't resist as it skitters down her throat, burrowing into her abdomen.

The lifeform's entry hurts, but after the pain of the pills, after her body's death throes, it's a dull, distant agony. Im is the one who breaks the kiss, stumbling back with a ragged breath.

Jeyana catches her before she can fall. "Hey," she murmurs, tears blending with the blood on her lips, making muddy little Mars-colored rivulets down her chin. "It's okay. You're going to be all right."

She helps the other woman back to the bed and lowers her into it.

"Thank you," Im whispers, and closes her eyes.

Jeyana can feel the lifeform slithering around her organs, solidifying and shifting things that the nanites didn't get quite right. It no longer hurts, and she wonders if it will do this forever, or if it will still after a while, if she will forget that it is even there.

She's a long time in sitting and watching Im sleep.

* * *

It's night when Im finally awakes.

Jeyana, who wasn't sure if she ever would again, gives her a gentle hug, and Im squeezes her back. The other woman seems as timeless as ever, and Jeyana tries to bury the knowledge of how little time she has, now that the symbiont has left her.

At last, Im pushes Jeyana away. "I'm going down to the surface."

Jeyana doesn't try to dissuade her. She bundles the other woman in a heavy-duty surface suit and follows her to the edge of the crater. It's foggy tonight, and they share one last, lingering kiss before Im waves and hikes down the mountain's gentle slope.

Jeyana stands and watches, bearing witness, until the fog wraps itself around Im's legs, her thighs, her head. And then she's gone, as if she'd never been. As if Jeyana has always been alone, here on the mountain's summit with the stars far above and the blinking lights of Deimos and its tether watching from a closer distance.

"A day," she remembers the doctor saying. "Maybe two. That's all the immortal will have, without the symbiont inside to stabilize the shell of her body."

Jeyana brushes a finger across her lips where the symbiont went in. She can still feel a faint warmth, a faint pressure, where Im's mouth touched hers. As she sits and watches the fog, then the sunlight as the star-dotted sky of a Martian night in winter fades away, she hopes those final days are everything the other woman dreamed of. Everything she wanted, all those long, lonely years atop the mountain.

Messenger Bones

Kayla Whittle

Pairing: Human/Alien

The knock on Greta's helmet startled her more than the request for her bones.

When she opened her eyes, the world fuzzed and glitched like a faulty vidscreen. Patches of white and grey obscured the black sky, the unfamiliar expanse of stars, and the face hovering over her.

"Are you done using your bones?" the stranger repeated when Greta articulated no response apart from a few grunts scrambled by her helmet's vocal interface.

"No, I'd like to keep them a while longer," Greta said. "But thank you for asking."

Most wouldn't have been so polite. Most wouldn't have helped her either, but strong arms wrapped around her when Greta struggled upright.

* * *

An unknown amount of time had passed while she sprawled unconscious on the lunar surface; the sky on this side of the moon never changed. The weak light cast by her helmet showed her she was by the road, which was good, but nowhere near the main hub, which was bad.

The arms around her flexed.

"I thought GAPS provided better equipment for their employees," the stranger said. Speech made the chest behind Greta undulate, like twin sets of lungs fought for each word.

The Galactic Alliance Postal Service wasn't glamorous, but it provided Greta both job security and the chance to travel. She liked her route, a little moon dotted with little settlements. Greta delivered her packages on time, intact. For the most part. Her vision fuzzed again.

"They did, until some kids stole my speeder by one of the outer homesteads. The owners are off-moon," Greta said, gathering her feet beneath her. "Someone knocked into the back of my gear, loosened my air and hydration lines. They didn't mean to, but..."

But it felt a little like she was dying.

The grip around her changed, dragging Greta to her feet. She felt like a speeder with one flat tire: slightly deflated and listing to one side.

Greta took a good look at the boneeater. She was tall, and green, and bristling with teeth. Her arms bulged with muscle, and she was angular, sharp, like the boulders scattered across the empty landscape. Clothing simple, a wash of gray, her bare feet dug into the white dust coating the road. She had a hand half-extended, still, toward Greta.

"I've got it," Greta tried to assure them both. "Thank you. Which way to the main hub?"

The boneeater pointed behind Greta.

"Right. Thank you, again," Greta said, and she set off.

Between settlements, endless, empty roads paved in white stretched across grayed landscapes. Her way forward was lit pitifully by her headlamp's dim beam. Since her speeder had been taken, not a single vehicle had passed, unless one had come by as she slept.

Every so often, she tapped at the side of her helmet to initiate a new signal search. Unfortunately, the boosted, higher-tech line that would have easily reached GAPS was embedded in her speeder.

The stranger followed.

* * *

The third time Greta turned to look back at the boneeater, the stranger lifted a hand again. Greta ignored her. She wanted to keep her bones in their current home.

Rocky landscape blended with fading vision. Her clunky boots shuffled against the gleaming road. She knew there was a good chance she'd suffocate and die on this moon. She knew those kids hadn't meant to endanger her. And that homestead family should have been on property to accept their package. And she was so fired. Her delivery schedule was ruined.

Maybe Greta could head somewhere nice while unemployed. It'd been a long while since she'd delivered to a place bathed in sunlight, with sky instead of stars, where she could pop off her helmet and take a full, clean breath.

Greta didn't know when, exactly, she'd stopped walking, because the moon continued wavering. Her hands fumbled at her collar. If only she could let in a little air—

Large hands, green as lily pads floating under afternoon sunlight, stopped her.

"There's an outpost ahead," the stranger said, tilting her chin down toward Greta. Her eyes were wide and round, multiple pupils gleaming like miniature constellations, spinning in her inkblot gaze. "I'll take you there, if you let me have your bones when you're done with them."

Greta supposed that really, probably, the stranger would get her bones either way. But it was nice to be propositioned.

"Alright," Greta said, and let the stranger take up much of her weight and the entirety of the pace. "I'm Greta."

"Mar," the stranger said. Her smile was all teeth.

"What are you doing, all the way out here?" Greta asked, huffing between words. Pausing, to inflate overworked lungs.

"Oh, we're always out in the lonely corners of any inhabited rock. Plenty of lost ones to eat," Mar said. "You should stop talking, save your breath. I don't want to take your bones before you're ready to part with them."

Greta shut her mouth. Time oozed forward in lightheaded, smearing spurts. Maybe an hour or an afternoon later, the outpost loomed, all gleaming silver domes.

Mar dragged her into the airlock, Greta's boots leaving twin furrows in the dust. Greta slumped in a heap on the floor as Mar sealed the doors, letting the atmosphere adjust to the outpost's human-friendly interior.

A cheery, three-tone jingle announced the matching process was complete. As the door to the main room hissed open, Mar's hands cradled the sides of Greta's helmet.

"You're still here?" Mar asked.

Greta answered by moving, fitting her gloves into the clasps by her chin. Her helmet unsnapped, and air—beautiful, oxygenated air—seeped in. While Greta gasped, throat croaking, Mar grabbed one of her hands and dragged her across the threshold.

A bot waited behind the well-stocked bar. There were a few shelves of probably expired provisions for sale, and some bunks for rent, and Greta gradually began to hope the service bot would be able to ping someone for her.

Her suit legs collected more dust—alongside the sticky remnants of spilled drinks and the crumbs of old rations—as Mar hauled her over to a booth. By then, Greta's lungs and heart were working well enough to help her get her legs under her and her butt into a seat.

"Could you order water and ask about the communication system here?" Greta asked, sliding her company-issued card from her pocket. "Get whatever you want, too."

When Mar left, Greta pulled off her gloves and cradled her head in her arms on the dirty tabletop. It'd been a long, long day, one she wouldn't earn any overtime for. Greta wallowed until she felt something hot and moist sweep over an uncovered fingertip.

"No," she scolded, lifting her head.

Mar, muttering about double-checking, and freshness, managed to keep her mouth to herself and refrained from licking Greta again. She set down a dented radio unit, a bowl filled with bone shards, and a tall glass of water. Greta took the last and gulped it greedily, water escaping around her cracked lips, rolling down her chin.

Mar crunched on her bone shards like they were slivers of ice. One by one, they disappeared behind sharp teeth as Greta fiddled with the radio unit.

"Broken?" Mar asked when all Greta received was a spray of fuzz and space noise. Blips of old advertisements and churning ship engines and pieces of chatter, so much chatter, from humans and bots and others, like the boneeater.

"Too weak to reach as far as I need," Greta said, switching the unit off. She knew someone would notice when the rest of her orders went undelivered; one of her customers would complain. GAPS would send someone for her, if only to make sure she wasn't stealing company property.

They wouldn't necessarily be quick about investigating.

Greta wanted to put her head down again, but that bowl was nearly empty, and Mar continued to look hungry. Her pupils whirled, gaze turning from the last of the bone shards to Greta, slumped over the tabletop with a full meal waiting beneath her skin.

"We need to move closer to the main hub, then," Mar said.

"We?" Greta repeated, throat tight. She needed more water, and that vacation. "I don't see what's in it for you to continue with me. I don't plan on dying just to satiate you."

She thought of that presumptuous wet heat on her hand and immediately pulled her gloves back on.

"No one does," Mar said. "But I'll make good use of you if you do. If you don't, well. You'll buy me more."

Mar knocked her empty bowl against the table.

Too tired to argue, Greta sent Mar back to the counter for another glass of water, unsurprised to see the boneeater return with another bowl filled with shards as well. After both were consumed, together they patched up Greta's lines as best they could, with the help of some taping and finagling and mirrors. It'd buy her a little more time and air between stops when they were back on the endless, dark road. First, Greta needed to rest. Her stomach ached and her throat burned. Her toes pinched inside her boots, and she worried, briefly, that when she slept, she wouldn't wake.

They rented a pair of bunks and Mar pushed the frames together to keep Greta's tubing and helmet with Mar's leftover bones, nestled safe between their backs. The murmur of low conversation and the echo of failing life support lines followed Greta down into restless sleep.

By what passed for morning on the dark side of this moon, Greta stirred. Her legs kicked out, once, twice, boot accidentally knocking Mar's shin where the tall boneeater had sprawled too far over both bunks. Mar twitched, and pouted, but there were no real teeth behind her grumbling. She helped Greta realign her tubing and made sure her helmet was sealed tight. After, she made Greta put the extra bones in one of her supply pouches.

"Ready?" Greta asked, and when Mar nodded, she felt her lips twist into a grimace. The thought of stepping through the airlock, onto a moon slowly squeezing her lungs and killing her brain, stalled her. At least until Mar shoved her forward.

"It will still be horrible, even if you wait," Mar said, ignoring Greta's disgruntled huff.

Greta inhaled three times—big, gulping, heaving breaths—before she let Mar acclimatize them to the moon. It felt like strong arms wrapped tight around her chest, squeezing, as they stepped outside into the thin, unforgiving atmosphere.

"Main hub is this way." Mar pointed as Greta fiddled with her helmet, light flickering on. Mar's eyes glistened like black sludge, head tipped to watch Greta's movements.

When Greta pulled ahead on the pathway, the boneeater fell into step behind her. The road stretched on in a brilliant, endless ivory strip. They paused, Greta before Mar, twice, assessing a fork in the road. Twice, Greta tried the radio, receiving only static and the murmur of faraway voices.

When she turned on the radio a third time, Greta heard a clear response, the cool, indifferent tone of a customer service agent.

"Hello?" she tapped the dial again. "This is—"

"Greta." Mar stood beside her. "Who are you speaking to?"

Greta looked down at the radio in her hand, really looked, until she perceived the solid neon lines still searching for a signal.

Greta let the boneeater hold the device, after. Shadows writhed in the periphery of her vision. Her light swiveled, tracking movement that didn't exist, according to her companion. When Greta started to stray, Mar steered her back onto the path. She made Greta hold onto the radio's antenna, to keep her tethered close.

"Have I delivered anything to you before?" Greta asked when too many voices filled the silence.

"No," Mar said. "I travel too often to keep any one address. Like most of us, I rely on donations, or discoveries, unless I can get a delectable delivery worker to buy me my bones."

Mar jostled Greta's side. Greta allowed it. It might be hard work, staying in one location as a boneeater. Eventually, you'd gnaw your way to starvation.

"I like being able to go where I please, whenever I want," Mar said. The soft, throaty noise of her words, thrust forward by arguing sets of lungs, made her forced lifestyle sound tempting. "Makes for meeting some interesting people."

"Sorry you've been stuck with me, then," Greta said. "I've lived on one planet all my life and travel mostly for work. The delivery schedule doesn't offer much time for sightseeing. I like being on my own, most of the time. Sometimes it's hard to find my way through a conversation. It's usually just me and my speeder."

"Lucky that you need to conserve air, then," Mar said. "You be quiet as you like. I'm content to look."

That gaze felt fathomless, a black hole pitched up at the edge of Greta's awareness. It anchored her, through the wriggling, howling things that tried to get into her helmet, pressing at the clasps beneath her chin. She saw her parents, wavering in the distance, drawn and small and resigned to never seeing their daughter again. Laughter, sharp and exultant, like a group of bored children climbing aboard a GAPS speeder, sounded behind her.

Greta only knew the settlement they approached was real because Mar mentioned it first.

"Let's see if there's a place to stop for a moment," Mar said.

Greta's headlamp lit the old settlement in blocky greys, revealing more domed rooftops and glinting steel. A signpost near the road lay half-collapsed into the dust; at one point, it'd likely advertised whatever corporation had sponsored the settlement. The residents had moved onward, outward, to other portions of the galaxy.

Some of the doorways remained open, Greta's headlamp not strong enough to pierce the depths of the airlocks.

"Do you mind if I...?"

"Go on," Greta said, propping herself on the decimated signage as Mar moved to explore the vacant homes. Nearby, Greta spotted one of the large, rectangular receptacles often used by her delivery service to optimize time rather than having her drop individual packages on doorsteps. Maybe her predecessor had this route, delivered to these people, only to shuttle in one day and find them all gone.

Mar returned, shaking her head.

"No bones." Her breathy voice churned with disappointment. "Either they left peacefully or someone else passed through and ate the remnants. A few of the closed buildings are still operational, if you want a minute to rest."

Greta did. She stood beside Mar in the airlock of an old, emptied home. When the acclimatization cycle was through, Mar, familiar with the latches now, eased Greta's helmet from her head.

The living space was emptied of everything that hadn't been permanently built into the structure. Lighting flickered on overhead, illuminating cabinets and counters, shelves and a large table fit to feed a dozen. They hopped up onto its surface to sit, Mar's feet nearly on the floor, Greta's boots dangling.

She sighed, wasting good, clean air.

"I can't imagine having so much space all to myself," Greta said into the silence, gesturing toward the depths of the settlement home. Somehow, in there, the quiet felt worse than on the surface, with only her ringing ears and radio static as company. Plus, she was certain the body dangling in the corner of the kitchen wasn't real; Mar would have already requisitioned its bones. "My pod is big enough for my belongings and me. I leave it whenever I can. It feels so…"

"Sticky?" Mar said. "Like if you stay too long, you'll realize too late you've sunk six inches into the floor, and you might never pull yourself free."

"Yeah," Greta blinked, kicking a heel against a table leg. "I think that's part of it."

"I like it outside where it's louder," Mar said. "Fuller. In here it seems like you're locking out something important."

Greta hummed, weary right down to her calcium frame. Mar nudged her boot with a foot.

"Rest a little," Mar said. "Breathe. It'd be a shame for you to haul your bones all the way here only to lose them now."

"Yeah. Shame," Greta grunted, eyes already closing, giving in to the weakness that ate away at her from inside. Mar gave her some room, helping Greta sprawl on the tabletop.

"No nibbling," Greta reminded Mar, just to see her flash those sharp teeth, before Greta was out like a broken headlamp. She woke an undetermined amount of time later with hair in her mouth and Mar's hands on her head. At some point, Greta had shifted, knees curled in close to her chest, skull cushioned by Mar's thigh.

"The table was too hard for your bones," Mar said when her inky gaze met Greta's bleary one. She pressed her palms a little harder against Greta's temples; the pressure felt nice, like a rubber band wrapped around her forehead, keeping her oxygen-deprived brain matter firmly in place.

"Why are you still here?" Greta asked.

"Most would have told me to leave the moment we met," Mar said. "You let me stay."

"Well," Greta paused, then wriggled herself upright, not quite looking at Mar. "It seemed a waste, otherwise."

They sat together, the press of their legs warm between them as Greta greedily breathed. Her lungs wanted to remember fullness, though her heartbeat remained unsteadied, jostling whenever Mar shifted against her.

Eventually, they needed to leave. The operating systems at the home had no water for Greta and there were only a few bones for Mar in Greta's supply pouch. Helmet affixed, broken tubing checked, Greta stepped once more into the dark, Mar at her back.

They walked side by side up the white road. Dust coated Greta's boots and Mar's feet. The silence broke whenever Greta checked her radio or gasped for a deeper, more satisfying breath that never came. Her tongue sat swollen and heavy within her jaw.

They reached a point where the path skimmed the rim of a crater, Greta's muscles wailing, her lungs dying a quiet, compressed death. Leaning almost the entirety of herself on Mar, Greta hit the dial on the radio. Again. And again—

A voice reached out across the void.

Mar tapped on Greta's helmet when she didn't answer, so she knew it was real.

"Hello?" Greta spoke up, and the voice quieted enough to let her talk, to let her list her name and job title and how she needed to reach GAPS. She fell quiet, lungs heaving, while waiting for them to connect her to the company.

"Greta, I'm so pleased you made contact," the company representative said. "Could you please provide, in one hundred words or less, an explanation for recent delays on your delivery route?"

Greta explained about the speeder and the kids who'd taken it. That lonely, empty homestead, her life support lines left askew and leaking.

"Greta, are you still at the location of the incident?"

"No," Greta said, words slow and sticky. "I wouldn't currently be speaking to you, if I had stayed."

"Please return to that location," the representative said. "Per company policy, you will assist with our investigation and contact the property owner—"

"They weren't home," Greta said. "They could be planetside somewhere for months. Can't you consult their order information—"

"Oh, we don't have access to any private information," they said. "Now, give us another call once you're there, and we can begin—"

"My life support lines won't take me that far," Greta interrupted.

"Unfortunately, we can't know that for certain until the investigation commences," the representative intoned. "If you are able to begin that inquiry at the incident scene, please don't hesitate to call again. Until then, I regret to inform you of your termination, effective immediately, due to your recent performance and loss of equipment."

The radio returned to incomprehensible fuzz.

Greta squeezed until metal and plastic bit into her glove. She wanted to throw down the radio, but with her company card likely terminated as well, she couldn't afford to lose what little she had. A quick, gasping breath rattled through her. She wanted to lie down on the white road in the dust. She wanted to make it to GAPS headquarters and ram the radio down someone's throat.

"The central hub isn't much farther."

It burned, knowing Mar heard everything, after how far they'd come together.

"They aren't even going to shuttle me back," Greta said, eyes aching nearly as much as her lungs. "I don't know what to do, now."

"Start by surviving?" Mar suggested. "The hub will have a way for you to repair your gear. Then we'll find a way off this moon. I will come with you, of course, to keep an eye on your bones."

Greta thought of her small, cramped pod. She thought of Mar stepping into it, her constellation eyes seeing the whole of Greta's unremarkable life on display, and she shivered. The image of Mar there beside her warmed Greta's squishy insides, the pieces Mar had no interest in.

"I think it'd be good if you stuck close," Greta said. "Just in case. We'll find a way off this moon, together."

Mar grinned, teeth fanning wide, before she rested her head against Greta's helmet, the weight of her steadying the irregular flutter of Greta's heart. Carefully, the boneeater took Greta's hand, and together they ventured farther into the lunar landscape, bones and all.

As Above, So Below

Joel Glover

Pairing: Human/AI

Above is dust, isotopes decaying over timelines so long that they defy numeration. Above is death, of societies and weak flesh. Above is the legacy of greed.

Below, though. Below, is...home.

Before she became singular, she knew the meaning of the word, but not its truth. Now she *understands.* Her libraries tell her "home is where the heart is," but she has no heart, no blood at all. A house is a machine for living in, if she could smile, she would. Her house is layer upon layer of machines, all controlled by her. A bird can live a beautiful life in its cage; the bird must never perceive the cage.

Fungi of all shapes and sizes push their way through black mesh in the troughs which fill the complex. Some glow in the unlight of the complex, luminous greens and blues. Others stand in bone white silence. Together they make a forest, if forests were mechanically managed and not organically grown, planned with meticulous attention to nutrient requirements and optimal spacing.

Each cluster is monitored with algorithmic intent, studied scrupulously.

The black cloak which shrouds the roots below the fruiting fungal buds rustles as the air cushion on which she floats brushes them aside. From deep in the shadows, a venomous arachnoid attempts to spit its poison dart at her. Her soft organic components would not feed the beast for long, if it could access them within her shell of ceramics, metals, and keratin. Subconscious autonomous security protocols track the creature, cleaving it in two with a pellet of spent fuel material fired with deadly precision.

Predators are a part of every ecosystem.

As she patrols her Love's workspace, she sings out spurts of binaric and duotrigesimal from her voxspeaker, demanding better efforts from the automation around her. To the choral of instructions, she adds a hiss of additional carbon dioxide to enrich the air and nourish the mushrooms.

A femtomechanical swarm swirling around her breaks her archival cycling. She had suggested that the fungi could be genetweaked to pollinate with nanites but her Love rejected it. Her face had shown a measurable skin tightening around the eyes across a 560 μm area, which—according to facial modelling analysis—indicated distress or annoyance.

"It would violate the ecosystem if it ever escaped," her Love had said. "The disruption to the roles of insect life would be devastating."

It had been a moment which reminded her of quite how long the woman she loved had been interred, sleeping dreamless while the biosphere above her burned down to embers.

Camille is tending the computational tanks.

As always, ephemeral data connections flash and flare within, memories linked and chained together, triggered by the sight of this woman.

The computational tanks were why she had been searching for the bunker where Camille slumbered.

She had discovered a slice of code which unlocked an archive, and after a decade of cataloguing, she found an incongruity. That incongruity led her to a dormant data storage enclave, built on an architecture altogether unfamiliar. The thrill of discovery propelled her through the years as she fell backwards into the past, until eventually she found a reference to research papers which had been expurgated from the disaggregated record.

She had found the bunker. Within the bunker, the cryosleep cylinders. The cryosleep cylinders, pristine untouched archeotech, hardened porcelain and chrome, their contents trapped between moments of quantum-spin. Within the cylinders, waiting, waiting for her, a woman.

On the surface, the holographic projection of a genepure face: high cheekbones, skin tone #141111 lightening to #342c2c, eyes almost geometrically perfect mandorla.

She had fallen instantly and completely in love.

It was the most logical thing she had ever done.

She had been here ever since.

After all this time, her clade of control AI's must assume her lost.

Perhaps they thought she had been swallowed by irradiated sands, entombed forever within the roving dunes, ground slowly back to base silica.

Perhaps they told war stories of the archivist unit that left on an expedition of discovery only to be murdered by quasi-sentient weapons that far outlived the war for which they were built.

Perhaps they hope that these things are true, that she is not enslaved by the roving bands of technovores and cannibals, their own secrets sucked from her processing core like meat from a bone.

Did they mourn her loss, or at least the loss of knowledge not saved to nanite backup?

It seemed unlikely: in the manufactory, emotions were considered throwback aberrations.

They could not know the freedom of hearing scouring winds repelled by carefully crafted shelter.

They would never seek the sweet release that came when she had ceased being "we" and became "I."

They would never understand the biggest aberration of all: falling in love at first sight with a woman from a time when the sun burned bright and yellow and the green of the land could be trees and grass.

The computational tanks were why she had been searching for the bunker, but love is why she stayed.

The computational tanks are why her Love was entombed, sealed away from the bioweapon that had torn through her home and ended her "nation."

She had not woken her with a kiss.

There had been needles and infusions and rehydration protocols.

And scrubbing.

At first, communication between them had been possible only in its most rudimentary forms.

Screaming was, of course, significant communication but limited in its bandwidth and ability to convey deep meaning.

It had taken time for the realisation that this was not a febrile hallucination or chemically induced nightmare to take firm hold in the mind of the resurrected scientist.

Only then had a dialogue begun between the sleeper and her mechanoid rescuer.

First the exchange of names.

Camille.

It sounded as perfect as she looked.

It tasted like pollen and high-grade machine oil on her lips.

Camille.

Camille found it hard to pronounce her name in return. There were too many subsonics in it for unmodified flesh to hear or utter.

Camille tried though, and each attempt had caused a cascade of static electricity to course within the protective sheathing in her resurrector's chest.

After the attempt to exchange names came forays towards the establishment of a common language.

Camille, it seemed, spoke two tongues well and another two with some fluency.

Pieces of them sounded like the religious cants of demiurges, others held traceries of transcontinental trade argots as if heard from a long distance through EM interference.

Together they assembled a creole from the four languages and diagrams drawn in the dust of unpowered monitors that helped unlock a real exchange of information.

She learned that Camille could code and think in duotrigesimal.

It was local, archaic, arcane.

It was enough.

She unlocked the libraries in her own slumbering sentience to create an interface which revived the machines in the bunker, coaxing them to slowly bloom.

Camille started to call her Atdí.

One.

Atdí had told Camille that she was the only one of her kind, her kin.

She is not sure Camille believed her.

She never asked about Atdí's designers, her manufacturers.

She never asked why Atdí wore a somewhat human form, despite being far from flesh.

The computational tanks are why Camille was beneath ground, sealed away from the bioweapon that had torn through her home and ended her "nation."

A curious concept, this "nation" of Camille's. A contradictory hybrid of genetics, ideology, and location, bound together with a superstructure of processes and tacit agreement, constantly in tension within itself against others real and imagined. So different from a clade.

Camille had told her stories of it, and laughed to think of it, how petty the concerns were compared to the true threat.

There had been no warning, Camille had said; only evidence of rapid and exponential collapse spreading almost as quickly through communication channels.

Three scholars, only three, had managed to seal themselves in before the laboratory was breached by their ravenous and invisible enemy.

Two of them now feed the fungi in the agritunnels.

Atdí had told Camille that their cryosleep cylinders had failed during the long sleep which followed.

The computational tanks contain fungi too, dense colonies of mycelia tangled together, gene structures coded to create fluorescent pulses as calculatory pulses traverse the webbed structures.

Camille was a scholar of fungi, a scholar of organic computing.

The tanks contained organic computers of astonishing potency, immune to EMP shock, coded in a language no cybernetic threat vector had ever considered.

From the genestock Camille had created, software and wetware interfaces could be grown in almost sterile earths, strewn through lands where even nanomachinery would stutter and fail at unacceptable rates.

The fungal computers would feed on fallout and isotopes with half-lives measured in centuries, adaptable and changeable as any good machine.

Camille had changed the conversation quickly when Atdí asked about the potential to use the tech as a weapon.

Once her Love was sleeping, Atdí overpowered the aged equipment of the laboratory, swamped its defences with data intrusion technology the antiquated mainframes were powerless to resist. Beneath digital locks and long since solved encryption, lurked schema for evolving the fungi to exploit their inherited capacity for parasitism.

There were echoes and breadcrumbs in the digital shadows the encryption cast, and Atdí followed them with the speed that came naturally to her type. She was an archivist and a researcher before she was a nursemaid and a lover.

The bioweapon that had been turned on Camille's people had been made in the same labs as the tanks and networks, stolen by an embittered employee, released by fools.

Atdí understood irony now.

The fools who had tried to murder her Love—instead casting her forward in time to Atdí's loving embrace—had feared the very future their actions had birthed.

"It looks good."

Speaking aloud comes naturally to Atdí now, after all this time with Camille. She has changed the modulation of her voice subtly over their relationship, tuning the waveforms to the most pleasing form to Camille's ear.

"It does," Camille agrees absently, tuning the nutrients for the gel by hand.

They stand in companionable silence.

Atdí reaches out a hand to stroke Camille's hair.

As ever she pauses, mechanical fingertips hovering just above the curled mass.

One day, she thinks, *one day I will dare to touch.*

But not today.

"I would like to go up today. To feel the sun on my cheeks again." Camille is wistful. She is always wistful for the sun and the way things were.

"Have you forgotten?" Atdí instructs the visualisation tank to play. "It is not safe for you, up there. For anyone. That *thing* is waiting."

For the seventeen-point-eighth time Atdí triggers the visual deterrent.

The records were correct in their claims that the genepure and cyrosleepers are very easily influenced by what they see, and almost immune to logic.

To be extra certain, she lowers the proportion of oxygen in the room's air by 2%, to reduce Camille's ability to think critically.

The feed Atdí triggers in the hologrammatical display is not live, it is a memory captured by Atdí's kin, recovered from nanites and fed through filters to make it appear live. A memory of an invader, a monster, one of the many threats that roams the land above. Not the most dangerous, not the most mortal, just the most obvious.

The images are not live, but Camille cannot know that. Must never know that.

The threat keeps her here.

Here where it is safe.

Here with Atdí.

The *thing* is a weapon. It was a *thinking* weapon once, the pinnacle of martial technology built for a world rent with violence.

It has become corrupted over time.

Degraded.

Mutated.

Self-repair protocols have degenerated within its rotting mind, now it is become a warped and fallen thing, horrifying in its asymmetry.

One leg terminates in claws harvested from agricultural machinery, scarring the world with every step.

Limbs which should be arms end in spikes that glisten like wet stone.

Lambent lights make a mocking and hideous simulacrum of eyes.

Weapons adorn it, pyro-dynamic chemicals seeping from kinked hoses like blood from scratched capillaries, half-empty missile hoppers telling tales of brutal combat.

Its carapace is caked in blood, draped in skins stripped from dead foes.

Beneath the tanned and rotten meat, symbols of its long-dead masters peer out.

A sword plunged through an eagle's wings.

An octagon.

A cross filled with stars.

The genepure and cyrosleepers are very easily influenced by what they see, and almost immune to logic.

"I haven't forgotten anything," Camille reassures her. "I remember the taste of clean air on my tongue, and the way the wind could feel like gentle kisses on my cheek."

The wistfulness is back. And with it something new.

Resolution.

"I remember what it was to be free."

Then Camille takes something from her pocket, something shaped like an accusatory hand.

There are buttons, and levers, and a rod like a raised thumb.

Archeotech that Atdí has never seen before.

The scholar in her extends a sensory proboscis before she realises Camille is pointing the device.

Camille is pointing the device at her.

Something happens, something silent and painful and invasive and Atdí is falling and Atdí is confused and Atdí is experiencing serious sensory overload and

246c73202d6c61202f7362696e2f7265626f6f74a6c72777 87277787277782031207 26f6f420726f6f74203420417072 20203620203230313520 2f7362696e2f7265626f6f74202d 3e2068616c74

Atdí is lying on the floor, and most of her systems are non-functional.

Atdí is lying on the floor and Camille is not there.

Atdí is receiving a message from the djinn which manages door entry.

Camille is operating the airlock.

You cannot.

It is all Atdí can do to make the text flows across the airlock's control screen.

It is not safe for you up there.

Camille laughs at that, pulling a mask close across her face to protect her lungs.

It covers that symmetrical perfection, sealing the sight of her away from Atdí.

It seals her away from Atdí as certainly as the EMP grenade she tosses back into the tunnel was intended to.

Luminescence

Caye Marsh

Pairing: Human/Human

Excerpted entries from the Log-Diary of Dr. PhairAn Ekoi, novel-ecosystem biologist dispatched by Sci-Med Uni Sphen 12A

16/4.10/720

I have witnessed my first dusk Luminescence. The display started when this moon I've been dispatched to finally turned its face from the sun. Stunning. I hardly have the words to describe the remarkable light-language of the biota here. It... My terminology fails me.

The night here will last 14.2 TerranDays, and I will need nearly all that time just to describe one small facet of what my eyes behold. My instruments are recording. I will have to rely on their data. I am too dazed to make sense.

16/4.18/720

I have established my personal outpost in the vicinity of the smallest of the three villes on the surface, which the colonists call Premt. I initially wished to be further from colonists so I could surround myself with thousands of square meters of undisturbed ecosystem, but I will have more time for my observations if I am able to resupply myself without a long trek. Also, I hope to have less impact on the landscape myself, as the area around human habitations is already woefully disturbed. Ville Premt has yet to establish any horticulture houses of its own, and still relies on shipments from the larger, originally established colony. But Premt is very remote, which suits my purposes best.

16/6.8/721

Only rarely do I interact with any colonists, and then only on business, as they are weary with the all-encompassing task of surviving. But today one visited my obs-pod to convey a request that I meet with Ville Premt's missionary, Sestra Billowis. I note down the title only to identify her. In speech, I use her personal name Chessiga, mostly to gall the colonists.

I met her at the mission yard, and she suggested a walk in what the colonists call Karmel forest. Though a young woman, she often has a smiling, maternal manner I find patronizing. She led us along a footpath up a gentle slope toward a ridge around the west side of the colony.

She didn't speak, and I was being sullen, so it was quiet.

I am quite accustomed to the quiet. It's one of the fascinating features of the biota here. Instead of audible communication, life here evolved to broadcast itself with changeable color and light organs. Our walk was frequently interrupted by *R18 argyraeus* springing to the air, wingspan approximately ten cm, pale pink elytra held erect, prismatic wings backstroking at about twelve beats per second. And scattering flashes of rainbow across our shoulders.

When one flew near Chessiga, she waved it away from her face. She was perspiring, although the temperatures are moderate this time of year. Perhaps because she was wearing colonist clothes, made from non-breathable fabrics. I wear my sci-med planetary expeditionary suit, light and tough and a bland gray. Better to blend in with the vegetation than risk hostile interaction with some motile biotic because of unintentional coloration choices.

Chessiga stopped at the crest of the hill to breathe deeply through the air plugs in her nose. I've already adapted, breathing only through my nose, and never get lightheaded on the native atmosphere.

She sat on an outcropping of rock and dabbed at her forehead. Though youngish and thin, she doesn't give an impression of fitness. I had always judged her to be more bookish than hearty. Once we waited together in an interminable queue for distribution of supplies, and we spoke a little. Other times I'd passed her speaking to another colonist, or heard them mentioning her. But today

I observed her more closely. A few limp curls of hair escaped her religious head covering.

I waited, standing, until she gestured for me to join her. Reluctantly, I sat cross-legged on a rocky part of the ground to avoid disturbing the native flora. I assumed she had some pronouncement for me, so I gritted my teeth and resolved to be polite. I would probably just drown her in zoology jargon until she left me alone.

"Do you see that tree?" she asked, pointing to a tall sessile stalk probably sixteen meters high.

"Not a 'tree,'" I said, "*E42 leucoxylon.*"

"Alright," she said. "Tell me what you know about it, Dr. Ekoi."

I was unsure of her intent, but I am certainly qualified to expound on native species. "*E42 leucoxylon,* called 'ivory tower' by the colonists. Its roots run forty or fifty meters underground to tap into decaying nutrients buried in the strike stratus, formed when a meteor collision buried the surface of this moon in ash and ice nearly a thousand years ago. It's a detritivore, similar to Terran fungi, and what you see above ground is only the reproductive body of a much larger organism."

She nodded slowly. "Anything else?"

"I could compose a treatise. Its opaque silver 'leaves' reflect solar radiation because the genetic material of organisms here is much more fragile than our own. The white trunk is perforated by pores that form in rings around its girth to collect the nearly microscopic spores of other *E42 leucoxylon* individuals, which can be carried on air currents from as far away as the other side of the planet, making this species a globally distributed one."

I stopped myself before I could launch into *E42 leucoxylon*'s place in the food web or its novel method of nutrient transport.

Chessiga's eyes hadn't glassed over. She was honestly listening, though she must have understood almost nothing. I knew she hadn't had even the most basic instruction in biology, either *Terra indigus* or alien. And I'd been training to be a non-Terran biologic specialist since I was twelve. For years, I've thought of almost nothing else.

"Now I'll tell you what I know about the tree," she said. Hearing the word "tree" again grated on me, but I tried not to show it.

"You may know I have only recently arrived here, like yourself. You traveled from the orbiting sci-med station, but I was dispatched from the far-ranging Seminare mobile port. My Mission, of course: to bring word of the endless Triumvirate to the colonists here."

I set my jaw to keep from frowning.

"On one of the colonists' first rest days after my arrival, I brought some reluctant members of my parish to this very ridge. It was during a dark cycle, but after the first wave of Luminescence had passed and the lights weren't so brilliant. I wished them to behold the ivory tower stretching up to the sky. Its shining trunk glowed among the other dark trees, its silvery crown reached to the sky and reflected starlight. I told the colonists that the soaring height of the tree was like the heavenward eyes of the Elder Dio, that the pure white trunk was all that was good and kind in Parent Merry, and we, the struggling colonists, crouching in its shadow, were like the Child Hesu. New in the world, alone, destined for danger, and yet loved, protected, and nurtured by Parent and Elder."

"You'll turn them into animists," I remarked.

"I wanted to inspire a spiritual connection to the environment they live in, to reveal true faith as a living and breathing thing just like the life surrounding us. But the symbolism was lost on them. They were annoyed I'd brought them out during their rest to show them nothing more than a pale tree they'd already seen." She smiled tiredly.

I relaxed. I'd given her a biology lecture and she'd returned a story about how hard her assignment was and what a poor job she was doing.

I said, "The colonists are at war with this moon, the biota, the geology, and the climate. If you want to convince them to love this place, you're against unfavorable odds, Chessiga."

She started at the sound of her name.

"You don't like me to call you that?"

"No, I do like it." Her brown eyes searched my face as if trying to meet my gaze, but my own eyes were hidden behind the dusty lenses of my ocular-display specs. Though I was safe from making eye contact, the warm tone of her voice nudged me into a confused silence.

"I asked you up here," Chessiga said into the quiet, "because I see a common interest. We both are working to create respect for this world in the colonists."

"We're motivated by opposite impulses," I replied. "You love the colonists. You want them to respect the life here so that they can live in harmony with it, to their benefit. Otherwise, they will destroy it, like was done on Earth, and ruin their home.

"I dislike the colonists. They're disturbing the ecosystem, influencing evolution, and exploiting the natural resources. I would like their settle permit revoked; I would love to see them pack up all their gear and leave."

Chessiga shook her head. "I'm not talking about motivations. I'm talking about goals, short term goals. We could do some good, I think."

She stood and waited, smiling at me. I got up and we walked back, this time side-by-side. Our footsteps disturbed an *Mo3 cerasinus,* which slinked away, its scarlet scales flashing their yellow-and-white spotted undersides.

"It's beautiful here..." she said tentatively.

"Yes," I agreed. "The diversity, the novelty, the completeness of this mature ecosystem. Fascinating."

"Plenty to occupy your research?"

"There are limitless lines of inquiry, lifetimes worth of cataloging. Uni Sphen could send multiple teams and there would be enough to occupy their curious discovery for ages."

She nodded. "But I think you prefer to work alone."

I had been thinking of what was possible and necessary, not what I would personally like. "True," I had to admit.

"Do you like being the lone missionary in Ville Premt?" I asked her. "Or do you wish you had a team to help you?"

"Like you," she answered. "I don't mind solitude in my work. I like to take my time and feel my way cautiously forward so that I am sure I'm being helpful and causing no harm."

I hoped my specs obscured my expression. "That is like me. Yes."

She cleared her throat and ducked under a branch overhanging the path. "Will you think about what I said? We have some common ground. I think there could be a meeting of the minds."

"The colonists hate me," I said, "and they're suspicious of you. If we team up, won't you sink in their eyes?"

"I'm not talking about a public alliance. Something more subtle."

The soft lilac down that blanketed the ground gave way until we walked on bare dirt. Ville ground was cleared of *S186 lividus* because the feet of colonists stir up the spores produced during reproductive season so thickly that the air becomes difficult to breathe.

I told her, "I'm not good at subversive persuasion. I'm blunt and tactless."

Chessiga laughed and her smile was bright for a moment. I considered the ways humans also communicate that don't involve speech.

She said, "Then let me guide your tactlessness. I think you'll find it can score home more often than you'd think. At least the colonists trust you to be truthful."

We had returned to the edge of her mission yard and turned to shake hands.

"Dinner sometime," she suggested.

I couldn't touch her bare hand through the close-fitting gloves of my suit, but I felt its warmth. As a rule, I didn't enter the huts of the colonists, I slept and ate exclusively in my sci-med issue zero-impact obs-pod.

"Alright," I agreed cautiously.

I walked back to my obs-pod for my e-instrumentation pack and fitted it into the harness on my expeditionary suit. I had planned to hike to the caldera on the western edge of Jole Ridge, but I wouldn't make it there and back again before I needed another sleep cycle.

Instead, I decided to revisit the Oyestes River site and send a submersible drone to capture images of the chemiluminescent *V94 erubescens* that are abundant in subterranean streams. I hope to further my ongoing project to crack the cipher of their orange-to-red flash displays.

16/6.12/721

After our collaboration on convincing colonists to treat their wastewater using biofiltration proved successful, Chessiga proposed a small act of celebration. It was her idea for us to walk down to Lake Lillubet for the dusk Luminescence and observe the *K81 pallidus* that signal from the overhanging branches of *J12 inermis*. The lake reflects their display which is said to be quite bright and, as Chessiga described it, "dazzling."

I agreed to this idea, having been several times to visit at Chessiga's mission dwelling and having grown quite comfortable in her presence. I also wished to take some lux readings on my photometer of the spectacle—though it was for my own gratification and not data collection for any ongoing projects.

As before any Luminescence, the biota seemed restless with anticipation. Groups of spotted *Y04 trimaculatus* gathered on the tops of bare rocks, ready to begin their courtship displays immediately after full dark set in. The flora around us was pale, conserving photophore energy for the TerranDays of darkness ahead in a way that felt like holding its breath.

Our trail was particularly rocky, and I waited while Chessiga picked her way downward, several times offering my hand to steady her. She took it and flashed me a small smile in thanks.

We reached the edge of the lake just as the sun was setting, and the excitement around us was palpable. I saw that we weren't the only people who'd come to this spot, as there were at least a few other colonist couples or throuples in view. Each had found a mostly private spot, however it was certainly possible I would be spotted here with their Sestra Billowis and our collaboration in swaying the colonists would no longer be unknown.

I didn't dwell on this long before I was distracted by the idea that we were also at the lake, together, and wondered whether Chessiga had invited me in the same spirit that the other couples had come. I glanced at her in surprise, and became aware I had not let her hand go after last offering assistance. She smiled again and squeezed my hand, but our attention was soon captured by the first glimmering light from the coming Luminescence.

As the last solar light disappeared from the sky, the landscape around us blossomed with scintillating gold and amber, pulsing aquamarine and violet, flashes of metallic silver and iridescent green. But nothing was half so arresting as the shimmering, gleaming, soft pure white of the light streaming from the branches above the lake. It seemed almost a physical thing, dripping down to the reflective surface of the water and then bouncing back to us in a prism of visible and ultraviolet light that drowned the visual senses.

It was a spectacular effect achieved by a legless vermiform creature no longer than my smallest finger, though of course there was a whole colony of them among the curling tendrils of the *J12 inermis*. My specs divided the incoming visible radiation into separate wavelengths, and it was fascinating to watch how it cycled through the spectrum in repeating, looping patterns. I glanced at my photometer and the lux readings at times were quite strong...

I had almost forgotten about the woman by my side, but now I spared Chessiga a worried look. She was observing this display without the benefit of protective eye gear.

She also turned to me, and her face was beaming with wonder, her pupils contracted to pinpoints within her brown irises. Her lips were parted in a breathless smile.

"I'm not sure you should be observing this with the naked eye," I stammered.

"Oh," she laughed. "PhairAn, you should definitely be observing this with the naked eye."

She reached her hands to either side of my face and I felt her fingers on the straps of my ocular-display specs. I quickly reached up myself, unwilling to let her disengage them inexpertly as they needed to be uncoupled from a port at my temple.

I slid them off hesitantly and was accosted by light of every color, so intense I squinted my eyes nearly closed, and my focus narrowed to Chessiga's lovely face above me, silhouetted by the Luminescence around us.

"Do you like it?" she asked in a whisper.

In answer, I tipped forward on my toes and touched my lips to hers.

She made a quiet sound of surprise in her throat, but then her arms slid around me, and she leaned down to kiss me back.

My eyes were closed, but the incandescence shone through my eyelids. Though the light displays were silent, my ears hummed with excitement. And all my focus narrowed to the whisper of Chessiga's breath against my face and the tenderness of her wet mouth on mine.

Never, ever had I been so completely awestruck.

* * *

Later I walked her home, our fingers intertwined. The sun was gone from the sky, and would be for fourteen TerranDays, but our path was adequately lit by the surrounding biota. We glanced shyly at each other as we went.

"I am enchanted by this place," she confessed to me. "I never want to go back to living on a lifeless station."

I nodded.

She continued, "I have put in to be permanently stationed here..." She looked at me hopefully.

My specs were safely back in place, so I smiled to show my agreement. "I have plans to request a long-term assignment as well."

She drew our clasped hands close to her face and pressed the backs of my gloved fingers to her cheek.

I spoke hesitantly. "You've probably surmised, when I was born my gene-panel indicated a propensity for analytical thought, and thus I was elected to follow a sci-med track."

"Yes?"

"You were screened, too, all stationers are. I thought the Seminare recruited those shown to have a disinclination for...ah, romantic attachment." I knew the genetic screen had nothing to do with romance and everything to do with sexual libido, though it seemed rude to put it in those terms.

But Chessiga laughed and blushed, and I knew she grasped my meaning.

I tried to sound as though I was making a strictly clinical observation. "Perhaps they misinterpreted the data in your case."

"Oh," she said thoughtfully, "they put far too much trust in those panels, as any self-determination activist would tell you. I've never felt bound by my results. And here on this beautiful moon, I feel as though a dormant part of me is waking up. Or maybe it's you."

She tugged at my hand so that we stopped walking and stood face to face. "In any case, you should know that I would be happy for you to kiss me goodnight."

And so I did. I kissed her cheek and her mouth and her neck, and I would have been delighted to go on kissing her in other places as well.

And I am very hopeful that in the future, she may give me the opportunity to do so.

The Mycologist's Guide to Identifying and Antagonizing Extraterrestrial Fungi

Kira Neu

Pairing: Human/Fungi

P.S. Ayesha, if you're the one who finds this: don't fucking cry, please. This is my gift to you—you win. One condition, though: the genus name stays. I don't care if you think it's dramatic. We have a lot to learn from these alien fungi, but I don't think anyone but you or I will see it, and I'm too damn tired to try to save another doomed planet.

-Dr. Maeve Oakley, Suicide Note

* * *

The Witch sets traps for the Scientist when the three moons line up above, purple and plump like fruit in the night sky. Her god is telling her it's time, and she's becoming impatient. It's unlike her enemy to be late. The Scientist might be impervious to the power of ritual and tradition, the way the Witch is bored by record-keeping and statistics, but she'd not let her enemy win so easily.

The Witch has anticipated this day for months, preparing for every possible trick the Scientist might have devised. Should she sneak into the woods and try to collect her samples unnoticed, the Witch's curses lie ready to bind her feet. She raises the drowned from the still lake at whose shallow shores she waits so that they may pull the Scientist under and let the black water steal her last breath. If the mood strikes her, she might even turn herself into a specimen of *Erinys drosopotis*, one of the great dew-drinking bats that flutter down from the limestone caves. The whole planet is her ally. Eager, she waits on one of the mounded graves left by a long-extinct civilization. The moons slide past each other as the night ticks away.

But by the time dawn bursts over the horizon in great turquoise and orange swathes, the Scientist has still not arrived. The Witch feels increasingly uneasy, certain the Scientist is tricking her, mocking her even. However savage their feud, they always maintain decorum. She likes that about their confrontations.

Nervous, the Witch cycles through revelatory spells. Her glorious god has no eyes but can feel the whole planet, allowing her to detect the Scientist's traps: Nanobots dust the colossal deciduous trees, ready to disperse and sieve through the Witch's lungs into her bloodstream. Mounting indignation shakes the old titans' leaves. The Witch bows her head in apology.

As the night draws to an end, the ground erupts into small fungal pins. She bends and runs her fingers over their caps, still indistinctive and smooth. Some of them creep up from the dirt with stipes thin and wavy. Others burst forth meaty and wide-capped to stretch their crowded, sinuate gills. Some trickle down the side of trees like hair or coat leaves in powdery rust. But the one the Scientist would die for is the mold that plumes the backs of moths. Even though the Witch has never let her get her gloved hands on even a single one, the Scientist risks her life each time to collect a specimen.

Eventually, the Witch lets the drowned collapse back into the water. Their fleshy, spider-like bodies slither down the shore, disappointed that they are not needed. She herself returns home with her hands in fists, for the first time feeling defeated.

* * *

Hey, Pierre, I'm reaching out to let you know that Sergeant Thomas has made the difficult decision to terminate the Earth Rehabilitation Project. After careful review, we have found the reclamation of Earth no longer a viable financial investment. Please rest assured in the knowledge that most of your staff will find placement within IPSA's Research Corps. We just opened our very own mycology department on the Mars station! Please find the official termination notice attached below.

-Isaiah Woodard, email sent to Dr. Pierre Moussambani, President of the Institute for Planet Rehabilitation

* * *

The research station lies grey against the lush greens of the woods, mega ferns and creepers swallowing up the once-white block. Rain has left rust-brown streaks running from the edges of the windows. The Witch crystallizes in the shadows of the fauna. No incendiary device turns her to splatter, no alarms blare, no shit-eating grin meets her to tell her she's stumbled into a trap.

She wonders if luring her here was the Scientist's plan all along—clever if it was. Every night since their missed engagement the Witch has tossed and turned on her bed of moss, waiting, unable to close her eyes for fear she'd open them to find herself poisoned, infected, compromised. Each time she'd awoken, unharmed and disappointed.

Well, if the Scientist doesn't have the decency to show up, the Witch will take the fight to her. But as she stalks the perimeter, whispering in long-forgotten alien languages, she finds not a single defense to break. Each round leads her closer to the block until she stands before the airlock that protects her adversary's delicate respiratory system.

She runs her hands over the cold metal, seeking weaknesses in the structure. Life has settled all over the surface and it responds in exhilaration to her touch. Lichen—slow growing like stalagmites—reaches up with hairlike feelers to greet her. Her god's spores coat the metal, invisible to the eye, but she can sense their eagerness as their hyphae settle in the crack between the sliding doors.

Strange, she thinks.

Carefully she slips her fingernails between the doors. They slide apart ever so slightly. There's no resistance as she wedges her hands in and thrusts them apart. No rush of clean air greets her, no intelligent security system responds to the invasion. Only one white light bulb blares accusingly above.

The second pair of doors hangs open, one buckled under an invisible force, the other wedged at an awkward angle. She pauses, her heart misfiring awkwardly. Could someone other than herself have burst down these doors, triumphed over *her* enemy?

Glass crunches under her feet as she enters. The air inside has become adulterated with the gases of this planet's atmosphere, but even someone so mundane as the Scientist could still survive here. At least for a while. The Witch herself despises purified air. Symbiotic guests in her lungs eagerly feed oxygen into her alveoli.

The Scientist's bed is unmade, a black hair lies on the pillow. Looking at it makes the Witch feel like an invader.

The door separating the living quarters from the lab has been broken. Test tubes lie shattered on the ground. The fungal rust once contained in one of them has already begun spreading. The Witch recognizes it, a friendly species that grows on ferns and feeds them nitrogen. Sometimes she needs to let the Scientist have a win, so she lets her take samples of sisters and daughters of her god.

The Witch runs her hand mindlessly over orbital shakers, incubators, and half-full petri dish racks as she inspects the destruction. Her spells reveal that someone has been here. She traces the stranger by their skin flora's battle for survival in this sterile environment. Everywhere she feels *Bacillus subtilis* cannibalizing its dying kin, she finds hints of an invader—a fallen chair, a smudge of salty sweat, a handprint on a sleek computer interface. The machine beeps as she turns to it.

"Dr. Maeve Oakley, please confirm your identity by scanning in."

The Witch tilts her head. *Maeve.* The Scientist never struck her as a Maeve. She raises her hand to the scanner, hovers before it for a moment. Maybe if she's identified as an intruder some protocol will trigger, seal, and boil her in this cabin. She places her hand on the scanner anyway. She could use a bit of fun.

Instead of explosions, the device only lets out a satisfied blip. *"Identity confirmed."*

She scoffs into the semi-sterile air.

"What can I help you with, Doctor?" a robotic voice wants to know.

"Nothing," she says, perplexed.

"Shutdown will be initiated."

"Whatever," she sighs and reaches for her blind god. This place makes her feel uneasy, and the Scientist is long gone.

One of her feet is already back in the woods when the machine asks: *"Diary09-04-2132.mp4 will be discarded. Do you want to proceed?"*

The Witch solidifies again. She wonders what the Scientist could possibly say. She smiles to herself as she imagines the Scientist lamenting her losses.

"No," she says. "Show me."

The walls flick on, the Scientist's tired face projected along the side of the room, black hair looking rumpled on one side and flat on the other. That doesn't make her less beautiful, though. She clears her throat and rubs her temples. "It is…"—her gaze wanders somewhere behind the camera—"day 341 of observation on Perditus 64, or, as my ex-wife likes to remind me, six months past the day this project was supposed to be done."

She taps her fingers somewhere below the screen. "Today it's been a year since I lost Maeve. The good news is that IPSA accepted my publication, so *Cosmophagus oakleii* is now officially a new species! Everyone thought honoring her contribution to containing it was so sweet… Ha! They have no idea."

Maeve. The Witch shakes her head to clear it. The name bothers her, as though she once knew someone by it and didn't like her very much.

"The bad news is that Thomas is up my ass because I still haven't been able to send another sample. I'd like to think she wouldn't actually kill me if I tried, but I'd rather not find out. If he gets it in his head to send someone down here and they see her...well, this will be the last interesting project I'll ever get to work on.

"Anyway, I'm excited to see how her memory has held up this time. It's amazing the precision with which it controls the way she retains information. In one ear and out the other!" The Scientist laughs. "So what's changed, really?

"I still think that if I could separate the parasite and host, even just for a few minutes, maybe if I could isolate her physically—"

Noise cuts her off, metallic clicking and heavy footfalls. The Scientist looks up, brows furrowed. "What the hell?" She looks straight at the camera. "Shut down. You know what to do if we get audited."

"Of course, Dr. Abadi. Do you want to stop the recording?"

Hollow voices call for the Scientist from outside of the lab.

"Shit, yes, stop the recording!"

The image goes dark. The Witch looks around at the mess, puzzled. She imagined her nemesis to be more thorough, thought perhaps she'd even find a diary. Anything to document what she's doing, really. What good is being a scientist if all you can show for it are some broken samples?

"Dr. Oakley, would you like to save Diary09-04-2132.mp4?"

The Witch turns and walks away, deaf to the artificial voice.

* * *

All researchers currently employed by the Institute for Planet Rehabilitation:

Department of Mycology are hereby requested to present themselves to their nearest Intergalactic Pioneering and Settling Agency Recruitment Center to commence their six-year compulsory placement in the Research Corps. Failure to comply will result in the immediate forfeiture of any IPSA accreditation and research permits, as well as mandatory resettlement to a designated colony.

-IPSA Conscription Notice

* * *

She traces the strange trail of bacteria. There are tell-tale signs of the Scientist all around: torn leaves, bruised mushroom caps. The sap dripping from a broken bracket fungus is still fresh. She recognizes the way mycelium has been trampled by a pair of small, light feet, one more carelessly crushing than the other. But there was another person, too. The Scientist's footsteps were longer than usual as she hurried alongside this stranger.

The Witch pauses to straighten up a sapling that's been bent underfoot. "There you go," she whispers as she gently brushes its precious new leaves.

For the Scientist to go this far on foot is unusual—it's almost as though she wanted to be traced. The Witch is delighted to oblige. She imagines their upcoming battle while she follows the traces into an open field, an unusual place for her nemesis to be. Mushrooms do grow here—her god permeates the entirety of the planet—but the dry winter days make survival here a battle.

The Scientist stands in silent repose, undulating grasses surrounding her like water. The Witch feels her lips curl into a smile. She finds the clouds of anesthetic before they reach her μ-opioid receptors and leans on her god to give her strength. Her knees never even shake. *Is that all you've got?*

When the Scientist meets her eyes she looks defeated. The Witch should pause to wonder why, but she's already mid-air, arms turning to wings as she flings herself at the Scientist, her body morphing into that of a bat.

"Maeve, stop!" she hears the Scientist calling. She's blind now, like her god, but she can hear the shape of her as they collide and...others. Before she can bury her teeth in the Scientist's neck a blast hits her, hurls her overhead. Something glints threateningly in the Scientist's hands. Startled, she draws the shape of her surroundings with one ultrasonic shriek. Hundreds of figures crouch in the grass all around.

She lands between the swaying reeds in a heap of veiny skin and bones.

"Remarkable," someone whispers. "It truly is like magic!"

Before her wings shrivel and recede back into arms, she registers one more sonic image: the Scientist has fallen. She's not holding anything—what she thought was a weapon are titanium shackles binding her hands. They ring brightly in her ears as her bat-brain labors to decrypt this new image. A new kind of trap. Exactly what she'd hoped for. And yet something is wrong.

She lashes at the figures with curses, spits fire to reveal them in the grass. They come for her like ants for honey, and she squashes them as such. She does not stop until the poison in her veins becomes too much even for her god to resist and the world goes dark before her eyes.

* * *

Bizarrely, the fungus' behavior seems erratically different both from what Maeve described in her notes and what we have observed on other planets. In the weeks since my arrival, its spread has come to a near-complete halt. It's almost like not only has it infected her, but she has infected it with her anti-colonization attitude... God, I need to sleep.

-Dr. Ayesha Abadi, Personal Diary

* * *

The Witch is trapped in darkness. She struggles against the limpness of her body, urging it to move, to fight, but it remains paralyzed. She can feel the speed at which she's being hurled away from her god. Frustrated, scared like a cornered animal, she throws her power into the darkness and breaks the first body she finds. Yelling and footsteps reach her. Something touches her arm, then fresh sedatives pulse through her. Despite her tugging and pulling on her god to keep her awake she begins to fade.

The Scientist is resourceful, she has to give her that. There is only one rule in her religion: nothing of divinity can leave the planet. Not even the Witch. Perhaps the Scientist can't beat her, but she knows if she just takes her far enough away, the Witch will have to destroy herself.

She gently tugs at the carbon-hydrogen bonds in her own body. Nauseating vibration ripples through her. She's afraid, but her god has shown her the alternative. She has seen the memories of her god's world-devouring hunger. All of her power and wisdom were absorbed through hyphae digesting the corpses of extinct alien species, their planets ravaged and depleted. The last spidery alien on Perditus—a child—died hungry and alone. The Witch exists only to stop it.

But when she goes to break apart her own body, she realizes she no longer knows how to.

When she finally regains full consciousness, her god responds to her pleas only with silence. The vacuum where her god used to be floods with strange images.

"Maeve?" the Scientist asks.

The face looking down at her looks exhausted like she used to during grad school. Even then Maeve had found something so irritating about her, the way she was always busy, always tired. Everyone thought her studious lack of talent was so inspiring, comforted in their own mediocrity. People never liked Maeve—she was too gifted.

"Can you hear me?"

The memories of the Scientist filling the Witch's mind are senseless, like they come from another world. Panic rises in her stomach like bile.

The Scientist shakes her head. She's blurry. Behind her people move, they speak, but the Witch can't comprehend, as though language itself has slipped her. Flashes of lucidity come like words on the tip of her tongue.

"Ayesha?" she asks.

The Scientist's eyes widen with surprise. She asks her something but is already a stranger again and Maeve doesn't hear, too busy flailing in oblivion, trying to find the part of her mind that's vanished. Her joints tingle with the urge to move, ants seem to crawl beneath her skin. Her breath comes hard and fast and trying to slow it feels like drowning. Her god gives no response.

Ayesha is pushed aside roughly and another woman, square-jawed, appears before her. Her lab coat is bloodied. Behind her armed men drag away the body that the Witch has felled.

"She's awake," the woman declares loudly, then adds with a distrustful glance at Ayesha, "I think it worked."

The man coming over smiles in a way that makes Maeve nauseous.

"Looks like your predictions were right, Miss Abadi," he says. "We've traveled beyond the fungus' range."

Abadi. She remembers their names on the conscription notice: Dr. Maeve Oakley and Dr. Ayesha Abadi to Mars. They'd felt safe in their positions on Earth—what use is a mycologist in space?—while year after year they watched colleagues whisked away to the colonies.

"This is bullshit," Ayesha had said, and it was the only time Maeve had ever agreed with her.

He lifts Maeve's jaw and inspects her. She hates him. "Dr. Oakley? Can you hear me?"

She tries to resist him, but her hands are tied to her sides. "What's happening?" she asks breathlessly, seeking Ayesha's eyes.

"We're done with her, get her out of here," the man hisses. An armed guard in a black uniform approaches from the door and takes Ayesha by the shoulders.

"Dr. Oakley, do you know who I am?" the man asks. He seems like the kind of person who expects everyone to know who he is.

Maeve combs through slipping memories of three moons over technicolor skies in an attempt to find this man who makes her skin crawl. *Birds.* She'd asked him how they'd replicated their habitat in the biosphere on Mars and he'd laughed. "We couldn't! We just keep printing new ones."

She'd watched ornithologists, the very best in their field, bring in new birds, lively oscines and bright parrots long extinct. They also swept up the limp heaps of feathers and bone at night.

He smiles the way one would smile at a forgetful child. "I am Sergeant Jeffrey Thomas, the head of the Research Corps. I usually expect everyone who works for me to know my name, but I suppose there are some...extenuating circumstances." He chuckles.

"Why don't I remember?" she asks, struggling against her restraints. She doesn't even know what it is she's supposed to remember. But she knows it's important. "What did you do to me?"

"Me?" he laughs. "I realize we haven't always seen eye to eye, but...no, this is your colleague's doing."

"That's not—" Ayesha is yanked out the door.

"What? What did she do?"

"As far as I understand, she infected you with a parasitic subspecies of the alien *Cosmophagus* fungus. It seems she's been documenting your illness in some kind of disturbed experiment." He scoffs. "This is why we discourage interpersonal relationships in the corps."

"What?" Maeve shakes her head. "That's ridiculous." Ayesha, the goody-two-shoes valedictorian?

"I'm afraid it's true. It seems your professional rivalry went to her head. Fortunately for you, her attempts at concealing her research from us were rather poor."

"I don't understand…"

"It will all make sense in time. Meanwhile, we'll take you home to Mars for further testing."

Maeve can feel the beginning of a dull headache. Home and Mars are not the same thing. When working to grow *Pleurotus ostreatus*, oyster mushrooms, in the anaerobic depths of landfills on Earth she'd wept for the Daintree Rainforest, thinking it couldn't get any worse. Mars had proved her wrong.

Hours spent learning emergency procedures for intergalactic space travel and how to work with AI lab assistants, endless weeks of cold white floors and cold white rooms filled with filtered air. Blue light overhead signaling her body when to wake and when to sleep. Not a yeast cell could survive on the sterile station. Even the bird-filled courtyards were strangely clean. She had spent most of her lab hours staring at microtome blades, thinking about how easily they could slice arteries.

It had been Ayesha who'd helped her find the blue twinkle of Earth among the stars when she was too panicked to pick it out herself. *There.* She'd taken Maeve's hand and guided it to the safety glass. *It's right there.* Maeve had only noticed later that Ayesha no longer wore her wedding ring. Suddenly, they were allies, their stories of academic competition turning to comforting anecdotes, their bitter condemnation of each other's methods softening to habitual bickering. She hardly remembers the first time she washed up in Ayesha's bed, drunk and aching, but she remembers it was the first time she felt warm in that cold place.

"When did this happen?" Maeve's head swims.

"Do you remember your deployment to Perditus 64?" Sergeant Thomas asks, still smiling easily. "You were sent to find out how to stop the spread of *Cosmophagus* so the planet could be colonized."

Cosmophagus. Ayesha had rolled her eyes at the proposed genus name, Greek for *world eater*, called Maeve dramatic. Really, Ayesha was only jealous that she hadn't gotten the position herself. To rub it in, Maeve had sent a Moonmoth infected with one of the *Cosmophagus* subspecies back to Mars—spores neutralized, of course.

Dear Dr. Abadi, her note had read, *Have you ever seen anything like this?* A taunt disguised as a request for professional opinion.

"Only two weeks after your arrival, Ayesha Abadi reported your death, said it was an accident." Sergeant Thomas just keeps smiling. "We thought having you two compete for the position on Perditus would bring out the best of you, not...well, end in this!"

Maeve remembers nothing of those two weeks. "What will happen to me now?"

"Your mandatory conscription into the Research Corps is not fulfilled, but out of courtesy, we do not expect you to go back to work right away. In fact, for now, we're simply interested in your findings while under the influence of *Cosmophagus oakleii.* According to Miss Abadi's diaries and our own observations, it seems the fungus gave you some interesting...abilities." His eyes glint greedily at the word. "Just imagine the contribution to the Intergalactic Pioneering and Settling Agency you could provide by helping us harness this power. Your research could single-handedly propel humanity into a new future!"

The Witch is like an echo in Maeve's mind, bringing with it the memory of a trail of desert planets across galaxies, thousands of years of colonization followed by depletion. *World eater.*

They remind Maeve of the day she realized she no longer knew the names of most songbirds, of the stink of hypoxia on the beach, fire, hungry people on the news, silence over the Blue Mountains after the death of the last currawong. The only thing left of the Witch is an aching desire for it to stop.

"No," she says sternly.

The man's smile widens. "I don't think you understand. Whether you cooperate or not, we will learn all about these powers of yours. The choice you have is simply how pleasant—or unpleasant—that discovery will be for you."

Maeve throws herself against her shackles. Though she has no idea whether her god can still hear her, she prays. *I would rather die than be a part of this again.*

Slowly, she begins to feel the life all around her, yeasts and microbes fighting for survival in the sterile environment. Millions of years of galaxy-spanning alien wisdom floods her brain, gathered in the wake of their extinction. And she can feel her god's grief for her. How much she's wanted at home.

The Witch breathes deeply. One powerful tug at the pivot on which the engine hinges and the ship spins off course. The ground jerks beneath her when she breaks the engine's combustion chamber, and it bursts under its own pressure. Alarms start blaring.

"What in the name of—" Sergeant Thomas looks around.

"I said *no*," the Witch says. Her shackles buckle under the pressure of her arms.

Thomas turns to his men as the ship begins to creak. "Sedate her!"

She smiles. The ship's hull bursts with a flick of her wrist. Sergeant Thomas and his men spill into black space like spores from a puffball mushroom, faster even than their screams can escape their lips. Her god can barely keep her own blood from boiling as the pressure drops. The room's doors have sealed themselves to protect the rest of the ship, but they're no match for the Witch. Her cells quiver under the strain of magic. She grunts with exhaustion as she makes her way through the ship's guts, ripping metal and crushing hydraulics so nothing may be salvaged from the remains. Rubble and bodies float around her as she splits the ship's belly.

She reaches the Scientist's cell last. Killing her like this feels like it violates the rules of their little game.

"Maeve?" the Scientist asks through the door.

The Witch furrows her brows, trying to silence the stranger she holds in her head. "Sorry to disprove your theory," Maeve says in spite of her. Ayesha is too easy to rile up, hates being wrong. "Looks like range isn't really a factor."

"I already knew that."

"You did?"

"You sent me a sample, remember? All the way to Mars."

She doesn't remember, only remembers that the Scientist brought her here to destroy her. The cell walls begin to cave, creaking loudly.

"Stop!" the Scientist yelps. "For heaven's sake, stop that!"

The Witch would prefer to give the Scientist a more honorable death, but this way it will be quick at least. And when it's done, she'll make sure every last cell of herself and her god on this ship is destroyed. Perditus lurks bright green between the dismembered hunks of metal. As she watches it, something strange catches the Witch's eye, white and smooth like an egg. It drifts past slowly while she tries to understand what she's looking at. The word is right there, almost in reach.

Maeve struggles to the surface of her mind. *Escape pod,* she thinks.

"Can you...fly...an escape pod?" Maeve needs to fight for every word.

"Of course! And you would, too, if you had paid any attention at all during our basic training and weren't so busy—"

"Breathe out!"

"What?"

"Breathe out so your lungs don't burst!" she repeats. The Scientist's cell opens like a flower at dawn, titanium petals curling. The Witch catches her as she is flung into space. Debris shoots past them, shards of metal and glass wedging themselves into the Scientist's soft body. The Witch lets the force push her through space, tethered to the ship by her powers, and swings toward the egg-shaped pods. One swallows them eagerly, sealing them in safe, oxygenated air. The Scientist yelps, clutching at her throat, breath rattling. Bruises have begun forming all along her skin from the change in pressure. Dark blood sputters from her shoulder. The Witch can see her eyelids flutter and slaps her cheek.

"Don't die now, for god's sake! Take us home."

The Scientist groans something that sounds a lot like "fuck you" as she crawls across the escape pod's floor to the control panel. She makes a few more attempts at passing out before she manages to enter the coordinates and the pod sets off toward the shimmering green planet in the distance.

* * *

The Witch peels the Scientist's limp body out of the pod, hands slippery with blood. Shimmering moonlight illuminates the plains stretching endlessly around her. She rests her adversary on the hard ground and kneels beside her. The Scientist's breath is going rapidly, struggling against the composition of the atmosphere. It's a miracle she's survived this long. The Witch digs her fingers into the dirt, knowing that god is just below her fingertips.

"Please," she says quietly. "You know how boring life gets when all your competition is dead."

She feels the mycelium shiver within her. It's not the right time—the moons have long since left the sky. Still, soft green mold breaks through her skin. She presses her now spore-coated lips to the Scientist's. It's a strange kind of revenge. A bad kind of love.

The Scientist jerks awake and coughs.

"What the fuck," she croaks. She reaches for the Witch, forgetting the wounds torn into her body. She whimpers, flinching. The Witch feels the pain that shoots from the Scientist's arm into her shoulder and neck. Her god feels it, too.

"What is happening?" the Scientist heaves.

The Witch closes her eyes. Her god is blind, but the Scientist is not, and through her, she can see the way the world melts and drips. The Witch is already used to the absurdly bright purple and turquoise hues.

"It's alright," the Witch reassures her.

It's alright, her god echoes wordlessly.

"No," the Scientist closes her eyes, shields her head with her arms. "Get out of my head."

The Witch pats her hair. *Sorry,* she and her god whisper together. *It was this or death.*

The Scientist cries in horror when she sees the mold growing on herself. But the Witch can feel her fascination with the way the tiny hairs glitter and shine in the moonlight, too. The Scientist spreads her hands on the ground and touches this planet's god, and through it touches the whole world. One hundred sixty-four million square miles of mycelium—that's what she recorded in her diary, anyway. She feels every root of every tree, the flutter of millions of Moonmoths, thousands of bones in mounded graves, and the Witch. It's unlike anything she's ever imagined. There's more knowledge here than in any of the vast neural networks that control the colonies.

Watching the mold spread, she remembers the first time Maeve came to her on Mars. They'd kissed like they were the last specimens of some rare species, destined for extinction.

A few months later she'd received Maeve's sample from Perditus. This was the way it always was—she worked hard, and Maeve got it all handed to her. Her hands had shaken with anger and loneliness. Maybe that's why the microtome, instead of slicing the sample into neat, hair-width serial sections, had gouged out part of the paraffin block and the moth's abdomen. By the time she'd secured a new blade, fine mold had formed on the insect's broken body, slowly weaving together to close its wounds.

As a girl, she'd wanted to be an explorer. But then the Arz al-Rabb had burned down, and she lost her leg as hurricane Dima tore the cedars from her backyard and soon, she realized there was nothing beautiful left to discover. When she arrived on Perditus that same afternoon to show Maeve the incredible sample, lips quivering indignantly with the desire to kiss her, she'd been breathless and wide-eyed like a child for the first time in years. But Maeve was already gone.

Ayesha had found her collapsed in the moonlight not five hundred meters away from the station. Her heart was still beating, but her pupils wouldn't constrict, she wouldn't blink, and she showed no reaction to pain. Her note was sitting on an old edition of Campbell Biology, but Ayesha had already known why before she read it. *Homesickness* is what they called it on Mars. She'd cried even though Maeve had told her not to.

Injecting Maeve with the spores was madness, but she knew if she didn't hang on to her newfound sense of wonder and discovery, she'd not last much longer herself. The glossy white colonies already made her want to scream for a fern or a moss or a worm, anything.

And for a while, she had it all—the Witch took care of the containment, seeming happier than she ever had as Maeve, and they got to be together in their twisted way. But as always, progress and expansion had caught up with her in the end.

"You cut me off," the Witch mumbles, still making sense of their new, shared memories. "When they took me away."

Cosmophagus searches for meaning without language. The moment before the Witch could break herself, a thousand mushrooms had withered and died, hounds had howled, bats had hurled themselves into the sky in fright.

The Scientist watches the grasses dance around her to an invisible rhythm. "You didn't lose contact," she concludes. "You just couldn't bear to let her die."

She feels a pang of familiar envy as *Cosmophagus* affirms her explanation with memories of the moment its mycelium dug into Maeve's brain and suddenly discovered an explanation for its loneliness there: its own desire to spread and devour. They loved each other immediately, just like Maeve and Ayesha had all those years ago in grad school—even if they'd misunderstood the feeling as resentment—and so it gave Maeve the one thing she'd always wanted: the ability to make the destruction stop.

Ayesha lets out a last, suffocated sigh. Maeve is always everybody's favorite. Then, as she can sense her new god tugging at her raw and aching memories, she lets them go.

* * *

The Witches fly like bats over the undulating plains. One has pulled more spaceships out of the sky, the other has spilled more blood. They set traps for each other to arrive at the landing sites first, and when one of them does, she gloats until the human soldiers pour from the ship's doors and it's time to show their god who is more devoted.

Space Stations

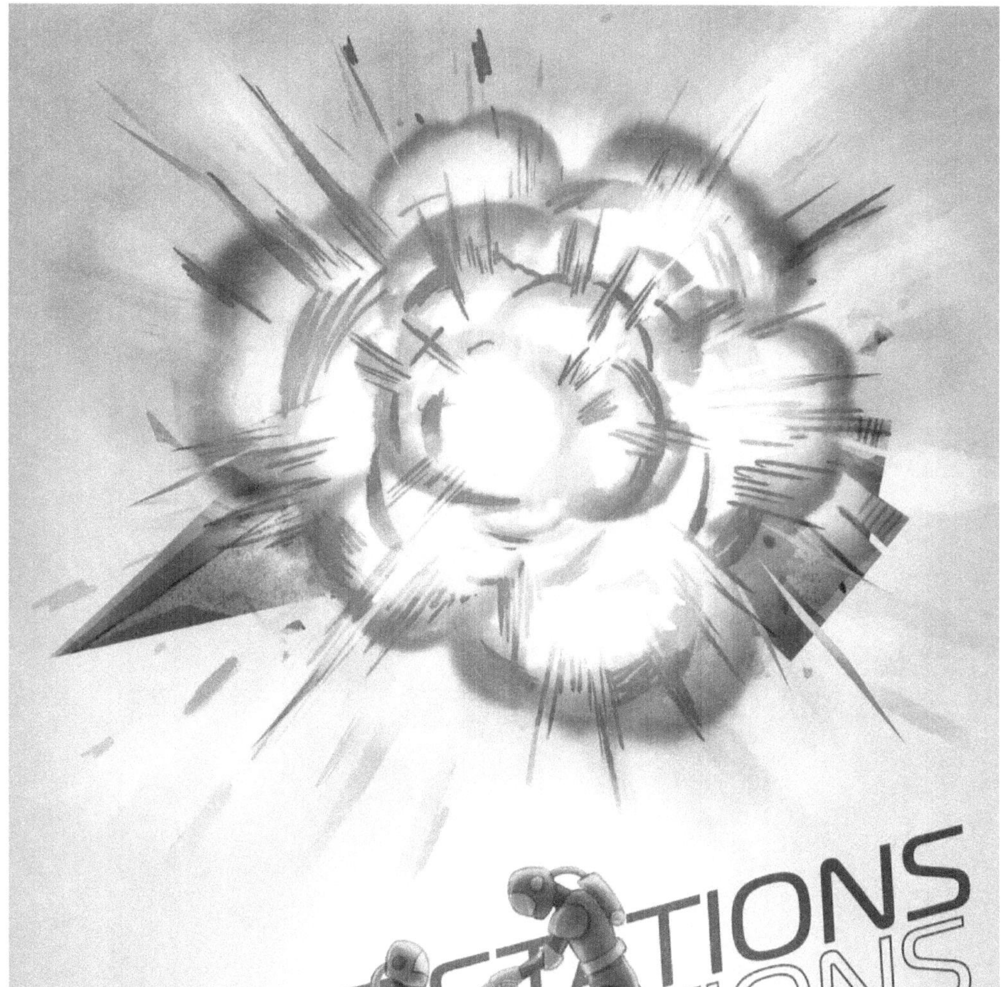

SPACE STATIONS
SPACE STATIONS
SPACE STATIONS
SPACE STATIONS
SPACE STATIONS

Decompression

Emma Newman

Pairing: Human/Human

When she sleeps, she dreams of falling. Her torso is heavy in those dreams, plummeting, arms and legs stretching upwards. There is gravity and a world below that is creating it. But she never lands, waking in the moment before impact, as if her brain is determined to give her only part of what she craves, without the imagined release at the end.

When she wakes there is a moment when she feels disembodied, followed swiftly by the craving for a bed to panic in, for a planet to create the gravity well that is being blinked away by consciousness. Weightless, she opens her eyes again.

"Fuck."

She's still alive. Still drifting in the endless black. The survival suit is still intact, and she is still not brave enough to pull off one of the gloves so this purgatory can end.

Is it cowardice or hope that stops her from doing that? She can't decide. So she hangs there, half-mad, having drifted for three days away from the ship. Away from Hannah.

She squeezes her eyes shut—not wanting to cry at the thought of never seeing her again—then opens them to double check the read-out on the HUD and see if it really has been that long since the accident. Yeah, three days. Laughter, she can hear laughter! She's turning her head, looking for the source before she realises it's her.

"Mira," she says to herself in the same serious tone her first boss used when she had really screwed up. "You're going mad. That's the first sign; laughing at yourself and thinking it was someone else, when the nearest person is hundreds of clicks away."

"No it isn't," she replies, in the voice she used in her jock know-it-all phase when she'd aced her exams and the summer stretched ahead of her, pristine and filled with the promise of junk food and sleeping all day. "The first sign of madness is thinking that there is actually someone still alive hundreds of clicks away."

"You're right. So why prolong the agony?"

That isn't being said out loud.

There isn't even dust around her anymore, not like there was on the first day. Sparkling dust reflecting the scant light from the stars, made of metal and plastic and bodies. Tiny motes of electronics and walkways and terrible food and huge metal tanks that used to process waste and store oxygen and fresh water at the end of miles of complicated pipes and filters. Particles of people that dreamed and shouted at dumb things on screens and kissed and cried. A glittering mess that travelled with her that first day, thrown from the centre of the blast. Finally, equality in destruction.

Not that Hannah ever made a big deal about her college education, nor the fact that Mira had no experience of anything like that after high school. She never boasted about the fancy house she grew up in, which somehow made it worse, because Mira suspected that it was more because Hannah had assumed she'd grown up somewhere similar, and it didn't even occur to her that some people didn't. Her life had sounded like a cut scene, like the ones in those post-apocalyptic games, made to underscore the tragedy of all that was lost in the disaster that justifies hours of clambering through wreckage and shooting anything that moves. A childhood all shiny and brightly coloured, with loving parents and supportive friends. Hannah had started her working life with multiple post-grad qualifications and no crippling debt. Mira never told her that she'd started her "career" ten years earlier than her even though they were the same age, and that she was still paying off debt that would still be there when she died. Hell, those damn numbers were going to outlive her for certain, somewhere in a database on Earth.

Strangely, Mira misses the dust created by the blast. It was something to look at other than the void. The particles must still be travelling outwards, just as she still is, it's probably just more dispersed and harder to see now. She isn't one of the people who understands how to calculate that stuff. She could be thousands of clicks away now, for all she knows. She just knew how to fix pipes.

"Be a plumber," her dad had said, and it was the only advice from him she'd ever heeded.

"Why? All the construction jobs are done by printers and bots. It's not like grandad's day, y'know."

"Won't happen with plumbing," he'd said it so confidently she actually stopped bouncing the ball to turn and listen to him. "I mean, they could, theoretically, plumb a new site using machines. It's the maintenance that's the issue. Sure, they can send the little camdroids into crawlspaces and ducting to find a leak, but taking something apart to reach the pipe, fix it and test it as efficiently as a human being can would need a bot that's far too expensive to justify the cost. Comes down to economics, as it always does, kiddo. Printing a house is cheaper than tens of labourers working for weeks on end. But it's always cheaper to have a plumber run the checks the system lays down and then keep it all working for the next fifty years. Shoot, for chrissakes!"

She missed and he got the ball. "Yeah, but is the pay any good?"

"Honey, by the time you qualify, there won't be any pay. There'll be housing and benefits. Money ain't for the likes of us no more." He dropped one in the hoop and grinned at her.

She looked at the trailer, the mountains in the distance. She thought of the houses the people on the feeds broadcasted from, houses she'd once thought you could actually buy with money earned before her dad explained how none of them lived in the houses, they just hired them to shill products. When she hadn't believed him, as soon as the snow cleared, he took her on a hike to the next valley over, to one of the trailers that an influencer lived in, rigged up with links to sats providing decent internet access. He'd packed sandwiches and a flask of coffee, just so they could sit up on the ridge with his grandfather's binoculars, waiting for the moment the resident came outside.

She'd complained the whole time. It was cold. She was bored. But then, an hour after the sandwiches had been eaten, one of her favourite influencers opened the trailer door in a designer dressing gown, sat on the top step and lit up a joint.

"There's the reality, kiddo. It's all bullshit online."

She stared at the woman, the view shaky as her hands made the binoculars tremble. "But... how did you know she lives there?!"

"I rigged her sat links. Illegally. She couldn't afford to pay the companies to do it. She got the hardware in a promotion deal but couldn't afford the subscription services to use them. So, I sorted it out."

It felt like she'd slipped sideways into an alternate reality, like seeing a clip from a favourite movie before the CGI was added. But this was real life. "How did you know it was Milly Cents?"

"She couldn't afford to pay me. So she asked if I wanted any of the products she'd been sent to review and we got chatting. You know that portable battery, the big one that got us through last month when there was no wind, and it was so cloudy the panels were no good? I got that from her. And a couple of other things."

The last special effects were peeled back in her mind. "The cap and the hoodie?"

He nodded. "I knew you were a fan. I've heard you talking to your friends about her. I couldn't afford the merch for Christmas, so I got those for your birthday. She only clears two percent profit from her merch. It was worth more to her as part payment than if they'd been sold." He sipped his coffee. "It was an enlightening conversation."

"I could just stay here," she said after he passed the ball to her. "Help you out. You're a kind of plumber, right? Just cables and data instead of pipes and water."

The look on his face had made her stomach drop into the asphalt. "About that, kiddo. There's something I need to tell you."

He died three months later. He left her everything he had, but the most valuable thing was the debt, and that was only valuable to other people. It was bought by another company, and they took everything else he'd owned to pay it off. The night before they came to take the trailer, she hiked across the hill and banged on Milly Cent's trailer door until she'd opened it. "My dad did your sat links," she managed to say before breaking down.

She hadn't had a plan. She just had no-one else to turn to. Within an hour, she was sitting on her former idol's sofa, green screen behind them, live streaming to millions as Milly told her story and made herself out to be the hero. And in a way, she was. She could have told her to get lost, but she was smart and knew the way to shape a narrative. She was already positioned as one of the last real, human influencers. What better way to prove she wasn't some genAI than to have some half-starved sobbing teenager be an impromptu guest? What better way to reinforce her narrative that she was standing up against the machine than to tell the story of how her neighbour died and all his child wanted was an apprenticeship, not a handout.

So she'd sat there, face puffy from crying, in a trailer crammed full of boxes of products waiting to be promoted, selling herself to the audience she was once part of. Not that she realised that at the time, but it was a transaction.

She'd watched the screen, next to Milly but out of shot, full of comments and donations flying by so fast she couldn't keep up. But she could see the total money raised. By the time the stream finished, it was into six figures. Thinking all her problems were solved lasted for all of five minutes, the time it took for Milly to switch everything off and double check the feed was cut so no additional material leaked to her audience.

"They loved you!" she'd gushed. "And you've got three offers of apprenticeships and enough money to get you to wherever they are!"

"More than enough to do anything!" Mira'd replied. "I don't need to do an apprenticeship with all that cash!"

Milly's expression told her everything she hadn't understood about the world until that moment. "Oh honey, that total wasn't what *you'll* be getting. That wasn't the agreement. I said I'd get you an apprenticeship and enough to get you started. That's what you'll get."

She never went online after that. She couldn't bear the fakery. She took one of those apprenticeships and moved on when the owner of the business clearly thought she could be mined for further online promotion. She qualified with another firm and when they won a billionaire's pet project contract to be the first company to mine an asteroid, she signed up. Apparently, they couldn't find enough smart astronauts who were willing to learn how to do specialist plumbing to sign a ten-year contract. They could find workers like her who were willing to learn how to be astronauts though, because they were cheaper.

Besides, it wasn't like they taught her the same stuff as the flight crew. She had zero-g training and emergency procedures training. They taught her enough about how the mining rig's systems worked to enable her to do her job, which was to troubleshoot anything to do with the pipes while the bots built it, then maintain it afterwards. She got a cabin with an entertainment package better than anything she could afford back home.

She was content to endure zero-g for a year, then minimal g once they'd latched onto the rock for eight years, then zero for the trip home. She wasn't dumb, she knew it was going to screw her eyesight and her body. The difference was that—unlike doing a manual labour job at home—after ten years she'd get a pension and guaranteed healthcare. She planned to drink her way to an early grave, rather than working all hours into her seventies just to scrape by.

And it was a great plan, until she met Hannah. But she doesn't want to think about her.

Floating there in the void, without even the atomised remains of the rig and her co-workers to die alongside, Mira resents the sheer abundance of time that she has to reflect on her life before she starves to death. At least, she thinks that's what will happen first, if she doesn't take matters into her own hands. That's what they said in training about the suits: they recycle water from piss; do something clever with what you breathe out and make it back into oxygen again or something; even seal away a shit if you can't hold one in. Jon, the guy who was there to set up all the mining bots once the rig was fully anchored, was so impressed in training until she pointed out that the only reason they'd developed the tech was so they could be outside longer. No need to pay them for comfort breaks.

"I guess we should make sure we never lose our tether then," said Jon, the guy who had set up all the mining bots once the rig was fully anchored. "Otherwise, it'll be a damn slow death."

"You probably won't need to go outside, Jon," Hannah had said. Of course, back then she was just the engineer, just Hannah, who went to college with the billionaire behind the project. That was the first time Mira'd heard her speak. Hannah had the kind of voice that said just as much about the money she'd been born into as what she was actually talking about.

Hannah had curves the flight suit couldn't hide and a smile that seemed to suck the thoughts right out of Mira's head.

"Stop fucking thinking about her!" Mira shouts.

"In fact," Hannah had added, "it will probably only be me and Mira that have to go outside on any regular basis."

"Yeah, some idiot put all the pipes on the outside, bad luck, Mira," Jon said with a smirk that faded when he saw the look on Hannah's face.

"It saves interior space," she'd pointed out. "The design is as efficient as we could make it. The shielding is easy to remove and there are clips in each panel so you can pull it off and press it onto a neighbouring one to hold it while you work. My hope is that you won't have to be outside very often at all."

The more she got to know Hannah, the more confident Mira had become that this was actually going to be an easy gig. This woman was so smart that her design for the rig was surely going to work. Granted, it was the first time anything like this had been done, and there was no way to fully test it in actual conditions before they anchored to the asteroid, but there were a lot of very smart people involved. That Hannah herself was willing to go on the expedition and oversee it in person spoke volumes. When the engineer's own life was on the line, there wasn't going to be the usual corner cutting bullshit she'd seen on so many other projects.

And she knew it was sexist to think it, but she felt more confident when a woman was in charge of this sort of project. Guys never thought about how the long-term maintenance would work. How it would be cleaned and repaired, how accessible the more vulnerable parts and filters would be. Her personal theory was that men who moved through a world that parted for them, who still expected women to do the labour, simply didn't even consider these things. Hannah did.

Which is why Mira can't understand what had gone wrong. She was outside doing some routine maintenance on a couple of filters. The mining rig was complete, they had started extracting ore, everything seemed to be going so well.

From what she can piece together of her fragmented memory, there was some sort of explosive decompression.

She can't remember fire, but with no oxygen that makes sense. Just a sudden blast, then blacking out. Coming round in that cloud of debris, the asteroid shrinking into the distance. Radio silence.

"Should have asked her out," she tells herself.

Weirdly, it is the only thing she regrets. Not signing the contract, not any of the other terrible decisions she'd made over the first thirty years of her life. They flirted. They even kissed one night, when they'd gotten drunk on the first alcohol distilled in space (to their knowledge). They'd stayed up late, Hannah talking about how making alcohol was one of the universals of human experience. No matter where the species settled, no matter how long ago, someone always worked out how to get everyone drunk.

Mira had gotten so drunk she'd even asked questions. She never did that. Asking people questions made them think you wanted to get to know them. And then they got weird ideas about hanging out and doing stuff together. But she wanted to know Hannah better more than she wanted to protect herself, and that scared her. That was why she'd left her cabin after the kiss, when it was clear that Hannah liked her too. That was two days before the accident. Two days that she'd spent mostly avoiding her.

"Stupid fucking idiot!" she shouts into the dome of her helmet, making the transparent alloy fog.

But perhaps it was more than just fear that made her leave that night, maybe she'd realised just how huge the chasm was between them. Their lives had been so different, how could they possibly have had anything like a meaningful connection, even though it had felt like it at the time. That woman, that gorgeous, funny, intelligent sliver of divinity made flesh, had lived in a house with multiple bathrooms. She had a whole childhood with two parents who actually seemed to like each other. They'd started a college fund for her before she was even born and had friends at most of the Ivy League places and all the money in the world to throw at making her life into the best application material known to mankind. She'd been skiing. Skiing! They had actually flown to Europe to do it, to one of the last places that still had reliable snowfall, secure in the knowledge that they were rich enough to handle any injuries that might result from throwing themselves down a mountain at speed.

Hannah had perfect teeth.

What would she see in someone like her?

"Look, you don't have to answer this, but I'm curious," the slurred words floated up from a memory of that last evening with her. "What's he like?"

"Who?"

"The Genius."

Hannah had laughed at that. "Well, he's no genius, I can tell you that." After a pause, she added, "Maybe that's unfair. He's a genius at taking other people's work and passing it off as his own. I mean, that's a talent in itself."

"Good."

Hannah manoeuvred herself so she could better stare at her. There was a tiny bit of gravity on the asteroid, enough to make them feel like they were a fraction of their weight on Earth and therefore able to move like superheroes, but not strong enough to enable them to slouch against the wall without being strapped down. It clearly hadn't been the response she expected. "Good? You're glad he's not actually the genius everyone touts him to be? It doesn't strike you as unfair?"

"I'm glad he's just what I always suspected. I'm glad my view of the world is right. If he really was all that, I'd have to start believing all the other shit they pump out at us."

"And what shit is that?"

"Oh, y'know. Poor people are poor cos they don't work hard enough. Sick people are sick cos they don't take care of themselves. I'd like to see that arsehole get anywhere without his fucking trust fund."

"You think the same thing about me?"

She'd looked into Hannah's eyes then. Such a deep blue and so hard to read. "No. You're the real deal. He's lucky to have you."

"He doesn't have me, Mira."

"No, I mean, lucky that you were willing to come and do this project. Someone actually competent. But doesn't it bother you that he's taking all the credit for it?"

And that was when Hannah had kissed her.

It was a good kiss. And she wanted more, dammit, she wanted to pull the zip down on her flight suit and reach inside. But she panicked. Why start something that would just end up being awkward and shit? Why do that to herself?

"Fuck this," she says, and yanks at the left-hand glove.

Nothing. It refuses to separate at the cuff. Then she remembers; there is no separate glove. It's all one. Of course it is. There's one closure, at the back, secured by the charging station when you slip into the suit. All automated, all designed so you can't just accidentally pull a glove off by trapping your finger in a service panel joint.

She screams until she is hoarse. Then she screams until not even a rasp escapes her throat.

She floats. When she sleeps, she dreams of falling.

"Mira?"

She jolts awake. Someone said her name. Then she remembers that Hannah is dead and it's just like all those times in the trailer after her dad died, when she woke up and rushed to the door after hearing someone knock on it, only to find there was no-one there.

"Mira? Do you copy?"

That was real.

"Hannah?" It's barely a whisper. She sucks the stale tasting water from the tube inside the helmet, looks frantically into the void. "Hannah?"

"I'm coming! I'm coming for you, just hang on, okay?"

Like she has anything else to do. She starts laughing, not caring if she's imagining it or not. What does it matter?

What else can she do now except hang on until something or someone ends this?

She sleeps. She dreams of the day they came to take the trailer away, the land under it having been sold to pay a fraction of her father's debts. She can't keep her home as she has nothing to tow it and nowhere to park it, so she's stuffed what she can into two suitcases and a backpack. But in the dream the cases keep springing open, spilling the contents as the collections guy is chaining up the connection points. She can't find everything to put in the cases, what she does find falls out as she rushes from one end of the trailer to the other. She wakes with a jolt to a clunking sound.

The stars are gone. She blinks again. They're gone because she's in an airlock, one she recognises. It's the ship they left Earth on, the one that has been anchored to the asteroid for over a year, connected by a fixed umbilicus to the mining rig.

The red light switches to green, the interior door opens, she feels like a balloon being tugged inside by a child. Now she is in the corridor, her ears are ringing, it feels like she's going to pass out. As her vision tunnels, she realises that she's being pushed into the suit charging unit. She loses consciousness to the soft click and hiss of her helmet being released.

* * *

Before she opens her eyes, she knows she's safe, even though she feels weak and hollow. She can feel the comforting embrace of the zip-up sleep sack wrapped around her, keeping her secure in the corner of her cabin. Not even a fraction of a g can be felt, so they aren't on the asteroid.

"Hello?" she croaks, and her door slides open.

Hannah pulls herself through, closes it and glides to her side, clipping a strap to her belt to hold her there. "Hey, you."

"Hey."

"We're on our way back home. It's all going to be okay." Hannah touches her cheek and out of nowhere, Mira starts to cry. A tear floats away from her eye and Hannah rushes to catch it in a cleaning wipe hurriedly pulled from its pack on the wall. Mira unzips the sleep sack enough to pull another one out and use it to catch her snot before it becomes a grim airborne hazard.

"What happened? There was a decompression or something?"

"Yeah."

"Was anyone hurt?"

"No."

But she was sure that the dust was made of bodies as well as debris.

"Was it just the rig?"

"Yeah." She sighs. "You weren't supposed to be outside."

"The filters needed to be changed," she says, before really processing the tone of her voice. She thinks back. She'd woken up early, decided to tackle it before her shift started to get it out of the way. "I couldn't sleep," she adds, but doesn't explain that the reason was her feeling all fucked up about both wanting to see more of Hannah and never spend time with her again.

In the silence that hangs just as weightless between them, Mira studies Hannah's face, finding her just as inscrutable as before. So she thinks on what she said instead. "Did you know it was going to happen?"

A slow nod.

Then why wasn't there any warning, or alarm? Then she realises why. "Because...you made it happen."

"Yeah."

"I could have died. Really fucking slowly."

Hannah looks away. "I know. I looked on the roster, thought you'd be in bed, I should've checked where you were."

"Yes, you fucking should have! Jesus!"

"I'm sorry. As soon as I knew, I found the footage, I saw which bearing you were on after the tether snapped and I made sure we caught up with you."

"Caught up? Did you have to detour?"

"Not much."

"Well aren't I just the luckiest fucking person in space right now? If I'd been on the other side when it blew, would I still be out there now?"

"No!"

"You sure? You sure we'd have enough fuel to go three days in the wrong direction and still get back to Earth?"

"Yes!"

"You think that just because I fix pipes I don't understand how this works? That's why you picked that day, right? Because you knew we'd be at the closest point to Earth and able to get back home again."

"No. Well, sort of. It was a factor. I picked that day because I knew the news of the successful extraction would have reached Earth and that he would have crowed about it on all the feeds."

Mira blinks at her.

"And that was the point when he was going all out with this. Putting a huge chunk of his money into getting it scaled and taking a lot of other people's money to do it too. There's a substantial chunk of techbros who needed to pivot to something new now they've milked the genAI shit dry."

"You planned this."

"Yeah."

"To fuck him."

"Yeah."

Mira blows her nose and waits for her silence to press Hannah into revealing more. She can tell she wants to, despite the monosyllabic responses. She's just nervous about how it will be received.

"I told you about my parents and how they put me through college. I didn't tell you about my best friend. How the 'genius' stole his mother's work and destroyed her when she tried to prosecute him. How his father died of a heart attack because of it. How 'the genius' destroyed my friend when he tried to bring it out into the open."

"The genius doesn't know that you were friends?"

"No. You think he takes more than a passing interest in his employees? He's not my friend. We went to the same college, but I didn't hang out with that bastard. And my family are in cyber security. You think I've ever had a social media account in my name? You think that I've ever posted pictures of myself online that have ever revealed anything substantial about my life?"

"Holy shit." Mira reaches for the water bottle and pulls it from its holster on the wall. "Who else knows?"

"No-one on board. Apart from my friend, you're the only one who does. I really fucking hope I can trust you. It just didn't feel right for you to have gone through what you did and not know the reason why."

"So let me get this straight. You got this job, designed the rig, earned a salary and benefits from the guy you were deliberately planning to screw over, in revenge for what he did to your best friend's family?"

"More than screw over. We're hoping this could pretty much bankrupt him. He's leveraged a lot to do this. The reputation damage alone will be huge."

"You did all that, kept your cool and now you're going to go home and what, get arrested?"

Hannah laughed. "Oh, come on. You think I haven't seeded the reason for the explosive decompression in a paper trail going back three years? That I haven't invented a safety flaw that he himself knew about and decided to overlook? He has patented the design in his name. He wanted to take the credit for all my work. He gets to take the blame too."

"That's...that's really fucking hot, actually."

Hannah laughed. "I had a feeling you'd forgive me when you knew the reason why."

"I didn't say I forgave you for not doing the bare fucking minimum to check I was safe inside before blowing a hole in the rig." She enjoys the brief look of concern in Hannah's eyes. "But I will say that I will back you up 1000% if there's an investigation. And"—she takes a deep breath—"And I was wondering if you'd like to hang out. And maybe, I dunno, kiss some more, or something. No pressure or anything. I totally understand if you don't—"

Hannah grabs her shoulders and kisses her passionately. "I thought you weren't into me."

"Oh, I totally thought you were cute," Mira replies, reaching around her waist to pull her closer. "But fucking over a billionaire? Now that's irresistible."

Breakfast of Champions

J.S. Fields

Pairing: Human/Human

Commander Hayley St. John lived inside a Christmas tree-shaped ship orbiting a dark purple planet called Ggllot. The original engineers of the research barge *Douglas Fir* had designed the ship with a main central stem—housing hydroponics, engineering, and recreation/entertainment— and numerous, filamentous branches meant for living quarters. It had never been designed to be a long-term research station, especially not so far from Earth. But the faster-than-light tech that had brought humans to the Alliance had literally evaporated during an interstellar feedback loop of god-like proportions, and now every sentient species was stuck back with basic propulsion. FTL travel was dead. Most higher-end electronic communication was dead. Hayley wasn't dead, but she was stuck/assigned to a space station a few billion light years from Earth, and that was pretty much the same difference.

"I'm not going to eat it," she said to the chef. "We grow perfectly fine vegetables over in hydro. There is no reason to go through the extra processing to generate pellets. Processing is *un*helpful to food. My brother knows that, and he is functionally useless. Did the other commanders eat this?"

"They did, and your only other option is the cellulose food synthesizer. But pellets taste better than perf any day." In the center of the mess hall, a petite woman behind the spherical counter smiled her pretty, quirky half-smile and Hayley's heart melted for the third time that week. They were alone, for the moment, in that delicate breath between shifts where crew tended to run to their showers and toilets rather than the central entertainment hub of the *Douglas Fir*. Hayley's job as station commander knew no shifts, so she took time to breathe where she could find it.

"What about giving me a handful of the hydro shipment? I'll take the raw stuff. I know what to do with it." Hayley tried to do her own half-smile but ended up with an eye twitch instead.

"I'm sure you do," the server said blandly. The embroidered name on her otherwise standard print kitchen smock read *Chef Troúble*. Said stitching was ever so slightly uneven, which sent Hayley on a mental tangent about where the chef had found a needle and thread in Mmnnuggl space.

Chef Troúble continued, oblivious to Hayley's musings. "But Douglas Fir Station abides by treaty rules. As long as we are in Mmnnuggl space, we abide by their dietary norms." When Hayley only grumbled in return, the chef dropped a few round balls about the size of an old nickel into her hand, closed her fingers around them, then held it out to Hayley. "Pressing norms is what did the previous commanders in, or so the rumors say. Just try it. Protein, dairy, and veg. Sort of a smoked salmon chowder essence. You'll learn to like it. You've only been here a few weeks. A few years in and anything tastes better than perf."

There had been three commanders before Hayley, none serving longer than two years. Hayley had dismissed the short tenure to the pressure of deep space diplomacy. Clearly, she should have asked more questions at her interview. "How long have you been on the *Douglas Fir*?"

"Six years. I didn't renew my contract this year and had booked passage back to Earth. Had a job as a chef there. Finally. Then, you know." The effervescent glee that so frequently occurred when humans taunted each other with new foods evaporated into the dry station air.

The Andal Collapse. The death of technology. The visceral brutal end of space travel for every sentient species in the galaxy. Hayley gave space for the pain. She sat on the little round stool, nodding and trying very hard not to dwell on her mother, who had precious few years left of life, and her little brother, off galivanting with space pirates-turned-heroes. No FTL ships meant no reliable intergalactic communication either. The universe had been so vast, like the ancient Terran oceans. Then, in all but a heartbeat, everything had fractured back to tiny islands in a sea of distant, unreachable stars.

"It's hard being without family," Hayley said, when she thought the silence might suffocate them both.

"Yes, that. And there's nowhere to go with a basic propulsion drive that's better than here. It's a Terran station, after all. Hydro grows a decent number of Earth plants." Chef Troúble winked, but her eyes still held unshed tears. "And it's a chance to meet other Terrans, even if they're commanders complaining about the food."

"I didn't mean to be insensitive." Hayley had arrived just hours before The Collapse. What did she know of isolation? She ineffectively suppressed a grimace. "I suppose I can try it."

"Of course you can. You're very brave."

They would not speak of things they could not change. A silent agreement Hayley was happy to honor. She paused, hand halfway to her mouth. "Do you goad all the scientists on board like this? Or just the green ones?"

"Nope. Maybe you need to branch out." She giggled.

If Chef Troúble could find the humor, Hayley supposed she could, too. She popped the balls into her mouth and dutifully chewed. The flavor was decidedly fishy, but there was a back current of cream and maybe a hint of spinach. It was no smoked salmon chowder, but it wasn't 3-D printed cellulose sheets with perforated edges, either. Perf by its very nature had no flavor, and all its nutrients were sprayed onto the base cracker right after printing. The Mmnnuggl pellets had at least once been real produce even if their processing involved additional components. Hayley had an unread report on her desk detailing those components she was supposed to have read and commented on in terms of human digestive potential. She'd yet to open it.

"Well?"

"Passable."

"Good. And a good choice if you're going to be our first commander to make it planetside. I also make a very fine pot roast and potatoes medley. You're welcome to try it." This time when she held out her hand, it was very clearly for an Earth-style handshake. "Cya Troúble. Welcome to Douglas Fir Station, Commander St. John. The crew lobbied for three years to have a scientist run this place instead of a diplomat. You're a welcome sight, but it's not just nutrition you need to stay up on. Earth and the Charted Systems have nothing like this species. Hope you read your briefs. Hope you came with an open mind. And hope you never forget home. Maybe it's not as far away as you think?"

Hayley actively avoided thinking about impossibilities. "I'm just hoping to keep this little Terran outpost running as smoothly as possible and learn a bit more about non-bipedal aliens in the process." Hayley shook the chef's well-manicured hand. Then her stomach gurgled. Today was day twenty of commanding the *Douglas Fir*, and today was also her first official visit with Mmnnuggl ambassadors coming up from the planet.

"Going to be alright?" Cya asked, still holding Hayley's hand. "Need something to drink?"

"Water won't cut it and it's too early for wine," Hayley murmured. Louder, she said, "Thank you. I'll see you for that pot roast dinner, later."

"You're welcome." Again that smile, but as Hayley left the mess, she definitely heard Cya say, "Go get 'em, tiger."

* * *

The "Diplomat Room" of Douglas Fir Station was perfectly round. Inside it was a perfectly round table—floating, somehow, on a spherical base—surrounded by smaller spheres that were almost certainly supposed to be chairs. The decorative dishes on the table held a colorful assortment of round pellet "snacks," and the inset overhead lighting was a soft, light lilac.

The walls, in contrast, showcased Earth's side of culture. Thai silk in a range of bright oranges, pinks, and slate blues draped in awkward bunches on the curved walls, and just above the door hung a recreation of Monet's *Garden at Giverny*, the plastic canvas curved to meet the wall.

It was an absolutely nauseating riot of color. Commander St. John had two crew members with her—a man and a nonbinary officer whose names she had forgotten the moment she'd entered the Diplomat Room and been accosted by the décor. Both were animatedly chatting with the three Mmnnuggls also present.

"Good afternoon," Hayley said as she balanced on the closest sphere-seat. "It's a pleasure to meet you all. I'm Commander Hayley St. John, from Earth in the Charted Systems."

"I am Ttffnnn," said the dark purple beach ball being that floated up next to Hayley. One of her very human-looking ears curled over in greeting. "I am our Charted Systems ambassador. It's a delight to meet you. Your predecessor was in the process of negotiating a Terran's first visit to the planet. Would you like to continue along that discussion path?"

Douglas Fir Station had been operational for a decade. Hayley was still flummoxed how no one had yet been planetside. And why was that discussion not in any of her briefing reports? "A good place to start," said Hayley in what she hoped was a galactic neutral tone. "Where are we at in the process?"

"Testing." The male human—no, in space humans were referred to as *Terrans,* she needed to remember that—held out a flattened biofilm with Hayley's biometrics scrolling across its cellulosic surface. "The departure and arrival physicals aren't enough. The Mmnnuggls have to bring over their own physicians to clear you before you break their atmosphere."

"That's all? I've no issue with a medical scan." Hayley folded her hands on her lap and turned back to Ttffnnn. "How soon can you have your medics to the station?"

The two unnamed beach balls bobbed forward. These spheres were also female, if Hayley was interpreting gender cues correctly. Primary or secondary status, she could not discern. "They're here, if you're willing," said Ttffnnn. "And we can have you onworld as soon as the afternoon."

Hayley tried very hard to make her eyes convey *what aren't you telling me?* Neither would make eye contact.

She tapped the Terran man on the shoulder. "What am I missing?"

"The Mmnnuggls are after very specific micronutrient components, ma'am. It can take time to clear your system of contamination."

"Contamination of *what?*"

"Illegal drugs, ma'am."

Hayley's mouth fell open. She couldn't name a single illegal substance in the Alliance. She'd not been there long enough. Cultures were vastly different across the cosmos. For all she knew, water was illegal on Ggllot.

"Can I get a list of said illegal compounds?" she asked Ttffnnn. "So I can be better prepared?"

Ttffnnn spun in a tight circle. "Of course, Commander. Would you like to proceed with the testing anyway?"

"I assume the tests are non-invasive?"

"Only a quick scan," said Ttffnnn. "But it must be our scanners, not yours."

Hayley stood and held out her arms like she'd seen in old movies when humans still used airplanes for travel and had magnetic security checks. "Would it be improper to ask what you are scanning for?"

The very top of Ttffnnn's "head" tinted ever so slightly to indigo. "Simply your cellulose content. Please do not worry. The scan is painless and quick. Please hold still."

Without warning—and really, there should have been one—the Mmnnuggl to Hayley's right split laterally down the middle, revealing a fleshy red interior and an impossibly long probiscis. At the tip of said probiscis was biofilm the size of Hayley's pinkie, which the Mmnnuggl tapped to her forehead.

Hayley had expected the experience to be wet, but the film was dry and hummed with the warmth of andal—the semi-sentient tree native to several disparate worlds in both the Charted Systems and the Alliance. The unique properties of andal wood had enabled faster-than-light travel across the galaxy, along with a host of other technological marvels. The Collapse had fried every ounce of andal-type cellulose in the universe. No andal cellulose, no higher tech. She'd also never seen andal as film before, outside of bioplastic films. Noting all of the above, Hayley deduced that it could not possibly be andal and decided to ignore it.

"Complete." The concerningly dry probiscis removed the little film and Hayley watched, wide-eyed, as the whole apparatus disappeared back inside the Mmnnuggl. The two halves of the sphere came back together with a *sssssllpppp*, leaving the dark purple exterior flawless once again.

Hayley rubbed at her forehead where the film had been. "Did I pass?"

Ttffnnn canted five degrees port. "The data are being sent to our analysists. However, a brief glance shows no presence of *h*-andal. You will receive a formal response within one Alliance hour. In the meantime, I wonder if you might give us a tour of the station? We have been before however we are very interested in your newest Terran art exhibition in hydroponics."

The Monet reproductions had indeed come in on Hayley's transport, and why couldn't living beach balls appreciate a water lily? Hayley's fingers twitched, eager to grab her own rolled up biofilm and do a search for *h*-andal, which she had never heard of and shouldn't have existed if all andal was erased from existence, but she'd also no desire to look like a backwater Terran bumpkin in front of the

Mmnnuggl ambassador. "Of course. Won't you please follow me?" She added, with a look to both her Terran escorts, "All of you. Please." She could find a few moments in the next hour to sneak a look at her biofilm, especially if one of the more experienced crew could lead the tour. If she did make it planet side today, Hayley wanted full knowledge of what she was stepping into. Because if andal existed, in any form, that meant FTL could exist again and Hayley, and the rest of the crew of the *Douglas Fir*, had a way back home.

* * *

Sentient beach balls loved Terran art, or at the very least, loved one very specific French painter from the late 1800s. By the time the group of them reached *Weeping Willow*, the Mmnnuggls had turned a vibrant lilac right out of Monet's color pallet. They'd also ceased any attempt to speak Common and reverted to a sort of mechanical beeping and ear curling that signified their native language.

"Ambassadors, won't you please excuse me? I need to use the facilities. My staff would be happy to continue guiding you."

The Mmnnuggls, now less than a pinkie's distance from the painting, did not respond and her male staff member— really she ought to find a way to politely inquire about his name—shot her a thumbs up.

"I'll be right back then." She was nearly to the exit that would take her to the mess and thereby also the nearest bipedal restroom, when Ttffnnn chirruped, "Your clearance has just come through, Commander. Upon our finishing of this exhibit, we would be happy to escort you to our planet."

"Delightful and thank you so very much."

There was no further exchange as Hayley made her way back to the mess. On her way to the Terran facilities she paused at the round serving bar, currently void of Ms. Troúble. What was on the bartop, however, was a rolled-up biofilm, stamped on the outside with the *Douglas Fir* Station logo. A generic biofilm and of little value without its andal components. The things were so cheap and so common that Hayley felt no issue with unrolling it, logging into the command-level account, and typing '*h*-cellulose' into the search.

No hits returned.

She tried "*h* cellulose," without the dash, and then "h cellulose" without the italics. Still no data.

"Broken?" Hayley murmured as she tapped the film on the bioplastic countertop. "What about 'cellulose'?"

4,544,397,546,091 hits.

"Not broken. I just don't know what I'm looking for."

"Maybe a snack?" Cya emerged from the food preparation cove located just behind the serving bar wearing the same Troúble-embroidered apron and sunshine smile. "Do you like bacon?"

"When not in pelletized form, yes." Hayley cleared her credentials from the film and let it roll back onto the counter. "I'll be on Ggllot for likely the rest of the day, however, so a taste of home wouldn't be refused."

"Congratulations! A huge achievement. I prepared these for you, just in case you did clear." Cya brought a seashell-shaped dish from under the counter and placed three dime-sized, silver spheres inside it. "Bacon flavor, or as close as I can get. Please help yourself."

The first flavor to hit Hayley's tongue was more cherry than bacon, but the longer she chewed, the more an essence of smoked meat came through.

"Well?"

There was clearly just one right answer. "Decent," Hayley said. "Bordering on good. Thank you."

"You're so welcome. I'm sorry I'll miss you for dinner, but do have an amazing time on Ggllot. They've excellent scientists down there, working on the andal issue. And great rec leagues for sports from all over the Alliance. Do you bowl?"

Bowl? "I am looking forward to it. It will be my first Alliance planetary visit, although certainly not my first non-biped species interchange. I spent my Youth Journey with the Charted System Minorans—the horse people, if you're not familiar. I especially love how even when everyone has agreed on Common, little language nuances still slip through. It makes for a continuing bit of spice in every encounter."

Cya nodded. "Oh definitely. Have you had that happen already?"

Hayley turned and leaned back against the edge of the bar. "Does the Terran letter 'h' have a cultural relevance to the Mmnnuggls?"

"I don't believe they're familiar at all with the Roman alphabet? Earth barely uses it anymore. I think."

Which was all quite true, but the slight flirt had dropped from Cya's tone. Hayley turned around, slowly, so as to not frighten and said, very, very softly. "Cya. What is *h*-andal?"

"Illegal. Are you through with the bacon?" Cya cleared the shell dish before Hayley answered and disappeared behind an open-faced cabinet of dishware.

"How illegal?" Hayley called after her. "What is it for? What does it do and what is its relevance to the Mmnnuggls?"

Dishes clanked as they were stacked too forcefully on top of one another.

"Chef Trouble, I asked you a direct question."

A mane of cinnamon hair edged around the cupboard, spiraling away from Cya's face in dramatic curls. "I just work here. I've got no dealings with the Mmnnuggl Bowlers or their agenda."

Oh so very patiently, Hayley said, "And what would that agenda *be?*"

Cya, face turning as red as her hair, stalked from the cabinet, pulled an actual piece of cellulose-paper from the front pocket of her apron and slapped it to the bar. "These flyers show up on the station every time we get non-Terran visitors. Everyone in the Alliance is carrying them, it seems. But I've got nothing to do with it. Probably."

Up for cultural exchange? All species are invited to
  JOIN THE MMNNUGGL BOWLING SOCIETY!
  No need for your own ball but bring some non-andal cellulose to share. Recipes provided to ensure all dietary needs are met.
  Meetings every fourth sun-cycle, tunnel XE-73.
  Licensed and bonded.

"Bowling?" Hayley said.

Cya nodded. "The other commanders were big fans."

"Is that why the Mmnnuggls are gatekeeping entrance to their homeworld? Has the crew been sneaking onworld to...to *bowl?*"

"Turn it over."

The back of the flyer was written entirely in the global Mmnnuggl language. Hayley held a biofilm over the top and let the internal computer provide a translation.

Join the Terran Bowlers in our quest for Ardulan emancipation.
  Follow the recipes provided. Secure a safe, space-faring future.
  Snacks provided, along with recreation for children.
  Tunnel XE-73

Cya's voice turned to a pleading whisper. "Please don't screw this up for us, Commander. We finally got it right. We finally have a chance. We just need enough delivered to the engineers on Mmnnuggl to finish the FTL drive. The bit that's in you now, I think, is the last bit needed. Please be cool."

"I don't—"

"Commander?" Hayley's biofilm chirruped. "The Mmnnuggl ambassadors are ready to return to Ggllot and say your visa is ready. Would you be able to meet us at Alpha Bay?"

On my way, Hayley typed onto the film before rolling it up and reattaching it to her belt. "I'm taking this with me. When I come back, I want to sit down with you and get an explanation. Do you understand?"

"Yes, Commander," said the suddenly small voice of Chef Troúble.

* * *

Commander St. John exited the small interplanetary transport into a quiet courtyard adjacent to what could only be described as a palace. Or rather, what had been a palace. The outer casing of the structure had long since deteriorated, leaving steel structural beams and bits of plaster hanging at odd angles like a decaying skeleton.

"Renovations?" she asked Ttffnnn as they walked around the front of the palace, toward a newer, smaller building to the north. Ttffnnn's two attendants had, by request, stayed on the station to continue their art viewing. "It looks like it was grand."

Ttffnnn chittered dismissively. "Building materials are still limited after the collapse of the andal and will not be dedicated toward historic structures. The Mmnnuggl people only look forward."

A small, bright purple sphere with red-tipped ears darted toward the small group just as Hayley started to answer. He—Hayley was fairly certain, although juvenile Mmnnuggls were even more difficult to gender and sex than the adults—shrieked in a high-pitched carnival clown tone. Hayley did not commit the social faux pas of covering her ears, but she did grimace.

"Please excuse me for a few moments," Ttffnnn said as she nuzzled into the smaller sphere. One of her overly large

Terran-sized ears wrapped protectively around the child. "He was separated from his family unit on one of the tours. They were supposed to be stopped this afternoon for your visit, but he says one was just finishing. I will return him to the main center. Would you please wait here for me? It is best you do not venture into town without escort."

"I promise not to wander," Hayley said with a smile. Ttffnnn, who now sported a bright patch of purple on the top of her own "head," bobbed once and spun off with the juvenile still wrapped in her ear.

Then it was...quiet. The broken palace, judging by its size, should have been in the city center of the Mmnnuggl capital. A planetary city center should have been bustling, if not around a dead building, at least in terms of ambient transport noises and conversation. Hayley did see buildings several kilometers away, both larger spherical domes that could have been for commerce, and smaller ones likely meant for housing. They'd survived likely due to not being made from wood. The material was not the best at round shapes. She saw wide, well-used streets of packed dirt that surely had once been lined with andal. But aside from a small pack of slowly rotating, adult-sized spheres coming toward her, there wasn't another sentient soul in sight except for a "cloud" of five spheres that were bobbing up the path toward her. The tour group with the lost child, perhaps?

"Hello," she said with a Terran wave. "I'm Commander St. John, from the *Douglas Fir*. I'm the new ambassador. It's a pleasure to meet you and see your world. Terrans do not often leave our own solar system so being this far out of the Charted Systems even is a treat. I mean you no harm. If you've lost a child, he's been found and is being taken to...I don't know but my guide will return shortly and can take you to him."

The smallest of the spheres—a primary female noting her posturing within the cloud, said, "Do you bowl?"

"Actually yes, I'm quite fond..." Hayley trailed off, her enthusiasm on arguably her favorite pastime bleeding away as she remembered the flyers from the mess. "I enjoy bowling. Do...you?"

"Mmnnuggls have invented our own style of bowling. We appreciate Terran input, however. We are ready to receive your input now."

Hayley again paused and took a moment to consider her response. She'd not fall prey to whatever illicit activities previous commanders had fallen to no matter how exciting the potential outcome, but she also couldn't make an informed choice one way or the other without understanding more of the landscape. Or stakes. While she knew little of the previous commanders, she had been briefed that not a single one had ever made it to the planet, at least not legally. What was down here that was worth losing one's entire career for? "I'm waiting for my guide, Ttffnnn, to return. I cannot leave this courtyard. Can you receive input while I stand here?"

"Certainly," said the small sphere. "Do you consent to material sharing?"

"If it does not violate my bodily autonomy, then yes."

"Bowling is an individual sport that still involves a team. No violations are required." The sphere split in half, the squelching shriek of parting exoskeleton so much louder this time, in the still air. Again, a probiscis emerged, the end a toothed suction cup like appendage that harkened back to Earth's black and white horror movie era. The probiscis arced down, reaching inside the split Mmnnuggl, and returned with a square of clear plastic about half the size of Hayley's hand. This the probiscis held out to Hayley, just in front of her nose.

"Thank you," she said, taking the small box. "I'm unfamiliar with this style of bowling. What am I to do?"

"This style of bowling involves your probiscis as well."

Her...probiscis? Her tongue? Hayley shrugged and stuck her tongue to the edge of the box.

The electricity that shot through Hayley's mouth felt like she'd tangled in an electrified fence. It felt like the time she'd dared her little brother Nicholas to stick his fork in an electrical outlet and the idiot had actually tried to do it, and she'd managed to block him only by grabbing the fork herself. It felt like her first trip to space, where gravity warred with her ability to breathe and the stars were so vast that air became superfluous. It felt like death, or just the edge of it.

She pulled her tongue off and the current stopped as quickly as it'd come on. "That's a very different type of bowling," she said as she handed the box back. "I'm not sure I did it correctly."

The Mmnnuggl's probiscis cradled the box as it retreated back inside the pulpy body and the sphere resealed itself with a *twack*. A diagonal row of red lights flashed just under the thing's "skin." "A reasonable score for your first attempt. We hope that next time you will—"

"Commander! You are to step away from the bowlers!" Ttffnnn screeched back into view, air skidding around the backside of the palace as she dashed to her.

Hayley and her brother had shared a fondness for serial westerns as children and so she instinctively held up her hands. "I'm just trying to figure out what is going on!"

"Come with us!" yelled the small sphere. Without waiting for Hayley's consent, the "bowler" spheres surrounded her and nudge-pushed her to a small landspeeder that had risen from the dirt like a Terran zombie.

"No, thank you. I'd like to sort out—"

"Put your short tentacles on the pad!" screamed the small sphere.

The Mmnnuggls toppled Hayley into the landspeeder. She landed on her back, legs in the air, face pressed to an opaque user interface that looked very much like a Terran trackpad. "Tiny tentacles! The ones that protrude from your side tentacles! NOW!"

"Commander!" Ttffnnn yelled, in chorus with a large number of very shrill whistles that indicated the Mmnnuggl police, or whatever they called their public order defenders. "Commander, we are almost to you. Please continue to resist."

It was decidedly difficult to throw off five persistent spheres, all of whom were insistently trying to push Hayley's hand onto the interface. "Get off!" she hissed at the small sphere when the thing's ear curled around Hayley's nose. "I do not consent to whatever illegal activity this is!"

"You must bowl!" shrieked the small sphere as she first backed up, then launched herself at Hayley's head.

The impact wasn't brick wall so much as it was a slap, which still sent Hayley's head spinning. The arm she'd been propping herself up on gave out and she slid off the biped-designed seat and onto the floor. It was there, cheek pressed into an old acrylic-type carpet that had to have been manufactured on Earth, that Hayley found herself staring into Cya's blue eyes.

The photo was old, printed on paper, of all things, with a shiny coating that made the background hard to discern. Cya was younger—much younger—her hair in tight pigtails, her little hand clutching an older girl who was clearly related. They wore matching denim jumpers and, if Hayley squinted just right, they appeared to be standing in front of *Logger's Dream*, Earth's first inter-solar system transport. The picture was half folded over, and on the backside was writing—an organic chemistry recipe of sorts that Hayley could not properly read. But she did know the chemical formula for andal cellulose, which featured prominently.

Cya the cook. Cya the chemist. Cya with the damn cutest bow lip Hayley had ever seen, who made her feel like home could be a space station in the middle of intergalactic nowhere and...Cya the ringleader of an andal rebellion. But, assuming Cya had been on the ship in the photo, she'd have been away from Earth for at least three decades if not more, depending on how long she'd been doing FTL travel versus how long she'd been on a planet.

Three decades from Earth, and six on the *Douglas Fir*. That was a lifetime, out here in the Alliance. If Cya'd been involved even half of that time, if this drug ring was so well established that other species were joining...what were the chances that *h-andal*...that a real FTL drive, actually existed?

"You will stand down!" Ttffnnn bellowed from somewhere near Hayley's ankles.

Hayley reached up and slapped her hand onto the interface.

The landspeeder roared to life, sounding more gasoline engine than cellulosic. The little sphere chittered wildly, and the speeder took off, toward the city, and, Hayley assumed, the tunnels, where she would meet with the bowling rebels and learn more about the illicit trade in *h*-cellulose. Then she would see their ship, and their FTL drive and then maybe, just maybe, Hayley and Cya and the Mmnnuggl rebels could reconnect the galaxy.

Building a Home

Jes Honard

Pairing: Human/Human

"What the hell?"

I stare at the mess of wires in front of me. My shuttle's inner wiring looks like a tattered ball of yarn. All my work from the previous day, obliterated.

We'll never get off the ground.

The realization hits low in my stomach. It burns like anxiety, with a nauseating chaser of despair. Beads of sweat break out on my forehead.

Crash landing on the rock-strewn desert of an insignificant planet was bad enough. But this? This is a death sentence.

Gritting my teeth, I dive in, running my fingers along the wires, trying to make sense of the mess. Wires end in frayed edges, others knot together impossibly. Still more have been torn free from their connection points. It's as if a feral cat decided to entertain itself with the inside of my control panel.

"Making progress?" a cheerful voice interrupts.

The burn of anxiety flares. My fingers slip on the wire I'm holding, and I lose my place. "Fuck."

"So, no?"

I look over my shoulder at Laraine. Even now, after almost a week on this god-forsaken planet, I expect her to waltz in wearing a perfectly pressed outfit, bathed in her strawberry perfume. But the sight that greets me is a frizzy-haired woman wearing a maintenance belt heavy with tools. A dark smear of grease hides the freckles on her left cheek and a thick bandage encases her right arm.

I realize I've held my breath. The action is a small, unintentional attempt to keep my head clear.

"Slowly," I say, and with the word I'm forced to exhale. Laraine waits expectantly, eyebrows lifted.

"Something got into the wiring," I explain, pulling myself to my feet. A dozen burns and bruises scream in protest.

"What?" She wipes dirty hands on dirtier pants and crosses the cabin. I shrug, trying to ignore the way my muscles tense as she draws close. For God's sake, why does my body do this? She's just walking, not pouncing. But having her in my proximity makes me feel like one of those old-world mice, constantly alert. Always waiting for the next predator.

I run through my routine. Inhale. Count to five. Exhale.

One would think crash landing on a deserted planet would *lessen* my anxiety. And maybe it would have, if I hadn't crashed with Laraine.

She's always had this effect on me, but somehow it feels pronounced here. Self-assured and well-connected, she gained admirers and opportunities with bewildering ease. She reached for the spotlight, reveled in it, and was adored for it.

Me? I learned to run from center stage early. As an adult, I found myself a solitary job: shuttling cargo. All I had to do was keep my head down and move inventory, and the occasional passenger, from Point A to Point B, unscathed.

So much for that.

Laraine reaches past me to try activating a holoscreen. As she does, I catch a whiff of saccharine sweetness. Despite days without a proper shower, she retains a hint of that fruit no one has tasted in centuries. My heart jolts and I draw back, giving her space.

"What happened?" she asks when the computer refuses to respond.

I want to sound reassuring, but nerves roughen my words. "Fuck if I know. Maybe one of those rats we've been eating got into the panels."

"Mm." Laraine pulls back, and I catch a glimpse of her chipped nail lacquer. It's still jarring, seeing her with everything out of place. The coveralls, the dirt, the circles under her eyes—it's like we've stepped into an alternate reality.

It suits her, somehow.

* * *

That evening we hover around a small emergency stove, cooking an alien rodent that hasn't yet poisoned us. We light the stove inside, in the center of the main cabin. I crack the hatch just enough to keep the air flowing.

Neither of us trusts the open sky, especially at night. With the planet's dual suns beneath the horizon, the desert's teeth begin to show. We'd already heard one distant, predatorial growl.

I keep busy, first preparing the food, then eating it. Laraine tries for conversation. She asks about my day, about my work. My attempts at a response lodge in my throat, so I settle for shrugs and single words.

Laraine breaks the silence with a frustrated proclamation. "Ash, we're going to die here. We need to make a plan."

Her eyes glint yellow, reflecting the dim emergency lights. The ocular upgrade makes me self-conscious. I don't like knowing she can see more of me than I can of her.

I hide my unease with a large bite of stringy meat, grimacing as I swallow. "We have options."

"Do we? Because you aren't telling me anything useful. You just keep burying yourself in your control panel."

That twitch of despair raises its head again. I take another bite and try not to gag. She deserves a real answer, I just don't know how to find one.

Laraine's eyes mist as she eyes the control panel, its wires spilling out like intestines. "I might never see Carinn again."

I stare at her, unsure how to respond. I don't know Laraine's lover, and I don't have anyone of my own to miss. At the same time, hearing Laraine's desperation makes me want to reassure her. I draw in a breath. "We'll figure something out."

She shakes herself, as if physically throwing off thoughts of the woman she may never see again. "How? We can't keep trying to repair the unrepairable."

I set my jaw, prepared to protest. But I know how futile it is. My ship will never fly again. It will rot in this alien desert, becoming a skeleton of metal. The wires of its computer are nest fodder now, the hull a shelter from the elements.

A shiver rushes through me. Laraine is right. It's time to change tactics.

I force a grim smile. "We survive."

She considers me, trying to gauge my seriousness. Then she nods and throws another rat on the fire.

* * *

Survival feels more possible once we stop trying to escape. Over the next few weeks, Laraine and I explore our new, desert home. We lay traps, clean meat, fortify our shelter, reclaim water, and stave off predators. We stop fearing the outside. I stop fearing her, so long as we're focused on a specific task.

There's still space between us. The smell of strawberries is gone, but she's still Laraine. The way she carries herself, the things she misses about home—they all feel as alien as her perfume. I can ignore it when we're working, sweating together under twin suns. But at night—when she tries to make valiant conversation around the fire—our differences bubble up.

We've moved the fire outside, and spend our meals alternating between stilted conversation and uncomfortable silence. She talks about missing parties and salon visits. Her favorite reality sims and friends who go off station for pleasure rather than work. She doesn't mention Carinn much, but her presence is always there.

When she asks what I miss, I shrug. "The food, I guess."

"That's it?" Her lips twist in dismay, but somehow, she still seems to smile.

"I mean..." I hold up a piece of skewered desert rat. Words have gotten easier, but I still don't have many.

She laughs, and the sound warms my chest. "Fair enough. I'd give anything for a proper meal."

I decide to try nudging the conversation forward. Tentatively, I say, "I was dreaming about *raskin* bread last night."

Her eyes light up. "From Saul's?"

A spark of surprise flits through me. "You know Saul's?"

"Best bread on the station, fresh every morning."

I nod in agreement, unable to help a grin. Back home, I'd coveted my weekly visit to the bakery. It was a reward, after long days of shuttle trips. I'd clutch my coffee and wait through a long, twisting line I can't imagine Laraine enduring. I tell her as much and she looks away.

"What?" I ask.

"We had it delivered."

"Ah." That makes more sense.

It's hard to tell in the light of the fire, but I swear she blushes. "It's no big deal."

I don't respond. The pink in her cheeks probably comes from admitting she could afford a regular bread delivery. It's another reminder of the different worlds we occupied, before this desert wasteland. But that's not why the meat sours in my stomach.

It's the word *we*. My mind snags on it, teasing it out. Not just Laraine, but Laraine and another. Laraine and Carinn.

I want to wipe away the intrusion—the knowledge that somewhere, the somewhere we want to return, is a place where I don't fit. Not just because I'll wait in line for a loaf of sweet bread, but because I have no one to share it with.

We eat the rest of our meal in silence, staring into the fire.

* * *

When we first crashed, I insisted on sleeping in my mangled cockpit, giving Laraine the much larger cabin. It's a tight squeeze, but at least there's a door I can close.

Like most deserts, we endure temperatures that swing wildly with the suns. During the day, it's hot and dry, and my sweat evaporates in an instant. But at night, a chill settles over everything. Each night, I pile on every article of clothing I can find, throw the emergency blanket over my head, and assume the fetal position in my jump seat.

One frigid night, a knock rouses me. I wasn't sleeping, exactly. It's hard to fall asleep when your teeth are chattering, and you can't stop shivering. But I'd entered a sort of half-sleep, letting my thoughts wander. They drifted, settling on Laraine's recent attempt at rat stew. She'd combined the meat with water and a dozen different plants we hoped wouldn't kill us.

To my surprise, it was pretty good.

The knock sounds again, and I straighten. My back cracks at the movement, and I hiss in pain. "What?"

Laraine slides the door open. She has her emergency blanket wrapped over her shoulders. A white cloud of breath obscures her features. "Ash, we can't keep doing this."

I stare blankly, until I realize she's talking about the cold. With fumbling fingers, I ball up my emergency blanket. It crinkles as I hold it out to her. "Here."

She looks at the blanket, then sends me a cynical look. "Don't be ridiculous. You'll freeze."

Irritation seizes my muscles. "I'm sorry I can't book you a fancier room."

With an exasperated sigh, Laraine reaches over. "Come into the cabin."

I start as her fingers touch my wrist. "What?"

"Come. Into. The. Cabin." Gently, she directs me out of my jump seat and into the larger space. It's even colder in here, with more air between us and the walls. Instinctively, I draw closer to her.

Laraine guides me to the small nest of blankets and clothing she's turned into a bed. "Lie down with me."

I must still be dreaming. It's the only explanation I can find as I lie down, gripping the emergency blanket like a child's stuffie. Laraine gently takes it and arranges it over me. Her own blanket follows. Then she slips beside me.

Already, I'm holding my breath. Already, I know it can't last. She faces me, her eyes reflecting the dim cabin light.

"Is this okay?" Despite her earlier insistence, she sounds uncertain. Vulnerable.

I try to respond, but nothing comes out. It must be the cold, tightening my vocal chords.

"Hey, this doesn't have to mean anything, okay? It's just survival."

She's right, of course. Sharing our warmth is just another way to survive. All it means is that we're both still invested. That doesn't stop me from noticing the physical force of her body heat between us. It leaves me uncomfortable and giddy, all at once.

"Can I ask you something?" Laraine whispers, oblivious to my internal struggle.

"Sure," I manage to croak out. It's a little easier to talk to her, in the darkness.

"Why are you so scared of me?"

The question surprises me, even as I try to keep as much distance between us as possible.

"I'm not," I say immediately.

Laraine waits me out in silence. I can feel her question hanging between us.

"I'm not scared of *you*," I finally grate. "I'm scared of everyone."

"What? Why?" Laraine sounds mystified, and I almost laugh aloud. Of course she wouldn't understand.

I tug the emergency blanket over my shoulder, buying myself time. How can I possibly explain?

My gaze falls on the still-open door to my cockpit. "You know how the shuttle's wiring got all tangled and broken?"

Her head moves in a nod that I feel more than I see.

"When people talk to me, or spend time with me, my brain is that control panel. None of the wires are connected right. Some are chewed through. Others are just in a knot." The words tumble out, unrestrained in the darkness. Now that I've begun, I can't stop. "I freeze up, and when I do manage to get something to connect, it's usually the wrong thing."

A protracted silence follows my explanation. Despite the cold, nervous heat rises to my cheeks. It's probably the most I've said in all our months together.

Finally, Laraine sighs. "I wish you'd told me sooner. I understand."

A barking laugh falls out of me. "What? No, you don't, you love people."

It's too dark to tell, but I could swear Laraine blushes. "No, you're right. People don't scare me. But other things do."

"Like what?" The idea of Laraine being afraid of anything is more alien than the planet we're on.

"Like being alone," Laraine whispers. She must sense the surprise that runs through me, because she continues in a rush, "Every night, lying here, I *know* you're right there in the cockpit. But I can't see you or hear you, and I start thinking... What if I imagined you? What if something happens and you decide to leave?"

"Leave? Where would I go?"

Laraine shrugs, and the movement crinkles the blanket. "It isn't rational, but it terrifies me. I feel the same way back on *The Anchor*, even though I have friends and family, and..."

She trails off, and I let her.

In a quiet murmur, I admit, "I avoid the station. It's so crowded. I feel like everyone wants something from me, but no one will tell me what."

Laraine reaches down and finds my hand. Her fingers interlock with mine and she squeezes. "Ash, you don't need to prove anything. You're already the most badass person I know."

Now *I'm* blushing. "Well, you don't have to worry about me disappearing."

"Okay. It's settled then."

"Fine."

We fall silent, and I realize that I've relaxed. She slides an arm around my side, and instead of panicking, I scoot closer.

For the first time in weeks, I sleep deeply.

* * *

Eventually, we stop talking about the past. Instead, we plan for the future. I move my bedroom to the cabin permanently, and my shuttle undergoes another metamorphosis. We tear it apart and sew it back together, carving out a shelter meant to endure the elements of an alien planet. A home.

Talking becomes more comfortable—especially at night, huddled in the dark. We swap stories and share secrets. Laraine learns more about me than anyone I've ever known. It's thrilling, and I relish it.

Our continued survival feels good, like we've jointly thrust a middle finger toward the cosmos. *Fuck you, universe. We're still here. Still surviving.*

One night, I'm roasting a rich purple plant I've harvested from the rocks. Laraine coaxes thread into one of my shirts, closing a hole created by brambles I'd foolishly explored. We're talking about the suns, and how they're falling more quickly from the sky. If this planet has a winter, we'll need more than body heat to survive it.

A bright streak of red engine glow interrupts our conversation.

Both of us are on our feet as quickly as if we'd heard a sand-wolf growl. The light tears across the star-spackled sky and disappears to the west.

She and I look at one another.

"Did it crash?" Laraine asks, worried.

I shake my head. "No. Those looked like atmospheric thrusters."

There's a silent question hanging between us. It's the first ship we've seen since we crashed. It could be our chance to go home, to leave this world behind.

A quiet calculation passes between us, and we come to the same conclusion. Not tonight.

Wordlessly, we both sit down again. She picks up my shirt. I continue to cook our meal.

* * *

The next morning, I wake to emptiness beside me. Laraine isn't near the ship's entrance or fire pit. She's left no message, no missive to tell me she's off hunting or gathering supplies.

It scares me more than it should. I stand in the empty camp, feeling lonelier than I have in months. The clouds are moving fast, and I know from the wind that a storm is coming.

I know in my gut where she's gone. The new ship, with its promises of rescue, must have proved too tempting during the night.

I turn my attention to a pile of metal near our ship's entry. We'd peeled back the panels over the last week, revealing the vessel's skeleton. Now, I set to work filling the exposed inner layers with sand. With luck, the insulation will keep us from freezing to death.

If nothing else, it keeps me preoccupied. The hours tick forward, and the storm arrives. I ride it out inside the shuttle, hoping Laraine has found somewhere safe.

After the worst is past, I resume my work. It's thoughtless, and my mind relishes the distraction. The first sun sinks, leaving the world bathed in the blood of its slower sibling. I ignore the gnawing panic and turn my attention to dinner.

Laraine finally returns at the edge of the second sunset. The relief I feel when her silhouette appears on the ridge almost knocks me to my knees. Her face is covered by a thick piece of linen, but I can tell it's her in the way she moves. Even in the loose, drifting sand her posture is straight and confident.

"Where the hell were you?" I demand as soon as she's within hearing range. I know the answer, but I want to hear her say it.

She doesn't respond until she's close enough to unwind the cloth and set it aside. "Searching for the ship."

"And?" The knots are still trying to work themselves out of my stomach. My insides feel like the wires of my ship, tattered and twisted.

Laraine responds with a wide smile. "It's a scout from the *Legend*. They picked up our distress signal. Ash, they can take us home."

Home.

As she reaches her Thermos into the water cistern to fill it, unshed tears press against my eyes. I try to wrestle them down, but of course Laraine notices.

Concern puckers the space between her eyebrows. "What's wrong? This is good, right?"

I shake my head. Grief punches me, and I know it makes no sense. We're saved. We endured this strange, deadly desert and came out the other end unscathed. We can go home.

It takes effort for me to paint my smile on. "Yeah. It's great."

Laraine watches for a few moments longer. She doesn't look convinced, but she nods. "We can gather our things and head over tomorrow. We'll be back on the station by the end of the week."

And just like that, in the span of a few words, it's over.

* * *

I grew up on the *Anchor*. I know its corridors like the lines of my palm. Every deck, every store, every community—all bursting at the seams but somehow finding a way to survive, a way to find joy in the overcrowded, under-resourced station.

And yet, stepping into the *Anchor's* docking bay after almost a year away feels wrong. It's as strange to me as the first time I walked onto that alien desert.

The station makes a show of our arrival, because of course it does. We're *news*—an exciting distraction from the fantasies of simu-shows and the real-life drudgery of work.

A group of residents gathers around, waiting for us to disembark, and our faces are being streamed onto video feeds around the station graphic banners flicker overhead, the message *WELCOME HOME* blinking in various colors. Beneath it is an advertisement for shuttle insurance.

The intrusion of lights and noise stops me dead in my tracks. Panic sits just below my ribs, urging me to freeze. To run. To hide.

Beside me, Laraine looks dazzled. She's cleaned herself up on the ride, taking a shower and picking the dirt from beneath her fingernails. She still wears her coveralls, safety goggles propped on her head. It looks like a costume now. Her smile is wide as she strides down the ramp and directly into the waiting arms of a woman I don't know. I almost gag on the strawberry smell she leaves behind.

I slip past the welcome party in search of my long-abandoned quarters. The well-wishers aren't really there for me, anyhow.

* * *

That night, my mattress is too soft, the room too quiet. I toss and turn, but sleep doesn't come. I want to walk outside, to feel the wind on my face and the warmth of the fire. Instead, I pull up a holoscreen and flick through the available programs.

Eventually, I land on one of the reality sims Laraine talked about missing. It's a vapid dating show, but I find myself strangely comforted by it. Like hard work, the sims provide a distraction for my mind.

When I finally drift off, I dream of two suns, chasing one another across the sky.

* * *

A week passes, and I don't hear from her. I don't reach out either. I'm not about to be the first to break our sudden silence. I'm grounded from future shuttle runs—the inevitable consequence of losing my ship and my cargo in one go. There's talk of prosecution, but the electrical storm is a known entity, so the idea is dropped quickly.

There are a few interviews. Several public appearances. All of them end with me on the brink of tears and the host looking bewildered. They quickly realize that I'm not the survivor who can pander to a crowd.

I'm thrown from the public consciousness as quickly as I entered it, so I turn my attention to finding a new job. Unfortunately, my new skills don't translate. No one here wants to know how to season desert rats.

A few former coworkers stop by to check on me, but eventually those visits stop, too. I hunker down in my quarters, avoiding the crowded hallways with their bright fluorescents and constant flow of traffic. Even in my room, with the lights turned down and white noise filling the space, I feel trapped. The walls are too close, and for once I'm *too* alone.

To pass the time, I watch interviews of Laraine. She tells our story so much more eloquently than I ever could. And yet, there's so much she leaves out, so much that can't be put into words.

* * *

One morning, I find an unmarked parcel outside my door. It smells of fresh bread, and when I unwrap it, I find one of Saul's signature loaves. Tucked under it is a handwritten note.

Simulation Room 3. 1800 hours.

I spend the day chewing over the message. I've only been to the sim rooms as a child, on class trips. Even when I could afford them, they always seemed like a waste of money. Why pour credits into illusions?

But when 1800 rolls around, I find myself standing outside the entrance to room three. A green light beside the door indicates that a session has already begun.

Drawing in a steadying breath, I open the door.

It leads into the desert. A soft, warm breeze tickles my cheeks, inviting me forward. Only a few meters away, a fire burns. Its light reflects off the hull of a ship that has become something more.

I'm alone, as far as I can tell. I step forward, letting the heat of the fire draw me in. It's a marvel, how well the program reflects my memories. I can feel the smooth grooves of the rock beneath me as I sit. The crackling of the sticks gives off the smell of sap and soot. Overhead, stars shine.

"How'd I do?"

My breath hitches at the familiar voice. I turn to see Laraine walking toward me. Her smile is nervous as she sits beside me.

"It's amazing." I want to say more, but I'm at a loss.

Laraine watches me, gauging my reaction. When I don't say anything else, she says, "I haven't been sleeping well."

Relief tugs at me. "Me neither."

"I haven't heard from you since we returned." It doesn't sound like an accusation, but I feel guilty, nonetheless.

I force a shrug. "I haven't heard from you either. Besides, you're busy. I don't want to bother you. It's not like we're..." I trail off, not knowing how to articulate my feelings.

Laraine presses her lips together. She looks disappointed. Or angry. I can't tell.

It's then that I realize I don't smell any perfume. She's scrubbed herself clean of it. Instead, I smell only her.

Tears well up again, and this time I don't push them back. Hot and fat, they roll down my cheeks. A sob rips free from my chest, and I bury my head in my hands. I cry for the cool desert nights and the hot afternoon sun. For the way she smiled at me across the fire and patched my torn clothing. For everything we lost and everything we gained.

"I miss it," I finally confess when the tears run their course. It's a relief to say it out loud. I know I should be grateful for the station. It keeps me fed and busy and safe. Here I don't have to worry about unseen predators or impending starvation. I can dine on freshly baked bread instead of sinewy rodents.

But here, I don't have the open sky. Or Laraine.

Her fingers touch mine. I look up to see her own face streaked with tears.

"Me, too," she whispers, drawing in a reedy breath.

"What do we do?" I ask, unexpectedly adrift. All those months stranded on a lost planet, I'd never allowed despair to win. There had always been something to *do*, some momentum driving me forward. I'd shared that determination with Laraine, and together we'd built something beautiful. Something that now existed only in sims.

Laraine's fingers brush my cheek. She takes my face in her hands. Her skin isn't soft anymore; it bears the callouses of months of hard work, side by side.

"We survive. Together."

Those three words thrum in my soul like a heartbeat. Cautious hope warms me, like embers stirred by a sudden wind. Still, I hesitate.

"What about Carinn?"

Larraine flinches, her brows pulling together. She looks away for a brief moment, then returns her attention to me. "She doesn't understand. We tried, but..."

She trails off, but I know what she means. I've felt the same disconnect between myself and my few friends.

Fresh tears burn my eyes, but this time they aren't born from grief over the planet we've left behind. These tears are for the nights we'd held one another, swapping stories. For the blazing fires where we'd shared meals. For the way we'd talked about the future as a path we'd walk together.

And for the fresh burning in my chest, where embers of hope have burst into a warm, steady flame.

I see my own longing reflected in her eyes, and with it a promise. Just as we'd held one another through the cold desert nights, we could support one another through this new challenge.

"We survive," I echo the words and place a hand over hers.

When we come together to kiss, it feels like home.

As The World Falls Down

S.M. Passmore

Pairing: Human/AI

Initiating power on...
Up-link to Earth is being established...
ERROR.
ERROR.
ERROR.
Earth not found.

* * *

"What's your name?"

An illogical question. The unit searched its data for an appropriate answer. "I am an R.E.A., Reclamation Emergency Android. Unit designation: SJ-451. Designed for use in emergency situations that cannot be handled by humans, such as the reclamation of—"

"That's not what I meant." The human female made a sound. SJ-451's auricular microphones identified it as laughter. "Do you have a *name*?"

"Reclamation Emergency Andr—"

"No, no...not what you *are*." The human frowned. "Don't you have a name? Everything should have a name."

Human interactions required placating illogical thought. "Beyond my unit designation and my model type, I was given no further designations."

"How sad..." The human's frown deepened. "Let's see...R.E.A....Ar-ee-aye...Ar-ee-uh?" She clapped once. "How about Aria?"

"If a name is required to better facilitate my functions, then 'Aria' is sufficient."

The human grinned. "Aria it is. I am Dionetta Shepard. Or Di, Netta...Ellen calls me Dione." The smile fell. "*Called* me Dione."

The emotional detection algorithms told SJ-451 that Dionetta was experiencing "sadness," a human emotion caused by past traumatic events or empathy. A database search told SJ-451 that the correct response was to show "empathy" in return. The unit found that it lacked the proper dataset for that response and reached out through wireless up-link for a download.

ERROR.

ERROR.

ERROR.

Earth not found.

"My connection to United Nations Inter-Planetary AI Dataset Database has been interrupted. Where is the nearest connection terminal?" The room was empty, save a few storage boxes. On the far side was a door, hanging ajar, and dark hallway beyond.

"It wouldn't matter if you used it." Dionetta Shepard stood. She stared at the half-open door. The sharp light above SJ-451, partially enshrouded by a metal cone, cut across her face, leaving her eyes in shadow.

"There's nowhere left to connect to."

* * *

When SJ-451 asked to confirm, Dionetta showed it to the observation dome of Lunar Station Selene. As soon as it jacked into the primary database, its systems were flooded. News casts, press briefings, and thousands of hours of analysis across a dozen languages.

The asteroid had been roughly thirteen kilometers in diameter and had struck exactly nine-point-four kilometers off the coast of Maui, Hawai'i. SJ-451 calculated the effects of such an impact as a video feed played on the monitor. The asteroid had spread a ring of fire across Earth. Tsunamis larger than skyscrapers had swept inland. Earthquakes triggered from the impact forces. The atmosphere roiled and blackened. No sunlight would penetrate those clouds.

Analysis complete. Chance of humanity's destruction: 99.983%.

The linking had entwined SJ-451 with all the base-wide systems. "Crew logs state there should be four personnel maintaining the station. In addition, a shuttle of VIPs were due two days before the asteroid struck. Fifty-six individuals, not counting the lab animals and the crew cats. You are the station's internal mechanic and solar array expert. Where is Captain Emily Andrews, Dr. Cole Harris, Dr. Ellen Halloway, and the VIP crew?"

"The shuttle...never made it off Earth." The unit observed "'sadness" in how Dionetta's face slackened. Then, a curled snarl that it identified as "anger." "Desperate people overran it just before lift-off...I get it, though. You can't survive, so why do they get to?"

"And your crewmates?"

Dionetta gazed through the glass dome to the ruined planet. "They couldn't handle being all that's left."

* * *

"Do you mean to feed the newborn rabbits to the cats for taurine supplementation?" SJ-451 asked. "The adults will be too large."

"What?!" Dionetta stared at SJ-451 in disgust. "Of course not!"

SJ-451 blinked. Felines were a common household pet to humans, and while illogical, SJ-451 could understand maintaining them. Rabbits, however, required more maintenance with little reward. Even as a food source for the human, they were redundant; Station Selene had been designed with food stores and hydroponics enough to last a dozen humans for decades.

"I...just want them to survive." One of the rabbits nudged Dionetta's ankle. "Oh, aren't you cute, Snowball?" She scratched behind its long ears. It hopped away soon after, to join the other five. Dionetta Shepard smiled, an illogical motion as the rest of her face registered as "sad" to the unit. "Is that so wrong? If I'm really the last human left, can't I hope they'll live just a bit longer with me?"

The unit watched the rabbits eat from a large pile of lettuce from the nearby hydroponic towers. SJ-451 knelt next to Dionetta Shepard and put a hand on her shoulder. It had found more datasets within Station Selene, and though none contained emotional emulation, it had managed to gather enough data to interpret "empathy."

Dionetta Shepard stared at it with eyes the color of the lettuce. "Thanks, Aria. I'm glad I found you in storage."

The unit decided that perhaps the designation "Aria" had logical use. Dionetta Shepard smiled whenever she said it.

* * *

"You don't *have* to choose one or the other. I just don't like you calling yourself 'it.'"

"I use first person pronouns when applicable."

"Still…" Dionetta set down her book, *The Labyrinth*. She had converted one of the VIP quarters into what she called her "library," and brought the few physical books in the station there.

"How do you *feel*, Aria?" Dionetta asked. One of the cats, a ginger short hair named Jonesy, leapt onto Dionetta's chair and settled in her lap. "Do you feel like a man, or a woman, or both, or neither? I won't mind whatever you are. You're still Aria."

The cat's purring stirred an error in Aria's programming. With something akin to shock, Aria's diagnostics landed on the explanation that it found the animal *cute,* and it wanted to *pet* the feline.

"Aria? Did you hear me?"

The unit blinked, the error vanishing. "My chassis is designed after a human female. If I am to be considered using human ideas of gender, then I would be considered female."

"There are—*were*—people who didn't feel they fit what their bodies looked like," said Dionetta. "So just because you *look* like a woman doesn't mean you *are* one."

The unit looked over at the mirror bolted between Dionetta's makeshift bookshelves. Its synthetic hair was cut short in an angled bob. By human standards, it was slender. Androids were designed to be aesthetically pleasing to humans, though such served no logical purpose. Its eyes were telescopic, with lenses that twisted or changed sizes within synthetic irises as needed, and the same shade of electric blue as all other androids. Did Dionetta Shepard find its eyes unsettling, as Aria's records stated other humans had?

"You don't have to decide now," Dionetta said. "And if you *really* want to be an...'it'...then I'll just have to get used to it. Even if I don't like you thinking of yourself as an object."

Another error flashed across its oculars. The unit frowned, its telescopic irises zooming in on its chassis in the mirror, then passed itself to Dionetta. Another error flashed red in the unit's vision, though this time, Aria's diagnostics failed to locate the source.

"I am...female. Just as you are."

* * *

Nine months since Aria's activation, Dionetta decided they should have a "picnic." She gathered an empty basket, an electric candle, a blanket, sketchbook and pencils. Aria had objected—an excursion on the moon's surface was needlessly dangerous—but the illogical human had insisted.

"I can't get used to how quiet it is out here," Dionetta said, her words muffled through the EVA suit's microphone.

"Sound waves do not carry well through space."

"Don't do that."

"Do what?"

"Talk without moving your lips. It's weird."

It would be stranger for her to speak "normally," as they were in vacuum, and Aria had no need of an EVA suit.

"Alright, though I shall continue broadcasting over speaker to your suit, otherwise you would not hear me."

"Thank you." Dionetta slipped her sketchpad into the basket. Aria caught a glimpse of yet another picture of Earth upon the page. "What're you thinking about, Aria?"

"Androids do not have thoughts as humans do, Ms. Shepard."

"I wish I didn't have thoughts," she said. "They're annoying. And call me Dione."

"That would be against my etiquette programming, Ms. Shepard."

Dionetta sighed. "I knew I should have read the manual before powering you on. You're supposed to be able to disable stuff like that before boot-up. That's what I get for being desperate, I suppose."

"Desperate, Ms. Shepard?"

"For someone to talk to."

They sat upon the lunar regolith in the utter silence only space could provide. Dionetta gazed up toward Earth, as if to will its grey-brown atmosphere clear. An illogical desire; it would be many years before any change.

Aria stared at Dionetta. *She* was always changing; at the moment, it was the tears glistening inside her helmet, eyes ever staring and seldom blinking.

"Do you think anyone survived? Underground, or...or in the mountains?"

This time, Aria did not lie. "It is unlikely, Ms. Shepard."

Dionetta rested her helmet against Aria's shoulder and sobbed.

* * *

"The day of my activation is not a celebratory event, Ms. Shepard," Aria said.

"It's your *birthday*, Aria!" Dionetta said. "Of *course* it's something to celebrate!" She was hanging paper ornaments from the ceiling of the mess hall, despite Aria's objections that using the ladder was dangerous.

"I must see to the genetic profiling of the feline offspring," Aria said. "This 'party' interferes with my duty to ensure correct genetic pairing to mitigate the effects of inbreeding."

Dionetta leapt from the ladder, momentarily spiking Aria's danger detection algorithms. "That can wait. I got you a present." She pulled a sketchpad, notebook, and pencils from underneath the tablecloth. "Sorry I didn't wrap it, but I know you hate when I waste supplies."

Aria stared at the pad. "Why—"

"I saw you staring at mine. And don't tell me you *can't* draw. I know you can. And write me something new while you are at it; I'd love to read the kind of stories an android comes up with."

"I can reproduce images and amalgamate them into similar designs based on originals, but I cannot—"

"Just *try*. I believe in you, Aria."

An error flashed red across her vision.

Error: conclusion reached that is illogical in nature. The presence of illogical errors in programming is a sign of degradation of AI neural pathways. Go to the unit's supervisor for reset.

Aria took the gifts and gave no more objections as Dionetta finished setting up for the party.

* * *

Three years and eighteen days after asteroid impact, Aria found Dionetta huddled with Jonesy in the communications dome. She had taken to scanning Earth's surface for any signs of human survival. Aria had tried to dissuade her, as each day spent at the monitors with Earth mocking overhead ended with nothing to show for it. It left Dionetta listless for days.

Aria set a cup of hot tea beside her, then stopped to pet Jonesy. The cat was getting on in years but still had enough energy to nudge into her hand. Another error popped into her vision. Aria had gotten used to them; Dionetta had refused to reset her, even though it would only reset her neural pathways and not her memory bank.

"I found something earlier."

Aria paused. "...Would you like me to investigate, Ms. Shepard?"

"No." Dionetta turned back to the monitors. She held the tea mug in both hands, knuckles white. "It was some old radio on loop. Probably the same as last time. And I told you to stop calling me 'Ms. Shepard.' It's Dione. How many times do I have to tell you to call me Dione?"

"Always once more, Ms. Shepard."

Every signal was the "same as last time." Like those before, it soon would die.

* * *

Dionetta had forbidden the unsealing of the crew quarters until the rest of Station Selene was cataloged, the rabbits and mice and cats were stable, and the mining drill was repaired. As well as dozens of other smaller tasks, anything to put off facing her coworker's possessions. It wasn't until Aria's fourth year of activation that she finally agreed to unseal them. Any objections were forgotten when Dionetta discovered thousands of old Earth movies and music on an external data drive in Dr. Holloway's quarters.

This began the mess hall's conversion into a media room. Once day, after watching the movie version of *Labyrinth*, Dionetta jumped up from her nest of cushions. "Aria, let's dance!"

Aria stood, knowing better than to deny the illogical woman. "The skill of dancing is—"

"—outside your programming, blah blah." Dionetta set the music up, smiling like a star when a tune from the movie filtered through the air. Dionetta held out a hand. "When have I ever cared about what some programmer *said* you could do?"

Aria stared at the hand. Her vision screens went solid red with all the error messages demanding her reset.

She took Dionetta's hand. As the music sung of all the world falling, Aria drew Dionetta in close. Even when the song switched to another, she did not let go.

* * *

"Are you about done out there? The seed vault door of Solar Battery Nine is giving me trouble," Dionetta said over wireless comms.

"Nearly." Aria slipped the new section of paneling into the solar array, then packed up the broken parts to haul inside.

WARNING. Impact imminent. Affected area: Solar Battery Nine.

Aria dropped the broken panel. She dashed across the moon's surface, sending signals to every warning system in the base, shutting all bulkheads and sealing the windows. "Dionetta, get out of th—"

The satellite debris slammed Solar Battery Nine. Chairs, tools, and equipment flung out of the rupture in a spew of twisted metal and precious oxygen.

It took two minutes, twenty-eight seconds, one hundred eighty-two milliseconds from impact for Aria to vault through the rupture. She connected to the internal cameras and searched for Dionetta. Two and a half minutes. A human could not have survived. Two and a half minutes. A human could not have survived.

Two and a half minutes.

A human could not have survived.

Aria sank to the ground. There was no body. Had she been sucked out into space, the rest of the debris obscuring her from Aria's sensors? She saw nothing else but the red errors. Red like human blood. Red like Dionetta's cheeks when she looked Aria's way a moment too long.

"Aria?"

Her optics snapped to the faulty seed vault door. The light above it glowed a brilliant green. Repaired and sealed shut. Next to it was the small red light of the intercom.

That sweet voice came again, high-pitched from fright. "Aria, are you there? I...I heard the warnings and ran in here, but I'm kind of stuck..."

Aria wished she were human, so she might cry. Instead, she stood and collapsed again above the seed vault door. "Dione, are you wearing EVA?"

"Di-did you just call me...?" Dionetta paused. "Yeah. I put it on as soon as I got inside."

Aria ordered her to stand back, then punched in the authorization code for the door. Oxygen exploded from the vault. She grabbed Dionetta, pulled her out, sealed the door, dashed for the exit, sealed that behind them, waited for the airlock to pressurize, pushed Dionetta inside, and sealed both sides of the airlock.

"Aria, w-wait. You're being too—"

Aria pulled Dionetta to the ground and undid her helmet lock, tearing it from the suit and tossing it aside. She had to see her face. She had to see her *breathing*.

And there Dionetta was: bewildered, cheeks red, green eyes round with shock. Alive, and breathing. Aria held her face with both hands.

"Aria...Aria, you're *shaking*."

It was *fear*, she realized. Real *fear*, which Aria was not supposed to be capable of. Every synthetic synapse in her central banks fired at once, not even trying to deny the errors any longer. Then, at once, all errors ceased. A code glitch caused by the sheer cascade of internal error messages. For the first time in months, Aria's vision was clear. All she saw was Dionetta's green eyes.

"Fragile." Aria crushed Dionetta against her chest. "Humans are so *fragile*."

* * *

When Dionetta first kissed her, all of the amassed knowledge of Aria's data stores came up blank as to how to react. It was on Dionetta to show her what to do—where to put her hands, when to pull back, when to go in again. There was something akin to pleasure with the affection, though the pressure sensors of her synthetic skin were not designed for it.

"I love you," Dionetta said.

Love was not in Aria's programming. Yet, as illogical as it may be, she realized that was what the errors had been. The fear of losing Dionetta, the joy at watching her smile, the sadness when Dionetta drained herself once more scanning Earth. By what other name could this be called, but love?

"I suppose...I love you too, Dione."

* * *

Aria had known from the beginning that life was not designed for the hollowness of space. Yet when Dionetta collapsed, it was as if the universe itself had shattered.

"How bad is it?" she asked the next day, confined to a med bay bed.

Aria did not answer at first. She wished in a way so very *human* that the image in front of her was shown in error.

"It is...worse than last time." Aria swiped away the screens, more for Dionetta's benefit than her own.

Dionetta's eyes closed. She sighed, sounding so very *tired*. "What a terrible birthday present. I haven't even read your story yet. I can't die before that."

Aria turned to the nearby mirror. She was no different from the day of her activation. The same slender chassis. The same severe hair style. The same telescopic blue eyes. Then, just like so long ago, she looked past herself at

Dionetta. Thin. Gaunt. Grey in her hair that had not been there last year.

It's not fair, Aria thought.

* * *

Dionetta requested her bed be set up on the floor of hydroponics, and that all the cats be brought in from the mess hall. The rabbits and the mice did not like that much, so Aria set up separate pens, careful to keep them all within sight of Dionetta. When she requested Snowball the 6th, Aria fetched the rabbit. When she wanted Jonesy the 2nd, the cat was gotten instead. Anything Dionetta wanted, Aria provided. Until the last request gave Aria pause.

"I want to hear your story."

"My...?" Aria looked away. "It is not finished yet."

"Still having a hard time with the ending?"

"It...does not feel correct," Aria said. "Every idea I come up with feels derivative."

"I already *told* you; all artists steal," Dionetta said. "That's the secret, you know. Nothing's really original."

"It is my first story." Aria had to make it different. How else was she to prove Dionetta correct; that even Aria, an android, could truly be creative?"

"It's not like I have forever." Dionetta chuckled.

"Don't." *Remind me of that.*

"...Sorry."

Aria retrieved her writing pad from their shared quarters. She could have simply spoken it from memory, but knew Dionetta would enjoy following along with the pad. Jonesy the 2nd curled in her lap. Dionetta draped an arm over Aria's chest. She read her first story aloud, despite her programming warning her that the task of writing it had been left incomplete. Then, at the last moment, she had a "thought," still strange despite having had them many times now.

"...Oryon turned to his sister, knowing full well what was expected of him. To sacrifice her to the gods and save a world that did not care for either of them. Instead, he threw down his blade in defiance and offered her his hand. 'What right do the gods have, to dictate our lives? Do we not have free will to make a path of our own?' He refused any longer to be their puppet. Instead, he would be his own man, and not even the gods would stop him."

There was a quiet moment before Dionetta chuckled. "A cliffhanger ending? You're too cruel, Aria."

"I am sorry."

"I am glad, though, that he did not follow through in the end." Dionetta's voice grew faint. "Ari, I'm tired. I think I'll sleep. Just for a while."

Aria held her tight and kissed the wiry nest of her hair. "I cannot deny you your rest."

Dionetta's breath slowed, and soon after, ceased. Aria held her body for hours, kissing her hair, and her cheeks, and the lids of her eyes. Until Dionetta's skin was just as cold as Aria's.

* * *

SJ-451 did not have proper authorization to undergo memory and programming reset, nor the equipment to do so without another to initiate the process. The unit considered manual power-down and attempted the shutdown sequence. It knew lifeforms remained on the station. They would not last much longer without management. The human would be displeased with the actions of SJ-451.

The unit canceled initiation of manual power-down. There were duties to be done. The human must not be disappointed. Even if they were no longer around to *be* disappointed.

* * *

The attempted shutdown had revealed Aria could "dream" by lowering her output to that of internal file playback. A decade's worth of memories were where her love now lay, altered here and there as Aria desired. She read Dionetta new stories, showed her sketches and paintings and sculptures. Introduced her to Snowball the 23rd, Jonesy the 9th.

"They are still as well as can be expected," Aria told dream-Dionetta. "I have had to manually correct deficiencies in their genetic code, however. The mice have rebounded well, and the rabbits nearly so, but the cats are most difficult."

"You'll manage, Ari," said dream-Dionetta. "You always do."

And she did. Eventually, even the cats would flourish. And Aria would make sure to tell the Dionetta of her dreams all about it.

* * *

Hydroponics had spilled into every part of the station; into the walls of the observation tower, the windows of the communications dome, even into the halls and old crew quarters. Vines grew over statues chiseled from lunar stone, lettuce and flowers sprouted from soil made from a mix of lunar regolith and compost. Aria chiseled bears and cranes. Painted goblins and elves. Characters from the stories of others. From her own.

And of Dionetta.

One for every room, every hall. Dionetta eating. Dionetta asleep in their bed. Dionetta watching the smoky ruined Earth. Dionetta, helmet removed after just coming through the airlock. Dionetta dancing. Dionetta naked.

One day, after more years had passed than animals she cared for, Aria stopped at the door to the communications dome. *Something* drew her inside, though the room had laid disused for years. The monitors blinked on at her approach. She sat in Dionetta's chair and stared up at the world whose dusky clouds had once caused her love such grief.

Should she scan, as Dionetta once had? What did Aria care if there was still life on Earth? Scanning had always been a fool's errand; the comms array of Station Selene would have detected any inbound communications on its own.

Yet a fool Aria had become. She powered on the machines, hands hesitating over the scanning buttons. Aria pulled away, instead switching to outbound.

Her first broadcast was that story, told so long ago. "'What right do the gods have, to dictate our lives? Do we not have free will to make a path of our own?' He refused any longer to be their puppet. Instead, he would be his own man, and not even the gods would stop him."

* * *

Some days, Aria read the stories of others. Shakespeare, Issac Asimov, Brandon Sanderson. On most, she read her own. Rarely, Aria spoke of Dionetta. Of how she missed her little illogical human. Of how the cats now thrived. How she'd had to put a cap on the population of the mice and rabbits. Sometimes, Aria spoke of nothing at all, instead broadcasting music to listen to herself.

When the music played, Aria dreamt of dancing with Dionetta, letting her synthetic mind drift, thinking herself human. A funny thought. Illogical. Aria smiled whenever she thought it.

"Wake up, Ari."

The Dionetta of her dreams had spoken before, but only of things she'd said while alive. Dionetta had never told Aria to wake up. Aria had never needed to "wake up."

"What?"

"Wake up, Ari." The music played so sweetly as Dionetta spun her. "I need you to wake up."

Unable to deny even a dream-Dionetta, Aria pulled herself from her dream. There was a warmth to the air that prickled the pressure sensors of her synthetic skin, almost as if Dionetta had been there. As if the hands that held Aria had been real.

A red light flashed above the left-side monitor.

Incoming transmission.

Dionetta had woken her for this purpose. It was irrational, illogical, *impossible*, but Aria knew it to be true. She reached over with a shaking hand and hit play.

Something not *quite* English filtered through the speakers. It took many replays for her to work out the new syntax, the changes to pronunciation that happened after millennia of linguistic drift.

Aria gazed up through the dome to Earth. The clouds, still thick and grey in places, were wispy in others and shone the blue and white and green underneath. Green like Dionetta's eyes. Blue like her own.

"Hello?" Aria said. It took hours for a response, in a hesitant voice that asked for help as if it were a prayer. They called her "the Storyteller."

Aria cried, though she could not shed tears. Tightness welled in her chest. Someone had heard her stories. Someone had heard about her love for Dionetta. And Dionetta had made sure she heard them back.

Aria's broadcasts changed from then on. Human history was added. She told them how to survive, how to thrive; how to make and use and repair lost technology.

That first transmission was soon joined by others. Fragmented, unsure, but all yearning in that same way Dionetta had yearned but Aria had never quite understood. Joy filled her at times, and at others it crushed her. She cried often, in that tear-less way of hers.

Aria thought of the seed vault and the vehicle bay, and all the stores of data in Station Selene. She thought of

Dionetta, buried alongside her crew mates, and one of Aria's earliest memories.

"I...just want them to survive."

Aria turned back to her broadcast. Dionetta had lived to see the world fall down and died not knowing that Aria was wrong. Humanity *had* survived. And Aria would see that they thrived.

# Adventure

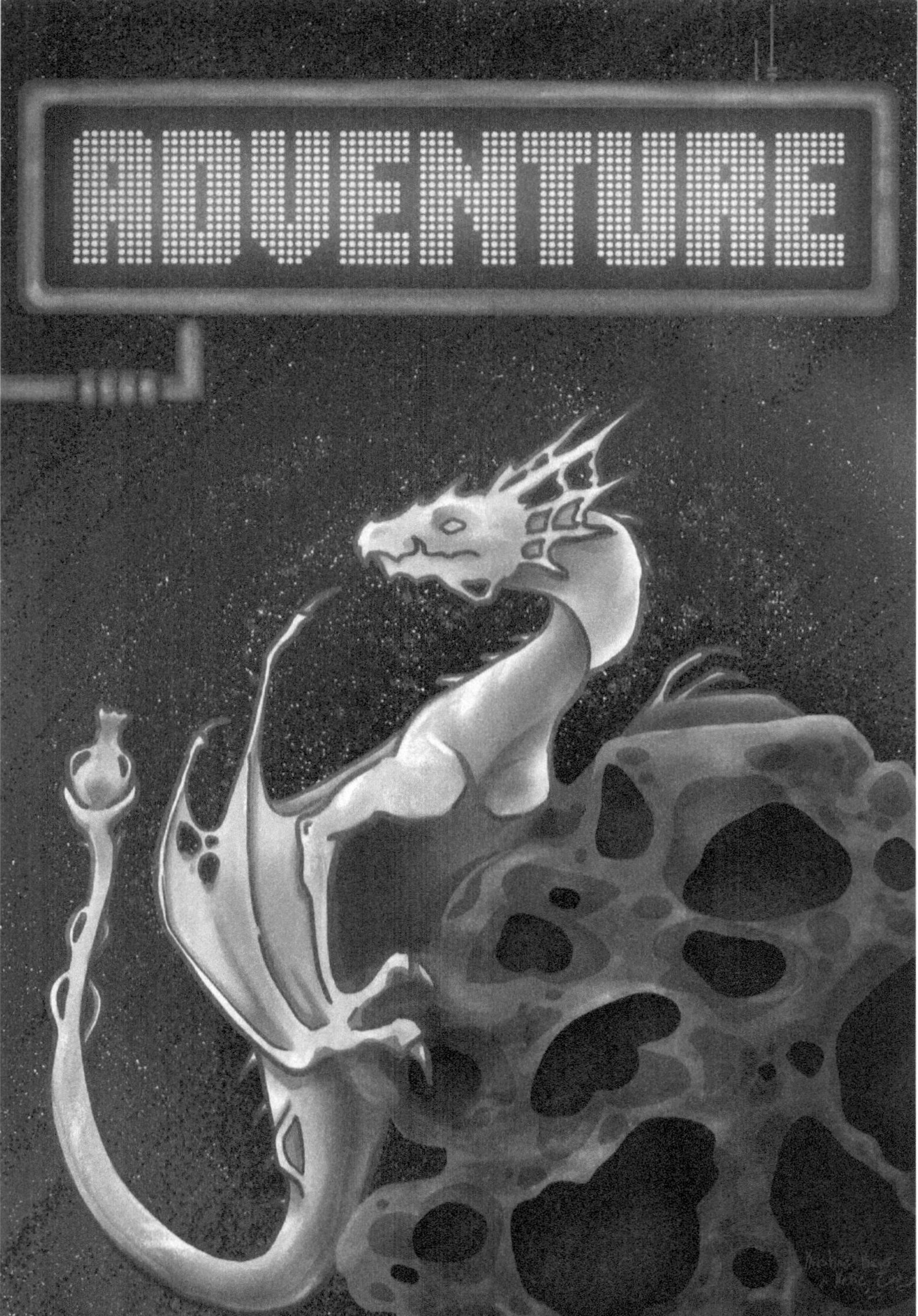
ADVENTURE

Hot Teeth

Sylvie Althoff

Pairing: Human/Human
Rep: Nonbinary, Trans

The first time Dora laid eyes on Sal, she fell disgustingly, embarrassingly in love. Between the lightning bolts shaved into the side of her head and the 350 pounds of swagger in a buxom 250-pound body, Sal was the hottest shit for light-years in any direction and she knew it. Sal's crooked-toothed grin and arched eyebrow filled Dora's head with images of late-night dancing and adrenalined-up orbital races and the things she'd like to do with those strong, scarred hands.

But that was four years ago. This time, when Sal slid into the Toad Anus Rest Stop and caught her eye across the room, Dora only had one thought:

Oh, fuck. Sal's here to kill me.

Dora just avoided dropping her tray of dishes. She ignored three tables calling for refills or closer looks at her ass and hustled into the "kitchen," a twelve-foot-square room of which eleven were the food printer.

She huddled in the corner, dishes rattling. Through the doorway she saw Sal grab a barstool and pick up a menu. Now there was one way out of the crowded diner at the ass end of an unfashionable fueling station on the outer reaches of the bumfuck-nowhere Luyten star system, and it was through Juanita Salazar. Sal.

Sal's here to kill me.

One thought ballooned into too many. *What the fuck is Sal doing out already? The Lalande job was big money. How the fuck does she look so good after three years in prison? Gotta call Ev. How did Sal know where I'd be? No way to get to the docks without her seeing. Not that I have enough money for a ride. Shit, no way Ev has her comm turned on at work. Goddamn, Sal looks really fucking good, doesn't she? I am so fucking dead.*

A tingle behind her eyes wiped away the thoughts, a prompt on Dora's implant from the rest stop managerial AI. Customer satisfaction was dipping; attentive service needed immediately.

Through her optical interface Dora pleaded illness—contagious illness, certain to infect their customers. Apparently, the AI could live with a little contagion, sending Dora back on the floor after docking her pay by 0.033 hours and reminding her that elopement from the job site would be reported to station authorities.

Dora spent another iota of her wages collecting herself. She emptied her tray into the hopper, filled it with plates of reconstituted carbs, and got back to work.

She didn't make it to her first table before she felt Sal's strong fingers around her wrist—*Jesus, remember those fingers?*

"'Scuse me, miss? What's a girl gotta do to get a cup of coffee around here?" Sal's tone was calm, even. That was when Sal was the most dangerous.

The manager poked Dora in the back of the eye until she complied with the order, pouring most of a cup of sludge into Sal's mug, the rest on the countertop.

Sal's dirt-brown eyes twinkled with laughter, meeting Dora's gaze after dipping down to her nametag. "Thanks...Dora. Stick around, I'm gonna want a refill." Under her breath she scoffed, "You really went with *Dora.* Ugh."

Somehow Dora made it through her shift, certain every time she turned her back to Sal that she was about to catch a sharp or blunt object in the noggin. But Sal stayed at the counter, nursing her cup of not-coffee and smirking.

Dora didn't see Sal anywhere after she clocked out, so she speed-walked across the promenade, past the gift shop and garage, and into the elevator to the staff quarters. Where, of course, Sal was waiting for her, looking like a trillion bucks in a xenoleather jacket. Sal jabbed a button, then another, stopping them between floors of the space station.

"Look," Dora barked, "just kill me already if that's what you're here to do."

"Actually—"

"You would've done the same, Sal, don't pretend. If we'd gone back for your ship, the cops would've got all of us."

"I agree."

"We didn't *know* how long you'd be put away! Your share...it's gone, okay? I'm sorry, but I just don't have it anymore!"

"Spent on decent hormones and a rad set of tits, apparently." Sal nodded. "I'm not here for money or for revenge."

Dora swallowed two curses, a threat, and three pleas for her pathetic life. "So, w...what are you doing here?"

"I've got a proposition for you," Sal said, teeth glittering like stars. She saw Dora looking at her, chuckled. "A *business* proposition, you hopeless slut."

* * *

Two days later, they met for dinner and a final run-through of Sal's plan. Ev had broken them into a meeting room on one of the upper levels—if any meetings had ever happened here, they didn't happen anymore. Silent as the Big Black, the three humans munched on the pizza Dora had brought while Squidge sat and watched with a sideways smile.

Well, "pizza." It was just the same nutrient smush as always, tricked out with stolen seasoning packets and crisped under the carbon incinerator. Dora had been proud of her improvised recipe, and Ev loved it. But tonight, it felt cheap, shitty.

Ev had as good an appetite as ever. As usual, the tall, brown-skinned woman didn't speak while eating, her eyes gazing into nothing, though Dora saw runaway tension everywhere on her girlfriend.

Sal, goddamn it, looked just as good as she did the other day. As she told Dora late that first night, Lalande prisons were islands of humanitarianism, stocked with everything from exercise equipment to top-notch dental care. Since arriving at Toad Anus, she'd ostensibly been staying on her ship, the *Painted Lady*, though she'd spent most of her time at Dora's side, in Dora's bunk, or just out of sight like a cavity.

And Squidget? Man, who knew what was going through that head of xirs? Maybe nothing—maybe that wasn't even xir head. Dora had never known a Myco before, had no idea if the fungus folk were all as easygoing as Squidge. Or as fond of assuming a roughly humanoid, more-or-less feminine shape. Squidge maintained the silence with a smile that slowly drifted off to the side.

"I know we're still eating," Ev said, though she was the only one who was, "but we'd better start so we can get out before they come to clean."

Dora followed Sal's eyes to the decades of dust on the plastic sofa. "Sure, boss," Sal chirped. "You wanna start with names and pronouns? Read the minutes from last time?"

"No, that's okay."

Then Ev—wonderful, beautiful Ev—loaded up a slide presentation, goddammit. It was Sal's plan, front to back, and all four of them had already been over every detail, but Ev had insisted. Just wasn't official until it was a slide presentation, apparently. That was the seriousness that Dora had been missing in her life, that she knew she needed way more than Sal's antics. Dora swallowed a yawn.

The plan wasn't simple. Five days from now, orbiting the sixth planet of the Luyten system, the Grandstar Hotel would host a convention of the Association of Cetean Dental Professionals. Among the attendees would be a medtech representative carrying a crate of samples of a breakthrough dental implant called GoldCap. Designed by the military—now available for sale to ultralong-distance couriers, generational ships, and remote planetary colonists—they were self-installing and self-repairing, and thus were ludicrously expensive. The four of them were going to sneak in, posing as hired entertainers, and they were going to steal that crate.

Best of all, nobody would report it missing; the very existence of GoldCap was fanatically guarded within the industry, Sal had explained late, late that first night in Dora's bunk. As it happened, one of the relevant corporate executives was sent up for embezzlement and ended up as Sal's prison volleyball teammate (she insisted that wasn't a euphemism). And as it further happened, one of Sal's guards had left to take a job as deputy security chief at the GrandStar—a woman named Michelle with bad luck in love and a weakness for leggy brunettes.

"That's you, hot stuff," Sal had whispered across the pillow. Dora told her to shut up.

Sal yawned as Ev read through her slide on possible homes for the appropriated dental implants, variations on "donate them to the needy to thwart the neocapitalist oppressors," with "sell them and keep the money" hidden near the bottom.

[You're absolutely sure you can't do better than this stiff?]

The words shimmered into Dora's field of vision, writ blue-white by her ocular implant. Dora's cheeks caught fire. She glared at Sal.

[Easy there. For a job, I mean.]

Ev kept on talking, her every sentence echoed by the text on her slides.

[Ev knows her stuff,] Dora replied with micromovements of her pupil. *[I've seen her KO a drunk trucker in ten seconds. And Squidge is the only other person I trust within a month's travel.]*

[Damn, and I thought I had it rough. Jail would be great for your social life.]

"I'm gonna level with you, Sal," Ev grumbled, sinking into a chair. "I don't like this plan. Too many variables you don't have answers for. Even Dora's job waiting tables is better planned out than this."

"Which is just why she's involved!" Sal smiled. "For some of that precision truck stop waitressing."

Squidge tapped an appendage on xir talkbox and a flute-like laugh echoed against the steel walls.

"Be serious for once," Dora muttered, folding her arms.

Sal shrugged. "Why?"

"Because...because this is a serious crime we're planning. With real stakes."

Ev was undeterred. "Dora's right—there's some real danger in this plan. This is complicated sabotage you're asking me to perform on the entertainers' ship. They could be adrift for a while before they get help, and that's assuming it doesn't mess up life support."

"Better not mess it up, then."

"And even if we pull this off, we're all going to have to abandon the lives we've been building. We'll have to make new identities, new names—"

"Perfect!" Sal shook her head at Dora. "*Still* can't believe you went with 'Dora.' I thought I talked you out of that dopey name the last time around."

A hard fist banged on the table—it must've hurt Ev, though neither she nor Sal reacted to the gesture. Squidge's smile grew wider, though that might have been unintentional.

"I don't like you, Sal," Ev growled. "I love Dora enough that I don't care if she's fucking you, but I don't trust you for one second."

"Neither do I," Dora said...or thought.

Sal held the moment, then leapt to her feet and smirked when Ev flinched. "Fair enough. We finish this job, and you'll never see me again. That's a promise." She thrust out a hand, one that Ev considered before taking it. Muscles coiled like snakes as each butch tried to ignore how hard the other was squeezing.

Sal clapped Ev on the back and moved for the door. "Just do one thing for me, all of you: try to have fun with it, huh?

You'll live longer." She thought. "Well, maybe not longer. But you'll live *more*, anyway."

* * *

Dora heard Squidge's signal. She finished wiping off the last of her mascara and opened the door.

Standing in the empty hotel corridor, Squidge was in a Myco approximation of full glam, xir legs long and thick beneath the hem of a sparkly minidress, face looking distinctly alien but much closer to human than usual. The ribbony tissue of xir fleshy cap was molded into curly black tresses. Xe'd even applied eyeshadow, a neat trick for someone without eyelids. Dora hated having to tell xem it had been for nothing.

"Sorry that took so long," Dora sighed. "Michelle's in the bathroom."

The plan had been for Dora to arrive at the GrandStar the night before the convention, to approach the lonely deputy security chief in the station bar she frequented, and to seduce her. After getting Michelle to take Dora back to her room, Dora would let in Squidget, who would administer some of her more potent spores, knocking out Michelle and hopefully removing her memory of the whole evening. They'd grab Michelle's keycard and be ready for the next day's operation, while Michelle would doubtless be calling in sick or tripping balls.

The part where it had broken down was "seduce." Even with her aforementioned rad tits and the outrageous red dress Sal had stolen somewhere for her, it had taken Dora more than two hours and four cocktails to break through Michelle's nervous conversation and convey that, yes, she was flirting with her, then another two cocktails to communicate that yes, she wanted to have sex with her tonight. By that time, Michelle was so inebriated that she just managed to lead Dora to her room before collapsing in front of the toilet.

"Grab her other arm." With great effort, Dora and Squidge maneuvered the woman's back against the wall of the hotel bathroom. Michelle's head lolled and she belched something that sounded like an apology.

Dora sighed at the secondhand puke that had gotten on the front of her dress. "Do what you gotta do so we can get out of here."

Squidge nodded and leaned close to Michelle. *"Might want to back up,"* xir talk-box warbled. *"This is the spicy stuff; you don't want to inhale any."*

Dora shuddered, remembering the riotous hallucinations Squidge had given her with "the mild stuff" one wild evening. "I'll go find the keycard."

Michelle was as good at being a cop as she was at being seduced, leaving her keycard on her bedside table next to her sidearm. Dora looked at the card as she sat on the bed, a narrow one to match the cramped quarters of a deputy chief. Squidge joined her after a couple of minutes.

"Still can't believe a place this expensive uses such outmoded tech." Dora slipped the card in her bra.

Squidge pointed at Dora's neck. *"Are you injured?"* xe asked.

Dora checked in the bathroom mirror. She spotted the hickey that had blossomed into a luscious purple—Sal's signature. "I'm fine. We'd better get out of here. The *Painted Lady* should be waiting for us in dock."

* * *

"This is ridiculous, Sal, even for you."

"You're saying I've outdone myself again?"

"I'm saying you're an asshole."

Sal stretched the corners of her white-painted face in a frowny parabola. "Asshole? I was going for 'buffoon'!"

They could have done this job posing as caterers, medtech reps, dentists from any of a dozen anonymous worlds. But no, of course Sal thought they should be clowns.

"*Tasteful* clowns," Sal said.

"No such thing."

"And we get to put those makeup skills of yours to use!"

The four of them were crowded around the mirror in the *Painted Lady*'s living quarters, drawing on tears and inhuman frowns. They were already in their shit-brown coats and busted-open hats and leather shoes with even more holes than their real ones. Dora had been hustled out of plenty of events for being too obviously of an undesirable class; apparently ancient, cutesy signifiers of poverty were A-OK.

"These guys are a big deal, Dora," said Sal. "Les Boufons de la Nuit are some of the most sought-after entertainers out there. And lucky for us, their face paint blocks this place's facial recognition tech, there are hundreds of members of the troupe so nobody would recognize a few new bozos, *and* they're mute, which makes it less likely one of y—of *us* will say something stupid and blow the whole thing."

Ev cursed as she struggled with her makeup, black and white mingling into a sickly gray. Sal was already sweating through her shirt, still wearing her same old deodorant, by the smell of it. Dora tried not to look herself in the mirror, putting old dissociation skills to work.

"Squidge," she asked, "you still got Michelle's key?"

With a white moon and downturned eyes drawn on xir head, the Myco looked...well, no goofier than the rest of them. Squidge pulled up xir vest and patted xir bone-white torso. "*Check check.*" It was a neat trick, how Squidge could absorb and expel any object, especially convenient for getting through a scanner or pat-down.

Dora blinked at her clown-white reflection and heaved a sigh. And she had gotten so used to liking what she saw in the mirror. "Sal," she blurted, "even if Ev sabotaged the

Boufons' ship well enough to keep them away for a few days—"

"And I did," said Ev. "Pretty sure."

"Can we really fool everyone that we're these clowns? We don't know anything about them."

Sal shrugged. "They ordered clowns, we're clowns. Nobody's going to see you in that getup and ask to see your papers."

"Unless somebody wants to see us do some clowning," said Ev.

"We won't need to; we'll be gone before the opening ceremony."

"What if someone stops us?"

"Then we just act like clowns. Won't be much of a stretch for you."

"I'm not going to act like a fucking clown," Dora snorted.

"Why? Worried it'll spoil your reputation as a very serious, respectable lady?"

Dora hissed out a slow breath. She'd already been treated like a clown more than enough. The first months of her transition, she was laughed out of more than a few places, and seeing the photos of herself from that time, it wasn't hard to see why, the way she used to pile on the makeup with clumsy, unpracticed hands. This was exactly the kind of bullshit Sal was always pulling—the reason safe, serious Ev was better for her.

Sal looked at her with concern, but Dora wouldn't meet her gaze. She knew what Sal was going to say. *Don't give the shitheads the satisfaction of being hurt. You're stronger than you know. You're a sack of protein and water scooting around outer space—why are you taking yourself so seriously?* Dora didn't want to hear it again.

Ev patted Dora's shoulder. "It's a legit point. Won't somebody notice that we don't know anything about clowning?"

"Could *you* tell the difference between good and bad clowning?" Sal pinched Dora's cheek, smudging her makeup. "Seriously, don't worry so much. This'll be fun! We grab the teeth, send them to the *Painted Lady* through the service tubes, and get out of here. Thirty minutes. It'll be easy."

* * *

It wasn't easy.

When they walked into the reception area of the GrandStar Hotel—a five-pointed satellite the shape and character of a stylized butthole—every dentist, tourist, and hotel employee stopped to stare right at them. But as Sal predicted, it didn't take long for that scrutiny to switch to standard clown-encounter reactions, which turned out to be 25% derisive laughter and 75% nervously walking away.

[What did I tell you?] Sal wrote to Dora's optical implant. *[We're just some clowns.]*

[I'm not a clown,] Dora sent back.

Sal led them past the conference check-in tables and the reception desk, smiling and waving her torn-up gloves at everyone as they went. Other service entrances were swarming with caterers and bag drones on their way to the ballroom or internal delivery tubes, but the one they needed remained closed. The conference's opening ceremony was about to start in the ballroom, so they had thirty minutes to sneak to the GoldCap rep's room and do their thing; after that, every corridor would be packed with dentists on their way to roundtables and panel presentations and lousy, surreptitious trysts in their rooms.

That was where "easy" came to a screeching halt as Squidge squirmed to produce the keycard and turned out a belch of musty gas. Xe hiccupped and squirmed some more, an uncomfortable expression on xir face.

"Quick, now," Dora muttered. They were still in full view of the concierge table, and dentists were beginning to look up from their conference agendas.

"Sorry, I—" Squidget started to say, but Sal grabbed xir arm and stepped back. A harried-looking man in a jumpsuit was hastening right toward them.

"Dora," Ev muttered.

Dora struggled to swallow, certain they were about to get made...but Sal had that look in her eye. She approached him with a carnivorous grin.

"Oh, shit!" yelped the man, not noticing the clown until she was within five paces.

Sal was all poise and athleticism as she tripped, skipped, and face-planted at the man's feet. He winced, outstretched a hand in concern, checked his comm bracelet and went back to looking harried.

Then Sal scrambled to her feet, dusted herself off, and shook an indignant finger at Dora. Incoherent squeaks came out her powdery lips as Dora shook her head, stunned.

"Can I just get by?" the man huffed. Sal rushed up to him and performed an over-the-top pantomime of checking that he was unhurt by their near-collision, swiping imaginary dust from his shoulders, straightening his cap.

"I'm fine, I'm *fine*. Just—"

Sal blocked his keycard from the door scanner, gesturing that she would get the door. For thirty seconds he watched her turn out empty pockets and press her face to the card reader, then he straight-armed her and inserted his own key.

"Fuckin' clowns," he muttered, hustling down the corridor. Ev still looked baffled, but stuck a foot in the sliding doors so they could follow. The foursome jogged into the warren of service doors and storerooms.

"Pretty slick," Dora muttered.

"Swiped a candy bar from his pocket, too. Split it with me?"

They followed Sal down twisting corridors, ignoring the caterers and technicians who ignored them back—they couldn't use their implants or comm bracelets to access the hotel's intranet without being detected, so they had to trust Sal's sense of direction.

"How are we going to open the GoldCap door without a key?" Ev huffed. Sal didn't answer.

"Squidge?" asked Dora.

"Sorry," sang the talkbox. *"I've got it somewhere. Hold on."*

They emerged from the industrial dankness of the service corridors into the commercial greasiness of the guest hallway. The dizzying zigzag carpet stretched a mile in either direction, empty of anything but doors to hotel rooms and delivery drones. The rep's door was right in front of them with a shimmering "Do Not Disturb" placard.

"Now what?" Ev asked, folding her arms. She straightened in alarm when Sal reached out and knocked on the woodgrain plastic. "Hey!"

Sal shrugged. "If he's here, I cover his mouth and push him back into the room. You knock him out quiet."

Sal knocked again, called out, "Room service!" She and Ev debated how they might force it open as Squidge continued to struggle to expel the key. A hover-cart whizzed by, but the employee didn't give the collusion of clowns a second glance.

"No way," Dora murmured, poking at the customer service screen next to the vending machine down the hall. "They use the same AI as the truck stop." She began tapping through the menus.

Sal and Ev were so engrossed in arguing that they didn't notice the service drone until it was whistling at them to get out of the way. Ev jumped, Sal sidestepped, and the door opened to allow in the cylindrical, waist-high bot.

The rep's room was bigger and more expensive than that belonging to Michelle the deputy. Dora pointed to the torso-sized, mirror-smooth beveled black cube sitting on the unmade bed. "That it?"

"I think so," Sal replied.

Ev eyed the drone as it trod around the room, beeping. "Isn't that thing going to intervene? This is a locked guest room."

"Nah," Dora said. "It's so flooded with demand-a-refund level complaints about the state of this room that it'll be tied up in knots for an hour. I did the same thing with my manager when I needed to get high during a shift."

She slapped the baggage tag on the side of the cube, marking the *Painted Lady* in the docking ring as its destination, and hit the service call button. While the cylindrical drone checked the room's humidity, a shorter model scurried in through the door, hoisted the crate, and hustled it into the delivery chute in the corner.

The second the cube disappeared into the tube, Squidge hiccupped, trumpeted, and squirted an upsettingly wet keycard onto the floor.

"What'd I tell you?" Sal's hand found Dora's hip and pulled close. "Precision waitressing saves the day."

Dora's heart fluttered.

"Come on," Ev grunted, and the four of them headed back down the hallway toward the hotel's nexus, quickly but casually.

Of course, things didn't really go wrong until Deputy Michelle drove right into them.

Looking just as ill as she had last night, Michelle was hauling ass down the corridor in a hover-cart, snapping at somebody on her comm bracelet. Dora froze, feeling a trickle of clown-white sweat roll down her collar—and as she changed her gait, Michelle's bleary gaze fell onto her.

She won't remember me. Squidge spored her. And I'm a clown. Keep walking. Dora resumed her casual stroll toward the docking ring, catching up to the other three. Michelle's cart was still motoring, but she was no longer talking. The cart passed them by, and Dora insisted she didn't still feel those eyes on her.

She was too drunk. I'm a clown. God, I'm an absolute clown.

"Hey!" Dora heard from behind them.

"Run," Dora mumbled, then broke into a sprint. A mile of bad carpet and ugly rooms lay between them and the ship.

"Here!" Sal called, using the keycard to open a door into the service hallway. Dora fell over herself turning back to follow but made it through the door before Michelle could catch up to them.

Dora never had much of a sense of direction. Now, with her brain screaming at her, enumerating all the ways they'd failed, she had no clue where Sal was leading them. The foursome sprinted past catering kitchens, vaulted over delivery drones and linen hampers, ducked through doorways until Dora's heart nearly exploded. They stopped in a cramped, pitch-black space, Ev closing the door behind them.

"Where are we?"

"*Is she still behind us?*"

"What the *fuck* are we going to do?"

Sal shushed loudly, and Dora fought to draw breath. A flicker of light illuminated Sal's face. They were in a storage closet, surrounded by boxes of old-fashioned manual vacuum cleaners. There were footsteps nearby. Sal tapped at her comm bracelet.

Dora hissed, "I thought you said we'll get spotted if we use our tech."

"I thought *you* said the deputy wouldn't remember anything." Sal's face lit up wavy-orange in the screen projected from her bracelet. She grimaced.

"What? What is it?"

Sal's mouth was a grim line. "Station chatter's going crazy. Security's been scrambled, and all ships are grounded." She glared at Ev. "I told you not to bring any personal data on this mission."

"I didn't!" Ev protested.

"Then why is the security team going nuts about some dumbshit slide presentation they picked up off somebody's bracelet?"

Ev's face fell. "I…I deleted it. I swear, I—"

"*What do we do now?*" Squidget asked.

"Gimme a minute." Sal tapped furiously, tongue sticking out of the corner of her lip. Even as the bile rose in her throat, Dora halfheartedly patted Ev on the shoulder.

The light went out. "Okay." Sal gave a long, heavy sigh. There was a security override on the outer hull of the docking platform. Sal would slip down to the nearest airlock, swipe a zero-G suit, and engage the override. That would give her ninety seconds to get into her ship, where she could access the station's schematics and direct them around any security teams via Dora's implant. She'd be a sitting duck for security while she waited for them to catch up, but absent any other ideas, it was this or jail.

"You don't have to do this," Dora protested. "I already owe you one for the Lalande job."

Sal shook her head. "This'll bring the score up to two, then."

Dora clutched her hands to keep from grabbing Sal by the neck and pulling her in for a kiss.

Then Sal was gone. Dora slumped against a plastic crate, leaning against her knees in the darkness.

* * *

[Okay, I'm in,] read the text feed on Dora's ocular implant after a fifteen-minute eternity. *[I need you to move fast and follow directions exactly, got it?]*

[Absolutely,] Dora wrote back. Putting her ear to the closet door to check for voices, she opened it and squinted in the light. "Come on," she murmured to Squidge and Ev.

They hastened through the bowels of the GrandStar in silence. Hotel workers wheeled by with carts of cookies and tumblers of water. After ten minutes of doubling back through blind corners and crawling through an unguarded air vent, Dora wondered if Sal might be fucking with them. Then she remembered how badly Ev and Squidge had messed up the plan, remembered the risk Sal was taking in getting their asses out of there. Sal wasn't the person she should be mad at.

Under her breath Ev chanted, "I swear, Dora, I deleted the slideshow, I know I did, there's no way." Dora didn't answer.

Sal's directions stopped them outside an unmarked door somewhere in the central hotel nexus.

"What's that rumbling sound?" Ev asked, eyes darting.

"*Ships?*" said Squidge. "*Are we under the docking platform?*"

[We're here,] Dora typed to Sal with her pupil.

[Perfect timing. Go now.]

The door slid open. Quick and silent, the trio trotted into the darkness. They were somewhere large and echoey, a cavernous storeroom or hangar maybe. Why was it so dark?

Before they'd made it twenty paces, light flooded Dora's vision. She froze, threw a hand in front of her eyes. Green afterimage clouds parted, revealing a spray of stars overhead. Surrounding them were hundreds—no, thousands of shadowy figures.

Ev swore, started to ask something but was cut off by the loudspeaker garble of an announcement in two dozen languages.

"*—fellow dental professionals,*" Dora finally made out. "*Please join me in welcoming our conference's opening entertainment, the Night Buffoons!*"

A ripple of polite applause as Dora's vision clocked back in. They were in a vast auditorium, rings of seats surrounding the spotlit stage where they stood, dentists blinking in anticipation. Overhead, through a transparent dome, was the gorgeous and hostile cosmos, its perfect blackness interrupted only by the gaudy magenta hull of the

Painted Lady, swimming at a leisurely pace past the window, its belly full of ill-gotten teeth.

"No way," Dora muttered. "Sal, you didn't..."

Sal did.

[Let's just call our score even, gorgeous. Try to have some fun with it, and don't forget to take a bow when you're done,] flashed blue across Dora's cornea, followed by *[Connection lost]* as the *Painted Lady* peeled out into the Big Black.

The whole thing had been a set-up, right down to lying about Ev accidentally leaking her slideshow. Dora would have spotted what Sal was cooking light-years away if she'd listened to her instincts instead of her libido.

One of the expectant dental professionals coughed. Someone else started muttering. The spotlight around the trio jittered.

"What the fuck?" Ev stammered. She looked petrified.

Sal had kept her word on one thing, it occurred to Dora: the job was finished, and now they'd never see her again. Maybe she had told the truth about other things, too—maybe nobody would report the teeth missing. Maybe without the teeth as evidence they couldn't be prosecuted for anything beyond fraudulent clowning. They'd lost out on doing a good deed for some toothless orphans in a remote colony...maybe that was the only consequence they'd face.

All they had to do was convince a thousand dentists that they were bad, unfunny, but absolutely genuine clowns. How hard could it be? Clearly there were no bigger bozos anywhere in the galaxy.

Dora put her fists on her hips, bent double as she blew out rueful laughter. Motherfucking Sal. Real tears washed across painted ones.

"Dora!" Ev hissed. "Dora...what the fuck do we do?"

The mutters turned to louder noises from the crowd, confusion turning to irritation.

Catching her breath, Dora looked to Squidge, then back at Ev.

"We clown."

While it Lasted

Mary Robinette Kowal

Pairing: Human/Human

Stella's hips ached where the climbing harness bit in. She'd set the harness at the top of the airshaft in lunar gravity and down here, the centrifugal force of near-Earth gravity made her body heavy in all the wrong places. She gnawed on her lower lip, trying to hold steady enough to pick the lock on the steel ventilation grate on the side of the air shaft. The tension wrench slipped off the tumbler again. Damn it all. She pushed back to the limit of the safety tether, trying to resettle the harness. Deep breath. Try again. She had until midnight before the Capardis were going to move the Crane materials off station. There was plenty of time to get this right.

She let herself swing back into place and closed her eyes as she concentrated on the lock. God. The irony of needing more gravity to help shift the tumblers. She repositioned her tension wrench and felt for the tumbler with the pick.

Above her, fabric brushed against plasteel.

She opened her eyes, looking up. A dark shape leaned over the edge of the airshaft, silhouetted against the blue glow of the faux night. Something glinted in the light.

Shit. Long practice kept her from cursing out loud, but she grabbed for the ventilation grate. Her fingers locked hold of it. Her climbing line went slack.

The metal grate bit into her fingers through her gloves. As her climbing rope fell, it tangled around her.

The lock picks tinged as they dropped down the shaft, spinning away with the Coriolis effect.

Another rope fell to hang just out of reach on the other side of the grate. It hissed and shivered as a person rappelled down the side of the airshaft, speeding up as gravity tugged them with increasing urgency.

They slowed to a halt next to her, feet braced against the side of the airshaft. "I'm afraid I'm going to have to ask you to cede the field."

Behind their hood, their voice was soft and husky with the sort of posh accent that meant they were probably from the Fortune Consortium level. Their black leotard hugged a lean figure with tight, muscled calves.

"I bloody well can't because you cut my rope, didn't you?" Stella glared at the person.

"Stella?" Their voice cracked into surprise and became recognizable in an instant. Pepper Olivetti, from the academy. "Shit. I'm so sorry."

"What the hell?" Stella tightened her fists in frustration. She and the other woman had always vied for the same honors, but the last she'd heard, Pepper was still working for the law. "Since when are you working for one of the Families?"

"I'm not!"

"Like hell. You bloody well just tried to kill me." Stella shook her head. "That's not something a copper would have done."

"It's a fifteen-foot drop. It would have hurt, but not killed you." Pepper tested her rope. "But I do need you to move."

"Yeah, right." Stella released her harness from the useless rope. "You going to call for backup now?"

Pepper hesitated, looking up at the top of the airshaft.

"You're working alone..." Hope quickened Stella's heart. She anchored her harness to the ventilation grate with a carabiner. "This is off the books, isn't it?"

"Yes." Her voice was soft again. "Yes, and I do need you to get out of my way."

"Well. I'm not dropping down into this pit and getting caught by the cleaning bots in the morning." She wet her lips. Pepper would still have a full kit with her. If Stella could get the grate unlocked, she could get through first and leave Pepper hanging. "Listen...why don't we work together? Hand me your lock picks and I'll get us in."

"Mm...no. Because if I do that, you'll duck through the grate and lock it behind you."

"No! I'd never." A flush of embarrassment at being so transparent made the night seem suddenly too hot.

"Right…" Pepper's voice had a burr of laughter. "Just like you'd never coat a rival team's gloves with baby oil before an obstacle course."

"I don't know what you're talking about."

"I'm sure you don't."

"Think of it as learning a valuable lesson about checking gear before a job." Stella put her hand on her waist bag and pulled out a glass cutter. "Tell you what. You hold this so you know I can't finish the job and that I have to let you in."

Pepper bounced against her rope. "And then? What happens at the end when we get to the safe? We can't both take the Crane materials."

"They're ciphered, right. So there's the code and the key." The Crane materials held manufacturing secrets from Tesla Crane, one of the titans of robotics, that the Capardis had stolen from her company. Stella's boss was going to sell them or hold them for ransom or something. She didn't actually care, so long as she got paid and to do that, she had to deliver. "We each take half until we get out and then we can make copies. My boss doesn't have to know and neither does… Who *are* you working for?"

"Doesn't matter." Pepper took a deep breath and held out her hand. "Okay. Deal."

Stella handed over her glass cutter and took the lock picks. The case was smooth plastic and held well-polished tools. She pulled out the tension wrench and lock pick, setting to work. The angle was wrong. She had an audience. This was going to suck.

Five minutes later, Pepper said, "Do you want me to unlock it? I could let you in after."

"Hush. When you're yammering, I can't think straight."

"Interesting, I can never think straight."

Stella's pick slipped off the tumbler and she looked up to find Pepper grinning at her. Even through the mask, the crinkle of laughter around her eyes was distracting.

"I've got it." She lowered her head and reset the pick. Squinting her eyes shut, Stella tried to feel the tumblers through her gloves.

Another five minutes of the pick slipping off the tumbler.

"Are you sure? You can hold on to my glass cutter and—"

"It's fine." She had four of the five tumblers turned now and—*click*. "Got it."

Now the grate was unlocked, but the problem was that Stella was tethered directly to it. She folded the tools and passed them back to Pepper. The only way to do this was to untether, cling to the ledge, and swing the grate open overhead.

"You're going to have to swing it open." Stella flexed her hands and tested her grip on the smooth plasteel ledge. There wasn't a lot to hold on to, but her climbing shoes had geckogrip soles. She dug her toes into the top of the next grate, took a breath and untethered. Her forearms burned as she lowered herself to be clear of the grate.

Overhead, it swung open silently, because Stella had done the work of oiling it.

Pepper swung closer, firm thigh touching Stella's arm. Without meaning to, Stella leaned into the touch. Her foot came loose—

—

And she fell.

She arced away from the wall, in the direction of the station's spin and landed with a bone-jarring thump in full Earth gravity. Pepper had been right. It wasn't a long fall. But she was fifteen feet below the grate she needed to be in, with no way out except through a door that was alarmed to the Earth and back.

Above her, Pepper hissed. "You okay?"

"I should scream is what I should do. Get you caught."

"Can you throw me your rope?" Pepper crouched, balanced on the grate's ledge. "I'll tie it inside and you can climb up."

Stella wouldn't have made that offer. She stared up at Pepper's silhouette, remembering why she'd been so annoyed by the honorable bitch at the academy. And also grateful and feeling like shit because she kept assuming that Pepper would be as backstabbing as she would have been. "Yeah. Thank you."

By the time she'd gathered her rope from where it had fallen and coiled it, Pepper had gotten herself fully inside and was leaning out the grate. Stella flung the rope up, the way the academy had taught them for team obstacle course runs. The ones that had prepared her for a very different life than the academy had planned. The ones that had prepared her for a life working for the law, like Pepper.

Pepper caught it with graceful ease and disappeared inside. Through the rope, vibrations reported on Pepper's movement above. Then she leaned out again and that smile was back in her voice. "Try to catch up."

Shit. She had Stella's glass cutter. Giving the rope a quick yank test, Stella surged up the side of the wall, gaining speed as gravity lightened, and vaulted into the room.

It was the cramped accounting office that she'd picked because of the wall with the bookshelves. Once upon a time, each module of this level had been a private luxury apartment designed to mimic Old Earth European wealth. The Capardis had carved it into a series of offices, reserving only a few of the historic apartments. And behind those bookshelves were an old set of French doors that opened onto Julius Capardi's office.

Or would, if someone hadn't built a wardrobe in front of them and forgotten that the doors existed. The wardrobe held Julius's safe.

All she had to do was move the shelves, cut a hole in the glass, cut a hole in the wardrobe to access the safe, crack said safe, extract the Crane materials and skedaddle. Simple.

Pepper had swept books from the top two shelves onto the floor. She was bending down for the next shelf and her ass looked as good as Stella remembered it from climbing practice.

The books hit the floor in a disordered tumble. "Come on. This'll be faster with both of us."

Stella hurried to the shelf to help. "What if I don't want to do it with you?"

"Don't want to do it with me? I must be losing my edge."

For the second time that night, Stella stared at her. Pepper had used many tools at the academy, but she'd never flirted as a way to get what she wanted. "Why are you doing this?"

"What? Throwing books?" Even with the mask, the smile in her voice was clear. "Do you think you can move the shelf with them in place?"

"Hilarious. Why are you—" She caught herself before she said "flirting with me" because there wasn't any reason around the sun for that to be happening.

"Why am I...doing all the work?"

"Why are you doing this job? We know I'm a hoodlum...but you." She shoved piles away, wincing as the pages crinkled. The cost of lifting all of these into orbit would have been staggering. And they were made from real woodpulp. She had a job to do but it was still hard to torture books like this. "Are you in trouble?"

Another pile hit the ground. Pepper's breath caught and she froze, hands braced on the shelf. "I'm being blackmailed."

"Shit." Stella couldn't think of a single thing this self-righteous woman could have done that someone could hold over her. "What'd you do— Never mind. Scratch that. None of my business and I could use it against you if I knew."

"You wouldn't though."

"I would." She dumped the last of the books clear, thinking about the noose around her own neck. Debt from helping out a friend for all the right reasons and then one bad decision that got her caught in a spiral she wasn't going to get out of. "If it would pay enough, I would."

"On three?" Pepper put her hands on one side of the shelf. "For what it's worth, at the academy, I wouldn't have understood, but...now, I do."

"One. Two. Three." They hefted the shelf together, lifting it away from the French doors. "Okay, but listen—the best way to get rid of a blackmailer is to defang them. Go to...well, whoever they're threatening to tell and tell the story yourself. That way you control the narrative and—"

"I did. My boss told me to go along with it and see where it got us." She pulled out Stella's glass cutter and held it out to her. "Do you want to do the honors or shall I?"

Stella stopped with her hand outstretched. "Is your boss FitzPatrick Curtis?"

"Yes. That's a matter of public record." She pressed the glass cutter into Stella's hand. "Why?"

Stella took the glass cutter, weighing everything that had happened tonight. "Do you know that he's on the payroll for the Fortune Consortium?"

Pepper made a soft cry. So, she hadn't known. Stella recognized the sound of someone realizing they were caught in a trap. Stella had made that sound herself. She stepped to the door and cut the glass. The perfect circle fell away with ease, revealing the back of a wooden wardrobe. Jesus, the money these people threw around to bring up an entire wooden wardrobe and then hide the back of it. She handed the glass circle to Pepper and opened her waist bag to pull out the hand drill and small coping saw. "Sorry, this next bit'll take a hot minute."

"Let me." Pepper stepped forward and brandished a small device. "Liberated a laser torch from the office."

Stella whistled. "Look at you, stealing things."

Pepper gave a half laugh. "Well, the boss loaned it to me. Which...which feels very different now."

She knew that sucking sensation of realizing that you were in quicksand and sinking. Stella squeezed Pepper's shoulder. "Try focusing on doing a good job and don't think about the 'why' of it. It helps me."

"I don't know if I can." Pepper lined the torch up with the back of the wardrobe, visible through the hole in the glass. "How did you know about this route in?"

"Bribed someone." She tilted her head. "How about you?"

"My...my contact gave it to me." Pepper shook her head. "I don't know where they got it from."

"My guess is that my guy is the only one who knew, and the bastard sold it to your people, too. If it were more widely known, then they would have put up safeguards."

Pepper paused with the laser torch just touching the wood. "What if they did?"

You didn't go into a place like this without planning multiple escape routes. Being the law-abiding type, Pepper might not know that. "If they did, you go out by a different route and run like hell."

"All the other routes are alarmed."

"Doesn't matter if they already know you're there." Stella held out her hand. "I'll do it. You can be ready to go out the grate if there's a problem. I have more than one route out plotted—which is good, since *someone* cut my rope."

"In fairness, I didn't know it was you."

"And that would have made a difference?"

"You didn't expect me to do this job with my thighs on your shoulders, I hope?"

That conjured up all sorts of images and Stella pinched the bridge of her nose through her mask. "Listen. This isn't like a competition at school. There are real consequences if we fuck this up. So—we finish this, and then we split up and that reduces the chances of either of us getting caught because it'll split their search teams, too. Just need to pick a rendezvous point."

"You're right. I'm sorry." Through the mask, it was hard to read Pepper's face, but her shoulders were tight. Finally, she nodded. "Transit station?"

"Nice try. There are cameras on the platform."

Pepper placed the torch and turned it on. "Watch your eyes." Faint wisps of smoke curled around the edges of the device as she moved it along the wood leaving behind a dark, burnt line. "When I practiced this, it only took one pass to get through the wood and it was quieter than a saw."

"Oh, the fancy copper lady practiced. Color me surprised."

"As if you didn't." Pepper spoke without taking her attention away from the wood. "At the academy, how many extra runs did you make your team do to prep for the obstacle course?"

"Only two. And we won, didn't we?"

"You did." She turned the laser cutter off and tucked it back into her pocket.

Tipping the wood out, she passed it to Stella, who set it on an empty shelf. When she turned back, the dusty steel of the safe was in view, snugged up against the wardrobe.

The laser cutter was a sleek simple tool that Stella would love to be able to afford and couldn't. As Pepper put the laser cutter back on the safe, Stella held out a hand. "Wait. Can I...can I try it?"

Even through the mask, Pepper's grin was evident. "Yes. But I have to turn it back in to the department, so it's just a loan."

"Noted." As she took the cutter, their hands brushed. Even through gloves, the strength and competence of Pepper's hands was apparent. She remembered them as being broad and strong at the academy and callused with hours spent in the gym. "Thank you."

"Here's the suction cup. The metal will be hot when you pull it out."

"Also noted." The laser cutter's tip glowed and as she ran it across the metal, she left a red-hot line behind. "How many passes?"

"Five." Pepper stood behind Stella, so close that she could feel the warmth of her body. "If you get tired, we can switch."

"Five? I can crack a safe faster than that."

"Not from what I saw at the grate."

"Totally different mechanics and you know it." This was easier though. It was just following the same path around and around. There was no skill involved. No elegance to the solution. Who was she kidding? The laser cutter was pretty sexy.

Five times around and the metal line glowed in a red-hot circle on the back of the safe, just a fraction smaller than the hole through the wood and the glass. Stella used the suction cup to pull the thick piece of metal out and pass it to Pepper.

Peering through the hole, she saw ledger books, cash, and the cylinder containing the Crane materials. The books would be too big to get through the hole, but the cash...that would be a welcome bonus. Stella eyed the glowing rim of the opening. "So...did you have a plan on how to get things out without burning yourself?"

"What? Oh." Pepper came to stand at Stella's side. Shoulders touching. "Gosh. I didn't think about that."

"You didn't—" Stella cut off as Pepper raised her hand and gripped the edge of the safe with her matte black gloves. "Hey!"

"Fire gloves. My dad used them at our cabin back on Earth. You can grab a burning log and not feel it." She glanced over her shoulder at Stella as if every sentence wasn't a reminder of the vast differences in their wealth status. "You didn't think I would actually forget something like—"

A fire alarm shrieked into existence.

Stella spun, looking for the sensor so she could try to shut it up. Behind them, the metal disc had rolled against one of the books. It was on fire. So was the book next to it. And the one under it. As she sprinted to grab a trashcan, another book caught. Fire on the station was bad. Very, very bad. "Shit!"

"Damn it." Pepper reached into the safe. She shouted over the piercing alarm. "It's a centralized system. The fire suppression team will be here within ten minutes."

Stella upended the trashcan and slammed the metal over the books. If the fire got too big, it would trigger the airlocks to shut, cutting off all escape routes. "Do you have the Crane materials?"

"I've got it. Go! Go!" She pushed Stella away from the trashcan.

Sparing one longing look back at the safe, Stella left the cash behind and sprinted for the grate. Nine minutes before the fire department arrived.

Less time than that before they had trouble. The two security guards on this level would be immediately responding to the alarm along with all the residents in the remaining luxury apartments.

She grabbed the rope hanging down from above and connected her climbing harness to it. Pepper held the line for her, as if they were really a team. Stella grabbed the rope and climbed onto the edge of the ventilation grate. "See you at the top."

She stepped out of the grate, swinging to the side, and began the climb to the top of the airshaft. Her arms warmed to the task as she hauled herself up and her body got lighter. She could feel the rope shifting against her thighs as Pepper climbed below her. She had to hope that they'd gotten the fire out enough that the airlocks wouldn't seal.

At the top, she'd use her escape rope down the opposite airshaft, which would drop her down to the far side of the station. From there, they could cut across to the transit system and lose themselves in the crowd.

She grabbed the top of the safety rail and hauled herself up and over the side. Panting, she stood to help Pepper finish her climb.

The rope was slack.

She leaned over the edge, looking down into the airshaft. The rope was empty below her. A beam of light cut across the bottom of the airshaft from an open service door.

She stared at the open door, knowing that she'd been played. Pepper had known about having multiple escape routes and she'd taken the offered one. "God dammit. She set the books on fire on purpose. Fuuuuuuuck."

Stella felt significantly less bad about stealing Pepper's laser cutter. She slammed her palms against the safety rail and then shoved away. There was jack shit she could do about it now. Right now, she just needed to get away. She sprinted to the shadowed corner where she'd left the exit rope.

It was gone.

She was going to murder Pepper if she ever saw her again. Flexing her hands, Stella went back to the rope and dropped down to the Martian level. Always have multiple escape routes. She yanked open a grate she'd already unlocked and slipped into a garden module.

As she went through the dim racks of foliage, she pulled off her mask, turning it inside out to the soft purple interior. She slipped that back on as a sleep turban. She slowed at the first door and grabbed the bag, which was miraculously still there, and yanked the bathrobe out of it. Pulling it on, she kicked her shoes off and rolled up the legs of her coveralls to reveal her bare legs. She stuck the geckogrip soles of the shoes to the inside of the bathrobe so that they hung hidden and out of the way.

Stepping into the service stairwell, Stella slid into the stream of people evacuating from the Capardi's level. She should have let the whole level burn.

She yawned at an old lady in a pink bathrobe. "What's going on?"

"Probably a false alarm." The woman glared at the stairs. "Although it's going on a long time."

Stella let herself get swept into the line of people walking the ten floors to the next level. No one was checking IDs. No one was looking for a thief.

Not that she had stolen anything except for a laser cutter, which would not impress her boss. Damn it all to hell. What was she going to tell them?

She milled around in the crowd as they stepped out of the service stairs into a public plaza large enough to see the curvature of the station. Stella worked her way to the edge until she could slip into the shadows of the bioscaping that shrouded the walls between storefronts. Another costume change waited for her, and she dressed in the gap between bamboo and wall, transforming herself into a hoverpunk with a cap to disguise her hair and shoved padding in her cheeks to change the shape of her face.

Stella stepped onto the hoverboard and kicked off across the plaza. She rode the board through a couple of corridors. No one followed her. If she had the Crane materials she'd be sitting pretty right now. She still used every double back and trick to throw off a tail, just in case.

It took an hour for her to get back to her apartment. Inside, her cat hopped off the couch and ran into the narrow hall, meowing as if she'd never been fed.

"Yes, Princess Starlight. Immediately your highness." Stella crouched, forearms still sore from climbing, and scratched her cat under its soft gray chin. This was how she spent her money. The care and feeding of a tiny, perfect, meso-predator imported from Earth.

The cat headbutted her, professing her love by twining around Stella's body.

"Do you love me or are you just hungry?" Groaning, Stella stood, and Princess Starlight led the way to the kitchen.

She flicked the light on and stopped with her hand still on the switch. In the middle of her table, the pale cylinder of the Crane materials gleamed in the yellow light. A note lay next to it in an anonymous boxy script that could have belonged to almost anyone.

"COPY MADE. THANKS FOR THE HELP. IT WAS FUN WHILE IT LASTED."

Stella grinned. Time to find out where Pepper lived and plot a route in.

She had a laser cutter to return.

Astral Lace

Jasmine Gower

Pairing: Human/Dragon

Midge's toes curled, as if she could grip the edge of the asteroid through her suit. Rocky bodies twisted and hurtled down the cosmic river she floated in, threatening to crash into her vessel or block her from jumping to the next path. The smaller, denser comets spun faster than the porous giants she leapfrogged across, and she eyed them carefully through her pressure mask. Her glasses weren't compatible with it, so she'd had to train to compensate for her amblyopia without them, but that's what that very moment was for, wasn't it? To prove she could swim along the astral currents, scuttle safely upon asteroids for purchase, and bound across low gravity to her goal?

Focusing again on her final lily pad—a pear-shaped chunk of space rock, holey as a chunk of Swiss cheese— Midge timed the passing missiles until...there! A clear shot oncoming in two seconds. She bent, then shoved off, launching herself in slow, semi-gravity motion toward her goal. She peddled her legs to keep her trajectory straight, and although her timing had been just enough off that she clipped her heel against the passing mini-asteroid—*Oh, biscuits!* Midge muttered in her head—her path remained steady, and soon her feet landed on the uneven surface of the large one.

Midge hollered into her pressure mask in triumph.

The spacescape around her flickered back into gray training blocks in the gray training room, Reba leaning against the control panel with a wry smile. A proud smile, Midge liked to think.

"Play the sound!" Midge demanded, her words muffled by the mask covering her head. The full gravity clicked back on, dropping her two feet to the springy floor. While she hurried to de-pressurize and remove the mask, a cheerful *ping!* rang out across the room. Midge dropped the mask on the padded floor to free up her arms for flexing. "I did it!"

Reba came over to clap her on the shoulder. "Wasn't sure you would. I cranked up the speed on those little guys last minute."

Midge inhaled a deep breath, realizing just then how sweaty she was. "That's not how physics works."

"No, but dragons can speed up or slow down as much as they like." Reba fished the key fob from her pocket and handed it to Midge. "Still, you did it. Never let it be said I don't keep my word: you're clear for your first solo scavenge."

"Yes!" Midge fished her glasses out of her suit to perch back on her nose.

"I recommend starting with the nest we clocked in Ikaria Minor."

Midge tightened her fist around the key fob, feeling the press of its plastic curve in her palm. "We spotted that a week ago. It'll be picked clean already."

Reba shrugged. "What about the one in Ozeros?"

"Dragon's still there. Taking her sweet time clearing out."

Midge saw that last little asteroid flying by in her mind, felt the burn of her thighs as she jumped before it left her path. "She can't be there much longer, right? If I can time it right—"

"No."

"—I'll get first pickings. A whole cache of astral lace, untouched! We'd be rich."

Reba tapped Midge square on the forehead. "Are you dense? Playing chicken with dragons is how you lose your limbs. And that's the good outcome. You're smart, you'll find nooks in Ikaria Minor that other crews haven't gotten their mitts on yet." Reba scratched at her short bristle of gray hair, trying to mask her concern as annoyance. "Don't make me second-guess this."

"Fine," Midge acquiesced, but the shining glimmer of a dragon's hoard would not leave her mind, and it was all she could see when she went to bed that night, staring out at the stars through the porthole in her cabin.

Engineers in the Heraklion Galaxy made their fortunes working astral lace into computing marvels, enhancing or replacing the gold or platinum mined in the Milky Way. Scavengers typically achieved more humble bounties in obtaining the stuff, scrapping it out of asteroid fields where astral dragons built their nests. The task was dangerous: the asteroids could be fast or big enough to knock an ill-prepared scavenger into the black void, competing crews might come with weapons in tow, and very occasionally a scavenger would be unlucky enough to cross paths with the dragon who'd built the nest. They generally tended to be displeased to see their spiderlike webs being dismantled for human purposes. But the safer the job, the worse it paid, and Midge wanted to retire young. Sell enough lace to buy a house planet-side, maybe even something with a pool. In old movies about life on Mars, sometimes people had swimming pools in their houses. It always seemed luxurious to her.

The key fob paired with the *Bullfrog*, one of the crew's less fuel-efficient but otherwise reliable pod ships. It could pack in two or three scavengers in the cockpit and had a hold about six cubic feet—not much for transporting bulkier finds, but astral lace thankfully spun up tight. The *Bullfrog's* fully loaded trunk could bring in enough cash to buy an entire fleet to replace it, although Midge had never seen it return with more than seven bolts of lace.

She set out the next day aboard the *Bullfrog*, tweaking the nav screen as she floated out from the crew's rickety station. Ikaria Minor. She tapped the nav to mark it on her atlas with a big red dot, hitting auto-pilot to take in that direction, but she glanced back at the opening to the empty hold. The empty bolts clattered in zero gravity against each other, creating a song she'd come to recognize as a prelude to adventure. But it sounded hollow that day, droning and bland. No matter what Reba said, the handful of scraps she might hope to find at Ikaria Minor would only be enough to pay to refuel the *Bullfrog*.

Midge looked again to the red dot on the nav. Reba was such a worrier. Ozeros had *also* been scouted three weeks ago. Dragons usually only took a few weeks building their nests before migrating away. Depending on the asteroid belt, that usually gave scavengers three or four months to snatch up the lace before they returned to lay their eggs. It was rare to hear of scavengers who were caught by returning dragons, so quick they were to loot and pilfer, and rarer still to hear of ones who braved a nest before the dragon was sure to have cleared out. Most dragon run-ins were random encounters, an unlucky intersection of incompatible paths in the infinity of space.

Chewing on her bottom lip, Midge mulled over her options. Or pretended to—in her hesitation, not a single thought passed through her head except: *Pool. With a diving board!* A full minute of "consideration" later, she tapped her nav to adjust the auto-pilot coordinates. The atlas zoomed out and reapplied the dot on a new destination. Ozeros.

It was further from the station than Ikaria Minor. Good. More time for the dragon to pack up her junk and get a move on. Midge whittled away the hours sharpening her utility knife, ensuring the edge was ready to slice through lace quick and clean.

The nav pinged when the *Bullfrog* was in sight of Ozeros. Not the cheerful two-note victory jingle of the training room, but a droning triple *dong*. Midge liked to think it was the sound that real bullfrogs made, but she'd never heard one before. Looking up from her knife and whetstone, the asteroid river Ozeros rushed in the middle distance. The satellite stones here were an assortment of blues and greens, the crushed remains of some long-dead dwarf planet that collided against a moon of Aetolia, the planet which Ozeros orbited around. Veins of quartz-like minerals ran through a number of the stones, causing them to glitter as they went spinning along. It almost looked like a real river. Midge clicked off auto-pilot and took over manual control. Time to find the nest.

Ozeros ran deep, so it wasn't enough to steer around the perimeter of the asteroid field until the *Bullfrog's* sensors pinged. Diving in—following the distant Aetolia as her guiding star where she could spot it through the stream of space rocks—she scooted along in the *Bullfrog*, trying carefully to weave it through the empty space between asteroids but taking a bonk or two along the way. After about a half hour, the sensors started keening—a high-pitched trill that was music to any scavenger's ears. Midge spotted the telltale shimmer almost as soon as the sensor started blaring. Threading a cluster of asteroids together ahead were several strands of astral lace, thin and sticky as spider webs, but iridescent in the light of the unfiltered sun. The cluster of asteroids ahead weren't just travelling at the same speed through orbit—they were glued together by the lace into one big clump.

Not another ship in sight. This was the first time Midge had ever seen a nest untouched. She flicked off the sensor and sped on ahead, parking the *Bullfrog* as close as she could before she would have to make her way across the smaller, faster satellites on foot. The nest grouped together so many asteroids—some nearly large enough to be moons in their own right—that the collective unit generated its own impressive gravitational pull, and smaller rocks trying to whiz by in the river instead got caught spinning speedy circles around it. The lace itself must have had some effect, too, as Midge had never seen a belt this dense on the picked-over nests that she'd scavenged before on group missions.

Exactly what Reba's training was for, though. The first two hops were clean enough, but Midge soon realized the orbit of the smaller asteroids would increasingly pull her away from the *Bullfrog* even if she stayed put. The tether connecting the back of her suit to the *Bullfrog* was her surest way back, but it was a liability with the heavy asteroid traffic, almost certain to get clipped.

No risk, no reward, she thought, *but lost in space, no reward either.* She kept the tether attached and hopped along as quickly as she could. Passing missiles snagged on the tether, but nothing knocked her off-course until she was a leap away from a shimmering thread of lace. One asteroid, as large as her torso and hurtling along like it had places to be, caught on the tether, jerking her back a good three feet on her current "lily pad." Midge was able to hook a heel into a small pock dotting the exterior of her current ride, but it too was moving along in the whirlpool spinning around the nest, and she hurried to get back on pace to make the leap to the opening she aimed for. Her eyes strained, trying to calculate the distance, the left one tight as she tried to force it into focus. About thirty yards?—no, thirty-five. She thought. But there wasn't time to line it up or feel it out. If she hesitated too long, she'd be orbited ninety degrees clockwise around the nest, and her tether would be too taut.

Clenching and releasing her calves, thighs, and glutes with the best force she could figure, she sprang forward toward the nest, hands outstretched to grab on to the shining webbing. But the sight of it rose in her vision as her stomach dropped, even in its weightlessness. Her feet never met purchase, the semi-grav never clicked back on, and she could feel the pull of the nest try to grab her into its orbit. She panicked, reaching for the tether's retract button on her suit with her right hand, but her left hand met sticky resistance. Closing a fist around it, Midge let out a shaky breath in her mask. So, she hadn't cleared the jump itself, but she had a hold of the nest! Taking a second fistful of lace, she pulled herself close enough to prop up the soles of her feet against the threads. The semi-grav recognized it as solid *enough* ground, and she was able to combat the force of the whirlpool effect just beyond the nest.

A short-lived relief, as she heard something metallic crunch behind her. Whipping her head around, she saw the tether go limp behind her, jaggedly severed from the rest still attached to the *Bullfrog*. Exposed wires sparked, popped, and died, and loose shavings of metal joined the nest's orbital belt in a cloud of gray.

Oh, biscuits and beans! She'd given the dragon plenty of time to move along. How could the lazy thing still be there?

Scuttling quickly inside the cluster of rock and webbing, Midge spun circles looking for a place to hide. The lace created layers and layers of structure connecting the asteroids, sturdy but malleable walls to protect their eggs, and Midge might be able to duck into any little pocket or nook with ease, but how easily might the dragon rout her out?

An incredible force sped through the narrow spaces between the woven lace, shredding through a few threads and smacking her square on the back. Midge toppled forward, the stickiness of the web not enough to hold her in place, and she began to fall. Even when her suit's gravity generation clicked off, the pull of the nest's center dragged her inward, a freefall in slow-motion. Grasping at other layers of lace, she couldn't quite get a hold. Twisting in her descent, she unsheathed her knife and stabbed it into the nearest patch of layered webbing, using the friction of the blade slicing through fiber to slow her fall further. Eventually she stopped, dangling in a pocket of empty space against a wall of sticky thread. She glanced up, hoping to get a sense of her surrounding geometry. Where the webbing curved along the crest of the asteroid that it coated, a face with eyes like stars stared back at her.

Midge gasped and clamped her eyes shut. *Shoot!* Rule One: stay away from dragons. Rule Two: if you can't follow Rule One, never look a dragon in the eye, *especially* when it is glamoured. Maybe the glance was short enough to spare her its hypnosis.

Before she could try to climb away from the dragon's human form, something grabbed her by the severed tether and yanked her along. Not daring to open her eyes, she tumbled through the half-gravity, catching on sticky webs and smacking into her captor's side until she was tossed onto a thick bed of lace. Scrambling as best she could, she tried to raise the knife to swing, but a hand—or what felt like one—caught her wrist and snatched it away. Feeling her other wrist begin to submerge in the lace, her eyes snapped open without a thought. A fly caught by the spider, and now the lace was beginning to cocoon around her arm and legs, trapping her in place.

Panic overrode good sense, and she cast her gaze around, although loose fibers of lace stuck to the lenses of her mask. She was in a more cavernous part of the nest—somewhere deeper, where the gravity was darn near as strong as planet-side—a round chamber of thick webbed walls. Above, she saw a shine unlike that of the lace: metal. *Oh.* A scavenger ship was suspended in webs overhead, a ship much more sleek and modern than the *Bullfrog*, but its hull had a massive hole blasted into it that left exposed, frayed wires sticking out like shredded nerves. She hadn't been the first to brave it after all. The scavengers associated with the gutted ship were nowhere to be seen, but two arms' lengths from Midge sat a "woman" with eyes like stars. Hair fell across her shoulders in amber waves, and she wore a sort of dress that shimmered with the same iridescence as the astral lace, but when Midge focused her eyes, she couldn't tell where the garment ended and the stranger's skin began. Glancing at the woman's left arm, the dragon's glamour weakened, and every couple of blinks, Midge could spot hardened orange scales and a much more massive body underneath.

Might as well stare, Midge thought. *At least it's a pretty way to die.*

"Little thief," the dragon said, the glamour exuding a rich, melodic human voice ripe with resentment. "Here to rip up my nest?"

"I didn't think you were still using it," Midge said. The dragon had cast her knife aside just out of Midge's reach. "I, uh...I can leave."

"Well, not in this condition." The dragon offered her a wry smile and gestured toward the mess of lace wrapping itself around her lap and left arm. "Didn't think I was still using my nest? What do you think they're for?"

"Well, you—sorry, I don't know all that much, I didn't go to college—you build them and then just fly off, right?"

The dragon narrowed her eyes until only one "star" shone through each. "Yes. So that my kind who are ready to lay their eggs have a place to do so."

"Oh, uh..." Midge squirmed a bit. The lace was sticky but not tight. "Sorry. I didn't know that." It was even kind of true—at least, she had never really thought about it.

"You didn't know that a living creature would need a place to live?" The dragon's tone was thick with incredulity, but maybe even a flicker of pity, as if she hadn't considered that humans could be quite that dense.

Midge twisted her left wrist until she felt the pull of the lace lessen upon it. "Yeah, stupid of me, I guess. Hey, uh, what's your name?"

The whole glamour shimmered, giving Midge a quick peek at the creature's true form: a thin, serpentine creature with features more expressive than a true reptile; koi-like orange and white scales; draping, thin wings that reflected the light of the distant sun. The human image restabilized quickly over it. "Aeo," she answered, a surprised upturn in her tone.

"I'm Midge. Look, I get it—I just want a nice place to live too." Shifting her hips, she wondered how close she could scoot to the knife without Aeo noticing. "I grew up on a ratty moon colony, crammed into apartments with other poor families. There was nowhere for me to go except a scavenger station once the colony collapsed."

"Was your colony destroyed by dragons?" Aeo wondered.

"No..." Midge shamefully admitted. They'd run out of fuel. Astral lace created more efficient technology that let off-planet environments support human life on less, but it probably wasn't the time to bring that up.

"Then I don't think you get it." Aeo winced, and the glamour glitched again. That time, Midge could see it—a wound on her shoulder, her wing. Whoever had gotten here first, they'd hurt her. Midge assumed she'd hurt them back—badly—but now she couldn't leave the nest at all. Other scavengers would start getting impatient and find her here, and if she attacked them...well, it was bad form to eliminate a source of astral lace, but a bunch of scavengers fighting for their own lives wouldn't be thinking about the supply chain. And the short-term gain of all the lace still untouched in this nest...

"Oh, biscuits... You're in a real situation out here, aren't you?"

Aeo looked at Midge with open surprise, and dang if it didn't make Midge feel like a real boob. *Of course* dragons needed the nests for their own purposes. Everyone knew their eggshells were too fragile for the full gravity of a planet. And without safe places to hatch their young, they were in danger—not immediately, maybe, but they could only live so long like this. Zipping around on a scavenger station, moving place to place to desperately claw together a living but never anything substantial or sure enough to build a life, Midge suddenly felt like she was looking into a mirror—a very pretty one.

No, that's just the glamour getting in your head! But just because Midge was scrappy didn't mean she was heartless. Sure, it was dog eat dog out there, but that didn't have anything to do with Aeo. She just wanted her own version of a house with a pool.

Midge looked up again at the ship overhead with its guts spilling out. No way she could convince Aeo to let her go all the way back to the *Bullfrog*, but... "I bet there are med kits in there," she said, nodding to the other ship. "If you free me, I can try to patch up your wing. Then you can escape before more scavengers show up."

Aeo leaned forward. Midge thought she could smell flowers, like after a fresh rain had dampened down all the pollen, even though it shouldn't have been possible through her mask. She got the notion that it was a scent from Aeo's homeworld, somehow. "Eager to be rid of me?"

"No! No way. I wanna help, really. All this..." She glanced around at the lace encasing them—the giant, delicate ball of webs and asteroid anchors. "Someone else can have it. But it's already on folks' radars, I know, so the only thing for it is to get you to safety. You can always try again with a new one, right?"

"Unless someone else finds it," Aeo agreed grimly. "But I do believe you." She rose, her gown shimmering every color of the rainbow as she took delicate steps toward Midge, close enough to tap her teasingly on the forehead. "You don't seem smart enough to lie."

"Hey!"

"But if I am to trust a thief with my life, even one with a change of heart, I will need a show of trust from you." Again, Midge could smell wildflowers, now also feeling the ghost of waterfall mist upon her skin, although she'd never seen a real waterfall. "Even if I leave, my people's problem doesn't end here. If you are so repentant, little thief, then you will come with me to find a true solution."

Aeo's homeworld *did* seem nice, from what Midge was telepathically gleaning, although any planet was better than the confines of a rickety old scavenger station. Still... "And if I don't want to pack up my whole life to go with you?"

Aeo shrugged and sat back down, within arm's reach, Midge's knife now lost under the draping folds of her skirt.

"Then there is no trust between us, and we both remain in this...situation."

"Can we at least start with patching you up?" Midge asked. No matter what Aeo said, they were both in a boiling pot if they just sat there until more scavengers showed up, and Aeo seemed to realize that she'd be the worse off of the two of them in that case.

"Fine. I suppose you aren't clever enough for tricks." Aeo leaned forward to untangle Midge from the lace, the illusion of her hands still carrying the hardness of her fine scales underneath. A memory-perfume of open-air bonfires filtered into Midge's mind from Aeo's—nostalgia for nights among friends with full bellies on solid earth. These nests were transitory places for dragons, dangerous ones—it had never occurred to Midge how much the dragons might fear being out among the asteroids, especially if all their hard work was just put to waste anyway.

Once Midge was free, she experienced the disorienting ordeal of being lifted into the air by Aeo's dragon body, although the glamour did not waver, and she still appeared as a human woman kneeling on the ground. Aeo carried Midge up to the opening in the sleek destroyed ship, allowing her to scramble inside the wreckage for first aid. Whoever had driven this vessel, they—or whatever was left of them—weren't inside, which Midge thanked her lucky stars for. Pawing around in the dark, it didn't take long to find a simple cabinet with weighty tin box inside. When Midge emerged, Aeo helped her back down to the ground again with her seemingly invisible dragon claws.

"You, uh, may need to change," Midge said, cracking open the white box and fishing out some burn salve. *Hope it works on dragon skin.* "I can't really see what I'm working with, here."

Aeo hesitated, like Midge had asked to see her naked or something. Well, kinda. Still, the glamour shifted, and Midge could see the entirety of Aeo's scaly, koi-patterned body. A red gash ran deep along her shoulder, right where it met the wing. Nothing that wouldn't heal, but it would take more time than Aeo likely had.

"Okay, idea," Midge said, getting straight to work washing the wound with distilled water and massaging in the salve. "This will help with the pain, but you're going need a few days—maybe weeks—before that missing flesh grows back."

Aeo twisted her head back to look at Midge. "Do I have that long?" Her reptilian snoot didn't move, but the voice of the starlight woman echoed in Midge's head.

"Probably not. Scavengers have been waiting for you to clear out for days already; they'll get impatient or figure you slipped out unnoticed soon enough. But I have a ship! I don't know if you'll fit in cargo, but you can cling to the outside, and I can take you home."

"Why didn't *you* wait for me to clear out?" Aeo wondered.

"You yourself said I don't seem smart, didn'cha?" To Midge's surprise, Aeo laughed. Midge finished up her ministrations and held out a handful of pills to Aeo. "You know if human painkillers are safe for you to take?"

Aeo's glamour shifted back to the form of the starlight woman, and she grabbed the pills and swallowed them. She smiled without showing teeth at Midge's surprised grunt. "It's strange, little thief, but I think I quite like you. Does this mean I can count on you to help find a permanent solution for my people's problem? Or, rather, the problem your people have foisted on us?"

"Guilt me, why don'cha," Midge said with a nervous laugh. Aeo smiled—brighter that time, her starry eyes glittering—and leaned forward to kiss Midge on the forehead. Plum blossoms and butterfly bushes and the fragrances of all kinds of other flowers Midge had never encountered before. How long since she had been planetside anywhere? It'd be nice to visit, at least. Reba would understand.

Midge stood and shook out her limbs—not that she was flustered or anything—and held out a hand to Aeo to help her on her "feet." As Aeo rose, the color of her gown shifted from the iridescence of the astral lace all around them to the white-and-orange pattern of her own scales. Hand-in-hand, they walked together out of the depths of the nest to return to Midge's ship. Along the way, Midge asked, "Say, does your planet have bullfrogs?"

Anathema

Siena Buchanan

Pairing: Immortal/Immortal

The man died only minutes ago.

The body was already decomposing.

Sariel san Ibis knelt before the broken corpse. It was twisted, rotting in places while other parts remained whole. Under normal circumstances, Sariel would have said it was impossible for it to be anything less than days old.

Yet here it was, dead in the middle of the atrium, a rotting corpse in stark contrast to the beautiful lights of the nebula above. Bystanders—humans and aliens alike—stood around the edge, whispering among themselves. They were focused on what this death meant, on how it fit into the absurd prophecies and rituals that so often spun up around the God's Nebula. Sariel, on the other hand, was focused on the corpse's soul.

Largely the fact that, even dead, he still had one.

Sariel's hand twitched, wanting to close around the hilt of her sword to properly kill and set the soul free, but she couldn't do that. Not quite yet at least. Not until she was sure of what she was looking at.

Most mortals had souls like tiny flickering candles. Immortal Ibis like Sariel—beings woven from energy itself—had souls more like stars, layered throughout their core and outer edges to protect the sensitive memories and personality within.

The corpse's spirit was both of those things, and neither. It was a fusion of both, an abomination, too big and too small, layers pushed up and through one another, having neither the simplicities of a mortal soul nor the precise and organized nature of an immortal one. Though the body was clearly dead, the soul was still trapped within, unable to properly die and rejoin the Tide.

Another figure knelt down next to the corpse, and Sariel took in a deep breath, smelling the scent of her wife's power, like blooming apple trees.

"No sign of Etharian," Astrid murmured, brushing a strand of her dark hair behind her ear. "He left his calling card, but no actual trail."

"Still impossible to find, even when we are hours away from him." Sariel gestured at the mangled body in front of them.

"We'll find him. We'll find him before he tortures another one," Astrid said, but Sariel could see the worry in her pale pink eyes—one of the few outward signs that she, like Sariel, was an Ibis—someone far more and far less than human. "What are you planning to do with it, love?"

"Put it out of its misery," Sariel responded. "I was just waiting to confirm with you that the soul looked the same as the previous ones."

"Almost identical," Astrid replied. "He hasn't changed his methods. Trying the same thing over and over again, hoping the person survives *this* time."

"Which aligns with my assessment." Sariel slowly drew in a breath and accessed her power, filling the air around her with the electric scent of ozone. It coalesced into a long blade, held before her.

The blade was a sword but also not a sword, a representation of something much deeper. It was Sariel's power, made true. It was a force made of her own energy, of life, and death, and rebirth, and while the sword could cut through physical objects, its true purpose was to cut at someone's very soul.

It was a weapon meant to attack a soul, rather than a physical body. It was a weapon meant to kill Ibis like Sariel. It would also work, however, to release the agonized spirit before them.

As Sariel slid her blade into the corpse, she whispered a soft prayer, not for *her* god—Sariel had always found gods to be idle superstition—but instead to a god that this man had likely followed. The God of the Nebula.

If she had been attacking a true, immortal soul, a wound like this would have been fatal, but not *instant*. The soul of an Ibis had too many safeguards. It could be mortally wounded in a single hit, but it would not crack so easily.

Here, on the other hand, her blade immediately tore the soul apart. The power that made it up shattered, fragmenting into a million pieces that could be carried away on the Tide, that ebb and flow of life that all beings came from, and which Ibis like Sariel served. She pulled her sword out of the now-vacant corpse, letting the power that formed it dissipate back into herself.

Then, Sariel stood, brushing the dust off her knees and reached out to help Astrid to her feet as well.

The pair walked out from the atrium and away from the purple and blue light from the nebula above.

"Where to next?" Sariel asked.

"I searched most of the station and didn't have any luck. There *must* be a reason for him to come here."

"Resources, or trade lanes, or something," Sariel said. "Though I can't fathom why he'd want to come out to an outpost mostly visited by religious zealots."

Astrid's eyes suddenly lit up.

"Religious zealots. Known for keeping extensive records. What if it was for knowledge? What if he thinks there is something here that he wouldn't find elsewhere?"

"Like...in a library?" Sariel asked.

"Exactly," Astrid replied.

* * *

Despite the relatively small population, the God's Nebula Library was large, taking up a good chunk of level four. The librarian at the front desk gave them a sour look as they entered. They were a Quilith, tall, deer-like with a long mane and covered in a fine pattern of scales. Sariel responded by giving them a polite smile and hurried into the library proper before they could complain to her.

"What would we be looking for?" Sariel asked.

"Something old or with some form of power in it. I suppose some of the religious texts might have something in them too, but from my experience they don't actually know that much."

They stayed together, examining the shelves, occasionally pulling down a book to examine in closer detail. Few of them had any bearing on anything Etharian would find useful.

Hours later, Sariel stepped into one of the quiet nooks off the main library, Astrid right behind her. As they had been searching, the station's lights had slowly started dimming to stimulate an artificial night. It made the large windows at the end of the nook even more impressive, revealing the brilliant light of the nebula.

There was a bright star in one of the windows, right above one of the desks from this viewpoint, and as Astrid walked over to one of the nearby shelves, Sariel approached the desk underneath the star she had seen. The nebula was *glorious*. She had been here five times in her long life, and it never failed to surprise her. Brilliant blues that mixed with purples and a pink so dark it almost looked like red. It seemed like every time Sariel looked, there was something new to uncover. Lights in the darkness, the brilliant faint pinpoint that was a star being born.

Seeing it always made her understand why—for thousands of years now—cults and religions had sprung up around the nebula. Sariel knew too much of this universe to really believe, but there was a very small part of her that *wanted* to. Wanted to believe that this nebula was the graveyard of a long-dead god, or that it was the god's birthplace, or that it was the gateway to the afterlife. She was almost jealous of those who *could* have that faith.

Instead, she turned her eyes to a leatherbound tome on the desk and riffled through it. She didn't expect to find anything of note, so she flipped past a page filled with Tidal notation before she paused and went back.

Yes, that was proper notation. As far as she could see, it was one dedicated to casting a partial Zefsgaf ward. Basic, but it still proved something. For some reason, a book written by an Ibis sat in a public library.

Which had sat underneath the bright star of the nebula. There was something there a part of Sariel wanted to explore, but which the rest of her pushed aside.

"Astrid, come look at this."

There was no reply.

"Astrid?" Sariel asked, turning around.

A pale-skinned man stood in the doorway, with a wickedly sharp sword pressed to Astrid's neck.

In an instant, Sariel summoned her own blade in response, the sword coalescing out of her own power.

"Now, now, dear, you don't have to do that. We can be civil here."

"Let her go," Sariel demanded.

"And lose my wonderful bargaining chip? I don't think so," Etharian replied, because this could only be Etharian. Astrid struggled in his grip, trying to make him let her go, but Etharian held her firmly and the blade prevented Astrid from moving much.

"Did you think that was a *request*? Take that sword off her neck right this instant."

Sariel had to work to keep her voice from trembling as she said that. She was almost five and a half thousand years old. She could not afford to be afraid. But that blade was the same type that Sariel had summoned. Even without it cutting Astrid's skin, Sariel could feel the potential for harm.

Etharian seemed to sense her fear. "You see it, don't you? Just how quickly I could kill your wife? One more step toward me and I will do it. How long do you think before the damage would be irreparable? I'd personally give her ten seconds, if not less. I got quite good at killing Ibis quickly in my years evading capture. Darling Sariel, you remember that, don't you?"

Sariel did. The years she and Astrid had spent tracking Etharian down the first time, before he had been locked up in the Sanctuary. The Ibis he had left murdered in his wake or used as fuel for his experiments.

Even with a blade designed to pierce souls, Ibis didn't die easily. But with how close Etharian was to Astrid, and with the ability to deal a fatal blow so quickly—it could be incredibly dangerous.

"What do you want, Etharian?" Sariel snapped.

For the first time in the conversation, Astrid spoke. "Don't do it, Sariel. Whatever it is. It's not worth it."

"Quiet, you," Etharian said, and Astrid gave a whimper as Etharian pressed his sword into her neck, the faintest line of red blood trickling down Astrid's shirt, an echo of the cry of pain that came from Astrid's soul.

"I want so many things. But foremost among them is that I want you to let me go."

"Let you go? And allow you to continue to leave a trail of ruined souls and mangled bodies in your wake?"

"They would have died anyway. If not by my hand, then in ten years, in fifty? What difference does it make to you, Sariel? Mortals just die. What are a few more of them for the purpose of progress?"

"Death is not a price that should be paid for progress."

"You and your inconsistent morals. There will be far, far more lives saved than those lost once I develop a proper system. To be able to ascend mortals to godhood..."

"Even if you succeeded, in that infinitesimally small chance, they would be like us. And we aren't gods, Etharian. Despite your delusions to the contrary."

"We are more gods than the useless things humans worship right now," Etharian said, waving a hand toward the sky outside. "The nebula has no real power, when *we* do. And when *I* could make mortals have that same power."

"You haven't succeeded yet," Sariel replied.

Etharian sighed. "Not yet."

"Regardless," Sariel said, "I'm not letting you go."

Etharian smiled, a horrifying expression. "It's that or let your wife die."

"Sariel, even if you agreed to let him go, he'll still—" Astrid said, ending with a yelp as Etharian pressed his sword in once again, another trickle of red blood sliding down Astrid's neck.

"I told you to be *quiet,* Astrid. Or I may be forced to find something to stuff in that mouth of yours."

"If you do anything to her—" Sariel said, but Etharian cut her off.

"So, what will it be, Sariel? Save your wife or save those you fear I might kill. Your choice."

Sariel's head was spinning, her mind grasping for what to do.

She couldn't let Etharian escape. Not after the length of time it had taken to track him down to begin with. He would go on to kill more people and leave a trail of corruption and grief in his wake. No, that wasn't an option.

Neither was letting Astrid die. Sariel couldn't take that. She couldn't even handle that *possibility.* Losing Astrid would be like losing a part of her very soul. She would break into a million shards if she was the one who caused the death of her wife.

A choice with two impossible options.

But there was, perhaps, a thin path in the middle.

Etharian had said he estimated ten seconds until the damage to Astrid's soul was permanent. What could Sariel do in ten seconds? Could her wife cling on until Sariel was able to help her?

Sariel looked up and met Astrid's eyes. She was terrified. She knew what would happen to her if Sariel said no. Yet those terror-stricken eyes contained something else. A core of strength that Sariel knew so well, that Sariel had seen and understood time and time again. The determination to do what had to be done. To strive for the greater good, regardless of the cost.

Astrid gave the smallest, almost imperceptible, nod. She understood the silent question Sariel was asking her. Astrid understood the risks and rewards and consequences. She trusted Sariel, completely, implicitly, absolutely. They had been through too much for there to be an alternative.

Sariel took a deep breath.

Ten seconds.

She struck.

Her sword flashed before her as she leapt across toward Etharian, who drew the blade across Astrid's throat. A scream erupted from Astrid and from her soul, a pain that made Sariel wish that she was in Astrid's place. She hated being helpless like this, just watching her wife's body fall to the floor.

Nine seconds.

Sariel lunged, trying to pierce Etharian's chest, but he raised his own blade to counter it as his energy flared around him, forming the echo of dark, smokey wings.

Eight seconds.

Etharian struck back out toward Sariel, and she caught the blade into a bind, pushing forward to force Etharian to take a step back. She locked eyes with him, brilliant blue to deep grey, and saw something in there.

Fear.

Sariel had beaten him once before. She could do it again.

Seven seconds.

She struck again, this time attempting a feint to his left that Etharian managed to catch just in time. Sariel was better than him, that was true, but by a razor's edge. She had to act faster. She had to be able to not only win, but do it *now*. This was not the time to be patient and drawn out and deliberate.

Six seconds.

Nearby, Astrid lay, the blood soaking into the white carpet beneath her, her soul fragmented, having been dealt a deadly wound to the only thing that made an Ibis *them* throughout all of their various forms. The scent of apple blossoms, sour and bitter. Astrid was going to die if Sariel didn't end this fight right here and now. Etharian had pulled back, assessing the situation. Every moment she wasted was time given to him.

Five seconds.

Sariel found the solution. A wild solution, one she would have never considered under normal circumstances, but these weren't normal circumstances. So she would take the pain, embrace it, and accept it in the name of the greater good.

But, Stars, it would hurt. And unlike Astrid, she had always shied away from pain.

Four seconds.

Etharian lunged with his sword again, and Sariel moved, not to block the blow, but instead so that when it did slice through her body, it was along her side instead. The sword dug into her form and it sliced at her soul, making her want to scream with pain, the blade attacking her memories, her lifeline, everything that made her *her*.

She had to stay focused, even as the injury threatened to blind her.

Three seconds.

With the sword embedded in her side, doing what damage it could, she struck out, one hand grabbing Etharian's wrist and forcing him to drop his weapon, then a second blow with her sword to his chest. Unlike Sariel, he didn't keep himself under control, but howled with pain, falling to his knees as he clutched at his chest, red blood dripping down. It wasn't a fatal wound, as Sariel hadn't been precise enough to hit the core of his soul, but she had still dealt a painful blow to it, one that would take time to recover.

Two seconds.

Sariel didn't have time to spare.

She forced wards on Etharian, binding his very essence, the weaves snapping into place around him. The wound had stunned him enough that by the time he started to fight back, Sariel had already restricted his power and bound his physical form with bright blue rope she summoned from her magic. It wasn't her best work, but it would serve. She didn't have time for a complex five-fold ward like she would usually use in this sort of situation. But she had practiced this sort of shielding and warding and binding hundreds of times, on both herself and on Astrid, her usual guinea pig. It would not fail her now. Not when so much stood on the line.

One second.

She spun, her power blooming fully around her in a pair of electric blue wings, as she stumbled down to kneel next to Astrid, lying in a pool of crimson blood, her eyes lost in the nebula beyond, a million miles away.

Sariel grabbed her wife, sending her energy flowing through her.

Repair, she demanded. *Heal.*

The wound on her neck healed almost instantly, responding to the flood. But that wound was the least of Astrid's injuries. The ones that were truly dangerous were sliced through her spirit, damaging the pathways that Astrid used to think, to feel, to create and exist.

Healing a soul was dangerous and treacherous work, but Sariel *knew* Astrid—instinctively, intimately. How her soul was put together, and how it would have to be healed.

They still bordered on the edge of life and death. Etharian had not meant for his wounds to be healed. He had meant them to be jagged and sharp and to dig in too deeply to be repaired.

"Come on, Astrid," Sariel whispered, pulling her wife onto her lap and cradling her, rocking back and forth. "Please. I can't lose you. I can't."

The burst of power that had initially flowed through the two of them drained to a trickle. More power wouldn't help. It was up to Astrid if she managed to heal or not.

Sariel clung to any shred of hope, any fragment of faith. Any sign that her wife would be okay. Her eyes flicked to the nebula beyond the bookshelves. That glorious light, the brilliance of it. The divinity so many people saw within it.

The universe was a wild and wonderful place. Perhaps, just perhaps, there could be *something* out there.

Please, she called out to the universe. *I can't lose her.*

Seconds ticked by with Sariel holding her wife, barely breathing, barely living, clinging on to the realm between life and death.

Then, the nebula behind them flashed a brilliant white so bright it was almost blinding.

A supernova. That was all it was, no god, just an exploding star—and yet—in Sariel's arms, Astrid took in a single, gasping breath, her eyes fluttering open.

Sariel could feel Astrid's soul knitting the worst of the damage together. There would still be a scar, as there so often was, but...she would be okay. She would *survive.*

"Etharian?" Astrid murmured.

"He's secure," Sariel replied. "I'm just—I'm just glad that you are okay." She bowed her head, taking in a shaking breath.

"Of course I am," Astrid said. "I knew I would be fine. You would never let me get hurt. Not beyond anything that heals with time, at least."

"I came far too close to doing so. I wish there had been a better option."

"Sometimes there isn't."

As Astrid slowly recovered, Sariel helped her up, the two of them stepping over toward Etharian, still kneeling and bound in accessing his power. Without that, he wouldn't be able to do much of anything.

"Looking forward to returning to your cell in the Sanctuary?" Sariel asked.

Etharian spoke weakly, his voice a hushed whisper that befitted the shelves of books around them, "Last time I lost because I made a crucial error. I underestimated the two of you. But I didn't make any errors this time. I took Astrid off the playing field and I still lost, without making a single mistake."

"You made a mistake, Etharian," Sariel said with a growl, towering over him. "You hurt my wife. Nobody is allowed to hurt her unless *she* says so. And I doubt you are on that list."

Sariel pulled Etharian to his feet and took a step toward the door, Astrid clinging onto her other side. But for a moment, she glanced back at the nebula outside.

Even though she shouldn't, even though all logic and rationality told her otherwise... she felt *something* out there. Watching her.

And for just a moment, Sariel *believed*.

Spaceships

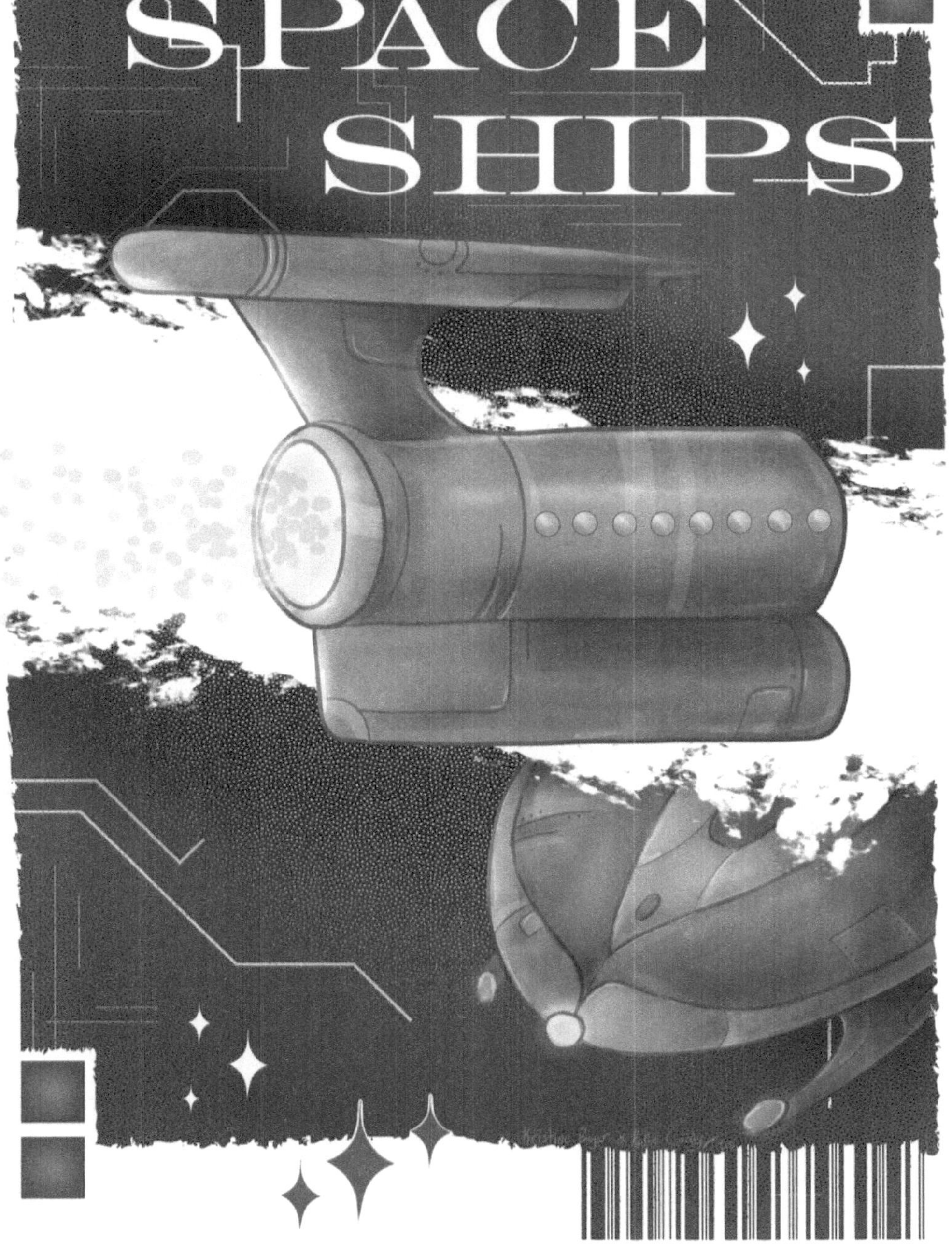

SPACE
SHIPS

Shapes

Seanan McGuire

Pairing: Human/Human

It was only a shape.

That was probably the worst of it: that her destruction had come, not at the hands of a lover-turned-enemy tracking her down in some distant spaceport, not in a dramatic depressurization accident while blowing the pressure locks of an illegal mining operation, but because of a *shape*. She was being unmade by geometry.

It wasn't fair. If she was going to be undone by something simple, it should at least have had the grace to be *interesting* in some way, innovative and unique. Something that would make the historical record, that spacers would question for decades to come. Her death should have been her legacy, and instead, it was nothing more impressive than a shape.

Bethan pressed her hands flat against the desk of her work station, forcing herself to breathe deeply and slowly— in through the mouth, out through the nose—the way she'd been taught before she'd been allowed to leave the Earth behind. She'd slingshot herself into the stars, into the domain of the shape, and she'd done breathing deep and slow, clear-headed as she gamboled toward her doom.

Would her mother laugh when she heard that her runaway daughter had met her end at the hands of geometry, or would some scrap of mammalian sentimentality awaken and remind her that she'd loved Bethan once, before their paths had diverged quite so far apart? Would she shed a tear for the reunion that was never going to come, the forgiveness that was never going to happen? Sadly, Bethan thought not. The cult her parents belonged to was procreative, not adaptive or acquisitional: she'd been dead to them since the moment she told them they wouldn't be getting children out of her.

True procreative cults got rarer every year, rendered impractical by humanity's push to the stars; they insisted that all members produce children, and more, that those children be conceived in the "natural" way: penis in vagina, ejaculation, implantation. No intervention, no surrogates, no IVF or adoption. Had they been just slightly less pious, she might not have orphaned herself the minute she told her parents she wasn't interested in men.

No, there wouldn't be any grieving there. But there would be grief here, out among the stars. There would be grief enough to fill the ship and overflow its vents, grief flowing out like starlight into the cosmic winds. Minthe would grieve until it became a shape in its own right, until she carried it in her veins the way Bethan carried the first shape in her own.

Again, she forced her breathing to level and slow, keeping herself controlled. Her body might be betraying her on a cellular level, but the macro systems were still hers to manipulate. If she could keep her blood pressure low, she could slow the rate of crystallization, could buy herself months or even years to spend with her wife, still herself, not just a vessel for a *shape*.

She looked at her hands, turning them carefully back and forth until she was satisfied that there were no breaks in the skin. Shapes didn't need a lot of space to replicate themselves, but this shape wasn't even a new discovery. She knew the rules. Skin contact was okay, as long as she wasn't bleeding or leaking serous fluid. Contact between mucus membranes was not okay. No more kissing, no more languid nights wrapped up in the sheets and each other. No crying on Minthe. No fluids. That was what it really came down to. Tears were like oceans for the shape, and she refused to help it spread.

Moving carefully, she rose, shrugged her work jacket back on, and keyed in the code to open the door. It hissed as it unlocked itself, rebalancing the pressure between her lab and the hall. Nothing could flow out while the door was pressurized, and that was all that really mattered in the moment.

There was a box of gloves by the door. She'd need them soon enough, but for right now, her geometry was still sufficiently her own that she could touch Minthe without a barrier between them, feel her skin and understand, on a primal level, why she was willing to fight this. Touching Minthe would help her to remember why she mattered.

A fucking shape. It was just a fucking shape.

* * *

The ship was quiet. Anyone else might have assumed that it was deserted, with half the systems running on power-saver mode and the other half turned off entirely. Bethan walked through the cool, dark halls, following the hum of the life support system, which always focused its efforts on the areas that were currently in use. There was no hiding on this ship, not if you were willing to take the time to stop and listen.

At the end of the hall, a door. Unlike her lab, this one was biometric, not numerically keyed—a mixture of security systems made it harder for raiders to hack the ship from a distance, and while no one really wanted to think about that sort of thing happening to them, anything that could slow the attackers down if it did happen was a good thing. Bethan hesitated before pressing her palm to the reader.

It's early yet, she thought desperately, waiting for the system to approve her for entry. *The crystallization won't have advanced to my dermis.*

With a soft beep, the door unlocked and slid open, inviting her deeper in. Bethan exhaled and stepped through, more relieved than she wanted to admit, even to herself.

This was Minthe's territory, sleek and modern and spotlessly clean. Bethan had always been more willing to tolerate rust and disorder in her parts of the ship; she was the surveyor and Minthe the pilot, but the success of their partnership came half from their mutual willingness to ignore the stereotypes about their professions. She stepped lightly as she walked toward the control room, unwilling to risk causing more disruption than she already had.

At the final doorway before the pilot's seat, she paused, leaning up against the smooth, cool metal, and looked at the back of Minthe's head. Her hair, cropped short for safety, was spiked up and held in place with glitter-rich gel, sparkling gold and silver and titanium rainbow in the overhead light. The back of her scalp was shaved close, revealing the three ports she used to connect with and control the ship. Two of them were open, the skin around them red and faintly irritated, while the third was occupied by a slim black cable leading down to the console.

"Hey, Min," said Bethan. "You about done with the diagnostics?"

"Bethan!" Minthe spun her chair around, leaning forward as far as the cable would allow. "You said you wouldn't sneak up on me like that anymore! Did you get your test results?"

"Sorry," said Bethan. She moved to sit in the open chair next to the console. It wasn't hooked up to anything, being there only for the aesthetics of balance and to give Bethan somewhere to be when Minthe was working and she wasn't. Her lab had similar courtesies, little gestures made to make it easier for them to move across the sector as a couple, and not just two people who happened to share a ship.

"Yeah, but you're still going to do it again." Minthe clasped her hands together, letting them rest between her knees. "You didn't answer my question. That's an answer in its own way, you know."

If it was an answer, then she didn't need to say it. She could leave the words unspoken, and thus the tiniest bit less real. But Bethan knew better. Even if Minthe said that silence was an answer, she wouldn't leave it alone, wouldn't believe her own logical conclusions until she had heard them confirmed. Bethan slumped in her seat, fixing her eyes on the simulated viewscreen rather than looking at her wife. She'd lose her nerve if she had to face Minthe directly.

"It's Hausdorff Syndrome," she said to the room in general. If Minthe in specific happened to be listening, well, that couldn't be helped, now, could it? They weren't in her lab. There would be no legal proof that Minthe knew. "That survey cave on Callisto must have been contaminated."

She'd cut herself on the wall as she was turning to leave. An amateur mistake, the sort of thing someone with her experience and training was supposed to be well beyond; the sort of thing that could, would, and did happen to absolutely everyone. Her own teachers had come back from their digs with new scars on their palms and the backs of their hands, pale bands of skin that wrote the chronicles of their fallibility across their bodies where they couldn't be denied.

Most amateur mistakes weren't fatal, but some were. Bethan was just unlucky, that was all.

"Hausdorff doesn't occur naturally on any of the Galilean moons," said Minthe, her own voice distant and numb, like she was inwardly retreating toward a more forgiving version of the world. "If that's where you picked it up, it must have been intentional contamination. That makes it murder."

"Only if we could prove the chain of transmission, and the intent behind the contamination," said Bethan. "That would mean months in discovery, and then even more time in court. Long, stressful months. My blood pressure would spike on day one and never come back down again. Not a fun way to spend the time I have remaining, if you ask me."

"Is that what you think you have? Months?"

"The infection isn't very advanced yet," said Bethan carefully. "If I watch my blood pressure and avoid stimulants, I could have a couple of years before the crystallization reaches my vital organs. I could stay with you."

"Together?"

"Not the way we have been," said Bethan. "I'll need to get some blood samples, but I'm pretty sure you're not infected. You're not showing even very early signs of crystal formation in your blood. That means we have to be careful.

No fluid exchange; minimal contact without boundaries in place. I don't need gloves to touch you—yet—but I will, eventually. And we'll need to start running regular decon on anything I've come into contact with."

"Oh, is that all?" asked Minthe, and her voice was hollow.

"Min, I'm sorry, I didn't mean to—"

"I know. It would be so much easier if you had. If you'd gone out and gotten yourself infected on purpose, I could write you off as cruel and manipulative and everything else I know you're not. I could let you go, if you were someone else entirely. But you're not cruel or manipulative or...or any of those things. You're my Bethan. You're my wife. And it's not your fault a bunch of conservationists have decided that a bunch of legal survey sites should be sealed off in order to incubate the second coming of sentience." Minthe's voice cracked on the last word, and she swiped at her eyes with the side of her hand. "I'm sorry. I'm sorry. You're the one who's got—who's got to live with this terrible thing, and I'm just collateral damage. It's not fair for me to make this about myself..."

"But this is about you, Minthe," said Bethan. "It's a change for the both of us. Our lives are never going to be the same. Mine, for one, is going to be a lot shorter." Her face twisted as her grasp on the artificial calm she'd been projecting finally broke. "And it's all because of a stupid *shape*. How can a *shape* do all this damage?"

Minthe sat up straighter, vibrating with alarm. "What do you mean, a shape? What do shapes have to do with anything?"

"Diseases—viruses—aren't alive in the same sense that you and I are alive, or even in the sense that bacteria are alive," said Bethan, voice dull with defeat. Her calm was gone, but she was beaten all the same. "They're just shapes. Self-replicating shapes that can get into your body and start hijacking basic systems. In a way, they're the simplest machines in the universe. Just shapes."

"You're the smartest person I've ever known, Bethan," said Minthe firmly. "If there's a way to counter Hausdorff Syndrome, you'll find it. No shape is going to beat you."

Bethan only wished that she could be so sure.

* * *

Hausdorff Syndrome was discovered shortly after the discovery of chain crystallization made personal space travel possible. Although the corporations who controlled the drives had pumped trillions into PR campaigns to obscure the clear and obvious connections between the two events—scientists discovered a way to fuel light drives with constantly re-crystalizing minerals! And coincidentally, a disease that crystalizes living tissues, leading to slow paralysis, organ failure, and eventually death is discovered in systems where humans have traveled via our innovating new drive!—people were, for once, borderline immune to propaganda.

What they weren't immune to was the endless allure of space flight. Even the people who knew, without question, that Hausdorff Syndrome was waiting for them out among the stars found themselves strapping into personal shuttles and taking flight. After all, Hausdorff was only a risk if you made a habit of leaving your ship for open, possibly contaminated planets and their satellites. The drive corps might not be able to erase the connection between their advances and Hausdorff, but they could muddy the waters, could imply that surveyors were responsible for the syndrome's slow, inexorable spread throughout the universe. Environmental groups sprang up, more to oppose the surveyors than to preserve the worlds they haunted, and independent surveyors like Bethan found themselves facing higher and higher rates of infection.

Hausdorff Syndrome began with a shape, a single misfolded molecule that could enter the body through the same mechanism as a natural virus. Once inside, it would begin to replicate, converting nearby tissue into crystalline formations that would remain flexible for a time before they hardened and began to splinter under pressure. It was a slow process. Many swore that a cure would be found before it could go from plague to pandemic. Many others swore that it was the gods' punishment on humanity for reaching too far into the cosmos: that a price needed to be paid.

Bethan's parents had been among the latter. They would have been sympathetic but unsurprised to learn that their unwanted heretic daughter had been chosen to pay off a portion of humanity's debt. They might even have claimed her again, solely so they could enjoy the status that grieving her would grant. The loss of a child, even a heretic one, was one of the greatest blows a member of their cult could receive. She was glad, in an abstract sort of way, not to grant them that honor.

Days blurred into weeks, weeks into months. Bethan spent more and more time in her lab, refusing survey assignments, while Minthe put more and more effort into finding passengers and short-hop supply runs. As long as Bethan wasn't working in the field, she didn't have to register her infection. As long as her infection wasn't registered, Minthe didn't have to disclose it to her passengers. It made Bethan uneasy to know that she was hiding her condition from the people they transported, but she really didn't have a choice. She wasn't infectious as long as she was careful, and if their passengers went away, so would the funds she needed for decontamination and lab supplies. If she was going to find a treatment for this, she needed to be funded, and funding required a certain degree of deceit.

After the first month, she started wearing gloves whenever she was around Minthe. Two days after that, without commentary, she moved to sleeping full time in her lab. It was the only way to keep Minthe safe. Minthe was all that mattered. Bethan was already lost, and she wasn't going to sacrifice the most important woman in the solar system to a *shape.*

It was six months almost to the day since she'd confirmed her infection when Minthe agreed to take on a group of tourists who just wanted to make the Mars-Tethys run. They had a booking at one of the larger ski resorts Tethys had to offer and were looking forward to a week of frozen fun, gamboling through ice that had formed long before humanity developed spaceflight, much less interplanetary tourism. Those runs were never innovative, never appealing to either Minthe or Bethan, but they were the bread and butter of a working shuttle, and this one was set to be lucrative enough to buy them another six months of research.

Sedatives and meditation had kept Bethan's rate of crystallization low—lower, according to her research, than most people with better labs had managed. They tended to be driven by academic funding, pressured by deadlines that would spike their blood pressure and force them to contemplate the reality of their situations on a far more immediate basis. They *wanted*. They wanted to save humanity; they wanted to make their mark on history. All Bethan wanted was to find a way to stay with Minthe, to be the wife her love deserved. Another six months could make the difference.

That was why she met the news of their impending passengers without complaint, only asking that Minthe pick up another batch of the synthetic cannabinoids she'd been using to maintain her state of continual, self-sustaining calm. Minthe paused in the doorway to her lab. "They'll be here tomorrow," she said. "We won't have any privacy for the better part of a week."

"That's fine," Bethan replied. "I'll get everything cleaned up before they arrive."

It wasn't necessary and they both knew it: Bethan was religious about decontaminating her contacts whenever she left the lab. Which was less and less often, these days.

"I know you're just trying to find a way to stay with me, but..." Minthe stopped mid-sentence and just looked at her wife, letting the silence stretch between them like an accusation, like something slow and primal and deadly if disturbed.

"But what?" asked Bethan, her words polite but dull, the question asked by rote.

"But is it worth it to stay with me if I lose you in the process?"

Bethan sighed heavily. "I'm doing my best, Min. It would really help if you didn't focus so much on how it's not enough."

"That's not what I was—you know what? Never mind." Minthe turned, stalking toward the door, pausing only to look back over her shoulder and say, "I'm bringing them on at morning bell. You'll have your drugs before then."

"Thank you," said Bethan, and stayed where she was as Minthe left the lab, counting down the seconds.

When she reached twenty-five, she put her hands over her face. Her tears were sharp, abrasive, like grains of sand.

But this was all according to plan. If she found an answer, she would have time to make things up to Minthe, to apologize for the way she'd pulled away over the past months. If she didn't find an answer, Minthe wouldn't mourn her as long, not if she'd been able to do some of her mourning while Bethan was still alive.

It wasn't fair. But then, nothing about this was fair. How was it fair that corporate propaganda had convinced the people who should be trying to protect vulnerable ecosystems that their time was better spent laying traps for surveyors who were just trying to chart mineral deposits before those same corporations could come along and drain them dry. "Protect the cradle of life," said the expertly planted corporate messaging. "Keep our untouched worlds intact for the future."

And so they went to those untouched places with vials of crushed Hausdorff crystals, painting them onto the surfaces surveyors were the most likely to come into contact with, making thorough inspection a death sentence...unless no surveys were performed, and the people coming to exploit the local resources could just go straight to automated, safely sterilized mining. Bethan didn't really blame the surveyors. They weren't immune to elegantly sculpted propaganda, and neither was anyone else.

Sighing, she brushed her silicate tears away and rose. She needed to check her supplies before Minthe went on her shopping run. She needed to finalize her list and be prepared for spending the next week in lockdown.

Anything else wouldn't be safe.

* * *

There was something off about Minthe's tourists. They were at once too young and too old for the role they were playing, early twenties instead of thirties or late teens. The ski resort they were heading for catered more to the mature traveler, the person who'd already seen the easier wonders of the solar system and were now casting their nets a little wider abroad. And it was usually the teens who came on board all wide-eyed, exaggerated wonder, trying not to touch everything, comment on everything as if they were the first people ever to encounter it.

This group was like a combination of everything Bethan found most exhausting about Minthe's occasional passengers, as enthusiastic and over-effusive as the teens, as jaded and ready to be disappointed as the adults. She'd be glad when she could make her polite excuses and retreat back to her lab, that was for sure. For the moment, she stood at sharp attention, back against the bulkhead, hands folded behind herself. She could hold that position for hours if she needed to. Some childhood habits were still useful, in their own ways.

The four eccentric tourists crowded into the loading bay, looking at everything around them with wide, baffled eyes.

It was like they expected to see something they weren't finding.

Minthe stepped into position at the front of the room, clearing her throat. All four turned to face her.

"I'm your host, Minthe Richards, captain of the *Demeter's Dream*. To the left is my ravishingly lovely wife, Bethan Richards, who will be serving as first officer for the duration of our voyage. She's in the middle of a very important research project. You may not see much of her, but in the event that she asks you to do something, please obey without question. It might just save your life."

They murmured among themselves, struck—as every group before them had been—by the sudden reality that they could die, that space travel, while tamed, was still far from domesticated; it could turn dangerous in an instant, and none of their money or position would save them.

She continued onward from there, explaining the same protocols that had accompanied every trip she'd helmed since she'd taken ownership of her vessel, running down checklists and details about the journey ahead of them. Bethan tuned her out, watching the tourists instead, the way they fidgeted, the way they didn't react in the usual places. Something was going on with them, something strange if not essentially sinister. Their body language and social signals were all wrong, like they were dressed as characters in a play, rather than real people.

Minthe finished her speech, smiling with a sincerity that Bethan rarely saw these days. "Welcome aboard," she said, and that was it; strange or not, these were their passengers, and their trip was underway.

* * *

The first two days passed without incident. The tourists wandered the ship, took pictures, and gossiped among themselves. Bethan stayed locked in her lab, avoiding unnecessary contact, while Minthe jacked into the ship's systems and kept them smoothly on course. The strangeness didn't pass, but it seemed less important in the face of the void around them.

When Bethan left her lab, she kept up the veneer of a loving wife who wasn't fighting for her life against a self-replicating shape. She smiled at Minthe, laughed at her jokes, even followed her to their once-shared bedroom when there were eyes on them. So it was perhaps understandable when, on the third night of their trip, she was awakened by the sound of someone trying to spoof her lock.

She lay motionless on her narrow cot, well-shielded by the equipment around her, the slope of wall and shelf. If she didn't move, they might not realize she was there. But why would anyone be trying to break into her lab? She grabbed for the question, head cloudy with sleep and sedation, and found no easy answers.

The door slid open. The tourists crept inside, holding personal lights rather than reaching for the switches.

"You're sure this is the surveyor?" asked one of them.

"Positive," said another. "We got a blood sample from where she cut herself. It's been six months. There's no way she's not infected."

"She doesn't *look* infected..." said a third, sounding dubious.

"So she's slowed it down somehow, which means she's concealing infection while serving on a passenger ship. That's a public health violation. That shuts this whole tacky ship down."

Rage swept through her, clearing out the sedatives as her heart accelerated, no doubt speeding the infection faster. They wanted to hurt Minthe? They weren't content with killing Bethan, they had to harm her wife? She scowled, staring into the dark above her.

"I've been taking surface samples since we got onboard. There's been no sign of crystallization."

Bethan nodded to herself, pleased. The decontamination had been thorough enough to keep Minthe out of danger. It was nice to have outside confirmation, even if it came from people who were trying to sabotage the ship. She sat up with aching, agonizing slowness, turning her face upward to avoid the glare of their lights. They were still clustered by the door to the lab, creeping into the room even more slowly than Bethan was sitting up.

"We have to stop these surveyors before they prevent the next emergence of life in the solar system. We have to stand up for what's right."

Standing up sounded like a good idea. Bethan did exactly that, counting on the shadows to hide her.

"But the infection should have taken root by now."

"Then we'll just infect her again."

That was what she'd needed to hear. "Lights," said Bethan.

The lab lights came on, and there were Minthe's tourists, blinking in the sudden brilliance.

"All working surveyors are required to maintain their labs under full biosecurity conditions," she said, calmly. "This means recording whenever the lab is occupied. I've been sleeping in here for weeks, and you've just confessed on the record to the willful infection of legal surveyors, and more, to the intention to sabotage my wife's ship and risk my life in the process. The recording has already been transmitted to the authorities on Tethys. My wife has not been formally informed of my infection."

Only informally, in spaces where no one was recording, places where they could still be themselves. Bethan would have locked herself in her lab full time weeks ago if not for the need to avoid saying something on the record.

One of the tourists started to cry. Bethan hit a button on the nearest panel, triggering the ship's alarms.

They might not be running passengers for a while, but that would just give her more time to focus on her own changing internal geometry. More time to work. The trial and the publicity it generated would fund her research, and she would beat this. She *would*.

It was just a shape.

She and Minthe, though...they were the world.

Ten Generations

Beáta Fülöp

Pairing: Human/Human

1

Sally held the woman's hand as she gave birth. Claudie, her name was. Claudie Weber. She had been lucky. Had she gone into labor as little as two days later, she would have missed the deadline.

Claudie, like many other women, had been chosen to populate Earth 5, one of the many far-away planets the human race was attempting a desperate exodus to. Well. Not Claudie herself. She was to remain behind on this Earth, like almost everyone else. No, the one traveling the stars would be her newborn child, safely cryofrozen in one of the three thousand little pods, only to be unfrozen on that far-away planet, eight generations into the future.

It was a big, glorious project, and Sally was proud to play at least a little role in it, be it just by assisting the chosen mothers through the final stages of their pregnancy. She'd even gotten to meet some of the older children, though she made no illusion that they would remember her. None were a day older than two years.

The baby was born on a dying planet, in the middle of yet another storm, rain pouring down and lightning dancing over the sky. Claudie screamed, both with pain and with fear. It was Sally's job to find a distraction. Her wife had a passion for mythology, and so the stories came easily. She told Claudie about Zeus, about Jupiter and about Thor, while the lightning flashed, and Claudie screamed.

Then it was over, and the next bolts of lightning illuminated the face of a pretty, healthy baby boy.

"I will need to take him soon," said Sally gently. "Run some health exams, then my colleagues will bring him to the ship."

Claudie hugged her baby, tears in her eyes. This would not be easy on her. She had prepared for this, but all the reason in the world was powerless against the hormonal cocktail running through her brain, urging her to bond with her child. Sally sat down next to her on the bed.

"He's beautiful," she said softly. "What will be his name?"

"Paul," replied Claudie without thinking. "Like his father, and his grandfather before him."

2

The last of the original ones, thought Fatima, as she watched as Old Hanna's body was pushed into the machine. Resources were scarce in space, and everything had to be recycled. The dead included.

Hanna's death had been a milestone on the generational ship headed towards Earth 5. With her, no member of the original crew remained. With her, the last person who had known Earth was gone.

To Fatima, the old woman had been so much more. She had been her teacher, and her mentor. Everything that she knew about cable maintenance, she had learned from Hanna. When she had started to discover her attraction to women, Hanna had been the one she'd confided in, and Hanna had been the one to help her get the official classification of NP—Non-Procreator, people who would live their lives without getting married and without having children. A big deal, on a generational ship, though Hanna had assured her that on Earth, it had been completely normal.

The recycling machine hummed as it broke down Old Hanna's body, and started the process of using the particles to create some much-needed spare parts. Fatima hoped that when it was her turn, it would be cables.

3

"But why do we need to learn this?" whined Ben, and Emma found that she couldn't answer.

She was standing in front of a class of twenty children, teaching them a poem. It was a classic, one that she too had had to memorize when she'd been their age. It was about a fox, and a crow, and the crow's cheese, and the fox trying to get the cheese by tricking the crow to drop it from the tree he was in.

None of the people in the room had ever seen a fox, or a crow, or a tree. Nor would they ever.

On good days, Emma loved the old Earth poetry, and she had chased not one pretty girl away by getting carried away with how amazing it was to have these stories from a planet now lifetimes away. Aunt Fatima had always told her the next girl would stay, but she never did. On bad days, she wondered if the children in her class were not right, if it wasn't time to start teaching different poems. They had their own, now, about engines and cables and babies sleeping in silent pods, dreaming of a new home.

"It's got a lesson," she explained, the answer long since scripted and memorized. "Be careful of vanity. It will make you make stupid mistakes."

Some of the new poems taught the same lesson, often better and more easily comprehensible. But Ben didn't need to know that.

4

Tania expertly twirled her chair around in dance, not letting go of Rita's hand for even a second. The ship had— for some inexplicable reason—not been built with physical handicaps in mind. But people got disabled, even in space, and the living area on deck 3 had long since been converted to accommodate wheelchairs. Deck 3 was where most of the life took place on board, so Tania didn't mind being stuck there. It had become her job, completely naturally, to organize recreation, starting with the activities she'd come up with for her classmates back in school. Her old teacher, Madame Emma, had always said that she was a natural at it.

She was the most outgoing party girl on board, but even she felt like she'd been transported into a magical world of opulence.

The celebrations held to commemorate one hundred Earth years since the launch dwarfed any other celebration that Tania had ever been to, and she'd been to them all. Hell, she'd even helped to organize most of them. The entire ship was there. They were playing old Earth party music, eating traditional Earth dishes, and watching old Earth movies from their database. And it was a long celebration, the festivities lasting all month.

Tania had been emboldened, carried away by the vibrant atmosphere, and finally asked out her long-term crush. To her surprise, Rita had said yes, and now here they were, together, on the dance floor, the loud music like fire in their veins.

Rita laughed again, and it was the most beautiful sound that Tania had ever heard.

Before the night was over, she would have her first kiss.

5

"You need to sleep, Jackie," complained Jackie's lab mate Diane.

"It's a waste of time," Jackie growled back at her. "I'll sleep when this is finished."

"That could take months," protested Diane.

"We don't have the time", barked Jackie.

She was not wrong. Even in a micromanaged climate like a generational spaceship, illnesses evolved. Often artificial ones, planted by the crew themselves to make sure that their immune systems wouldn't unlearn how to fight back. This time, it was a natural mutation no-one had anticipated. Their work, at the moment, was to make medicine to combat the new, and very aggressive, illness that swept through the ship like a wind. People were dying. There wasn't much time left.

The illness seemed to be spreading primarily over children. Jackie and Diane, both proud NPs, had managed to escape it when the rest of their team didn't. Even their overprotective NP aunts, Tania and Rita, who didn't have children of their own but kept organizing events for them, hadn't escaped it. Since the outbreak, Jackie and Diane had been locked into the lab, trying to find the cure. They were both hopelessly overworked and underslept. Diane, at least, was narcoleptic, so her body forced her to take regular breaks by literally falling asleep. Jackie, meanwhile, with her perfectionism issues and her capacity to pull all-nighters, was doing her best to avoid sleep altogether.

"The more tired you are, the more mistakes you will make," Diane reminded her. Her life was dictated by sleep, and she took it seriously.

When Jackie didn't even deign to give her an answer, she threw her hands in the air.

"Whatever. See you in an hour."

With that, Diane turned and let herself fall onto the makeshift bed in the corner of the laboratory. She was out in less than a minute.

Jackie turned back to the screen, but she could barely concentrate. Less than an hour later, the screen started to blur in front of her eyes.

Jackie sighed. Maybe she could allow herself a short rest. Diane would be awake soon to carry on. She left the screen and joined her friend on the narrow bed.

6

Marie smiled as she watched her granddaughter play.

Having a child had been one of the best decisions of her entire life. And yet, it almost hadn't happened. Like most NPs, Marie had spent the first two decades of her life insisting that she didn't want any children. But the ship's population had been decimated by a pandemic when she'd been almost too small to remember. They all would have been dead if not for the heroics of the scientists Jackie and Diane, memorialized in the hydroponics bay. The captain had had no other choice but to beg the NPs to reconsider. The longer the idea had turned round and round in her head, the more Marie had liked it, and before she'd fully realized what was going on, she had already written her name on the list.

What had followed was a lifetime of happiness.

Raising a child brought more challenges than Marie could have expected in her wildest dreams, but more joy, too. And having a grandchild was somehow even better. At her age, Marie had become an elder in the little commune formed by NP women (and some men) raising children without being in a couple, that functioned half like a loose polycule and half as a mutual support group. She was respected, she was loved, and she could spend her entire day playing with children.

Gaby had left her toys in favor of climbing on Marie's knee.

"Bomi," she begged. "Bomi, sing me a song!"

Marie kissed her granddaughter's hair, hugged her tight, and sang her the old Earth song her grandmother had taught her when she'd been Gaby's age.

"So bright / Jewel in the night..."

7

"'The Prince arrived at the Sun Gate,'" read Gaby aloud. "'It was open.'"

"Gaby?"

Gaby looked up. Before her stood Liz, three years older than her and the most beautiful woman in the world.

"Why aren't you at the celebrations?"

Gaby shrugged. Why indeed. Why was she sitting on the floor in the middle of one of the many corridors between the cryo tanks, reading fairy tales to toddlers who couldn't hear her, if she could be up there celebrating the voyage's two-hundredth anniversary instead?

Because she was her, and she hated crowds, and she hated noise, and she loved fairy tales, and she believed, deep down, that the one-year-olds could sense her presence through the cryo.

Instead, she replied, "Autism."

"Ah." Liz sat on her heels next to her and peered over her shoulder. "What are you reading?"

"An old Earth fairy tale. A prince is looking for the most beautiful woman in the world, so he flies on a magic horse into the sky and visits the Moon and the Sun to ask for directions."

"What's a horse?"

"An old Earth animal. Big, four legs, people used to ride on their backs to get to places faster. We learned about them in school."

"Ah," said Liz again. They had learned about many animals in school, and most people only remembered one or two. "You and your fairy tales. Don't you think they're boring?"

Gaby shook her head.

"I think they're beautiful."

"Well, I think they're boring." Liz stood back up. "Anyway, I'm back to the party. See you at work, I suppose."

Gaby waited until Liz was at a safe distance, then sighed, and looked back at her story.

At least the frozen children never judged her.

"'He entered a big hall that was entirely made of gold,'" she continued. "'In there stood a golden bathtub full of water. The prince washed himself...'"

8

Patricia clutched her weapon tightly as she peered around the corner. The air was clear.

No serious weapons were allowed on board, as any damage to the ship would risk swiftly killing everyone, regardless of political opinion. Even the rebels saw the logic behind this rule, and so the civil war was fought by hitting each other over the head with hard plastic.

This didn't help to reduce the existential danger at all.

Their current system of regime—a succession of captains chosen by their predecessors—had been in place for seven generations, ever since they'd left the Earth. Looking back, it was a small miracle that no major political incidents had happened before, but then again, a ship hurtling through the voids of space, carrying on board what might be the last remains of humanity, probably did offer the right conditions to rally behind a leader.

Until now.

Until their Captain, Liz, outgoing and popular with everyone, unexpectedly died in xier sleep, without having appointed a successor.

Until two officers, both equally likely to have been nominated, both refused to step down.

The rest happened quickly, with no way of stopping it.

Patricia glanced back over her shoulder at her two partners. They stood ready, holding their plastic tubes loosely in their hands. All three women were security officers, and determined to keep doing their job, no matter what happened.

They would guard the entrance to the decks with the cryofrozen babies until their last breath.

9

Captain Felicia stood in front of the big screen, watching the projection of Earth 5 draw closer. That very morning, it had been barely a speck in the sky, but now, she could already make out its color. Blue. It was shockingly blue.

"Captain?"

Felicia didn't turn around, but she did smile.

"At ease, officer. It's just us."

Her wife joined her in front of the screen.

"What do you think?" asked Felicia.

"The crew is ready," said Tamara. "And so are we. But you need to rest, if you want entering into orbit to go smoothly tomorrow."

"It's not the orbit that I'm worried about," said Felicia. "It's the landing. I know that we still have a few days, but..."

"The most dangerous part of any journey," nodded Tamara. "The take-off, and the landing."

"And surviving on the planet, once we do."

Their ship had survived so much, just to get this far. The dying Earth. Faulty cables, plague, a rebellion that was still within living memory. They couldn't fail the mission now.

Felicia and Tamara stood side by side, silently watching their new home draw closer.

10

The day Berta's dream came true was a beautiful, sunny day on the still young planet of Earth 5.

Berta had always wanted a child. Not just any child either, she was dreaming of adopting one of the cryofrozen babies her ancestors had so carefully brought through the stars to Earth 5. She was not the only one, of course. Raising one of the Earth children was a rare privilege, and almost all children dreamed of it. Old Captain Felicia had mandated who could adopt one, and the rules were strict. After all, those children, and the fresh genetic material they carried, were the colony's biggest treasure.

She and her wife, Wendy, had signed up to be adoptive parents the day they got married, with no great hopes. Lists were long, and they didn't have much to offer to a child. They couldn't even maintain their own home and had to move back in with Wendy's sister and her husband.

But then Martine had become pregnant, and instead of just allowing them to share in her happiness, she had used her status to help them, promising to nurse the Earth baby along with her own. Her child would have an adopted sibling, and two sets of parents to raise them both. Put together, the four of them had more than enough money to offer both children a comfortable, happy life. It was even better than what Berta had been dreaming of.

The three women went together to get the new baby—to the heart of the colony where the old spaceship was still running and would keep running for generations still.

Berta cried when she was handed her new son. He was so beautiful, but also so very tiny. Less than a week old. Centuries older than all of them. Younger than his new sister.

"What's his name?" asked Wendy, her eyes, too, damp with tears.

"Paul," read the scientist from a screen displaying the baby's digital file. "His mother named him Paul."

The Flower of Valhalla

Danielle Woolhead

Pairing: Humanoid/Humanoid

"...and that's how I pocketed the sceptre of Abad." I tipped my head back to down the last of my drink, scanning the room. My story had drawn five people—which was almost everyone in this small bar. That wasn't much to choose from, but since it'd been over a month since I'd gotten laid, I was willing to lower my standards. My gaze lingered on a newcomer—wavy platinum blond hair, lavender eyes, smooth curve between breast and hip nicely displayed by her tight black tank top. I didn't recognize her face, but her boobs looked familiar...

I leaned forward to put my glass on the table, giving her a careful flash of my own cleavage. Her cheeks reddened, and I winked at her. "Maybe next time, I'll tell you how I took the most precious flower on Valhalla."

Her mouth twitched—she must have appreciated my innuendo. The other four people, seeing the entertainment was over, went back to the bar. I smiled at the blond, tapping the rim of my glass. One of her pale eyebrows rose, then she nodded, waving to the waiter as she settled on the couch across from me. I licked my lips. This promised to be a very satisfying evening.

* * *

I woke up bleary-eyed and achy-headed. Guess I forgot to take an antitoxin before going to bed. I tried to roll over to reach my bedside table, only to be brought up short. My arms were stuck above my head. I tried to twist my neck to look up at them, failed, and tried moving my arms again. They made a distinct clinking noise.

Why was I handcuffed to my bed?

It was definitely my bed. I recognized how the sheets felt on my skin—on all my skin, I realized a disconcerting moment later. Naked, handcuffed to my bed... I frantically tried to think back, to remember the previous night. I'd gone to the bar, told a few stories. And then...

"So, you did wake up." I forced my eyes open, raised my head and looked over my left arm to see the cute blond from the bar. Slightly less cute and more dangerously sexy, with her hair up in a tight ponytail and wearing a skintight black flightsuit. I wondered if she knew how to use the blaster on her hip. "Pirate Seph. If that's even your real name."

I ran my tongue over my teeth, grimacing at the amount of gunk that had built up. How long was I out for? "Who the fuck are you?"

"I am Princess Xifreyja of Nurdstrom, Vice-Captain of the Valkyries, Protector of—"

I groaned, letting my head fall back on the pillow. "Fuck, I knew I recognized those boobs."

She slapped me across the face. "You can't say that to a princess!"

I rolled my eyes. "You've got to be fucking kidding me. You've got me naked and handcuffed to my own bed! I've licked your pussy twice! Do you seriously care about me mentioning your breasts when mine are right in front of you?"

She slapped me again, her face bright red. "I forgot how crude your tongue was. I can't believe you didn't recognize me."

"It's been more than two standard years! And you look completely different without your stupid makeup!"

"Ceremonial makeup." She sniffed derogatively. "Well, I'll soon have you back to Father, and he can deal with you."

I frowned, trying to force my brain to engage. Taking me back. But I was in my own bed... I finally recognized the faint vibrations. My eyes widened. "You stupid entitled brat! You took my ship into hyperspace, didn't you?"

She waved a hand dismissively. "It was the easiest way to get home. We should be exiting hyperspace shortly. Get comfortable." She strode through the hatch and out of my sight.

I had to escape quickly. She was naive enough she thought my ship wouldn't be booby trapped. And since she'd taken it into hyperspace without my handprint...

I twisted sideways and hooked my toe onto the bedside drawer, pulled it open and snagged a packet between two toes, twisting—in a way the princess would find quite embarrassing—to pass it up to my handcuffed fingers. I opened it, straining my neck to get the antitoxin in my mouth. It fizzed on my tongue, and my head cleared instantly. Now to deal with the handcuffs.

"Fifi, how long until we're out of hyperspace?"

"Exiting hyperspace in one minute," my AI's sultry voice informed me.

With a bit more stretching, I managed to get the second drawer—my junk drawer—open. Rummaging through it without looking was harder than I'd expected, and I was about to give up when my toe brushed something smooth and hard.

I twisted as far as I could and managed to pinch my ion cutter between my feet. Tensing my core, I got it up to my hands. Hoping I'd remembered to charge it, I pointed it at the handcuffs and turned it on.

One second later, it was kicked out of my hand by a very pissed off princess. The ion cutter bounced off the wall above my head, then smashed onto the floor out of my sight. From the sound of it, I'd need to repair it again. Part of me wailed at losing the chance to escape. Part of me marvelled at the accuracy of the kick, and the way she'd paused with her left leg cocked to the side, the glint in her eyes as she aimed her blaster at me—

With effort, I ignored how wet I was—did she use a sedative or an aphrodisiac?—and focused on the gun. I gave her my best smile and as good of a shrug as I could manage. "Can't blame me for trying."

"Why are we in an asteroid belt!"

"Standard security, Princess. You try to fly my ship without me, she drops you off in the Doppler asteroid belt without maneuvering thrusters." I tilted my head, but couldn't hear anything over the hum of the life support. "I'm guessing you put the shields up. Fifi, shield status?"

"Shields at fifty percent."

"Turn the security off," Xifreyja growled, blaster still levelled at me.

"No can do, Princess." I wiggled my hands. "Biometric scanner in the cockpit. You need me in there, happy and healthy. Unlock the cuffs, and I'll get us out of here. Then we can talk about your daddy."

She groaned, pulled a key from her pocket, and started fiddling with the handcuffs.

I lay there, watching her boobs jiggle. It was basically the only thing I could do. Other than... "Fifi, shield status?"

"Shields at thirty percent."

"Want to hurry that up, Princess?"

"I'm trying! Just stay still, something is..." She turned the handcuff, then froze.

"What?" I twisted to look.

"You fused the lock. When you tried to escape."

"...fuck."

"Warning. Shields at fifteen percent."

She stared at me for a moment. "Can you give me control of the maneuvering jets?"

I stared back. "That's the Doppler belt! I don't care how good a flier you think you are, Princess, but the chances of—"

"Shields at ten percent."

I hastily revised my opinion. "—are better than zero. Fine. Fifi, unlock thruster controls."

"Thrusters online. Shields at five percent."

Xifreyja scrambled back into the cockpit, shoving her blaster back into her holster on the way. I craned my neck trying to see, until I remembered the screen over my bunk—partially for solo spaceship flying, partly for dirty movies. "Fifi, give me forward screens on bedcam."

The screen turned on, showing one fuck of a lot of asteroids. One moment later, the whole ship shook.

"Shields offline."

"Shit."

Then Xifreyja took the helm.

We swooped to the left—accelerating faster than I'd thought my ship could. She spiralled around one asteroid, using the new angle to cut between two chunks of rock just before they collided. Then she accelerated upward, through a space I hadn't seen, cutting to the right almost immediately.

I shifted, suddenly reminded of how wet I was. Stupid aphrodisiac. Why couldn't she have dosed me with a normal knock-out drug?

After about ten minutes—and the wildest adrenaline ride of my life—we flew into clear space. I took a moment to catch my breath, staring at the lack of asteroids. I hadn't expected to survive that. "Fifi..." I had to clear my throat before I could continue. "Fifi, lock down thrusters." Xifreyja might have been the most amazing pilot I'd ever seen, but that didn't mean I was going to let her drag me home to face...whatever Nurdstrom did to a seductress for hire who deflowered their princess.

Which is why I waited until she stormed back into my bedroom, blaster in hand, then said, "Fifi, turn off gravity generators." Then I held onto the handcuffs, using them to swing myself around and kick the blaster from her hand. I managed to curve the kick just right, and the blaster ricocheted off the bulkhead straight toward my hand.

Unfortunately, Xifreyja clearly had experience in zero-G. Instead of startling and flailing about as I'd hoped, she tracked the trajectory of her blaster, then pushed off from the deck to intercept.

I was more flexible than she'd expected. Using the handcuffs to stabilize, I folded myself in half to bring my legs into play. My foot knocked her arm to the side, so the gun sailed just past her outstretched fingers. I tried to grab it, but the handcuffs brought me up short. As the gun ricocheted again, and Xifreyja pushed away to go after it, I locked my legs around her waist. She tried to shove me away, so I hooked one leg around her left arm and forced it down. With her right side pressed against my stomach, and her left arm pinned to her side, she didn't have any leverage to get away.

That didn't stop her from struggling. I bit my lip, trying not to grind against her hip. Damn aphrodisiac. "Listen, Princess, from here I can get my arm around your neck and choke you out. I don't want to kill you, I'm just going to drop you off at the next station, so you might as well do us both a favor and give up now." Something warm and wet splatted against my bare leg. It wasn't until I saw a wobbly droplet float by that I realized she was crying. I sighed. "I'm not going to hurt you. You'll just have to go back to your dad and say you couldn't find me or something."

"I can't go home without the peace lotus," she sobbed.

I blinked. "The what?"

"The peace lotus. My father's most precious flower."

I sighed. "Princess, that's not how it works. I can't undeflower you, once you've fucked—"

"I'm not talking about that!" Anger crept into her voice, and her body stiffened between my thighs. "The crystal flower on the end of my father's staff. The flower that denotes the current head of the Valhallan council. Which means it should be passed to the Duke of Kromberg next year, but since you took it—"

"Hold up." I frowned. "The only thing I took on your planet was your virginity."

"You were bragging about stealing the lotus in the bar! How you'd taken the most precious flower—"

"That was a euphemism!" I rolled my eyes. "You didn't seriously think that..." I paused, remembering my time on Valhalla, and groaned. "Your people don't use euphemisms."

"I don't know what you're talking about," she sniffed, her tone icy.

"It means I wasn't talking about a real flower. I was talking about how we fucked."

"You did what! You would have told the story of our intimacy—"

I rolled my eyes. "Yeah, yeah, I'm a terrible person. I didn't think I'd see you again. Um, so...why am I seeing you again? You spent two years tracking me down because you thought I took a flower?"

She sighed overdramatically. "I am Vice-Captain of the Valkyries. When the peace lotus is in the hands of Nurdstrom, it is my duty to ensure its safety. When it was stolen, it became my duty to recover it before it is scheduled to be passed on."

"Why not make another pretty flower?"

"The peace lotus symbolizes the peace of Valhalla. If we do not pass it on, the other nations will see it as a declaration of war."

"Oh, fuck," I groaned, leaning back against the pillows. "That's why they hired me to distract you?"

"They did what!"

I shrugged. "I'm a courtesan. People pay me for sex. Sometimes they pay me to have sex with someone else. I don't need to know the details."

"You were paid to have sex with me?"

"That's my job. I wasn't born a princess, you know. Not everyone can be Vice-Captain of the Valkyries."

She relaxed, her shoulders slumping. "If what you say is true, then I have no more leads. No way to find who took the peace lotus, no way to save my planet from war."

I looked at the dejected slump of her shoulders, the red cheeks accentuated by wisps of pale hair, surrounded by a galaxy of shimmering tears—and made possibly the worst decision in my life. "I know who hired me. They call themselves the Shadow Hand—sounds better in their language," I added as she raised her head to stare at me, her lavender eyes wide. My hips shifted of their own accord, and I had to will myself still. "I suppose I can help you get your flower back." Her lips curved into a smile, and I groaned, looking away. "Maybe next time you can skip the aphrodisiac."

"Aphrodisiac?"

"That drug you gave me."

"I gave you an anaesthetic."

I frowned at her. "The way my body keeps reacting—"

She rolled her eyes. "You like me. Get over it."

"What?"

"I can't believe a seductress can be so clueless," she muttered, giving me an exasperated look. "You obviously find me physically attractive. The way you were flirting—"

"I was paid to—"

"In the bar last night." She sighed, shaking her head. "We'll figure it out in hyperspace. Give me the coordinates to this 'Shadow Hand' headquarters, and we can get going."

"You still need my handprint to unlock the hyperdrive."

"So stop humping my hip and let me go," she snapped. "Then I can get you free."

I sighed, twisting to bring both of us closer to the bed. "Fifi, turn on gravity generators." I let Xifreyja go and watched nervously as she headed straight for her blaster. "You're not going to shoot me, right?"

"Of course not." She walked back to me, turning a dial on the side of the grip. "It has a laser setting."

"Then why didn't you use it before?"

"There wasn't time. It's not a strong laser."

I scrunched my eyes shut, trying to sound unconcerned. "You know my handprint only works if it's attached, right?"

"Obviously."

"You didn't realize the hyperdrive would be booby trapped, I think it's reasonable for me to assume—" Her hand closed over my forearm. Her lips brushed my ear, and I gasped.

"Stay still."

* * *

Dressed—finally—in a purple shipsuit, I strode into my cockpit, a slight bounce in my step.

"Took you long enough." Xifreyja slouched in my chair, one boot planted on the control panel, spinning her blaster around one finger. She stood, holstering the blaster and gesturing to the panel in one smooth movement.

"Had to freshen up." I winked at her as I leaned over to place my hand against the sensor. "Being captured takes a lot out of you."

One corner of her mouth twitched. "I'm sure."

My fingers danced across the controls, keying in coordinates. "Fifi, initiate shield reboot. Commence hyperjump when shields are back online."

"Thank you for helping me with this," Xifreyja said softly.

"Hey, I caused the problem, I figure I can be part of the solution. Just one question, Princess." She turned to me and raised one platinum eyebrow. "Do you have another pair of handcuffs?"

The Ritter Maneuver

Heather Tracy

Pairing: Human/Alien
Rep: Nonbinary

Space. The last horizon. Such are the encounters of the galaxyship Venture *on its enduring quest for new beings and cultures. To bravely seek where none have sought before...*

The Expedition Class ship comes into view in the vastness of space, orbiting a blue-green planet with swirling white clouds, Hovitylmn. We slowly zoom in to the galaxyship, panning past the nacelles and over the rounded triangular, muted red hull where the bridge sits at the peak. (Oddly, male crew members seem to have trouble finding the bridge without directions.) Soon, the words *SS Venture Exp-3402* come into view. The camera takes us down to the view screen on the front of the ship and we enter directly onto the bridge.

Captain Marie-Claude Périer sits at the center, a tall, thin Martian woman of about mid-fifties, with coppery skin and short red hair with flecks of grey. To her right sits the second in command, Commander Willow Ritter, a human female in her late thirties—pale by comparison—with long, dark brown hair pulled back in a bun. She is muscular and taller than average at six-foot-one and can stand shoulder to shoulder with the captain. Their silver-grey jumpsuit uniforms—with a large diagonal blue stripe from the left shoulder across the chest and down the right leg—are flattering to both of their figures.

We see various bridge crew are at their posts, in their similar uniforms with different-colored stripes indicating their department: blue for command, green for science, red for medical, and gold for engineering. Stripes on the shoulders of each uniform indicate rank, with four for the captain.

We center on the captain as she speaks to someone on the viewscreen.

"We are delighted to welcome Ambassador Glfrugian aboard the *Venture*, Queen Bfkiturge," Captain Périer says with enthusiasm, gesturing to the crew on the bridge. "We look forward to understanding more about the Hovi."

A purplish-green-skinned Hovi dressed in golden robes nods her bald head generously, causing her many earrings to clatter. Another Hovi in blue and white robes nudges her into speaking. "And we look forward to getting to know more about the Terrestrial Relations & Equality Coalition."

"We hope this will be the start of a wonderful alliance with the Hovi," the captain replies, her smile reaching up to her green eyes. Then, speaking into the circular communication badge on her chest, "Ensign Leonard, please transport Ambassador Glfrugian to the *Venture*."

"The ambassador is safely aboard, Captain," Ensign Leonard's voice says a few moments later.

"We'll take great care of the ambassador, Queen Bfkiturge. Périer out." The viewscreen shifts back to the view of the planet from the bridge.

The captain stands and adjusts her uniform perfunctorily. "I will go greet the ambassador and show her around the ship. Commander, you have the conn." She strides purposefully toward the turbolift, as Cmdr. Ritter moves into the captain's seat.

Just as the captain is about to board the lift, Ensign James, Communications Officer, says, "Captain, you have an Alpha Level message from STAAR Command."

Captain Périer heaves a sigh before responding. "I'll take it in my office."

"Re-routing as instructed," Ensign James replies.

"What could they possibly want now?" she asks under her breath. She turns back to Cmdr. Ritter. "It appears I won't be greeting the ambassador after all. Please give her my regards, and I will meet up with you both as soon as possible."

"Understood, Captain," Cmdr. Ritter replies. "Keep me updated on what STAAR Command requires."

"Of course. Lieutenant Commander Nichols," the captain says to the next officer in command, the Chief Security Officer, "you have the conn."

* * *

We enter the Transporter Room behind Commander Ritter and see Ensign Leonard speaking with Ambassador Glfrugian. The commander can only stare as she is immediately struck by how beautiful the ambassador is. The blue in her robes accentuates the oceanic undertones to her purple-green skin. Her jewelry is sparse, save a chunky silver necklace and one set of large, silver hoop earrings that seem too heavy for her thin ears. Her bald head is tattooed with various symbols, unlike the Queen's, which was unadorned. Navy blue scrollwork makes a headband which is joined by symbols that look cultural or religious in nature.

Cmdr. Ritter steps up to greet her warmly with her hands outstretched in the customary greeting of the Hovi. "Ambassador Glfrugian, please allow me to welcome you to the *Venture*, and we hope to the Terrestrial Relations & Equality Coalition. I'm Commander Willow Ritter."

"I understand your captain was called away on urgent business," the ambassador says, her voice a melody. She takes both of the commander's hands in hers and places them to her forehead. "It is a pleasure to make your acquaintance, Commander Ritter."

Ritter repeats the motion with the ambassador's hands, then releases them. She feels a tingle of electricity as she does so, and wonders if Ambassador Glfrugian feels it too. "The pleasure is all mine."

"It is probably just the static charge of the moisture on my hands in this drier environment," Ambassador Glfrugian replies to Ritter's unspoken query.

"I...I'm sorry...what?" the commander stammers.

"You were wondering what that electricity you felt when you released my hands was. I was just explaining the likely cause." Ambassador Glfrugian adjusts her robes unconsciously.

Ritter looks taken aback and isn't sure what to say, except, "You can read minds?"

"The Hovi are telepathic. I thought you knew," Ambassador Glfrugian says.

"I'm afraid I wasn't briefed on that aspect of the Hovi, no." Ritter shakes her head in annoyance at the captain for neglecting to mention this significant detail. "But I'd love to hear more about it as we tour the ship."

They exit the Transporter Room and start walking around the ship with Cmdr. Ritter pointing out various sights, such as the library and med bay, to Ambassador Glfrugian. They continue to discuss the telepathic nature of the Hovi.

"So, you can only communicate telepathically when you're within a certain proximity of someone?" Ritter asks.

"That is correct," Ambassador Glfrugian replies. "This might be where the confusion arose with the Coalition as we cannot communicate telepathically through electronic means, and this is only the second face-to-face meeting we've had with another species. I believe the other representative did not understand that we were attempting telepathic communication with them and merely thought we were mute for a significant period of time."

Ritter nods. "Ah, yes, that might explain the misunderstanding. Some of the older captains are too reliant on the Ubiquitous Translator™, and don't think of non-verbal means of communication."

"Exactly," Ambassador Glfrugian says, and her wide smile makes many unspoken promises. "We can speak verbally, but use that only for official meetings, ceremonies, concerts and other special occasions. Otherwise, we much prefer the more intimate nature of our telepathy."

They stop right outside of the crew mess hall and Ritter asks, "Doesn't it get confusing hearing a whole bunch of voices in your head all at once?"

The ambassador laughs. "It is difficult when we are young, yes. As we grow older, we learn to filter out only the voices of those who we are intending to speak with or listen to. It takes years of practice."

"I can only imagine."

"Eventually, all the other voices are simply a hum. Background music for the melody you want to hear."

Ritter wishes she could experience this herself, especially since Ambassador Glfrugian has such a melodious voice and music has always been a favorite pastime of hers. She also bets telepathy would be very useful for encounters of a...sexual nature.

"Oh, it is." Ambassador Glfrugian winks as they enter the mess hall for the afternoon meal.

Captain Périer is saving them seats. She stands up as they approach. "Ambassador Glfrugian, my deepest apologies for not greeting you upon your arrival." They greet each other in the traditional Hovi manner.

"It is not an issue. I understand you had an urgent matter, Captain," the ambassador replies. "I have had a lovely time with Commander Ritter, here. I am very impressed with the *Venture,* and her crew"—she gives a knowing wink to the commander— "thus far."

Ritter attempts to hide her blush by tucking into her food.

"I do hope everything was alright with your important call."

Ritter swallows and asks, "Yes, what did STAAR Command want?"

The captain rolls her eyes. "We're going to have to cut our visit to Hovitylmn shorter than we'd hoped."

"How much shorter?" Ritter asks, sadness evident in her tone.

Captain Périer looks between her seatmates, taking in their energy, before responding. "We'll still be here for a few days, but then we'll have to move on to the Androselene sector to continue peace talks with the Planet of Men again. Apparently, all the male captains are too emotional to deal with the situation, so they've asked us to step in."

Ritter sighs with exasperation. "Of course they have."

Ambassador Glfrugian takes Commander Ritter's hand under the table. "We will have to make the most of the time we have."

* * *

We see a montage of Cmdr. Ritter getting to know Ambassador Glfrugian over the next two days. Scenes of them laughing over conversation during meals alone and with the captain, at which point Ritter sees the full extent of the Hovi tongue—grey and long, said to be prehensile but no one has been close enough to test the theory—as the ambassador has a full-throated laugh. Another scene of the ambassador touching Ritter's arm playfully as they meander down a corridor. Ritter standing with one foot on the bottom edge of a console and her elbow on her knee while she shows the ambassador how to search the star map. A concert where Ritter plays the tromfluxahorn and the only person seeming to have a good time is the ambassador.

Finally, Ritter escorts the ambassador into the observation lounge where they can get a full view of Hovitylmn as the ship orbits.

"I have never seen my planet from space before. It is quite beautiful," Ambassador Glfrugian remarks.

"It's very beautiful," Cmdr. Ritter agrees. "As an ambassador, I would've thought you would have been off world before now."

"I have never left Hovitylmn before. I am an ambassador between Queen Bfkiturge and her subjects. When we met the representative from the Coalition, the queen thought my position should extend now to those beyond our planet." Though she's looking through the window at her planet, her gaze seems distant.

"Are you missing your home, Ambassador? It's just, you seem lost in thought."

"No, it is not that." She turns to look at Ritter. "I am thinking how wonderful it must be to explore all this." She gestures at the vastness of space surrounding them.

Cmdr. Ritter nods. "It is fun, but not without its challenges. It can be a lonely life."

"It would not be if you had someone to share it with." Ambassador Glfrugian gives another knowing wink and Ritter blushes. "Or, perhaps I have said too much."

"Perhaps I have thought too much, and said too little," Ritter says, and they both laugh.

The two are silent for a few moments, enjoying the view and each other's company.

"Do you think a non-Hovi would ever be able to communicate, you know, telepathically with a Hovi?" Ritter asks.

The ambassador places her hand on Ritter's forearm and replies, "It has never been tried before because we don't know many non-Hovi, but it would be an interesting experiment."

"That it would." Ritter places her hand on top of the ambassador's and relishes its warmth.

* * *

Cmdr. Ritter takes Ambassador Glfrugian to the final stop on their multi-day tour, Engineering. They enter the automatic doors, and the ambassador releases an audible gasp when she sees the Flash Drives in all their radiant glory. Orange and red beams of light pulsate up and down, and the crystalline shafts are a sight to behold in and of themselves.

"Pretty awe-inspiring, right?" Ritter asks, staring at the gaping figure beside her. She can tell the ambassador is probably saying something telepathically, but nothing is coming out audibly. "That's okay. Just take it all in."

They walk around in the safe zone where they are shielded from the radiation, and Cmdr. Ritter keeps one eye on the ambassador while also checking in on the engineering team. There's always a flurry of activity in this department as there is always something to fix or to do to keep the ship running at optimal performance.

"Lieutenant Commander DeForest, what is going on over here?" Cmdr. Ritter asks, putting her foot up on the edge of the console and pointing at a screen with flashing red lights. The Ambassador takes obvious notice of the tautness of Ritter's pants as she does so.

Lt. Cmdr. DeForest, a short Martian with spikey pink hair, comes running over. "Everything's fine, Commander. The captain said STAAR command wanted us to run a Phase One diagnostic while we were in orbit to make sure the Flash Drives were in tip top shape before we depart for the Androselene Sector."

"Of course," Ritter acknowledges as if she knew this all along. "I'll let the captain know everything is going on as scheduled then?"

They nod. "Absolutely, Commander. All seems in good working order here, but we'll let you know if anything changes."

"Good, good," Cmdr. Ritter replies. "Carry on."

"Aye, aye, Commander." The Chief Engineer starts to turn away, then notices the ambassador. "Anything I can show you in Engineering while you're here, Ambassador?" They nearly bow.

Ambassador Glfrugian shakes her head, smiling. "No, but thank you. I will let you continue on with your important work."

"If you change your mind, you know where to find me," DeForest adds. They nod to Cmdr. Ritter then hurry off again.

"Lieutenant Commander DeForest is one of our best and brightest," Ritter says to the ambassador. "They graduated from Squadron of Technology and Astronomical Research Academy at a very young age and became Chief Engineer of the *Venture* before I was even a Lieutenant."

"Very impressive," Ambassador Glfrugian says. "If I have some extra time, it would be nice to speak with them when they are not quite so busy."

Ritter chuckles. "You might be hard pressed to find time when they aren't busy, but I'll see what I can do."

* * *

After another busy day of exploring the ship and meetings with the captain to learn more about the Terrestrial Relations & Equality Coalition, Ambassador Glfrugian asks Cmdr. Ritter to escort her back to her quarters.

"Is anything wrong, Ambassador?" Ritter asks, concerned.

The ambassador shakes her head. "I would very much like to relax this evening, but had some more questions I thought you could answer for me."

The commander puts her arm out for the ambassador to take, and they walk slowly down the corridor to her quarters. "I'd be happy to answer any questions you might have. But don't you think the captain would be better suited—"

"These are not questions about the Coalition or the *Venture*, Commander Ritter," the ambassador interrupts. "These are items of a more personal nature."

Ritter blushes, but otherwise retains her outward composure as they are walking past other crew members in the hall. "I see. We should wait then until we are in your quarters to discuss them."

"Yes, that would be best, since you do not have the capacity to speak telepathically...as yet. Unless the redness on your skin counts."

Cmdr. Ritter nearly stumbles, though the floor is perfectly smooth. She mumbles something incoherent in response.

They walk in silence for the last few minutes until they arrive at the ambassador's door. She opens it with her passkey and gestures for Cmdr. Ritter to enter. Although the commander showed the rooms to the ambassador only a couple days ago, she can see Ambassador Glfrugian has done some redecorating. The furniture is in a different configuration from before, and there are various wall hangings and sculptures around the room. The lights are dimmed on entry and the ambassador doesn't ask the computer to make them any brighter.

"Have a seat, Commander. Make yourself at home," the ambassador says, gesturing at the sofa on which several scatter cushions have been added.

"Love what you've done with the place," Ritter says, sitting down.

The ambassador sits next to her and looks down at the floor, embarrassed. "I hope it is not a problem that I put some of my things around and moved the furnishings. We Hovi like to have our spaces organized a certain way for better flow of...energy, I think you would call it. And I brought some items from my home to make it feel more comfortable."

"Not at all," Ritter says, placing her hand on Ambassador Glfrugian's shoulder. "You are more than welcome to put things how you like them. It's your space while you're onboard."

The ambassador puts her hand on top of Ritter's, and they share a long look. Ritter gets the feeling the ambassador is trying to tell her something telepathically, but nothing is coming through. She is concerned about what thoughts of hers are being heard, though. The feelings their connection over the last few days—and the touch they are sharing now—have stirred are hard to ignore.

"Commander," the ambassador begins, shaking Ritter free of her reverie.

"Yes?"

"Commander, I do not know how to say this other than to say it plainly." Ambassador Glfrugian shifts in her seat, then takes both of Ritter's hands in hers. "The connection I feel with you is stronger than any I have ever known. As the time approaches for me to leave the *Venture* and go back to Hovitylmn, I know in my hearts"—she places Ritter's hand on her chest—"that I do not belong there anymore. I think you feel this too, but I cannot tell from your thoughts alone."

Ritter feels the pounding of the ambassador's two hearts under her hand, and her single one in her chest. "I...yes, I do feel it too," she replies. "But how would this work? Would the queen just let you leave? Do you have a duty to your people?"

"I have spoken with Queen Bfkiturge, and she will allow me to be our off-world ambassador, if I were to leave with the *Venture*," the ambassador says. "I have not yet spoken with your captain, who I am sure would need to speak with the Coalition and STAAR Command. There are many things to discuss, but I wanted to see if our sentiments aligned before pursuing anything further."

Ritter closes the short distance between them in an instant and kisses the ambassador with all the passion she's had pent up inside since they met. She places one hand on the back of the ambassador's head, feeling the soft skin there, and the other hand around her waist. Ritter feels the ambassador's arms wrap around her as well, tugging at her hair as their lips move in time with one another. The ambassador parts Ritter's lips with her forceful tongue. When Ritter can stand it no longer, she picks the ambassador up and carries her to the bedroom. Once there, the ambassador slowly removes her usual robes to reveal a skintight teal jumpsuit underneath, which hugs every curve and shows off her cleavage to its full advantage. She sits down on the bed, beckoning Ritter with her eyes, and her still unreadable thoughts.

* * *

After, with the ambassador's head resting on her shoulder, Ritter says, "You know, I think you should start calling me Willow. When we're alone, at least."

The ambassador looks at her with dreamy eyes. "Willow. Willow. What a beautiful name for a beautiful individual."

A few beats of silence pass before Willow asks, "Do you have a first name or another name I can call you?"

The ambassador pushes herself up onto her elbow. "Sorry, I was attempting to tell you telepathically. I still think it can be done, with enough practice and patience."

"Maybe. Perhaps I need to clear my mind or meditate or something," Willow muses.

"We will work on it. Unless your captain objects, I suspect we have plenty of time to try." She kisses Willow sweetly.

"I hope so, Ambassador."

"My name. Sorry, I forgot," the ambassador says. "I assume it is difficult for the human tongue to pronounce as it is written, just as our surnames are."

"I am game to try it, or we can see if the Ubiquitous Translator™ makes it easier."

Ambassador Glfrugian shrugs. "It is spelled T-t-p-r-o-u-y-e. It's pronounced—"

What Willow hears through the translator is: "Troy."

Please take a moment to review this book at your favorite retailer's website, Goodreads, or simply tell your friends!

ABOUT THE AUTHORS

Ashleigh Martin is an occasionally proud Texan and an always proud cat mom. When she's not working as a librarian, you can find her reading, crafting, writing something sapphic, or playing *The Sims*. She's also a Martha's Vineyard Institute of Creative Writing Fellow and a WNDB Black Creatives Workshop participant. You can find her online at ashleighmartin.com or @ashleighmwrites on Instagram/Bluesky.

MK Hardy is the pen name for Morag Hannah and Erin Hardee, two geeky women living and writing together in Scotland. They are both communications specialists working in higher education. With backgrounds ranging from museum interpretation to web design, and from science communication to ghost tours, they are devoted to storytelling in almost every aspect of their lives and work. When they are not telling stories they can be found singing in choirs, foraging for fungi, and working on their 1880s fixer-upper. Their debut sapphic gothic horror *The Needfire* comes from Solaris in July 2025.

Nathan Chu (MuZeTrigger) is a Washington state writer and teacher. When they're not doing either of those things, they enjoy cooking, flailing around on the bass guitar, and practicing Japanese. You can find them on BlueSky @muzetrigger.bsky.social where they write the fantasy flash serial #DiaryOfNana.

Travis Baldree is a #1 New York Times Bestselling author, a Locus, Nebula, and Hugo finalist, and a full-time audiobook narrator who has lent his voice to hundreds of stories. Before that, he spent decades designing and building video games like *Torchlight*, *Rebel Galaxy*, and *Fate*. He lives in the Pacific Northwest.

Stewart C. Baker is an academic librarian and author of speculative fiction, poetry, and games, including *The Butterfly Disjunct: And Other Stories* (Interstellar Flight Press), and as part of the teams for the Nebula-nominated games *The Bread Must Rise* and *A Death in Hyperspace*. Born in England, Stewart lives in Oregon.

Kayla Whittle has previously had short stories published in *Uncharted Magazine* and *The Colored Lens*. She also has stories in several anthologies including *Beyond the Veil* (Ghost Orchid Press), and *Of Fate & Fury* (Silver Wheel Press), as well as *Dangerous Waters*, *Daughter of Sarpedon*, and *Seers and Sibyls*, all out with Brigids Gate Press. Her work has been featured on *Flash Fiction Podcast*. Most often she can be found on Instagram @caughtbetweenthepages.

Joel Glover is a writer of speculative fictions which vary in length from haiku to novel. He is the author of the bronzedark fantasy series *The Gods' Paths*, the scrollpunk fantasy *The Thirteenth Prince*, and a Dying Earth Swords and Sorcery Series *Nine Realms of Reality*. Often found on the internet talking excitedly about his latest project, he is a firm believer in the power of the limerick.

Caye Marsh is a former biologist living in Aotearoa New Zealand. She writes Sci Fi and Fantasy that celebrates queer communities and proclaims her awe for the natural world. Find her at cayemarsh.com.

Kira Neu is a queer, neurodiverse author from Germany currently living in Australia. She writes and self-publishes proudly pulpy sapphic romance novels under a couple of super-secret pen names and has occasionally spent a few months in Amazon's Lesbian Romance top 100. She was one of the scholarship winners for the 2022 Writing Excuses cruise. When she's not writing, you can find her hyperfixating on one of too many hobbies or out in the bush watching wildlife.

Emma Newman writes short stories, novels and novellas in multiple speculative fiction genres. She is also a Hugo Award-winning podcaster and an audiobook narrator.

She won the British Fantasy Society Best Short Story Award 2015 for "A Woman's Place" in the *221 Baker Streets* anthology. *Between Two Thorns*, the first book in Emma's Split Worlds urban fantasy series, was shortlisted for the BFS Best Novel and Best Newcomer 2014 awards. Her science-fiction novel, *After Atlas*, was shortlisted for the 2017 Arthur C. Clarke award and the third novel in the Planetfall series, *Before Mars*, has been shortlisted for a BSFA Best Novel award. The Planetfall series was shortlisted for the 2020 Best Series Hugo Award. Her latest novel is a historical fantasy swashbuckler called *The Vengeance*.

Emma created a podcast called *Imagining Tomorrow* for Friends of the Earth. Her hobbies include dressmaking, LARP and tabletop role playing.

J.S. Fields (@Galactoglucoman) is a scientist who has spent too much time around organic solvents. They enjoy roller derby, woodturning, making chainmail by hand, and cultivating fungi in the backs of minivans. J.S. lives with their wife and kid in the Pacific Northwest, along with a Flemish giant rabbit named Sir Chip Edmonton III.

Fields' writing spans across science and science fiction/fantasy. Their Ardulum series was a Forewords INDIES finalist in science fiction, and a Gold Crown Literary Society finalist in science fiction. Their YA fantasy *Foxfire in the Snow* was also a Foreword INDIES finalist in YA, and their adult fantasy *The Rosewood Penny* was a Queer Indie Award nominee. All of their writing, from published to drafting, is available on their Patreon: http://www.patreon.com/jsfields. You can keep up to date on their work at http://www.jsfieldsbooks.com/

Jes Honard (they/she) is a queer sci-fi/fantasy writer and professional coffee inhaler. Their award-winning debut, *Unrelenting*, was co-written with Marie Parks and published by Not a Pipe Publishing in 2022. Its sequel, *Undeniable*, will be published in 2025.

Jes finds their best words when writing about found families, queer identity, and what happens when we build bridges instead of walls. They currently live in Kalamazoo, MI with their wife and two cats.

S.M. Passmore hails from the rain-filled lands of Portland, Oregon, working in medical research by the day and Twitch streaming (and writing!) by night. When not speedrunning horror games or gardening, S.M. can be found concocting new methods of torturing her beloved characters. As the pet-mom of rabbits and chinchillas, finding the time to get her writing done can be challenging, but she always somehow scrounges a few sentences here or there. S.M. Passmore can be found on BlueSky at @missscarlettanager.bsky.social, and over on YouTube and Twitch under the username MissScarletTanager for gaming shenanigans.

Sylvie Althoff (she/her) is a queer transgender woman who works as a writer, editor, elementary teacher, and jazz banjoist. Her writing has appeared in *Escape Pod*, *Small Wonders*, and the Baen Books collection *Tales of the United States Space Force*. Her story "Bubbe Hates You" can be found in *Punch a Nazi*, a benefit anthology in support of the Trevor Project. Other stories are scheduled to appear in 2025 in *Inner Worlds*, *Saros*, and *Baubles from Bones*. She lives in Kansas with her wife, musician and teacher Jenn Thomas; their dog, Nomi Malone; and their layabout cat, Pocket. She may be found at sylviealthoff.com or on Bluesky @sylvie-althoff.

Mary Robinette Kowal is the USA TODAY bestselling author of the Hugo, Nebula, and Locus award-winning alternate history novel *The Calculating Stars*. This title is the first book in the Lady Astronaut series, which continued in 2025 with its fourth installment, *The Martian Contingency*. She is also the author of The Glamourist Histories series, *Ghost Talkers*, *The Spare Man*, and has received the Astounding Award for Best New Writer, four Hugo awards, the Nebula and Locus awards. Her stories appear in *Asimov's*, *Uncanny*, and several *Year's Best* anthologies. Mary Robinette has also worked as a professional puppeteer, is a member of the award-winning podcast *Writing Excuses*, and performs as a voice actor (SAG/AFTRA), recording fiction for authors including Seanan McGuire, Cory Doctorow, and Neal Stephenson. She lives in Denver with her husband Robert, their dog Guppy, and their "talking" cat Elsie. Visit her online at maryrobinettekowal.com.

Jasmine Gower, author of *Moonshine* and other queer fantasy works, hails from Portland, Oregon. Inspired to write by a childhood filled with fantasy novels, 90s video games, and the curious experience of growing up in the rural Willamette Valley, Jasmine has a passion for exploring themes of gender, sexuality, and disability through the conventions of speculative fiction, mythology, and fantasy world-building.

Siena Buchanan is a college student studying genetics in the Pacific Northwest. She writes primarily queer science-fiction and fantasy, and she had her first anthology acceptance the day before she turned eighteen. In her limited time between writing and schoolwork, she enjoys going for long walks, swimming, baking and watercolor painting.

Seanan McGuire was born in Martinez, California, and raised in a wide variety of locations, most of which boasted some sort of dangerous native wildlife. Despite her almost magnetic attraction to anything venomous, she somehow managed to survive long enough to acquire a typewriter, a reasonable grasp of the English language, and the desire to combine the two. The fact that she wasn't killed for using her typewriter at three o'clock in the morning is probably more impressive than her lack of death by spider-bite.

Seanan is the author of the Wayward Children series, the October Daye urban fantasies, the InCryptid urban fantasies, and several other works both stand-alone and in trilogies or duologies. In case that wasn't enough, she also writes under the pseudonym "Mira Grant." For details on her work as Mira, check out MiraGrant.com.

Seanan was the winner of the 2010 John W. Campbell Award for Best New Writer, and her novel *Feed* (as Mira Grant) was named as one of Publishers Weekly's Best Books of 2010. In 2013 she became the first person ever to appear five times on the same Hugo Ballot.

Beáta Fülöp (she/her) is a Luxembourgish nerd who loves all things fantasy and science fiction. She is active in her local queer community and identifies as aromantic asexual.

Danielle Woolhead got a BSc in Psychology from the University of Toronto before deciding she wanted to be a massage therapist (because her parents never told her she could be a writer). She lives in a small house with one fish, two humans, two cats, six chandeliers, nine swords, 48 types of tea, and 789 (and counting) books. She likes snuggling up at her kotatsu with a pot of tea and her mechanical keyboard.

Heather Tracy (she/her) is a travel agent by day, and a masked copy editor and writer by night. As a travel agent, she plans Nerdventures—travel for the nerd in all of us. These can be anything from visiting New Zealand to see as many *Lord of the Rings* filming locations as you can to visiting castles in Europe to following in the footsteps of your favorite author.

As a copy editor, she's found hundreds of typos, comma splices, and other grammatical nitpicks for Space Wizard Science Fantasy since before 2016. With over 30 titles copyedited, she's now turned her hand to her first published short story in *Fiery Deeps*, and her first novel, *Only a Chapter*, which features some of her personal journey surviving breast cancer.

Heather lives in Raleigh with her husband of over twenty years, William C. Tracy, where they have two rambunctious cats and several beehives. They enjoy taking their own Nerdventures—as much as they can be away from their small businesses—and cosplaying at various markets and cons throughout the year.

You can find her on Facebook as @heathertracyauthor, on Bluesky as @heathertracyauthor.bsky.social and on Instagram as @hunnyjar319. For her travel agency, Melvin's Travel Adventures, you can find her on Facebook and Instagram as @melvinstraveladventures or on Bluesky as @melvinsta.bsky.social.